Praise for Apr

GOOD

"Evocative and b
drumbeat of the

"Smith has create
and has a superb
telling."

"Spellbinding, fu
ments that make
missed."

"This stunner of
in the details: A
still packs a punc

"[Smith's plots] are so fast, harrowing, and breathtaking
that they are like skiing down the expert slope while jug-
gling vials of nitroglycerine." —*New York Sun*

"April Smith is a writer with a laser eye that can record
with cold precision the details of the daily life of her
crime-solving subjects." —*Chicago Tribune*

APRIL SMITH
GOOD MORNING, *Killer*

April Smith is the author of *Judas Horse*, *North of Montana*, *Be the One*, and *White Shotgun*. She is also a television screenwriter and producer. She lives in Santa Monica with her husband and children.

www.aprilsmith.net

ALSO BY APRIL SMITH

APRIL SMITH

GOOD MORNING, *Killer*

AN FBI SPECIAL AGENT ANA GREY NOVEL

VINTAGE CRIME/BLACK LIZARD
VINTAGE BOOKS
A DIVISION OF RANDOM HOUSE, INC.
NEW YORK

FIRST VINTAGE CRIME/BLACK LIZARD EDITION, NOVEMBER 2011

The Library of Congress has cataloged the Knopf edition as follows:
Smith, April
Good morning, killer / April Smith.—1st ed.
p. cm.
1. Government investigators—Fiction. 2. Fugitives from justice—Fiction.
3. Santa Monica (Calif.)—Fiction. 4. Kidnapping victims—Fiction.
5. Women detectives—Fiction. I. Title
PS3569.M467 G66 2003
813'.54—dc21   2002035917

Vintage ISBN: 978-0-307-94760-4

www.vintagebooks.com
www.weeklylizard.com

Printed in the United States of America
10 9 8 7 6 5 4 3 2 1

For my father

Part One

PROOF OF LIFE

One.

I t was winter and I was swimming laps in the rain.

I have found it a privilege to swim outside in the rain, a perk you get in return for living in Los Angeles that not many appreciate. You have to like being extremely wet, and enjoy the feeling of smug superiority because the canyon air is forty degrees and you're in a relatively warm bath. You have to appreciate the subtle play of vanished circles on the water and the dance of droplets off your goggles, blurring the shapes of redtail hawks resting on a telephone pole and deer moving close to the houses.

I did not know about the girl.

I was doing the backstroke, looking up at the clouds, trying not to get pushed into the lane lines by the county lifeguard who was working out beside me, with the tapered legs and the chest of a manatee. He was gray-haired, with a stroke so smooth it never seemed to break water, as if propelled by some internal muscular power known only to yogis. In fact the lifeguard was a kind of spiritual seeker and would speak of "the breath" as if it were a living thing.

My personal meditation that day was on a briefing with the senior superintendent from the Hong Kong Police Force. It would be a lunch with twenty other folks, a long ungainly table in Distefano's, everyone trying to look spiffy and smart—a total waste of time when I had to get my files in order for an upcoming ninety-day file review, an assessment of open cases as pleasant as a cross between a migraine headache and spring cleaning. When you work the kidnap squad you find a lot of cases—mostly missing children—stay open forever.

When the red hand on the workout clock brushed 6:55 a.m., I hauled out of the water and hightailed across the frigid pool deck, raindrops popping off my silicone cap. Checking the pager hooked inside the swim bag, I found it was blinking: *Code 3-PCH-AB*.

Emergency.

I stood alone in the freezing cinder-block locker room, dripping freely and staring at the numbers with a secret smile. It was a message in police code from "AB" (Detective Andrew Berringer), which usually meant not a life-and-death emergency but an emergency of the gonads, which I could feel responding as I peeled off the cold clinging bathing suit and headed for the open shower.

The two other women who had been swimming in the rain (both lawyers) came hurrying in, shivery and goose-bumped, absorbed in chatter about book clubs, children, different types of olives, someone's half-demolished kitchen, as a wild mix of botanicals—mint, eucalyptus, citrus, rose—swirled in the steamy vapor and they lathered unabashedly and shaved and loofahed, while I stood under the hot pounding spray with head bowed in thanks because of this sudden unexpected gift of seeing Andrew, even more delicious if it were to take place, let's say, behind the locked rest room door in Back on the Beach, a café down on Pacific Coast Highway.

Where, I thought, the emergency was.

Good thing I had those ten extra minutes.

In the parking lot of the YMCA facility I passed the lifeguard, who carried nothing but a small satchel while my shoulder was crippled under the weight of a swim bag loaded with fins, towels, hair dryer and an enormous makeup kit. I was wearing a slim black pants suit and heels because of the luncheon with the superintendent from Hong Kong. The lifeguard wore nothing but a T-shirt and shorts.

"Come under my umbrella."

He shook his head. "How'd you like your workout, Miss FBI-FYI?"

"Good."

"Make sure you get enough air." He inflated his lungs. "Air," he said.

"Air," I agreed, and got into my car to the silent buzz of the Nextel cell phone on my belt.

"Ana?" It was my supervisor, Rick Harding. "Where have you been?"

Lost in an erotic delirium, I had forgotten to check the Nextel also. Two missed messages.

"Underwater. Sorry."

"Tell me about it, the freeway was flooded, took an hour and a half to get in. We've got a kidnapping on the Westside. The police department requested our assistance. You're next up."

Next in line to be case agent. The senior in charge.

So much for ten minutes in heaven.

"What's the deal?"

"The victim is a fifteen-year-old female missing since yesterday. I'm going to the police department. The techs are on their way to the family residence."

He gave me an address on Twenty-second Street, north of Montana Avenue, the Gillette Regent Square section of trendy Santa Monica. Kind of like the tenderloin of the filet mignon.

"Is that why we're all over this?" I asked. "High-profile neighborhood?"

"It's the 'new politics,'" he replied, which meant yes.

"We're sure about the kidnap? It's not just a runaway?"

"Mom and Dad got a call early this morning."

"Ransom?"

"The girl was pleading for her life. Then they hung up."

"Works for me."

"Just get over there."

I barreled down Temescal and took a quick detour south on PCH, swinging through a puddle at the entrance to Back on the Beach. The muddy water rooster-tailed up about ten feet, completely obscuring my windshield.

Andrew was not there to witness this dramatic arrival. His burgundy unmarked Ford was parked facing the ocean, empty, doors locked. The restaurant hadn't opened yet. Patio tables were glassy and jumping with rain, and I knew if I took one step onto the bike path my black heels would instantly become stained with saturated sand. So I waited on the asphalt under the umbrella while impertinent gusts blew at my knees and under my arms, wishing I had taken the time to blow-dry my hair, which had become uncomfortably damp in the sideways mist. I began to sneeze, that smug superiority cooling down fast, as a yellow county rescue truck, red lights pulsing, came north across the beach.

Where the hell was he?

Against the unsettled ocean and the bluster of the blue-white sky, I watched as the heavy truck pitched stubbornly over rises in the sand. Its slow progress seemed to make a statement about law enforcement: *We shall override.*

A pitiful thing to take for comfort.

The truck stopped past the restaurant, just out of my sight. I could hear the deep idle of the engine and feedback on a police scanner. I stepped onto the bike path. A hundred yards away I could see Detective Berringer in his trademark black motorcycle jacket, kneeling beside a bicyclist wearing bright regalia who had skidded out.

"Andrew!"

He waved me back, yakking it up with some county lifeguards in fluorescent rain gear who were bringing out a spine board. Claps on the back, handshakes, long-lost pals. Now the wind was wrapping around my legs, and I could look forward to clammy panty hose the rest of the day.

Finally, he jogged over, brushing off his hands.

"What are you doing?"

"Waiting for you. Hi, doll," giving me a smooch. "See that life-guard? The tall, skinny guy? That's *Hank Harris!*" he said wonder-ingly.

"You know him?"

"I know his *dad!*" Andrew shook his head. "When you turn fifty, things get weird. That kid's supposed to be *eight years old,* playing Little League!"

"You're not fifty."

I never knew anyone to *add* to his age, but Andrew was several years ahead of himself in an apprehension he had about "getting old," which was ridiculous. He was adorable. Not perfect-looking (nose like a stumpy old carrot, not the tightest chin), but a rough-hewn charisma you would definitely pick out at a bar—dark wavy hair cut short and greenish eyes that could bully or tease; a face that could be a mask of detachment, then open up like a kid who just hit a home run. I believe this was the reason—an extraordinary ease with his own emotions—that Andrew was often picked by the department for pub-lic relations gigs. He was a seasoned street detective who apparently was not afraid to show what he felt. Therefore he would not likely be afraid of the deeply awful things that had happened to you. When Andrew gave workshops on bank security the female tellers would write down their phone numbers on deposit slips. He would call them back, was my understanding.

That's how we met. Working the same bank robbery, dubbed "Mis-sion Impossible" because the bandit came in through the roof. We don't always catch the bad guys, but we're great with the nicknames.

Andrew took the umbrella. I put my arm around his waist even though his jacket was cold and slick. We were walking as fast as possi-ble, an inelegant pair, since I am five four and he was six one, outweigh-ing me by a hundred pounds. He was built like a football player and cared about it. He owned a bench and read weight-lifting magazines.

"So what happened?" I asked of the bike wreck.

"I don't know why assholes go out in this weather."

"Because they're—"

"—The sand is all soggy, look at this, like riding in peanut butter."
The wind picked up. We ran for it.

"Come into my office." Unlocking his car. "Normally we don't let
Feds in here. But I have something special for you."

"I have to go."

"So do I."

But we paused, very close, under the umbrella.

"I'm crazy about you, you know that," he said.

"Yeah, well, you *drive* me crazy. Is that the same thing?"

The rain drummed on our makeshift roof. In the frank light our
faces were eager, ruddy, his high round cheeks shining like a choir-
boy's. In those days it lifted me to be with him. It just lifted me, like a
kite off the ground that wants to return to the same spot in the sky.

His eyes half closed and I rose up and he leaned down to kiss me
and we did and the umbrella tipped and rain went down our necks.

"Fuck this shit," he said, fumbling for his keys.

"I have to get out of here. You know about the kidnapping?"

"Let me see. Do I work robbery/homicide, or is it Hal's Auto
Body?"

I laughed. "Sometimes a toss-up, huh?"

"I've been at the house since four this morning!"

"*You* have?"

"First it was a critical missing, then they got the call around three."

"How are the parents?"

He shrugged. "Distraught. The girl never came home from school.
They contacted her friends. Nothing."

"'*Not like their daughter not to let them know where she was,*'" I
guessed.

"Not like their daughter," he agreed.

Our few words implied a complicated professional speculation
about who these people were and how the girl had disappeared.

"So what were you doing there?"

"I caught the case."

"It's *your* case? It's my case, too!"

He snorted indulgently as he often did when I would say things that showed I was missing the precision of what was happening.

"What the hell did you think that page was all about?"

"There were . . . other possibilities."

He tried to get past a smile. *Code 3-ER-AB.* A supply closet in a certain hospital emergency room. *Code 3-RVM-AB.* The Ranch View Motel.

"I was giving you a heads-up, in case it worked out."

"I guess it did."

But I wasn't so sure.

"Get in the car, I've got more."

"Is this a good idea?"

Teasing. "To get in the car, or to work together?"

Right then I didn't like it.

"Andrew, how are we going to do this?"

"What do you mean, how?" He was hurt. "I thought it would be good for you at the Bureau. I thought you would get a kick out of it."

"I did. I do. It's very cool."

I smiled and touched his hand, pushed up his sleeve to look at his watch. A kidnapping is a federal crime. The FBI has jurisdiction over the local police. He had to know I would be his boss.

"We better get over there."

I had become aware of sirens. They might have called an ambulance for the fellow with the bike. Or maybe it was another wreck. Suddenly the light was hurting my eyes, hard off the ocean, steely blue. It was going to be one of those sickening days when the sun comes out after all.

Two.

Juliana Meyer-Murphy was in ninth grade. She came from
a stable home in which the parents had been married seventeen years, neither previously divorced. There was a
younger sister. The house was a two-story Spanish with cast-iron balconies and fat curves and bits of colored tile set at odd places in the
stucco. There were fan palms and potted flowers and even a fountain,
as if the owners were Hollywood aristocracy instead of manufactur-
ers in the garment business. The front door was painted purple.

The tech vans pulled up to the residence at the same time Andrew
and I arrived in our separate cars. A blue sky was shining through
a maw in the clouds while fine spray sifted across the rooftops like
million-dollar rainbow dust. I grew up in this neighborhood, but these
new mini mansions could have eaten our little cottage for breakfast.
Like the Meyer-Murphys', they each had at least one sport utility vehicle in the driveway and a sign for an alarm system on the lawn. A private security patrol car sat side by side in the middle of the street with
a unit from the Santa Monica police.

Yet there was also a hum, a sense of ordinary family life, not so different from the days of the blow-up pool in our threadbare back-yard. Kids left their trikes out. There was a handmade tree house, an American flag. The lofty pines on adjoining streets were old, with large heavy cones. How peaceful it would be to push a baby in their fragrant shade. A child could walk to the public school, a teenage girl chill on the curb with her friends, even after dark. The cars that passed would carry TV celebrities or dot-com money or entrepreneurs; well-meaning professional folks, if somewhat disengaged.

Maybe. Let's hope. Nine times out of ten.

The FBI team assembled on the sidewalk. The full-bore response was part of the "new politics" Rick was talking about, an effort to position the LA field office as responsive to the diverse communities it served—especially the wealthier communities, whose constituents hired lawyers to make their hurts known—as well as to reinvent our image as "good neighbor" to local law enforcement.

We were convincing—a clean-cut group, sporting an assortment of windbreakers and trench coats, cropped hair, ties, khakis, neat as flight attendants, the female installers wearing ponytails and lipstick. We looked like cops—what else could we be? Poised, scanning the quiet street in every direction.

Ramon Diaz, the twenty-eight-year-old tech wiz, said it first: "Surveillance is going to be a bitch."

Every other house seemed to be under construction. Today we had a break because of the rain, but tomorrow there would be laborers' vehicles and Dumpsters obscuring the sight lines, making it impossible to know who belonged where, what was different, if the bad guys were watching the Meyer-Murphy home.

"The street can be secured, people," commented Andrew with a patronizing smile.

Heads turned toward the big guy in the leather jacket.

"Do I know you?" answered Ramon, giving it a little strut.

Ramon, like me, was new LA. My dad emigrated from El Salvador, my mom grew up here and was Caucasian. With long wavy black hair and pale almond skin, you would take me for white. Ramon, on the other hand, was pure second-generation Salvadoran, no doubt about it—dark complexion, step haircut and aviator sunglasses, drove a huge black mother truck, married to a Mexican dental assistant with lined lips and attitude.

Andrew made his business card appear between his fingers with a *flick*.

"Santa Monica . . . I'm down for that," Ramon acceded, shaking hands.

Ramon had only been playing, working out the tension, but as we marshaled toward the house he leaned in close so I could smell wintergreen gum.

"Why you siding with *that* white boy?"

Mrs. Meyer-Murphy opened the purple door with feverish anticipation.

"Officer Berringer!"

When she saw the rest of us her eyes narrowed and she began to blink rapidly.

"What's all this?"

I stepped forward and offered my hand. "Ana Grey with the FBI."

Mrs. Meyer-Murphy continued to squint as if she'd suddenly gone blind.

Andrew touched her shoulder.

"Remember, Lynn, I told you? We were bringing in the FBI?"

She'd been pumping my hand with both of hers. Autopilot. Cold, long fingers. She was tall and strikingly underweight, short black hair with short bangs that kind of triangulated out over the ears. Sassy. On a good day. She wore a mismatched yellow cardigan over a T-shirt and blue nylon track pants. She was tired and wired at the same time, sallow skin, and the circles underneath her eyes profound. She was in that state of fluid grief where tears just come and go. But now the nervous blinking stopped. She peered at me with all the spirit she could muster.

"Thank God you're here."

"We're going to do everything possible to get your daughter home safely and quickly. May we enter the house, ma'am?"

"Please."

She stepped back.

The gang, which had been pawing the driveway impatiently, trampled through the door.

It was like opening day at the big sale at Target.

In a matter of minutes they had fanned out through the house, hoisting metal briefcases and coils of wire.

Mrs. Meyer-Murphy stared. Strangers were chugging up her steps and opening her closets.

"What are they doing?"

"We're taking over your home."

Wide-eyed. "You are?"

"Where is your husband, Mrs. Meyer-Murphy? Who else is in the house?"

Inside the door a heap of helmets and Rollerblades sat underneath a hat rack. She led me through a living room dominated by a fireplace of river rock. Family pictures on the mantel. I would get to those. A Santa Monica uniform was leaning over a coffee table, reading off the top of a pile of newspapers that had spilled onto a rose-patterned rug. There were shoes all over the place, kid sneakers and grown-up running shoes.

"My little one's at school," said Lynn Meyer-Murphy. "I took her to school, was that wrong?"

"Not at all. I'll send an agent over."

The tears—"I didn't know what else to do!"

"It's okay, Mrs. Meyer-Murphy. Beautiful home."

There were gingham-covered sofas, distressed-pine tables, quilts and old-fashioned brass lanterns—artfully arranged but incongruous. The country style of the inside seemed to have nothing to do with the Spanish style of the outside. Or maybe the purple door held a symbolism that I missed.

"This morning, around six o'clock, I actually drank a martini. Is that crazy?"

"Understandable."

"But it had absolutely no effect."

As we passed through an arched doorway I noticed a cluster of miniature watercolors—tiny corsets and hats and high-button shoes. Commercial quality, obviously trained.

"Those are nice."

"They're mine. I'm a clothing designer and my husband is the manufacturer. A good idea at the time," she added dryly.

In the kitchen the husband was half seated on a bar stool, talking on the phone. Lynn threw up her hands at the sight of him.

"Ross. Get off."

He held up an index finger, telling us to wait while he continued to talk, focused on the floor.

"Ana Grey with the FBI." Badging him. "I need you to hang up the phone immediately."

He lowered the receiver. "It's my phone."

I stayed cool. I did not engage his anger.

"The lines need to be clear in case your daughter calls."

"Oh, really? I never thought of that."

He had the body type where the fat goes to the shoulders, round and bulky on top, a waist pinched by a belt too tight for those fancy jeans, stocky powerful legs. Balding. A light beard, color indiscriminate, which he was rubbing up and down.

"This is my husband."

"She's Meyer," he said dolefully. "I'm Murphy."

I gave it a smile.

Ramon hustled in, whipping a screwdriver from his tool belt.

"The police already hooked something up," the dad said, indicating a small tape recorder attached to the phone.

"I know, sir, but we have to install our own equipment."

"How are we doing?"

Now Andrew entered the kitchen, trailed by another Santa Monica police officer, statuesque, with blonde hair in a French braid. She had been the first responder. Her arms were strong and capable beneath the tight-fitting midnight blue uniform but her broad Slavic cheekbones were oily, eyelids heavy with fatigue. She had been on her feet for hours. Seeing another female on the job was a relief for both of us; we exchanged brief smiles.

"I just want to say one thing." The dad pivoted on the bar stool. His chin was up, weary eyes defiant. "You already know this, Andrew."

I cringed. Police officers like to be addressed by their rank. So far neither one of the Meyer-Murphys had gotten it right.

"Juliana is loved. She comes from a loving home. She is a good kid. She doesn't drink, doesn't smoke—*anything.*"

Andrew said, "I hear you."

The police officer put a fist on her hip and shifted weight, keeping her expression neutral. She had heard it, too.

"Juliana has never even been *late* without calling," the dad went on. "Something happened to her, because she would never do this to us."

"We *know* something happened to her," began the mom a little desperately.

"Do you have a recent picture of your daughter?"

They had already been to the shoe box with the sheaves of family photos like a mixed salad of time—trips to Big Bear and fifteen years of Halloween—and pulled the standard school portrait, one of those cookie-cutter images that reduced the victim to an everyday teenager with long brown hair and a pleasantly chubby face, along with a black-and-white full-body shot of her holding on to a tree, an exaggerated pose with her butt sticking out, imitating a model, with a tight self-conscious smile.

"Has Juliana ever run away?" I asked.

The dad rolled his eyes.

"I know you're tired and you've been over this—"

He put up his palms in submission. "No. *Okay?* My daughter has never run away."

"Does Juliana have a boyfriend?"

"Are you kidding? She has no friends at that school."

"She's doing fine," countered the mom.

"What school are we talking about?"

"Laurel West. It's a private academy." Ross seemed to like the word. "She just started there, just when we moved into this house."

New house, new school. *New money?* I was making handwritten notes.

"How is Juliana doing at Laurel West?"

"Maintaining a C average," the dad said with some sarcasm. "In middle school she was pulling A's."

"How do you account for the change?"

Neither parent had an answer.

"Can you give me a general idea of her activities?"

They looked at each other. "Well," said Lynn, "she likes to hang at the Third Street Promenade."

"Was she at the Promenade yesterday afternoon?"

"Not yesterday. Yesterday she was going over to her friend Stephanie Kent's house. She *does* have friends. He thinks he knows her. He doesn't know her at all."

"I don't know my own daughter?"

Lynn ignored him, gripping the back of a bar stool.

"They had to work on a science project," she continued deliberately. "They had to make a car out of paper."

Ross: "For this we spend fifteen thousand dollars a year."

That was it. Lynn crumbled and Andrew was there to catch her, just as he had been for the pair of terrified bank managers on the Mission Impossible job. He'd had both arms around them—one male, one female—as they wept on his shoulders after the ordeal of being held in the vault. I had been impressed to see that. With quiet patience he now held Lynn Meyer-Murphy through the present wave of anguish, his face closed down and solemn.

"Why don't we sit?" Andrew said finally, indicating the breakfast nook. "When was the last time either of you had anything to eat?"

Lynn opened a drawer, pulled out a bag of bagels, put them on top of the counter and forgot about them.

Spread before us on the breakfast table was evidence of a family in the midst of a life too hurried even to sort out: mounds of magazines, catalogues, homework pages, *The Silver Palate Cookbook,* spelling tests and piles of mail still in rubber bands.

"What is that hammering?" Ross was staring at the ceiling.

"We're putting in direct lines to the Santa Monica Police Department."

"What for?"

"We're setting up a command post over there. But we will have agents in your home, twenty-four/seven."

This, also, was "new politics."

"Twenty-four hours a day!" cried Lynn in a panic. "Where do they sleep?"

There was some drama happening across the room where Ramon was messing with a phone jack.

"Excuse me," the uniform was saying. "You can't just go ripping out our stuff." She was holding the discarded tape recorder by the wires. She thrust it at him like a dead rat.

"Lady," said Ramon, "the Bureau always puts in its own equipment—you never worked a kidnap before?"

"It's *Officer Oberbeck*—"

The parents were watching. Andrew scrambled to his feet.

"Sylvia . . . ," he called.

"We were here first." She jabbed an acrylic fingernail.

"It's our jurisdiction." Ramon angled the screwdriver.

"The right hand doesn't know what the left is doing," Ross commented grimly.

"Sylvia," said Andrew, walking over. "Take a deep break."

"Don't let them talk to you like that!" Lynn chimed in. "Just because you're a woman!"

Officer Oberbeck suppressed a smile. "I'm really okay."

"You're more than okay—she's *terrific!*" Lynn declared to the room. "When we got that hang-up call, I thought I would go over the edge—"

Me, alert: "A hang-up? A *second* call? Did anybody monitor it?"

Negative, according to Officer Oberbeck, and there was nothing on the tape.

"So nobody logged the call," I said heatedly.

The police officer straightened, wiping an arm across her forehead, midsection held in tight. I could see her in basketball shorts playing hoops with the boys.

"I'm going home," she said, adding kindly: "Don't worry, Mrs. Meyer-Murphy. By dinnertime Juliana will be sitting here, and you'll be yelling at her for scaring you to death."

Lynn started blinking rapidly again.

It was twenty minutes into Day One and already I was corked.

"A call came in that we missed, people. We don't know who it was or what they said? *What the hell is going on?*"

"It's chillin'," said Ramon. "We got it under control."

Holstering the screwdriver, he left.

His emotion, my emotion, none of it mattered. The pressing absence of the girl was making itself felt even in the confusion of the kitchen: A leopard bag with ruby beads hooked on a chair. *A Tale of Two Cities* in paperback, a pink marker stuck in the pages. Blue nail polish. Size-eight pool thongs. These things, obviously Juliana's, had become Day-Glo talismans, striking my eyes with mocking urgency as we took swipes at one another in frustration and landed on our butts.

There was a moment of bleak silence.

"Cream cheese or butter?" Andrew asked.

You had to love a guy standing in the center of a room, holding up a bag of bagels.

The dad's eyes slowly rose.

"She's Meyer, I'm Murphy. You figure it out."

"No problem," Andrew replied crisply. "My first wife was Jewish."

"I didn't know that," I blurted.

"Lots of things you don't know about me." Untwisting the bag.

I hoped they thought we were being entertaining for their benefit instead of slip-sliding into the wrong movie.

I flipped a page in my notebook. The phone calls had come four hours apart. Maybe there would be a pattern.

"The next time the phone rings, who is going to answer, Mom or Dad?"

Lynn slowly raised her hand.

"The guy says, 'We have Juliana and we want a million dollars ransom.' You say, *'I want to talk to my daughter. Put my daughter on the phone.'*"

"I don't ask where she is or anything like that?"

"You want to *hear her voice,*" I repeated calmly. "Before we even get into any type of negotiation, we need to know she's alive. We call it 'proof of life.'"

Lynn looked stricken by the implication. Her fingers went to her throat. "'Proof of life'?"

"Anyone else, tell them nothing, get off the phone."

She caught her breath.

"What if it's my mother? I can't tell her what happened. I can't say, *Mom, your granddaughter is missing, we don't have a clue where she is, but we're good parents, we really are.*" She was twisting her wedding ring.

"Where does your mother live?"

"Florida. She moved there after my dad died."

Ross: "After *the loser*"—making an elaborate point of gesturing to himself—"took over the business."

Lynn's cheeks were suddenly flushed. "You don't understand. She's very critical."

"There will be a negotiator sitting right there, wearing headphones, listening to the conversation, passing notes on what to say."

"A team of professionals," said Ross, "trained to deal with your mother. God bless America."

"I can't do this."

"For Juliana," Andrew prompted. "Come on, you've been very brave."

Lynn looked up with brimming eyes. She almost believed him.

"I'd do it," said Ross. "But I hear that bastard's voice, I'm gonna go ballistic, tear his fucking throat out over the phone . . ."

Then he saw something in his wife, a deep, sick fear he perhaps had never understood.

"You're a good mom," he said firmly. "*Never* let *anyone* tell you different."

Lynn held on to her husband's hand.

I asked about their manufacturing business.

"Business is fine," answered Ross briskly, rubbing his beard. "Andrew went all over that."

"We still need to look at your records. It would be helpful if you'd allow access to what's on your desk."

"My *desk*?"

"Employee records, ledgers, address books . . ."

"Fine," said Ross. "How about what's up my ass?"

Lynn said crossly, "Oh for Christ's sake."

Ross put his hands flat on the table and tilted back on the hind legs of his chair.

"Goddamnit, we are not the criminals."

"In most kidnappings, the victim and the suspect know each other," Andrew reminded them. "Someone in your world might have taken Juliana."

Ross's eyes went out of focus.

"I can't do this. I can't do this anymore."

We waited.

"I just want her home."

The scrambling went on around us. You could hear them working in the walls. Ramon appeared at the doorway, got the vibe, and backed away.

"Why," whispered Lynn, "would someone we know take Juliana?"

"A grudge." Andrew was watching her closely. "A threat."

The mom's cheeks flared even brighter.

"I'll tell you who it is!" Ross snapped his fingers. "I should have thought of it before! David Yi."

David Yi was a trusted employee who turned out to be a member of a Korean gang that worked the downtown garment district. He figured out the alarm system, broke into the plant and stole three hundred thousand dollars' worth of spandex. Ross had testified against him.

"Good. We'll check out David Yi. Next."

It is a statistical certainty that the longer a person is missing, the smaller the chances of recovery.

"Stephanie Kent. The girl Juliana was supposed to meet. Do you have an address?"

Lynn said she did, and I followed her up the bare oak stairs to get it, she in her blue running pants moving heavily, I in the black suit, impatient. I wanted to see the daughter's room. To touch her bed-clothes and breathe her teenage hibiscus perfume.

It was my job to know the victim as if she were my own flesh and blood.

In that way, I would know her abductor.

"I see Juliana swims." Spotting a suit and towel hanging over the banister. Remembering the thongs.

"She was on the swim team," replied the mother, "but she quit. Another thing she quit." Her voice was faint. "I guess we should have told you."

"It's okay. We're only at the beginning of this."

I shouldn't have said that.

She pushed on the door, and Juliana's world opened up to me.

Three.

The Kent residence was on a walk-through street in a "transitional" part of Venice, which meant you could pay six hundred thousand dollars for a tear-down and still get hit by a random gang bullet.

Andrew and I stayed in contact on the cells all the way over. Cell phones and pagers were our thing. Because of our schedules sometimes we couldn't see each other for a couple of weeks, but we'd talk, weaving in and out of a never-ending conversation about police work, police gossip, police movies, police screwups and the Dodgers. Tension would build. Then would come the teasing call, the secret beeper code: it is surprising how sexy you can feel driving a tan Crown Victoria.

"Think the parents are in it?"

"I'm not ready to rule them out."

"Me either. What about the dad? Think he's molesting the girl? That's why she split?"

"I don't know, but the guy was pretty stuck on that spandex theft. We should check it out for insurance fraud."

"Would you wait on the polygraph?"

"Kind of early," Andrew agreed.

"But what about the two of them? Lynn and Ross?"

"It's an old marriage. You can smell it. Rotting meat."

"Oh, Andrew!"

"What?"

I mugged so Andrew would see me in his rearview mirror and was rewarded when the top third of his face broke into a smile.

"You are so cynical about relationships."

"I've been there," Andrew said into the phone wedged between shoulder and ear. "In fact, I've been there so often my name is permanently inscribed in the relationship crapper."

"Is that supposed to be inspiring?"

"I never make promises."

"Really?"

We had pulled up and parked. Our car doors slammed and we drew in our jackets against the uncertain weather. The sky was full of moving clouds like squirting inks, charcoal and mauve. It was 4 p.m. A brief white light struck the puddles platinum.

"I thought you promised to move in with me," I said. "Sooner or later."

"Wasn't it the other way around?"

"I don't want to lose my lease."

We crossed the street. When he spoke again, his voice had dropped to that somber *do-not-argue* pitch. "It's my father's house. I can't sell it."

"Isn't that *love*?" I poked his ribs.

"Isn't what?"

"Giving it up?"

When I looked over he was watching me deeply, enigmatically.

"I'm just looking for safe passage, hon."

"Meaning?"

"An expression my dad used to say when he had to tell us something. *'Give me safe passage.'* And you'd say, *'Okay.'* And he'd say, *'I know you're smoking cigarettes and it ain't gonna cut it.'*"

"Like, don't get mad at me."

"Like, help me through this."

"So, Andy—is there something you need help getting through?"
He laughed sardonically. "The fucking day."

The walk-through streets, a maze of lanes too tiny for cars, had become prized for their bohemian hipness. Five years ago this area was a slum, but entertainment and foreign money was moving in, building eclectic houses like the Kents'—small, but well-proportioned and impeccably postmodern, with a Xeriscape garden made of cacti and rocks.

"What's the point of a garden," Andrew asked as we walked up the gravel path, "without flowers?"

"Saves water."

"These people can't pay for water?"

Andrew was an azalea man. The shade garden behind the one-story cottage in Sunset Park was the legacy of his father, who had also been a Santa Monica police officer. Sergeant E. Prescott Berringer, originally from North Beach, San Francisco, made his own beef jerky and brewed his own beer, and so did Andrew, who maintained the backyard meticulously, a shrine. You could eat off the potting table, and you never saw so many different-sized clippers and shears oiled and sharpened and hung in their places. Sunday mornings, when we first started going out, I would try to be cheery and helpful with the weeding and whatever, but it didn't come naturally, like tending someone else's child. Andrew took my tools away. "That's okay," he'd say, "I'll do it," and ignore me for a couple of hours.

One day Andrew told me he had been adopted, and I applied that like a balm to his remoteness and silences, all my discouragements and puzzlements and questions. It made the bond to his father sizzlingly poignant. There was a photo in the bedroom of Andrew (eight years old) and E. Prescott, both wearing Dodger jerseys. He said they often dressed alike. Mom was meek, and Dad, I guessed from the curly blond hair and cocksure posture, played around. The father-and-son photo hung next to a plaque Andrew received when he made detective. It read, "The Homicide Investigator's Oath," and listed Ten Commandments, including "*Thou Shalt Not Kill.*"

At the time, I took all this to mean that Andrew was a person of discipline.

A frosted glass door was opened by the mother of Stephanie Kent, the girl who Juliana was supposed to have met at the bus stop yesterday. Mrs. Kent, hearing our business, wrapped her arms around her waist, as if we had brought an icy wind.

"You mean Juliana isn't back?"

"We're optimistic that she will be."

"My God, what could have happened to her? Anything could have happened! I have to tell you, this is not like Juliana."

"No?"

"How is Lynn doing? I haven't talked to her since last night."

Andrew gave the compassionate cop shrug. "Hard times."

"The longer Juliana's missing, the worse it is, isn't it?" said Mrs. Kent knowingly. "My husband is a TV director. He's done episodes of *Law and Order* and *NYPD Blue.*"

Andrew's mouth twitched which was like an electric shock to the pelvic giggle nerve. I had to look away not to pee my pants.

"We understand Juliana and Stephanie were friends?"

"She was new, we were just getting to know her. But she seemed like an awfully nice girl. That's one of the things I am so proud of with Stephanie. The way she reaches out to other kids."

"Can we talk to Stephanie?" I asked.

"She's in her room. With the Boyfriend."

Mrs. Kent could not help rolling her eyes.

"It's very important that you not discuss Juliana's disappearance with anyone. If there are rumors in school and it hits the media, her life could be in danger."

The mother wore Levi's and a plaid shirt; agile and loose in the body. Her face was pert, small gold-rimmed glasses, red hair cut radically short like a man's, and I thought Miss Stephanie lucky to have a cool mom, wondering if Juliana liked it better here, the artsy Craftsman feel of red maple trim mixed with severe white walls, earthenware dishes still on the table and the lingering scent of curry, as opposed to the repressed tension of her parents' disordered home.

"You have my word," promised Mrs. Kent. "This is just so terrible. It could happen to any of us."

A hip-hop bass was coming from behind Stephanie's closed door, which had pearly plastic whorehouse beads hanging in front of it. I knocked and there was no reply. I knocked again.

"Give them a break, they're getting dressed," Andrew said.

Finally a female voice called, "Come *in*!" with exaggerated brightness.

I opened the door and poked my head through the chattering beads.

"Ana Grey with the FBI. This is Detective Berringer, Santa Monica police."

Andrew said, "What up?"

Stephanie and her friend were lying together, fully clothed, on top of her bed. They did not jump up in embarrassment or even look surprised but regarded us with a low-grade curious disdain.

"What up wit' you?" replied the boy, whose name was Ethan.

"We need to talk to you about Juliana Meyer-Murphy. She didn't come home last night. Any help you can give will be very much appreciated."

The girl sat up, hooking long blonde hair behind her ears. She wore skintight jeans with a snakeskin pattern and a short top that revealed a flawless abdomen with navel pierce.

The room smelled like burning raspberries.

"Is Juliana all right?"

"She's still missing."

"Really?"

Stephanie sat up straighter, surprised.

"We're hoping she's all right."

"Me, too. Definitely."

But Stephanie's hands were laid along her thighs so the elbows stuck out and the thumbs pointed down. In the Comprehensive Coding System for Emotional Recognition, should we be taping this interview and running it through a computer, we would call it a backward sign, like nodding yes when saying no. It meant there was some emotional leakage in that heartfelt answer.

"You guys are friends?"

"We chill." She glanced at the boy.

"We don't know her all that well," he added.

Andrew was leaning against the wall, arms folded. He had made himself very still.

I sat down on the desk chair in front of a computer where instant messages were popping up like pimples.

```
r u down for cj's?
when?
you are all a bunch of fucking gangsta homo-
   sexuals!
```

"You know this person?" reading the screen name. "*Sexbitch*?"

"Not a clue."

Stephanie jumped up and pumped the keyboard, fast, to get back to her screensaver, which turned out to be a blue mushroom. Thinking better of that, she shut the thing off completely.

There were a lava lamp and enormous plastic daisies and all sorts of furry accessories that shouldn't have been furry, such as an orange furry phone. We let the music thump along until the tension in the room built nicely, and then I reached over and cut the sound with the touch of a button.

"So what do you want to talk to us about?" Stephanie asked.

Now they were both sitting apprehensively on the edge of the bed.

"Juliana was supposed to meet you the day she disappeared. What can you tell us about that?"

"We were going to do homework. We had a science experiment. We had to make a car out of paper."

Andrew, as if we hadn't heard this already from Mr. Meyer-Murphy: "How in hell do you make a car out of paper?"

"It's stupid," Stephanie replied. "The teacher gives you the answer."

"What about Juliana?"

"She just never showed up."

"Where were you supposed to meet?"

"At the bus stop."

"What did you do when she didn't arrive?"

"Called her cell. Got a recording, so I figured, whatever."

"You called her from where?"

"A pay phone."

"You sure?"

"Uh-huh."

"You could show us which one?"

"If I could remember."

Her cheeks were hot. She knew I would check it out.

Ethan was fidgeting with a silver chain that went from his belt loop to his wallet. He began flipping the wallet open and shut.

"What's this?" asked Andrew, holding up a small black cone.

"Incense."

"What's wrong with incense?" demanded the boy.

"Watch out," I told him, "or you'll grow up to be a lawyer."

"My dad already is a lawyer."

Andrew nodded sagely and took his time replacing the incense on the little china plate. The boy's eyes followed.

"What do you think happened to Juliana?" Stephanie was anxiously hooking the hair behind her ears with both hands now.

"We're working on some theories. Tell me what it's like at Laurel West."

She shrugged. "A lot of people think it's cold, but it's really a good school. The teachers really care."

"A lot of homework?"

They nodded in unison.

"Lots of pressure?"

"If you're motivated, you'll make it there."

"And you're motivated?"

"I want to get into a good college."

"What about Juliana? Was she motivated?"

Ethan, carelessly: "She tried too hard."

"Like how?"

"With the other kids." He was suddenly uneasy. "I don't know."

"She'd invite you for a sleepover," Stephanie jumped in, "and if you couldn't come, she'd like keep on asking. Incessantly."

"She could be a pest?"

"She didn't mean to be. She was just—"

Andrew: "Out of it."

"Kind of, socially . . . I don't know. I don't want to say *retarded*."

I was becoming more and more impressed by the way Stephanie reached out.

"We were on swim team together. She tried to be friends with the wrong people, and it just didn't work."

"She was playing the violin?" said Ethan. "And the bridge just flew off."

They chuckled.

"Once, she couldn't even get the case open. I felt sorry for her."

Stephanie was holding something in her hands, a contraption made of lined paper and fasteners and rubber bands.

It is not unusual for people to give themselves away unconsciously. Once I interviewed a suspect who was wearing a white gold chain he had taken from a drug dealer he had just stabbed to death.

"What is that?" said Andrew. "Is that the car? Can I see?"

"Sure. It had to really work."

Andrew twisted a paper clip, which torqued the rubber band up tight. He put the thing down, and it scurried across the red maple floor like a beetle.

"Cool."

He had to retrieve it from under my chair.

"And what does that say right there? Looks like 'Stephanie Kent and Juliana Meyer-Murphy' and—what else? Help me out, I don't have my glasses."

He handed the car back to Stephanie.

And forced her to read the date she had written on the wheel, a date that was two weeks before.

"Is that the day you turned the project in? Two weeks ago? So you and Juliana weren't working on it yesterday, were you?"

"We had other homework."

"But why did you tell us, first thing, when we walked in here, that you and Juliana were getting together to make a paper car?"

Andrew and I seemed morbid and heavy with our serious questions and oversized adultness in that fluffy room. I wanted to go home and throw on a pair of jeans.

"*Why did you say that, Stephanie?*"

Stephanie's creamy complexion turned pink. All at once.

"I don't know—"

"Don't trip," Ethan warned.

I stood up. My back was stiff from wearing heels all day. "I think we'd better get your mom in on this."

"No. You don't have to."

"When are you going to tell us the truth?"

Stephanie said nothing, trembling lips compressed. Her fingers held the denim coverlet, trying not to trip.

"If you're not telling the truth about a silly car, how can we believe you're telling the truth about something as important as what was going down with Juliana?"

"Obstruction of justice will look real impressive on your college application," I suggested.

"That's bullshit."

"Bullshit makes the world go round," Andrew shrugged.

"You can't do that," Ethan insisted. "We're minors."

"Ask your dad." Offering my Nextel. "Call him up."

"You know what, kids?" said Andrew. "This is bush. A girl is missing. You want this on your conscience the rest of your lives? Or does that not mean anything to you? Never mind. You have five seconds."

He looked at his watch.

"See what I told you?" Ethan said to Stephanie in a high panicked voice. "She did not have a clue."

"*Juliana* didn't have a clue? What did she not have a clue about?" I asked with magnificent restraint.

This is the value of training.

"First of all," said Stephanie, her clear eyes filling with tears, "it's not our fault."

Four.

They lied. Of course they lied. They had no intention of meeting Juliana at the bus stop after school. The plan was for Juliana to score some weed and meet them at a diner called Johnny Rockets.

It wasn't Stephanie or Ethan or Kristin or Brennan or Nahid's fault that yesterday Juliana went to Crystal Dreams, a New Age store on the Promenade, and never came back. Privately, they thought it was a hoot. Only "some fool" would be so "ghetto" as to go to a public place of business and think they could just walk in and buy drugs. Like what was she going to do, go into the back room where they were smoking crack or whatever, and they'd all be so happy to see little Juliana with her piggybank full of quarters? It was "awesome" to imagine someone so "dumb" not getting ripped off, anyway. Maybe that's what happened, Stephanie suggested, through beet red sobs: someone got paranoid at Juliana's "totally tourist" attitude.

No way they *asked* her to score. They only showed up at Johnny Rockets mainly as a goof, because, as Stephanie and Ethan insisted over and over, they and their friends did not smoke marijuana. In fact they were sure Juliana hadn't even tried it. That's what made the whole thing "whack."

Later, we found a stash in Stephanie's locker at Laurel West Academy.

To me, it was beautiful. But then, I like TV shows about beauty in nature, such as those South American frogs whose dazzling vermilion skin secretes a deadly poison.

We could now establish Juliana's location yesterday at approximately 3:30 p.m.—and there had been a van, Stephanie and Ethan disclosed when Mrs. Kent had joined us, arms crossed stonily, in her daughter's Day-Glo hip-hop cradle—a green van parked in a delivery zone at the north end of the Promenade. It pulled away when a Brink's truck elbowed in. The kids had laughed when it was chased again by UPS. *"Dork."*

Andrew and I grabbed a noodle bowl and jetted over to the Promenade. The crowds were light for a weekday night because of the rain, which had sucked away the popcorny city stink of pigeons and cheap hamburgers and cigarette smoke, and freed some walking space where there were usually impenetrable ranks of bodies.

The Third Street Promenade was a successful outdoor mall geared to fourteen-to-twenty-five-year-olds, anchored by a couple of big bookstores, a deli, some multiplex movie theaters. Clothing chains and street performers and carts selling dance-music CDs had replaced the aging dry goods stores and five-and-dimes from the sixties. Dinosaur fountains and artsy banners were supposed to make you feel safe.

(I had to chuckle when a crime scene instructor, formerly a Chicago homicide detective, who was out here from Quantico to conduct a seminar in which he showed slides of beheaded babies and disemboweled and maggot-encrusted bodies, found our homeless population less than paradise. "A lot of creepy people around here," he said.)

A gate was drawn and Crystal Dreams was dark when we arrived. I'd have an agent over here at first light, but right away we checked exits and entrances, the upper stories—and the parking structure and alleys for a persistent green van.

"It would have been three in the afternoon," I reminded Andrew. He nodded, peering up. "Exterior video cameras?"

I scoped the cornice of the brick frontier-style building. "No such luck."

Peering through the gate I saw polished spheres and tarot cards in the window of Crystal Dreams, along with a cockamamy assortment of straw hats, brand-name backpacks, headphones and handbags, most likely stolen. I took out my pad and sketched the scene, indicating the vitamin store that was adjacent, the greeting card shop on the other side, making note of the position of the fountain and the shuttered carts where a stalker could hide. I sat on a bench and let Juliana's presence come to me: an unformed girl with an ordinary longhaired look who doesn't want to feel ordinary.

"Her A-list friends are waiting at Johnny Rockets the next block down. If she has the goods, no problem. If she doesn't, she's sitting here, scared out of her mind about how she's ever going to show her face in school."

"Maybe she doesn't care," said Andrew.

I shook my head. "She's vulnerable. Needy. Her violin fell apart, for God's sake. She can't go back to the cool kids with nothing."

Andrew sat heavily beside me.

"I'm too old for this."

"Get outta town," I said of the empty Promenade. "This is the most exciting part."

"I'm just saying, don't get carried away."

"With what?"

"Overidentifying. You don't know anything about this girl."

But I felt that I did. I knew something. She was an outsider who wanted to belong.

"What if she gets on a bus?" I riffed. "Winds up on the Strip. Or the Beverly Center, runs out of steam. She's a good girl, doesn't do this kind of thing. It's late, she better call Mom, but she doesn't. Why?"

Andrew: "Because she's come into harm's way."

We sat in silence. A wind blew up. Strings of white lightbulbs flexed and dipped.

"What do you say, baby? Let's go home."

I snuggled against him. "How about Amsterdam?"

He had heard such improbabilities before and indulged me with an arm around the shoulder.

"Although," I considered, "I'd take the Sandpiper motel."

"The one up the coast? That was just a shitty little beach joint."

"No, it wasn't."

He was silent, fingering my hair, and we watched the lights, like birds caught in a net, straining to release a flight of radiance from the gloomy trees.

I wish I had asked how he really felt about what happened at the Sandpiper, but I was afraid to push. I sensed he was backpedaling from the idea of living together, and that made me tentative. Still, it was a mistake. I wish I had understood more about the things he said up the coast in Cambria. I wish I had taken that quiet moment on the bench, before everything broke loose, to ask the questions that kept nosing up like shoots too green to tell what fine—or hideous—flowering might unfold.

"Come on, it's freezing."

I took his big warm hand. "I hope Juliana isn't on the street tonight."

I had become aware of a homeless African-American man on a nearby bench, fists in pockets. Every time his eyes fluttered closed, he jerked himself awake. Now another transient, a white guy with a huge belly, was lumbering toward a doorway.

Andrew was suddenly on his feet.

"Where're you going?"

"That's Willie John Black. Hey, Willie!"

The man looked over slowly.

Andrew said, "Remember me?"

"Sure I remember you," he said, but seemed to need a little help.

"Detective Berringer."

"Of course." The man raised a hand, which was weighted down by a small, filthy, formerly yellow day pack. "How are you, Detective?"

"Good. How are you, my man?"

"Well, I was just going to claim this doorway. It's a double, you see."

It was the entrance to a vintage clothing store with side-by-side glass doors, room enough to lie down and stretch out. Willie lowered his small pack and a bedroll.

"Just put down my gear . . ."

Every move was shaky and painfully deliberate. I made him for fifty or sixty: matted white hair and a full white beard stained yellow around the lips. He wore a clean blue sweatshirt that said *Beverly Hills 90210,* paint-splattered pants and enormous round-toed boots with red nylon laces that were loose because he could not bend to tie them.

"You're not going to bust me?" Willie said.

Andrew laughed and patted his shoulder.

"Last time I busted you had to be eight or ten years ago, when I was on the street."

"You remember that?" said Willie shyly.

"Sure do."

"I remember you, too. You were always nice. Always a gentleman. Even when you arrested me."

"This is Willie's doorway," Andrew explained, with a significant look because it was directly across from Crystal Dreams.

"Used to be a bookstore," Willie said.

"You hang out in this doorway a lot?" I asked.

"Sometimes I go up to the 7-Eleven. Up near Saint Anne's. They've got a serenity meeting and a men's room I can have access to. Sometimes I go down to that place behind the Holiday Inn. They've got soup. You can get a paper bag lunch."

It was hard to see what was going on underneath the hair and beard. His face was ruddy and weathered, and his eyes—I tried to find his eyes—were flat disks, faintly green. They slid away and came back to me.

"What's *your* name?" he asked. I gave him my card and we shook hands. His was heavy and rough and imbedded with hard black grime.

"You go up to the 7-Eleven, but you come back?"

"Sometimes I penny-cup for a meal. A lot of people pass by here."

That made sense. There would be crowds from the movie theaters and pedestrians streaming from across the street.

Andrew showed him the picture of Juliana.

"Did you ever see this girl?"

The paper trembled in Willie's hands.

"Yup. I've seen her. Many, many times."

My heart kicked up.

"Where?"

He seemed lost in the picture.

"Have you seen her around the Promenade?"

"Oh, yes," said Willie. "She's a regular."

He handed it back.

"Look," said Andrew, "can we buy you some dinner?"

Willie looked around. "Don't want to lose my place. The man said it's going to rain again."

He swayed, tired on his feet.

"Willie," I said, "this girl was kidnapped."

"Kidnapped?"

"We think she was here, yesterday, sitting on that bench in front of Crystal Dreams."

"Did you see her," Andrew prompted, "sitting on that bench?"

Willie squinted through the hazy light.

"Yup. I've seen her. Talking to that man with the camera."

Sometimes you hit it. Sometimes the silver dollars tumble right out into your hands.

"Can you describe him?"

"Oh, he's been around here. I think he must be a tourist from Arizona."

"How do you know?"

"We talk."

"You and the man?"

"Oh, sure. He gives me a hard time about my gear," said Willie, moving the grimy pack aside with a big round toe. "Told me to get it disinfected for bugs."

Andrew and I were like hounds baying on the leash.

"Tell us about him."

"What was his name? What did he look like?"

"White fellow."

"How old?"

Willie shrugged. "Young."

"What kind of camera?"

"Pretty fancy camera. Called him 'Arizona' because he was always talking about Arizona. Wanted to go back there. Didn't like it here in California. We had some deep talks. I told him he could count on me. You have to take care of your own."

"Was he a transient?"

Willie considered what it meant to be a transient.

"Never saw him up at the 7-Eleven."

"Did he have a van? A dark green van?"

"Van? Don't know. Never offered *me* a ride. But he did seem eager to leave."

"What didn't he like about California?" I asked.

"Wanted to go back to where he came from. Just like me. I'm originally from New Orleans. That's where I've been trying to get back to, soon as I can recover my property."

"But you saw him talking to this girl." Andrew put the picture in front of Willie's nose. "When?"

"On and off."

"Yesterday?"

"Might have been."

Willie lowered himself slowly and with great weariness, hands feeling along the glass door, until, with a sigh, he found that he was sitting on the bedroll. He was finished.

"Thanks for all your help."

"I want to help out," echoed Willie, and his eyes rolled up at us with a serious and sad expression. Everything he said had borne the same monotone, as if the world he saw through those colorless eyes was only gray-on-gray.

Andrew was gazing down at him.

"It's going to rain, buddy. Let me give you a ride to the shelter."

"That's very nice of you, but I'm waiting for a dude named Steve. We're going up to Malibu. He has access to a propane stove," said Willie with a meaningful raise of white eyebrows. "It's better to stay together because of street violence. That way we can maintain a reasonable situation."

"You're not going up to Malibu tonight."

Willie thought about this and nodded his shaggy head. "That's true, I have to work."

"What kind of work do you do?" I asked curiously.

"I travel around America for the national Defense Department," he said. "I have an ID which the El Monte police took away. That's what I'm talking about, trying to regain my property. They also impounded my vehicle. My job is to drive randomly throughout the United States and data-process sponge cake in the U.S. population."

I had the woozy feeling of being lifted up and set back down, like bobbing in a wave.

"Sponge cake?"

"'Sponge cake' is a code name that refers to Patricia Hearst, who was an individual from the Soviet Union who was being data-processed to be a high warden in the NOBD. That's what I was trained to do, you see. Sometimes I would encounter a candlelight situation."

Andrew was looking away. A damp breeze lifted up the back of his hair.

"A candlelight situation," Willie explained, "is an entity case where the future and today merge together."

I thought for a moment, just one moment, he was pulling the greatest joke of all time. Then it all drained out of me.

"Willie," I said gently, "have you ever been in a hospital?"

"Oh, yes. Yes. I was flying a Cobra and slammed into a mountain in Wyoming called Devil's Ring. They put me in the hospital."

"Did they give you medication?"

"They just give me medication and you talk to someone and they release you. I'm taking medication right now," said Willie. "I'm a depressed person right now. I personally knew Sylvester Stallone in the HBD. He was killed in nineteen seventy."

Willie said these things with the same measured dullness as before. I felt as if I were in the presence of something enormous, like the pulsing of the stars.

I gave him ten bucks and said, "Take care of yourself."

"What did you say your name was?"

I gave him another card.

"Thank you. I'm generally around here, if you want to talk to me."

"God bless," said Andrew.

We left him sitting cross-legged in the doorway, a mound of bedroll and scraggly white hair.

"Sometimes they whip up a vehicle and leave me someplace," he called after us.

As we walked through the deserted street, I laid my head against Andrew's shoulder, certain that they did.

And I dreamed we were in Amsterdam, walking hand in hand, and it was wet and cold and there were lights on the canals.

Five.

Out of nowhere came the smell of cooking onions and the low chatter of the TV. I sat up in bed, awake, heart pounding, late for something I could not remember. Stocks were being traded in New York, but here it was still dark, a little after 6 a.m., Day Three. And the girl was still missing.

We had spent the last two nights in my apartment in Marina Del Rey, averaging about four hours' sleep, which meant you were never out of the roar. Your eyes might be closed, but case points kept flipping through your brain: Jumpy parents. Employee records. Tax returns. A man with a camera. Sylvester Stallone. Rich kids talking rap and smoking weed and a voice in the night, fifteen years old, begging for some hopped-up piece of shit to bestow upon her the privilege of her life.

We had a bulletin out on the van that had been hovering around the Third Street Promenade: a dark green 1989 Dodge, identified separately by both youngsters, Stephanie and Ethan, after looking through police files. The Korean gang member, David Yi, who had stolen a load of spandex from the Meyer-Murphy factory and had been convicted, at least in part by testimony from Juliana's dad, was at present serving four years in state prison on a plea bargain and not considered to be a suspect.

We'd had briefings every day at the police station, in a windowless lounge next to a kitchen that our techs had transformed into a command post: secured phones, a white board on an easel, a chain of laptops to input Rapid Start—software designed to track every byte of information relevant to the investigation, from interviews to lab reports, photos, computer searches, archives and dust bunnies under the bed. Rapid Start was a cutting-edge tool for examining the particulars and getting the overview. One pair of Big Eyes would be responsible for reading every page of Rapid Start every day: looking for patterns, searching out disconnects—the unanswered questions and the links.

Big Eyes. That would be me.

The case had a name:

UNSUB

Juliana Meyer-Murphy—Victim

Santa Monica Kidnapping

And that's all we had.

Halfway out of bed I stole one more moment, to inhale the slow rich bloom of coffee and listen with pleasure to Andrew banging cabinet doors in the kitchen. My grandmother's quilt lay on the carpet where it had been kicked; jasmine-scented massage oil stood, uncapped, next to a vibrator in full view on the nightstand. I slipped it back under the bed. We had been short of time that morning, forced to take the express route—which, in a tender way, seemed in keeping with our newfound teamwork on the job. He had been right, at the beach, in the parking lot, when he said it would be a kick. More than right. We were free and we were flying. We were hanging in that buoyant pocket in the sky.

I swung into the living room. Milky white light was coming through the curtains. As I drew them back, rows and rows of boats docked at the huge Marina were becoming visible in random jigsaw pieces out of a pale mist—hulls, rigging, motors, masts.

"Sleep well?" Andrew wiggled his nose with obnoxious smugness, then went back to assembling breakfast burritos.

"Pleased with yourself, aren't you?"

He said, "Aren't you?"

A fresh copy of today's *LA Times* lay on the counter. Flipping to the local section I saw no mention of the Santa Monica kidnapping.

"Looks like we still haven't made the news."

"From your lips."

Mortified that her daughter, Stephanie, had sent Juliana on a fool's errand, spunky Mrs. Kent organized a "community response," apparently believing that she and her TV director husband knew more about crime fighting than we did. Laurel West Academy parents came running, with posters, fliers, search parties at the ready and showbiz contacts speed-dialing the story to the national news—exactly wrong. I thought we had been clear on Day One that she would not discuss the case. You didn't want to panic the suspect, have him escalate to murder if the victim wasn't already dead. Special Agent in Charge Robert Galloway had not been pleased. This was not the slick "new politics" of an efficient Bureau. This was anarchy. I had to go back to the Kents' and kick privileged ass. Get them to understand we had a media blackout in effect on this case.

"Don't you like my new furniture?"

"Yeah," said Andrew absently, "it's nice."

I put my arms around him. "Nicer than that dark old stuff in your father's place."

"You are like a little terrier," he said. "Don't you ever let go?"

Holding tighter, "Nope."

I had finally sprung for a whole new deal, all at once, on sale at Plummers. I am a klutz with colors, it was the worst day of my life, but three hours later I staggered out of there having committed to a blonde wood (actually particle board) entertainment center which faced a couch and two small wicker love seats on either side of a coffee table.

The coffee table was a dark varnished rose with a dandy drawer in which I kept a Colt .32 my enlightened grandfather had given to me when I went to college, as protection against what he called "the blacks," as if I were to single-handedly hold off a revolutionary siege at UC–Santa Barbara. When I was arranging the furniture, I stowed the gun in the drawer. Poppy would be proud. The apartment was fortified.

The matching cushions on the love seats and couch were a bold tropical pattern in deep plums and greens, which more or less went with the dark gray carpeting. I had one of those curving chrome lamps you can bend all the way down to read by and some glass vases with dried flowers, which I bought at the farmers' market that weekend, giddy with success. The entertainment center almost had enough shelves for the hundreds of mystery and sci-fi paperbacks I was always trading and borrowing, no longer in piles along the wall.

The place looked like a grown-up lived there. A grown-up who kept tonic and limes in the refrigerator, turkey bologna, hummus, some very nice imported Colby cheese, one percent milk, OJ with calcium, always a couple of beers, usually a leftover pasta primavera or soggy salad in a box, fruit in the bin and Zen muffins in the freezer, along with a slew of frozen diet entrées. A grown-up whose most-used appliance was the blender, with an industrial-sized crock of vanilla protein powder at the ready.

And there was this man in my kitchen, wearing a black short-sleeved knit shirt that had to stretch to get around hard, polished biceps, a zipper at the neck with some logo dangling off, tight jeans with a thick belt that pushed his alleged love handles up (sleek as a bull, he was always fighting ten invisible pounds), loafers, no socks. Long, crazy hours had taught Andrew to keep a change of clothes neatly folded in a gym bag in his trunk.

He had skinned a grapefruit and set perfect pink sections, no stringy white stuff, on each plate.

"How'd you do that?"

"Sharp knife."

"I don't have any sharp knives."

We were sitting at the glass dining table. Glass wasn't such a good idea, but I liked the bamboo legs. He pulled a ring of keys out of his pocket, including a contraption that fanned out like a geometric puzzle into screwdrivers and ice picks, featuring an impressive blade.

"Surgical steel."

He then folded each tool back with a meticulousness that reminded me of the way he ordered the pruning shears. Andrew had a talent for mechanical things.

"What's the program?" he asked.

"Rick thinks it's time to polygraph the parents."

"Cool. I'm going to walk the Promenade. Canvas the merchants again."

"I've assigned an agent to do that," I told him.

"My job."

"I think it should be one of our guys."

He looked up from mixing salsa with the eggs. "What is this, pulling rank?"

"I just know Rick is going to want it covered."

"Do what you need to do. I'm going to look for the transient, Willie John Black."

"What for?"

"Take him in for a composite."

"Good idea. If you want to know what they look like on Mars."

"He's been helpful to me in the past. You can't discount everything he says. A social services guy told me they can be lucid. Their delusions are a defense."

"Against what?"

"Whatever their personal terror might be."

We were picking up the dishes. "Andrew, why? I need you at the Meyer-Murphys'. You know they're going to freak about the polygraph."

"You can handle the M&Ms," Andrew said, "and besides"—he leaned back against the sink and drew me close—"I have to ask you something. Do I have safe passage?"

"You have safe passage."

"It's a favor."

Sighing hugely, "Okay, what do you need?"

He laughed. "You sound like my lieutenant. Only he's nicer."

"I'm nice."

We were nuzzling.

"Yes, you are."

"What kind of favor?"

"I'm a little short right now, and some unexpected things came up. Do you think you could loan me nine hundred bucks?" Then before I could answer he winced self-consciously and added, "It's for the Harley."

He might as well have said it was for a poor starving child in India since that is how he felt about the stupid bike. He worked on it every weekend; he did the Love Ride to Lake Castaic every year.

I knew all that, and yet sometimes you see a vision of the person as he was or will become. In Andrew's pleading eyes there begged a young boy in the shade garden of the home of his adoptive parents, a pretty place, and yet he is unsure about the ground on which he stands. Something is unstable in his world, something he cannot trust, as basic as his name. He wants this thing so desperately, whatever it is, a little toy car, so he can hold it in his fist and it will tell him who he is. Worthy. Powerful. Comforted. Strong. And loved. *Oh give it to him.* I know how it feels to ask.

Lynn Meyer-Murphy was sitting cross-legged on the kitchen floor, wearing the same track pants and sweater she had on since Day One, surrounded by pots and everything else she had taken out of the lower cabinets. Grocery bags were stuffed with mismatched plastic containers and grimy shelf paper.

"Good morning, ma'am."

She turned and I almost flinched. Bright half-moons of scaly pink skin had popped up at the sides of her mouth like a horrible clown grin.

"Any news?"

I shook my head. "But we need to talk. I asked Special Agent Shaw to get your husband."

Eunice Shaw was one of the most grounded people I have known. She had a light about her and spoke and moved in her own time. She was a churchgoing Baptist from Georgia, and even though her hair was straightened and rolled under, circa the civil rights movement, and even though she always wore a dress, even the bad guys wouldn't dis Miss Eunice. She had iron poise. Because of this, she was a born negotiator and an almost religious presence for those, like the Meyer-Murphys, whose suffering had brought them to their knees.

Lynn's fingers were massaging the inflammation. It looked itchy and mean. "Stress," she explained. "Last time I had it this bad was my wedding day. What does that tell you?"

I smiled empathetically while rehearsing how to best inform the parents that they were now under suspicion in the disappearance of their child. Juliana had vanished too completely, with too few leads, for too long a time not to suspect foul play close to home; to consider the case a possible homicide.

"Why do I need this?" Lynn pushed a muffin tin into one of the garbage bags. "But Juliana likes popovers." She pulled it out again. "Not that I ever make popovers."

She sat there with the muffin tin on her lap.

Eunice appeared in the doorway with Ross Murphy. He looked like an eighty-year-old man who just had open-heart surgery.

"Did you get that bastard David Yi?"

"I told you, Mr. Yi is no longer a suspect."

"He has friends," Ross insisted. "*Friends in prison,* have you ever heard of that? It's that bastard Yi. He calls again, you better not let me on the phone!"

An eighty-year-old man waving small weak fists. All puffed up because he was helpless.

I took a breath. "Folks, my supervisor has asked me to bring you in for a polygraph today." When they looked blank I added, "A lie detector test."

"*Us?*"

Eunice left the room to answer her Nextel.

"Standard operating procedure for anyone who might have come in contact with Juliana in the days before she went missing."

"Bullshit," said Ross, "and I resent the implication."

"Oh Ross," snapped his wife, "it's the real world."

"Don't I know it. Doesn't get realer than this. We're her *parents*," he exploded. "We love her! Okay, yes, people chop up their children and put them in concrete. Did we? *No.* Are we dying here? What the hell do you think?"

Lynn was staring at the muffin tin.

"I know you've been through it. But we have to ask the tough questions and there is no question we will not ask, and nobody who will not be scrutinized."

"We have *no problemo* taking your test," Ross hissed, "because we have nothing to hide, but what really pisses me off is the fact that I *gave* you the guy. *David Yi.* Why doesn't anyone listen to me?"

"You're a broken record," murmured his wife in a monotone.

"Hold it," I said. "Everybody take a deep breath."

Lynn had covered her ears with her hands. They were trembling. Then, in slow motion, she keeled over.

"Lynn?"

Sitting cross-legged, she had folded forward until her forehead pressed the floor, as if assuming some kind of yoga position.

Her husband said, "Are you all right?"

"No test."

"What?"

"No reason," she mumbled.

I had to get down on my hands and knees to hear. We looked like two mental patients with ears to the ground, listening for Indian hoofbeats.

"Can you speak a little more clearly?"

Her nose was squashed against the oak flooring. "I should have told you before. I'm sorry I was not forthcoming, but I tried to believe it wasn't true. I didn't want it to be true, but now I'm so afraid because Juliana's still not home."

"What the hell are you talking about?" Ross cried impatiently. He was bent over in a squat, hands on kneecaps, head cocked toward his wife.

"Eunice!" I wanted a witness. "Take it easy, Mrs. Meyer-Murphy—"

"I had an affair!" Lynn sobbed quietly. "I had an affair in Milan, with a buyer from Nordstrom."

Ross closed his eyes and shook his head with a look of perverse satisfaction, as if he had always known this punishment would come to him.

"He took my baby!" Lynn was now convulsed with tears. "Oh my God," she kept saying. "Oh my God, oh my God."

Eunice was back, hooking the cell phone on her belt. She took in the scene with a knowing sigh.

"Why would this man kidnap Juliana?" I was asking.

"He was very, very angry with me—"

"Why, honey?" Eunice crooned. "How could he be that angry he would take your child?"

"Because he's mean, and possessive, and I ended the relationship."

"You ended the relationship?"

"I sent his underwear to his wife."

"*Who is this?*" demanded Ross. "*Who are you talking about?* Is this Ed Hobart?"

Lynn's whole face went crimson, and she was making coughing, barking sounds. Eunice and I were kneeling beside her and speaking soothingly, but it was impossible to unfold her from that repentant pose. Her body was like locked steel. Where was Andrew with his melting embrace?

"It's Hobart," said Ross with a tight, tight smile. "Head of the whole wonderful overseas Nordstrom operation. Good. Good choice. Go fuck Hobart. I guess there's no need for *the loser* anymore."

He straightened up and left. A door slammed. Eunice and I exchanged a look and she darted after him.

"Tell us about this man and we will check him out."

"He lives in Seattle," Lynn gasped, "but he comes down here all the time. Oh, what if he has Juliana? All I can think about are terrible, awful, horrible things—"

"Ana!" Eunice interrupted sharply. "We have a situation. Dad locked himself in the powder room."

"You must think we're a bunch of lunatics," sniffled Lynn.

I dragged her to her feet and into the foyer with the hat rack and the pile of Rollerblades beneath it and a small Oriental rug.

"Is there a window? What's in there?"

"I don't know," she whimpered. "Bathroom stuff."

"Ross." I banged on the door. "What's going on?"

"Ross!" called Lynn hoarsely. "Come out."

I heard the toilet flushing.

"You all right, buddy?"

No answer.

"Talk to me, Ross. Or I'm going to have to come in there to make sure you're all right."

"Screw you!"

"Listen to me. We're making progress—"

"You don't know what the fuck is going on. You don't know if my daughter is alive."

"We don't have anything that says she's *not* alive."

Silence.

"Let's come out and talk about it, Ross." Nothing. "You'll work this through with your wife. You're both under a lot of stress right now—"

"I'm sorry, Ross!" Lynn cried. "I love you. I'm sorry! I never meant to hurt you, but I had to tell. I had to tell to get Juliana back. She's the only thing that matters, please—"

"I'm tired of this bullshit. Nobody listens to me."

"*I'm* listening to you," I answered boldly. "What is bullshit, Ross? Your definition. Tell me what that is."

"Bullshit is not getting anywhere. Bullshit is farting around and dicking around when I *told you to go after Yi.*"

"I hear you about Yi. What else is bullshit?"

Silence.

"Are you thinking of doing something to yourself in there, Ross? Are you thinking of committing suicide?"

"Fuck you. Fuck everybody!"

"You haven't answered my question. Do you want to kill yourself?"

Eunice said, "I think we should call for backup. Get the guys outside—"

"I know," I said, "but I'd rather—"

Suddenly the door flew open. My hand went to my weapon.

Eunice yelled, "Watch out!"

Lynn screamed, *"Don't shoot my husband!"*

We ducked and rolled.

Ross was standing in the doorway of the bathroom, holding a gun.

"Easy! Easy!" he cried. "Don't shoot! Jesus Christ!"

"Put the weapon *down* on the ground. *Now.*"

He put it on the ground. It was not a gun. Worse. A cell phone.

Six.

An emergency briefing was called for 5 p.m.

The Santa Monica Police Department was housed in back of City Hall, in a white Moderne building with blue trim that suggested sand and sea. The police department was in the lee of the building, away from sand and sea, looking at an overpass. If you narrowed your vision to exclude the high-rise hotels, condominiums and gangland ghettos, you might get an idea of what they saw when they built this public works project in the thirties: a sleepy little beach town sparkling with optimism in which all that would be required of the local police would be the management of drunks and theft of the occasional Packard.

They built it small and it stayed small—quaint, by today's antiseptic standards. The vintage sixties station in Long Beach, where my grandfather, Poppy, served, looks hip by comparison, and the Bureau downright millennial, I thought, quickening my pace across the Civic Center plaza. It was four-thirty and already several Bu-cars were lined up in the lot.

The entryway held a couple of metal chairs and drawings on the wall by schoolchildren. Turn right and a brown arrow led to the hold-ing cells. The hallway to the left was short and dully lit, lined with cases of patches and awards. Over a doorway swung the kind of lacquered wooden sign they used to have in Western movies over the saloon, only this one read *Licenses*. I hoped they never remodeled the place. I hoped they turned it into a museum.

As I hurried up the staircase leading to Investigations, a woman clattered right into my arms.

"Ana! All the computers went down!"

Margaret Forrester, the police liaison working with the Bureau on the kidnap, had a flair for the dramatic, but as she gripped my elbows, eyes wide, it was clear she was not kidding.

"I am in such trouble!" she stuttered. "Where is your guy?"

She was a beautiful woman, about thirty years old, with layers of glossy brown hair and a face too decorative, too perfectly formed, with its strong dark eyebrows, squarish cheekbones and egg-white skin, to belong in a police station. You had to wonder at the natural selection that produced such a striking girl from a pair of alcoholic dirt-poor Oklahoma drifters, who, according to her, literally lived in the dirt, picking apricots and peaches in the San Joaquin Valley. Nobody at the station looked like Margaret, nobody dressed like Margaret, in a well-cut camel sheath with a shawl collar, low-slung belt and suede boots. Her usual accessories were an ID tag and a water bottle. There was a tinkle about her I would later identify as seashells. She had a business on the side: fashioning natural objects into "body adornments" that she sold to stores. She often wore her own creations. That day it might have been a concoction of abalones, or Native American bracelet charms with feathers.

"Which guy are you talking about?"

"The tech. There he is—Ramon!" she called up the stairs. "Come down here, sweetheart, I'll show you where the circuit breaker is!"

Ramon's work boots thundered out of the dimness and he ap-peared, holding a flashlight.

"I think it might be under there." Margaret indicated an unlikely hatch beneath the staircase. "But your computers are what's causing the problem."

"It ain't *our* computers, Chiquita," Ramon said disdainfully. "It's *your* freaking wiring," grimacing as he pried at the warped door.

"Hope you like spiders," I called humorously.

Ramon answered with a Spanish phrase he knew I would not understand. Margaret's hands were still somehow all over me as we chugged upstairs. But then she was all over everyone, shouting, *"Congratulations! I heard Brian made the soccer team!"* to a busy secretary, or giving the thumbs-up to a baffled cadet behind the desk. The waiting area was basically a wooden pew underneath a pot of fake begonias furry with mold, the yellowing walls smudged with finger marks, as if people had been crawling up them for decades.

Lean bicycle cops and sour overweight detectives were going in and out and Margaret had a word or a touch or a hug for each. Following in her wake was like looking through a camera in which smiling fish-eye faces loomed and fell away. The smiles were tolerant, and I wondered why. She had no experience and was no help to me. Working with the locals was tricky enough—they already resented the Feds. You hoped your contact person would be a professional, but here was an individual better suited to hostessing a martini bar.

When I said something like, *"What's with that Margaret Forrester?"* Andrew responded with a sharp rebuke that Margaret Forrester was a police widow. Her husband (they called him "the Hat" because he shaved his head) had been one of Andrew's closest buddies, an undercover narcotics detective murdered by a gang; but he had been assaulted and killed while off-duty, and therefore his pension benefits were denied. Out of compassion, and because the Forresters had two young children, the department gave Margaret this job.

"I hate spiders!" she confided. "They eat my cashmere sweaters."

I have never owned a cashmere sweater or a new gold Lexus sedan, but Margaret Forrester had these things. They lived in a tiny cottage in the wrong part of Venice, but she would throw birthday parties for the police chief at the swank Loew's Hotel, only the *select people* invited.

She had been, according to the careless scuttlebutt you pick up at two in the morning, stunningly ambitious for her husband, to the point of leaking stories about his cases to the press so reporters would call and include his name. But now, according to the blue code of sacrifice, we were all supposed to cut Margaret Forrester a lot of slack.

We entered a single space where twenty investigators were jammed together. A lot of them wore telephone headpieces to block out the noise. Since they redesigned our offices I missed the camaraderie of our old bull pen, but in this arrangement you had to smell your neighbor's aftershave all day and look at the ass end of his computer monitor slopped over your desk. In fact it was hard to see where one desk ended and another began, as they seemed to work on one square surface billowing with papers and personal clutter. The walls were brick and the window blinds maroon. It felt like we had walked into a bad TV crime show from the seventies.

Our team was arriving for the briefing, talking in small edgy groups. Everyone in the field was fired up about something, hoping their little piece would complete the mosaic and be remembered as the one link that led to the safe recovery of the victim. You don't make big salary jumps based on big scores at the Bureau; merit accrues from the steady accumulation of good choices and the intelligent analysis of details, most of which goes into a file that nobody but a supervisor will ever see. Briefings in high-visibility cases give the rare opportunity to show your moves in varsity play.

Computer techs were crawling under the table as two agents frantically tried to re-create the timeline by tacking brown butcher paper on the wall, unrolling it over notices of bake sales and group discounts to Universal Studios, while two others followed with marking pens and printouts from Rapid Start, copying in large letters the sequence of developments in the case.

Big-time federal agency.

Rick Harding strode in a few minutes short of 5 p.m., wearing a navy blue suit and wraparound sunglasses that made him look like a corporate president on steroids, sliding his briefcase down the conference table past a row of computer screens showing odd cascades of numbers.

"People?" he called.

We began to settle, in the close wood-paneled room with the soda machine droning on, next to a kitchen where someone was using a microwave. There was the black-and-white of Juliana holding on to the tree and a blown-up school portrait of her looking out in the tired ocher light, with the glassy expression of martyrs too young to have known the passion for which they died. At the last minute, Andrew appeared in the doorway. Two rookies stepped aside for the senior detective.

"Let's start," said Rick, ritually hanging his jacket on the back of the metal chair.

I took my place beside my supervisor. Forty-seven, a former navy pilot, Rick wore his mustache neat and blond hair clipped. He always looked tight, but today he was pretty well steamed. You could tell because he unclipped the handcuffs from his belt and started tapping them on his thigh.

We are all fussy about our handcuffs. You are issued one pair that can last your whole career if you're smart enough not to lend them. Like any other tool, they become worn with handling and acquire an idiosyncratic feel, so you can tell which is yours just by touch. Nothing is more straightforward than a pair of handcuffs. In times of stress they are a comfort; you will often see several people in a high-intensity meeting worrying and working their little rings of power.

The only problem with handcuffs is sometimes they fall in the toilet bowl. If you are a woman, especially, this will happen when you're in a hurry and you forget to lift them out of the back of your waistband before lowering your pants. Then you will hear behind you the unmistakable, heart-stopping sound of metal falling on porcelain.

All of us have heard it, more than once.

"What's all this?" Rick asked of the brown paper snaking around the walls.

"Computers went down," chorused several people.

He nodded grimly as if expecting one insult after another. "Now we've got a media leak, is that right, Ana?"

General groans and shifting in chairs.

"Right. The dad called channel five."

Eunice chimed in. "He locked himself in the bathroom and used a cell phone. He believed that if he could get the daughter on TV, it would lead to her recovery."

"Was it not explained to the gentleman there is a media blackout on this case because it might escalate the suspect?"

"Yes," I cut in, "but he was crazed because his wife had just admitted that she had a boyfriend. She thought this guy might have taken Juliana for revenge. I asked Special Agent Jason Ripley to check him out. *Jason?*"

I said it so harshly the poor kid jumped. He had been an agent only eight months—skinny and ginger-haired, still so eager he wore a three-piece suit every day.

"The suspect's name is Ed Hobart."

"He's not a suspect yet," I reminded Jason gently. Since when did I become a mother hen?

"The *subject*. Sorry." His acne flushed pink. "Upstanding, church-going father of six. Mr. Hobart is a senior buyer in ladies' fashions, who oversees a budget of five million dollars . . ."

My Nextel was vibrating, then the pager. It was Special Agent in Charge Robert Galloway, messaging me to return to the field office immediately.

"As for Mr. Hobart's current whereabouts, the Seattle field office should be getting back to us within the hour . . ."

"Rick," I said softly while Jason went on, "gotta go."

"What's up?"

"Galloway paged me twice."

"What does he want?" Rick whispered back. "If it's about the media leak, tell him we can handle channel five—"

We were talking with heads averted, so everybody knew something was going on. By now a lot of people packing guns had crowded into the room, including Andrew's lieutenant, Barry Loomis, who wore a walrus mustache and a Superman tie, and Officer Sylvia Oberbeck, impassively chewing gum. She looked put together, just going on shift: heavy mascara and a freshly braided bun. At one point I tried to make eye contact, but she did not seem to remember who I was. There was the rustle of seashells, and Margaret Forrester suddenly pushed through, swinging the water bottle, stepping over legs.

"Damn! Computers still out?" Fanning herself at the collective menthol-scented body heat. "What did I miss?"

"Case closed, go home," someone replied disagreeably.

"There's been another development, Rick," interrupted Special Agent Todd Hanley. He was a reliable sort. Narrow-faced, with horn-rimmed glasses, achingly serious, he wore tweedy sport coats and spoke only when it was relevant.

Maybe he was a spy.

"It also concerns the dad."

Rick: "We are so past the damn dad."

Nervous giggles. Bored, cynical looks.

"Just so you know, legal says Mr. Murphy has threatened to sue. Claims he sprained his back during the altercation with Special Agent Grey."

Thirty sets of eyes went my way, including Andrew's.

"What altercation?" I said defensively. "He tripped on a rug."

Rick now was ratcheting the handcuffs with a rhythmic, grating sound.

"Oh, please," I went on, "I admonished him about the cell phone, he took a swing at me and slipped on a Chinese rug. He was fine."

"When he was barricaded in the rest room," Rick seemed to have to ask, "why didn't you call for backup? There was a surveillance team outside."

"What were the ladies supposed to do?" cracked Andrew. "Bring in the artillery because the guy was taking a good, long shit?"

Amazement. Big laughs. Margaret squealing: "An-*drew*! I'm going to kill you!"

I wanted to crawl under the table. *Don't make this a fight!*

Andrew must have stuck his head under the shower in the locker room because he looked refreshed. His thick dark hair was slicked back; he wore his shield on his hip, a hand-tooled leather gun belt and a fresh lilac blue shirt with a monogrammed cuff through which you could see the sculpted moves of his shoulders.

Still, I wanted to throttle him, especially when, as I pushed away from the table to leave, he said, "Where are you off to?" as if we were the only two people in the room.

"Back to the office."

"What about 'Arizona?'" It sounded like a code. People were watching us.

My gut clenched. "It's premature to talk about 'Arizona.'"

Margaret shook her hair and took a long throaty draw on the water. "Sounds like Ana doesn't want to share."

"It's a promising lead but needs to be developed," I said dismissively.

Andrew replied, "Bullshit."

"It is bullshit," I repeated, now confused. We had not discussed this. I was not ready to present some half-baked theory based on the statements of a crazy homeless person.

Rick: "Could you two clue us in?"

"Sure," said Andrew. "The source is a transient named Willie John Black."

It was a bad moment, as I feared it would be. Andrew's own people guffawed and began offering comments on their encounters with Black, who apparently was famous in the world of social services for his movable collection of wire hangers, coils of nylon tied with the precision of a yachtsman, cereal boxes, gloves, strips of fabric, milk cartons and the occasional flag mounted onto a trio of bicycles tied together, upon which he had somehow secured a full-sized camping tent. They didn't let him take it on the Promenade so he kept the thing parked in an alley across the street.

"Black puts the victim with a young white male," said Andrew, who seemed the only one at ease in the room. He held a small investigator's notebook, to which he did not need to refer, and spoke with an authority that held the respect of a bunch of disbelieving, over-tired cops.

"We know Juliana went there to buy marijuana. I make the suspect as a dealer. He has a camera, which he uses as a cover. Black says the guy is from Arizona, so I want to use narcotics investigators on the local level to identify this individual. We should reach out immediately to law enforcement in Arizona."

Nobody spoke. Margaret Forrester—peacekeeper and liaison—was mouthing the water bottle, big eyes gone bland, as if she had nothing to do with any of this. My heart was jackhammering; I was hoping Rick would not force me to make the call.

"Sounds like a poor use of resources," he said. "Mr. Black is obviously a questionable source."

"That's your judgment."

"Of course it's his judgment," I said nicely. "This is an FBI investigation."

Andrew shut me down with a cold-blooded look—"Now you're telling me who's in charge?"—and my overbeating heart clutched at the shock of his anger.

His lieutenant intervened: "We'll employ our own resources to follow up on Detective Berringer's recommendation."

"Thank you, Barry," said Rick.

The pager went off again.

"This is whack," I cursed under my breath, quickly shouldering handbag and canvas briefcase.

Rick had given up on the handcuffs, which lay splayed upon the table. The mood was suddenly wilted and depressed. There was no more oxygen left in the room, and what did we have? No new ransom demands. A half-assed boyfriend and a schizophrenic.

"Keep me informed," said my boss. "And watch your back."

I went out through the kitchen exit to avoid passing close to Andrew.

Seven.

The fog was a surprise, but along the coast it often comes up quickly. When I left the police station, sometime after six, everything smelled of water. The air wasn't air but cold humidity that had congealed. From inside the car, the windshield was impenetrable. I let the defroster blow. According to the dashboard readout, the temperature had fallen to thirty-seven degrees.

Someone was rubbing a clear circle in the driver's side glass. Fingernails scratched and a round face peered close, spooking me. When I lowered the window I saw that it was Margaret Forrester. With hair frizzed out by the mist and some kind of seashells on a thong around her neck, she looked like a creature hauled out of the sea, a siren, regarding me with dark eyes that seemed to shine with strange compassion. Steam curled and vanished from her small-sculpted nostrils as she considered what to say.

Finally it was just, "Drive carefully."

"I will. You, too."

She smiled sympathetically and reached in and patted my hand on the wheel. I grinned like a cat until she had withdrawn and the window rose again and sealed off the vaporous outside.

What was her concern? Was it for Juliana, disappeared into the dark psychic stink of America? The fog was blanking out the street lamps, making the night unnaturally dim, a guttural gray through which they shone just faintly. But sometimes the fog would be a lens, diffusing a pair of headlamps passing behind a tree so its outline would spring out, monumentally visible, each twig and leaf in flashing silhouette as if etched by a laser.

I wished for that same shocking clarity in our search for Juliana, even as I fought a growing instinct it would not occur. There was uncertainty beneath the frenzy of the briefing, a stain of helplessness that seemed to be numbing Rick. We were all giving in to the fear that we had failed. Look at us, Andrew and me, fighting in public like dogs over territory.

I dialed his pager: *Code 3-AG.*

Emergency.

It was ten long minutes of creeping through fog until he called back.

"Still in the briefing?"

"That's been over."

"I'm sorry for what happened back there."

When he didn't gush, *Oh my darling, I'm sorry too,* my instinct for compromise evaporated.

"We never talked about going with Willie John Black." My voice was hard.

"This is not working," Andrew decided abruptly. "Let's forget it."

"It's a little late, don't you think?" I listened to his impatient snort into the mouthpiece. "This is what I told you would happen on the beach."

"I work independently. I don't report to the lieutenant every time I take a crap."

"Now you're accusing me of pulling rank."

"That's not what I'm saying."

"But you've *said* it, about this very thing, Willie John Black. *'What is this, pulling rank?'*"

"When? When did I say that?"

"This morning, at breakfast."

Now there was silence. I knew what he was thinking: just like a woman to start whining about personal shit.

"Andrew? We're still together on this, am I right?"

"Sure, baby," he said with penetrating indifference. "Doesn't matter to me."

"What doesn't?"

"Kiss up to your boss, that's cool. Just stay out of my business." He hung up.

Sometimes the temperature drops and you are blinded. All that I could see in front of me was swirling white and not the labyrinth beyond—the sudden drop-offs, veering alley walls and bottomless puddles into which whole cars could up-end and disappear—creeping inch by inch all the way to Westwood, and the police scanner was jammed with accidents, hit dogs, frightened seniors lost at indistinguishable intersections, reports of a fire.

A bus had rammed a car in front of the Federal Building. Traffic was stalled and lights were blinking idiotic green. When I finally pulled into the parking lot, I was surprised to find it still half full. People must be waiting it out. You could see the red throat of the stuck freeway from the upper stories of the tower.

The stark brightness of the institutional lobby gave little relief from the mayhem outside, only serving as a reminder that steely measures were required to keep things in order; there was no room for soft upholstery of any kind. We were the Department of Justice, not the Department of Comfort. The elevators were sterile, and the turnstile where you swiped your card a floor-to-ceiling cage of bars that rotated loyalty and discipline in, individuality out.

We all used to work together in an open bull pen. The supervisors had window offices around the rim, the grunts labored at traditional oak desks pushed together in the center of the room, like the detectives at the Santa Monica Police Department. There were no walls or encumbrances, you could see at a glance where everybody was and who they were gossiping with, and you could feel fine about important work being done by decent people, even though most of them were middle-aged men in white shirts who kept their shoulder holsters on.

You damn well knew where you were.

Then the elders started to retire in waves, and the rest of us watched with apprehension as a generation of experience and chops walked out the door, while the technology to replace them walked in. Some android in the administrative division got rid of the oak and installed workstations covered in charcoal acoustical felt arranged in "pods" like alien seedlings, and we were all supposed to sit in front of our computer screens and germinate, nothing to look at except the constellation of pushpins on our mini bulletin boards, also covered in charcoal acoustical felt, where the messages we posted were only to ourselves.

This reduced the sound level to a few shuffles and the occasional belly laugh, and chopped up the social space into a confusing stew. Once sight lines were cut off nothing was clear. You couldn't just look up from your desk and with one sweep register the current pecking order, or instantly see who was making it with whom. The new kids, like Jason Ripley, didn't seem to have the time or imagination to fool around anyway. My pod was occupied by raw rookies with fast agendas who considered me an old fart even though I had only ten years in. Naturally, I distrusted them, too. In the new configuration, our time-honored FBI paranoia grew like a fungus in the dark.

I had not been back to the office since I met Andrew in the parking lot and gone straight to the M&Ms. I found myself moving through the darkened space with customary informality, like unlocking the front door and walking into your living room after a long trip. The collection of plastic trolls on my work surface was reassuringly in place, chair stowed. The in box had acquired three days' worth of debris, the

cartons of court papers and files I pulled for the ninety-day file review
as untended as before. The stress I had been feeling about the review
seemed remote as I zigzagged through the charcoal matrix toward the
executive suite, where the lights were still on.

Special Agent in Charge Robert Galloway, originally from New
York, was an expert on organized crime who brought a rock-solid
street savvy to the fluid complexities of LA. For a long time he sat up
there on the seventeenth floor with his dead cigars and trademark
turtlenecks, steering the field office through terrorist threats and internal scandals like a captain in a season of squalls, until his wife, an elite
mountain climber, left him for another elite mountain climber, and he
sank into a terrible depression.

How do I know? I once saw him in his car, in the far reaches of the
garage, sobbing.

After a while he seemed to regain some balance, joked about taking "herbal supplements," which I guess meant antidepressants, but
still, he could be irritable, and irrational, and susceptible to scrutiny,
more sensitive than ever about the Bureau "looking stupid" in the
media, which is why he'd come up with this "new politics" idea. He
also had a seventeen-year-old daughter devastated by the divorce who,
rumor was, had been arrested DUI.

I found him in the corner office with the soft carpeting and real
furniture, behind an old-fashioned four-legged desk. A bookcase held
his New York City horror show collection of Statues of Liberty, bound
*Playbill*s, NYPD mugs, a whip, a miniature guillotine, a human skull,
a severed finger, possibly real, a dusty centennial quart of Guinness ale,
a black wig and a replica of Poe's cottage in the Bronx. The walls
were taken up with celebrity photos: Galloway (a younger man) with
the mayor, senator and Bobby Kennedy; Galloway on the tracks in
front of a subway car, inspecting the remains of a jumper; signed cast
photos from TV cop shows shot in New York; a plastic box contain-
ing yellowed memorabilia from the opening of Mickey Mantle's restaurant, including a champagne glass with giddy lettering—*Spavinaw,
Okla!*—and a matchbook signed by the legend himself.

"Glad you could make it." He looked at his watch, a chrome Rolex. "What'd you do, take the bus?"

"Fog. It's bad. Don't go anyplace."

"Where do I have to go?" shrugged Galloway.

Self-pity was now the norm. I learned to ignore it. If you attempted to commiserate about the state of his emotions, he would savage you.

"Got an alert from HQ. It's come to their attention about the situation in Santa Monica. High visibility, especially if it goes south. They wanted us to be aware that they got three hits on VICAP, which might link Juliana Meyer-Murphy to three other missing juveniles. In each of these cases—Georgetown; South Beach, Florida; and Austin, Texas— you have a teenage girl disappearing from a youth-oriented area like the Third Street Promenade."

I had become distracted by a young woman I had never seen before who was sitting in the visitor's chair.

"Ana Grey, meet Kelsey Owen."

She looked like part of Galloway's quirky collection. Bureau folks wear suits. Black, brown, navy. Kelsey Owen went for ethnic—long, tiered Mexican skirts and oversized sweaters. Once, even a straw sun hat. She was late twenties, nice skin, long curly dark hair like a folksinger's and just chunky enough to appear nonthreatening.

We shook hands.

"Kelsey is over at NSD," Galloway explained. "But she wants to get into the Crimes Against Children Unit."

"You're a new agent?"

She nodded. "This is my second year. I just love it."

"Isn't that great?" Galloway jabbed the unlit cigar. *"Enthusiasm!"*

I gave him a sardonic flick of the eyes. *Enthusiasm?* What the hell did he think was going on over at the command post, twenty-four/ seven?

He gave me the printout from headquarters, including photographs of the other victims, aged fourteen to sixteen. They all resembled one another: dark, shoulder-length hair and smooth, hopeful faces. The others were still missing; only the girl from South Beach had been recovered alive.

"Kelsey is a trained psychotherapist. I think we should pay more attention to the psychology of the offender."

"We do. It's called criminal investigative analysis."

It used to be called profiling, but the term sounded too much like racial profiling, so they figured out a way to make it incomprehensible altogether. After completing several hundred hours of advanced instruction at Quantico, I was selected to be a profile coordinator. I learned how to analyze a suspect by age, profession, marital status, sexual history, style of attack, IQ, social adjustment, appearance and grooming habits and a host of other factors in order to come up with a hypothetical portrait. Profiling is not about whether the guy was potty-trained too early. It's a working description that narrows the field.

As soon as we had a couple of freaking facts, *of course I was going to look at the psychology of the offender!* I was groping for it now.

"I'm talking the *causes* of why things go sour," Galloway went on. "We don't pay enough attention to what happens in relationships."

Relationships? This was not Galloway-speak. "Kelsey can provide some insights."

"I really want to do what you do," Kelsey said.

"I've been doing it ten years," I replied darkly.

"I hope to learn from you," she swooned, "and not make the same mistakes you made."

Just the kind of insight I needed.

Galloway tapped the unlit cigar in a clean ashtray. "What's the status over there?"

"You mean the Santa Monica kidnapping?"

"No, the Lakers game. Jesus Christ, Ana, don't give me a lot of shit."

Irritable.

"All the mechanisms are in place but no new ransom calls. We're developing two suspects: one is the mom's ex-boyfriend, the other a white male seen with Juliana on the Promenade. With the information we have right now, we believe the suspect may be a drug dealer from Arizona, which doesn't rule out the unsubs from the east—"

"Is this a high-risk victim?" interrupted Kelsey Owen. "Is she known to use drugs or prostitute herself on the street?"

I gritted my teeth. Why me?

"*No*, she is not high-risk, and *yes*, we know all about the victimology. These are questions we have asked, and continue to ask, since Day One. Believe me, we are living with it night and day."

I realized from Galloway's narrowing expression I had better put the brakes on my Inner Bitch.

"The Santa Monica police are developing the lead on Arizona," I said flatly and finally. "It'll all be up on Rapid Start. Do you know how to access Rapid Start?"

"I'll find out," Kelsey promised brightly.

I gave her a worn-out smile; that's what it's like up here in the stratosphere.

"I wanted you two to meet because it's an interesting case and I thought you would get along," Galloway intoned. "Sisters in crime."

I had stopped listening. I was thinking about a Subway sandwich and a bag of chips.

"And on top of that, Ana is a natural to be a mentor."

"Listen," Kelsey was saying, "it doesn't have to be a formal thing—"

"What doesn't?"

"—because I'm still officially on the national security squad, so you can copy me the material and we can have coffee whenever you—"

I was prancing like a little kid who had to pee. *Don't do this to me!*

"This is really not a good time—"

Galloway was mouthing the cigar thoughtfully. "You say Santa Monica is handling the possible link to Arizona?"

"Yes."

"I want us to do it."

"Why?" My stomach tightened. "They've got a senior detective on it, very competent guy—"

"Doesn't matter," Galloway replied. "Headquarters is going to want no doubt about who makes this case."

"What happened to the 'new politics'?" I was riled. I was pissed. I did not want to have another conversation about this with Andrew. "I thought we were supposed to share."

"Sharing is good. As long as we get the bigger piece. You have a problem?"

"I guess it's been a while since I was in the sandbox."

The phone was ringing. Kelsey was giving me a sisterly shrug.

"Yeah, Rick," said Galloway, dismissing us both with a wave of the stogie. "What've you got?"

The surveillance team had been in place. That night it was a pair of rookies, I don't know their names. As usual there had been little movement on the tranquil street since the last of the dog walkers, around eight. Lights were on in the Meyer-Murphy home, where day and night had merged into what Willie John Black would call a "candlelight situation," wonderfully descriptive, if you think about it, of a halftone state in which the present and future are equally without meaning or illumination.

The first verbal report stated, "Someone is walking up the street."

This was transmitted to walkie-talkies inside the house and recording equipment in the Bureau and command center.

"Walking slowly. Weaving. Possibly intoxicated."

Someone muttered, "Ten-four," to let the guys in the car know somewhere in the city another human was listening.

"I think it's a female. Can't tell in the fog." More alert: "She's heading up the path."

In reply, Eunice Shaw's voice from inside the house was sharp. You could sense her bearing down since the cell phone incident.

"I can see somebody out there," she confirmed. "Who is it?"

"Coming your way," warned surveillance.

"To the front door!"

"Can't see shit in this fog—"

"Get out of the car," she ordered, *"right now!"*

And they were, in a heartbeat, because out of the heavy mist drifted a hollow, dirt-stained face with feral matted filthy hair—a crippled figure Eunice first made as a homeless alcoholic or some demented member of the kidnap outfit—until she came underneath the exterior lamp, and Eunice saw the T-shirt was hanging open like a vest, for it had been slit down the middle, and the torso had been wound with bloody gauze.

"Oh sweet Jesus," Eunice breathed and opened the door and drew the girl inside. "Don't be afraid, Juliana. I'm Eunice Shaw with the FBI. We've been looking for you, baby. Your parents are waiting for you, right upstairs."

Juliana swayed, listless, lightweight, as if about to float off her feet. She was pale and shocky. For a moment Eunice froze with hands on her shoulders, holding her upright, and made eye contact over her lolling head with one of the stupefied young male agents who had skidded through the doorway and Eunice's black eyes were pleading and accusatory and infuriated and without being told he radioed 911 while the other agent went scuffling up the stairs to stammer to the parents that their little girl was home.

Eight.

The parents were like strangers, sitting on opposite sides of the hospital corridor. The minute you saw them your heart sank.

Their anxious bickering had at least been a connection. Now, at this unimaginable moment, when they needed the comfort of rabbis and saints, these two could not even bring themselves to touch each other's hand.

He, wearing a shiny purple jacket that said *Laurel West Academy,* as if it were Juliana's swim team practice instead of a rape exam at one in the morning, hauled himself up from the seat. In the harsh light I noticed how the jaw drifted slightly to one side, as if years ago someone had taken a good and accurate slug at him.

"You all did a great job."

"I'm glad we could be of help."

She, back in control of her public self, had dressed in businesslike khakis with a blue sweater and spotless white tennis shoes, but looked, if it were possible, as if she had lost another ten pounds in the last twelve hours. Wordlessly, she put her arms around me, and I could feel the fragile shoulder bones.

"It isn't over," Ross warned. "You've got to get the guy."

"Believe me, Mr. Murphy, that's the plan."

"Who," said his wife, eyes communicating her private torment, "do you think it was?"

"I couldn't speculate right now."

"But you'll keep us informed?"

"You'll be informed."

"I just want to say—," but Ross couldn't say it. He ducked his head and swiped at his eyes. "If I acted badly, I didn't mean to cause any trouble . . . I was just trying to get my daughter back."

I nodded, eyes stung with empathy. "It was a difficult time for everyone."

"If there's anything we can do for you," he began stalwartly, "on a personal level—"

"No, no, no—" I may have blushed. "Please."

"I understand." He put up a meaty hand as if he were a kingpin in the Russian mafia. The fluorescent lights glinted off his gold spectacles. "Just know it's there."

What is? I wanted to say. The automatic doors blew open and Andrew came through on the hustle.

Ross greeted him with some kind of white suburban power handshake and a dozen claps on the shoulder of his leather jacket.

"She's back, huh? She made it! She's a survivor, that kid! I feel like I should be handing out cigars!"

But there was a contradictory sadness behind Ross's bravura. We all knew, standing there, the life of this family had been kicked off track and lay twisted and skewed like a toy train, smashed by the heel of someone who resented its ordered path around in a circle; the perfect miniature town inside.

"Ana, they want you."

Ross: "What's going on?"

"Procedure," Andrew explained. "They like having law enforcement in on the initial interview so the victim doesn't have to go through the story twice. I do it all the time with rape victims, but Juliana requested a female."

I had an ungracious thought: Had he been trying to edge me out?

"I'm glad Ana will be with her," said Lynn. "My daughter's never even been to a gynecologist." Her voice faltered. "And for this to be her first examination . . ."

"Listen," said Ross, "we're lucky she was only raped."

Andrew and I exchanged a look. The guy was at the beginning of a long road.

"She did not sustain major injuries aside from the superficial cutting, but she has been sexually assaulted and brutalized," Andrew stated emphatically. "We'll find out to what extent in a couple of hours."

He had my respect. He was patient but firm, and despite his often-repeated credo *Bullshit makes the world go round,* he was not bull-shitting here. I wondered how many parents, husbands, siblings and friends of rape victims he had made this same speech to, in this same corridor, over twenty years as a cop, and if the competence and authority that went from the leather soles of his work shoes firmly gripping the floor to the priestly intertwine of his fingers resting like a bowl held out toward the family had brought any comfort at all.

"Detective? Can we talk?"

We moved aside, and I took a deep breath and asked where he was on the Arizona investigation.

"Just getting off the ground. Sent a bulletin to Phoenix, they'll post it statewide. Why? Checking up on me?" he added, half kidding.

"No." I smiled, glad he could joke. "This is not my idea, okay? I fought for you. But the SAC wants the Bureau to take the Arizona connection from here. He wants all the marbles, and it's his game." I ran a hand through my hair. "I'm sorry. I hoped we never had to bring this up again."

Andrew shrugged. "Doesn't matter to me," he said tonelessly.

I chose to believe him. "See you later?"

"You bet." He nodded toward the doors. "Be with Juliana. Go."

"How is she?"

"One tough cookie." Andrew put his fists in his pockets. "He tortured her, you know."

Juliana Meyer-Murphy, still wearing her own clothes, was sitting up beside a nurse-practitioner on a sofa in the Rape Treatment Center clinic at the Santa Monica–UCLA Medical Center. I expressed my joy and relief that she was safe, as we had been working very hard to get her back.

Many things were working on me in the first moments I met Juliana. Andrew's caution not to identify with the victim had already gone by the wayside. She boasted none of the arrogance of her friend Stephanie Kent, but was, achingly, a child, whose first steps into the adult world had been slammed by a bully—not unlike my own experience, growing up without a father in a household dominated by my grandfather's eccentric punishment of my mother and me, not by fists but by a kind of psychological enslavement to his authority, keeping us isolated in the one-eyed brick house on Pine Street. I still thought of the house that way: one of its two staring front windows was covered by a bush.

"A lot of people care about you," I told the girl.

"That's supposed to make a difference?" rasped Juliana in a strange, deep voice, like a person with emphysema.

The shock of that voice made me want to make this girl believe that somebody would care for her wounds, unconditionally.

"It does make a difference. It *will*."

The nurse introduced herself. *Nancy Reicher, RN, NP,* it said on her tag. She was petite, with eyebrows plucked in two thin arches. She wore a knee-length white lab coat with a stethoscope in the pocket, small gold earrings and a garnet ring. Her manner was practiced without being cold. She explained again to Juliana who I was and asked if it was okay if I was present at the medical interview.

"Are you comfortable with that?"

"All right, whatever."

"Thank you," I said. "Everything you can tell us will help to track, apprehend and prosecute the offender."

Juliana looked younger and less robust than in the enlarged school photograph that had been keeping watch over the command center. Here instead was a drawn, delicately featured girl whose quiet aliveness in this tranquil room struck me as one of nature's most resounding miracles.

And again, something hopeful: we were, at least, in a rape treatment center of the kind that did not always exist, where the revolutionary message was that the hurts you cannot see are sometimes the most devastating, but that even inside the deepest hurt is the promise held, like the easy abandon of the redtail hawks, of a gorgeous liberty.

Juliana sat with head averted. She wore smudged eyeglasses with girly rainbow frames, dirt-encrusted jeans and a large zippered sweatshirt with a red wool plaid scarf (her mother's) wound around her neck. Her brown hair was up in a careless twist that did not catch every greasy strand. Her hands and fingernails were filthy, too. I was greatly reassured that they had not allowed her to change or take a shower.

It was hard to see the expression behind the convex lenses under which her enlarged brown eyes seemed to stare, then drift away, as if they could not process such a suddenly disorganized world, even though the room had been designed to be an oasis from the impersonal passageways of the hospital, from phobias that might have been triggered by the attack. The light was low, provided only by table lamps, as in a normal setting. There was a poster of flowers above the oatmeal-colored couch, draped with a soft white woven afghan. Juliana's body was living and breathing in this space, but her soul was folded up somewhere. In my imaginings I had invested her with sadness, loneliness, laughter, aggression, embarrassment, but now, as a person, dynamic, across from you, she projected only one wavelength, unremitting fear.

Nancy gestured. "Sit down, Ana."

I had been unconsciously keeping my distance, as if Juliana were not a normal teenage kid but a brittle specimen that might become contaminated by human warmth and breath. Still I chose the opposite couch, to give her space. I noticed Nancy sat close, knees almost touching the girl's. She held a clipboard thick with forms.

"I'm going to give you a complete medical examination to make sure you're okay. But first, I'm going to ask some questions about what happened, so I know what to look for. Just tell me as much as you can."

At this point all we knew was Juliana had been let out or escaped from a vehicle somewhere and had somehow made her way back to the M&Ms. She might have been released a block away. It might have been Van Nuys. It might have been the abductor. It might have been a friend.

Juliana said nothing. Nancy said nothing. We sat in silence for a very long time. I tried to make myself still. I looked at an orchid.

Finally Nancy tried again. "Whatever you can tell me is helpful. If you don't remember, that's okay."

Juliana crossed her arms and legs.

"A few hours ago you got out of a car—was it a car?"

I could barely hear when Juliana murmured, "A van."

Nancy said, "Okay, a van."

"What kind of a van?" I asked. "Can you describe it?"

She shrugged. Her head was down.

We waited.

I offered some prompts without replicating Stephanie and Ethan's description: Was the van old? New? Color? Did she notice the stereo, or some CDs lying around? It was very foggy tonight. Could Juliana tell where she was when she got out of the van?

"Can't we just, *please,* get this over with? My parents are freaking *out.*"

Before I could respond Nancy silenced me with a look. She stood up and pulled a leopard from a shelf of stuffed animals.

"I love this guy," she said. "He's so soft."

It wasn't a new leopard. Its spots were yellowed from much handling. She handed the thing to Juliana, who clung to it greedily.

"Let's talk a little about your general health," Nancy began again casually. "When was the last time you saw a doctor? Are you taking any medications? How old were you when you got your period?"

She was able to get Juliana to occasionally respond with one-word answers, each time in a voice so injured I found myself staring at the plaid cloth around her neck, telepathically communicating to Nurse Nancy, *It hurts!*

Still she pressed gently on, asking if Juliana had consensual intercourse in the last seventy-two hours.

Juliana answered, "No."

From her wide-eyed reaction to the question, I knew she'd never had consensual intercourse, even once. Right then, I thought I would lose it.

She had been a virgin.

My concern had been to protect her life, I hadn't worried about the fine-tuning, but now there was another reality that hit me like a body blow, and everything came unloose inside. In one smoldering moment I saw her innocence ignite with a *whoosh!* like a huge gas flame; and inside that flame there had been such bright wholeness.

This would be Juliana Meyer-Murphy's first *oh-my-God* experience with a man. Whatever happened during those absent days to strangle the voice out of her would now become the core image of sex this young woman would take with her through life, where the rest of us fondly, or even ambivalently, carry the saga of the first boyfriend, the parents' bed—or the beer party, the mosquitoes and the riverbank.

Whoosh.

Nancy had seen it, too, and was assuring Juliana that her first sexual experience with someone she loves would still be special, would still be her choice. The girl was nodding, but I wondered how much she was able to take in.

"Can I have one of those guys?" I indicated the stuffed animals.

"A puppy, or a loon?"

"I'll take the loon."

A loon is a striped bird like a duck with a fat round body that, if soft and stuffed, fits just comfortably under the arm. I recommend holding on to one.

"Did he have sexual intercourse with you?" Nancy waited. "Did he penetrate you with something else? Each act is a different crime, okay? I'm going to ask more questions than your doctor usually asks, not only because I want to account for every crime that happened, but to help during the medical exam."

"I can't say. After I first got in."

"You mean, first got into the van?" I said eagerly. "When he first made contact with you?"

She was shaking her head no. I was desperate. *No, what?*

"Do you want to take a break?" Nancy offered with an easy smile.

"I *really don't.*"

"Don't what, Juliana? Don't remember? That's all right."

"I'm not in the mood," whispered the girl.

Nancy put the clipboard down. "We can continue this later."

"Wait!" I cried without thinking.

Nancy turned to me with the same compassion she had shown the victim. Obviously we were both in need of guidance.

"It's up to Juliana," she said.

"I know, but—Juliana, honey—we really need your help in remembering everything you can—"

"I'm sorry," Nancy said more sharply. "*Juliana* can decide if she's comfortable or not or if she wants to go on."

I had to sit there, gears spinning, waiting as Juliana continued to gnaw on the leopard's ear like a three-year-old until it turned dark and wet. She was making speaking noises that were buried in the fur.

"What is it?" Nancy asked, leaning forward. She seemed to listen, but it was more than listening. "Tell me."

Juliana shook her head.

"What's your very worst fear? Your biggest concern?"

She didn't answer.

"Juliana," I said, and she looked at me. "I'm an FBI agent, and I carry a gun, but things still scare me—I'm not even talking about on the street but things that are inside. I still wake up, sometimes, and I'm all by myself. Man, it would be a relief to have someone to talk to."

Finally, tentatively, Juliana lowered the animal.

"I'm scared . . . because . . . I might not ever . . . be able to . . . have a baby."

Her words, barely audible, dwindled to a mewing wisp of nothing.

We were on our way to the examination room to collect the physical evidence. Nancy said she could have a support person present, and Juliana had silently pointed to me, a gesture that flooded me with gratitude.

Just outside the doorway I touched Nancy's arm.

I understood the enormous vulnerability of the sexual assault victim, the need for sensitivity and emotional support. But also I had a team of agents and policemen with technical backup ready to roll. If I could get hard information from Juliana about the offender or offenders—method of approach, control, display of weapons, threats, what kind of physical force—we could mobilize right now. Otherwise, Rick could rightly argue we'd recovered the victim and it would all go away.

"I need a narrative account of *what happened to her,*" I told the nurse quietly.

"There's a period of time she can't remember. It's possible she was drugged."

"Drugged?" Fear snagged me.

"Roofies. We see a lot of it."

Rohypnol and GHB are two "rape drugs" you can buy on the street. Put into a drink, they will render the victim unconscious, then he or she wakes up, mauled, in another part of town with no memory of how it happened. Because these drugs can metabolize quickly without a trace, they are currently the preferred weapons in sexual assaults.

"*No*," I moaned and trotted after her. "You understand why I have to ask questions."

"She has the right to decline to answer."

"I know all about her rights. I'm not suggesting we traumatize her further in any way. But in order for the investigation to move forward—"

"Nothing is going to happen to her that she doesn't want to have happen," reiterated the nurse in the same calm tone.

"I see that, but, with respect, I think we can press just a little harder, given the fact this guy is out there and likely to do it again."

"You're impatient, and I don't blame you."

The door to the exam room was open and Juliana was just inside. I could tell from Nancy's preoccupied look she was not about to leave her alone for more than another few seconds.

"I'm asking for your cooperation," I said urgently. "You're the expert, you know how to get her to disclose."

"I'm impatient, too," Nancy said. "I want to proceed with the evidentiary exam so she can go home and be with her family. But she has the right to withdraw her consent at any point in the examination, and if she does, I will stop. She needs to feel comfortable in her medical care."

"I need to move. I've got a task force ready to go—"

"I don't give a shit what you need to do," Nancy said, still serene.

S till, every doorway holds an opportunity, and inside the exam room there were two.

Juliana's body: a crime scene. Evidence would be recovered, as in any crime scene, and as in any crime scene, a story would be told.

Juliana's trust: she asked me to be in here. In the long run her confidence would be invaluable.

It was another carefully muted room, not like the bus terminal where I see my gynecologist at the HMO. Pale wood. Beige-on-beige, a subtle cloud pattern embossed on the wallpaper. There was a computer in a corner and an examination chair in the center where you could sit up and look into your nurse's eyes. Her mom would be relieved to know that Juliana did not have to lie back on a paper-covered table with stirrups.

"You're worried about being able to have a baby." Nancy was close, maintaining eye contact. "You're worried about the injuries inside your vagina. I'll have a better idea when I take a look. I'll tell you what I see. I'll never withhold information. I'll always tell you the truth."

Juliana scanned the room.

"How . . . are you going to look?"

"Oh!" said Nancy brightly. "We're going to see it all right here on this screen," and she patted a monitor on a cart, which held a VCR and a video camera. "If you want to watch, I'll explain it to you as I go. But that comes later."

Later, Nancy would explain to me it was a colposcope, a camera at the end of a long stalk that magnifies sixteen times. She would flick switches and point the lens at the pattern on a sheet covering the examination chair, slowly zooming in on a teardrop-shaped paisley, and I would watch on the monitor as the paisley became a country with green boundaries, a continent of blue, a universe of emptiness; until we were looking at the spaces between the cotton threads.

Later, we three strangers would become linked by the shared sight on the TV screen of the lacerations inside Juliana's vagina—invisible to the naked eye but vast as crimson canyons when magnified—and deep, mysterious half-moon cuts in a row.

The livid marks of a man's fingernails.

But now Nancy broke the seal on a rape kit and began to unpack white envelopes for evidence collection.

Step one was *debris.*

Step two was *dried secretions.*

Step three was *external genital examination.*

Step four was *pubic combings*.

There would be nine steps in all.

"Would you feel comfortable taking off the scarf?"

The girl unwound the material, revealing a necklace of water-color bruises in wine and black.

"How did that happen?" Nancy asked without any kind of inflection, which might have indicated outrage or alarm. Obvious marks of strangulation are rare.

"I don't know."

"Okay. Can you open that sweatshirt a little and sit here, and I'll take your vital signs?"

The ER doctor had ordered X rays to rule out fractures of the larynx and scans to check for soft tissue damage. The bruises would be photographed, and analysis would show the suspect had used a metal chain as a ligature to strangle Juliana several times to the point of unconsciousness or almost death. When she revived, he would perform sex acts and then strangle her again.

As Nancy pressed the disk of the stethoscope to Juliana's chest she smiled tenderly and said, "You have a kind heart."

My knees buckled.

I felt an unreasonable amount of love for Nancy Reicher, RN, NP, with the plucked eyebrows.

"Let's come over here and take off your clothes. We're going to need to keep them for evidence, so afterward"—Nancy opened a cabinet—"you can go home in one of these."

Inside were shelves of royal blue sweatshirts and sweatpants and rubber thongs in ascending sizes.

"There may be evidence on your clothes. Dirt or fibers, stuff like that. We need you to undress carefully. I'm going to put down some pieces of paper on the floor to collect anything that falls out of your clothing, and then we're going to collect everything you have on and put it in this bag. Let's go behind the curtain."

She drew some fabric across a track so a quarter of the room was hidden. I stood by the counter looking over the evidence packets. It would be a slow and meticulous examination. The oral cavity. The swabs for sperm. Examination of the buttocks, perianal skin and anal folds. Drawing blood to test for pregnancy and sexually transmitted diseases. The careful cataloguing, signing, dating, sealing of every piece to maintain the chain of custody.

"I need your underwear, too," I heard Nancy say from inside the curtain. "Are you okay?"

How many times was she going to ask if Juliana was okay? I was aware that my pits were damp. I was thirsty and wanted someplace to sit down.

"Now I'm going to use a long-wave ultraviolet light called a Wood's lamp," came Nancy's voice. "All kinds of stains show up that we couldn't see under white light. We're going to scan your body for evidence. But first I'm going to turn out the lights. Are you all right out there, Ana?"

"Fine."

The windowless room went pitch black.

Inside the curtain a purple light went on.

"I'm just going to scan your body with this lamp."

It was hot and close and surreal in that room. Shades of purple light danced above and below the curtain like a gruesome attraction in a carnival of perversions.

"It's like a black light," Nancy was explaining. "Do you know if he ejaculated outside your body?"

I could not hear Juliana's reply.

"Well, here are some dried secretions, and you can tell they're semen because they turn yellow under the Wood's lamp. I'm just going to swab it. Turn around for me. Thanks." There was a pause. Then, "Would you mind if I asked Ana to see this?"

Juliana's voice was faint with exhaustion. "Yeah, sure, I don't care."

With the chill clatter of metal rollers, Nancy slowly swept the curtain aside, and I saw Juliana Meyer-Murphy standing naked in a violet column of light.

She had her father's slope-shouldered slump, with his tendency to spread at the hips, but the long legs were her mother's; soon the baby fat would go. They had put clean dressings over the area on her chest where the offender had cut meticulously with a fine instrument, cross-hatching, like an etching, to draw a steady beading of blood. On the Tanner classification of sexual maturity, a five being a fully mature adult woman, Juliana would rate a four. She had no pubic hair, not because it had not developed but because it had been shaved off; you could see the raw raking furrows of the razor.

Under the tinctures created by the lamp—cobalt, ultramarine, magenta, rose—her body looked like a Romantic sculpture splattered by a madman in a purple haze. It made me feel ashamed to see her so exposed, and yet I kept on looking, because the more I looked, the more I could see the assault in progress, as if it had been conjured.

"What kind of shoes did the assailant wear?" I asked.

"I have no clue."

"Were they sneakers? Sandals? Boots?"

I already knew the answer.

"Boots," breathed the girl.

She was right. "Anything special you remember about them?"

"They were clean."

"New?"

"Polished."

I nodded.

"Thank you. Thank you very much."

"I was thinking you might want a forensic photographer to document this," Nancy suggested.

"Yes, I would."

Blunt-force injuries such as those sustained by hammers or shoes create rapid tissue compression, which results in bruising and bleeding below the skin. The contusions on Juliana's back would have been clearly visible to the naked eye, but the impression of the weapon used to cause them would not. Now, out of the anarchistic splotching, there appeared a glow-on glow, a ghostly memo, as if sent by the offender in almost-invisible ink.

"What?" Juliana asked, craning her neck. "Where is it?"

"On your lower back," Nancy said.

"What's the big deal? I can't feel anything."

"He left a partial imprint," said the nurse matter-of-factly. "It's pretty clear. It's the sole of a shoe. At some point he must have stepped on your back."

Stamped on her back, while Juliana lay on her stomach, unconscious. *Stamped,* she should have said, since she had promised to tell the truth, *trampled* or *stamped,* using the full weight of the boot with his body behind it, blunt-force heavy impact.

Juliana's mouth turned down, and she emitted a series of guttural screams.

"Get it *off me*! Get it *off*!"

A Wood's lamp is a coherent light that causes materials and messages to luminesce. This particular message was clear as day: the offender had declared that he was a powerful and commanding man and the rest of us bugs under his feet.

Juliana wanted the impression *"off!"* like a spider crawling up her back, *"off!"*—and her cries were hideous and freakish squawks; her twisting, flailing arms kept beating us away; the curtains buckled, the lamp, discarded, rolled upon the floor, spinning wild purple rays around the darkened room.

The lug-soled design of a size-ten boot floated in and out like a wondrous charm.

Nine.

S omething happened to Andrew and me that night. After Juliana was released, we came back to my place and drank enough tequila to shine our own black light on those illicit dungeon doors—the ones that appear only, under the right conditions, in total darkness. Once you find them and you enter, certain things are left behind that cannot be reclaimed between two people.

Most of all, after the physical ordeal of the case, I wanted comfort. I wanted us to bleach our sins with astringent soap and scalding water, and make love, and fall asleep like new puppies in a box full of clean sheets. I wanted the relief of knowing that despite the roughneck ride we were on, we could always return to the kind of private shelter we had discovered at the Sandpiper, the very first weekend we went away together, where, at dusk, on windswept Moonstone Beach, we had walked until our fingers froze, and came back and lit candles and lay in the bathtub in the steamed-up motel bathroom, hot as a sauna, and told our secrets. I remember resting my head against a sopping towel laid over the edge, and how we faced each other, my legs inside his, the strong heavy bones of his shins buffering mine against the cool porcelain, surrendering to our nakedness and the dissolving boundaries between us, the comfortable bubbly water, letting go inch by inch, until I was able to accept, at last, his enduring offer of safety. There is no deeper luxury.

In the canyon of those forgotten hours of the night, half senseless after bearing witness to the interminable rape exam, I craved that luxurious feeling of safety again, even ran a bath, as if Andrew and I could both fit inside the half-size plastic shower-tub of the apartment in the Marina. But we were too drunk, at odds, on the job, did not have time for luxury, had seen so many borders violated it seemed useless to defend them. He turned the water off. He wanted me to do it on my knees on the floor, like a hooker. I didn't want to; he made it a challenge; so I did, as if wild submission were the same as wholehearted surrender, as if it could take you to the center of the labyrinth. I couldn't find where we were on the bed, up, down or across. He wanted me to slap his face. He got up and came back with a belt. It had never been like this before. When I had an orgasm, I cried. I didn't know what it was about. He held me, panting.

Now I see why I had been so desperate to be sanctified by water, by touch. Andrew and I had become profoundly contaminated by the materials we were working with. (The Bible talks about cleansing with blood; Andrew believed it, but I have never known true atonement to work that way.) Like a chemical reagent that causes evidence to glow in the dark, the alcohol had made that contamination observable for a brief period of time, but the kind of perversity that had acted on Juliana Meyer-Murphy, and therefore on the two of us, does not go away with daylight. You carry the toxins. Maybe he was angry at being reassigned from the Arizona investigation, had to put me in my place for a lot of reasons; but there was something about the purposeful way he took us to the edge that hinted he knew all about dark places, and savage unrestraint.

*   *   *

After Juliana went home, we withdrew from the M&Ms', shut down the command center at the Santa Monica Police Department and initiated a nationwide manhunt for the suspect from a war room at the Bureau.

The war room consisted of a disused space near the lavatories: two old windowed offices with the dividing wall taken out and lined with metal shelving that held somebody's collection of administrative operations in thick unreadable binders and textbooks called *The Biology of Violence* and *Ransom,* probably not cracked since some of the World War II vets were laid to rest in the VA cemetery across the way. In a contemplative moment your eyes could travel from those shaded white markers north to the lustrous Italian marble of the Getty Museum, perched like a mythical griffin over the mountain pass.

We had our own artwork going. A real exhibition. The tattered old timeline from the command center had been reinstalled upon the wall, beginning when the 911 came in and listing every event—when the police responded, when the Bureau was called, who was interviewed, when each polygraph was done—all the way up to *"Someone is walking up the street"* in the fog. There were aerial photos of the Promenade obtained from the satellite facility at headquarters and location shots of the storefronts. Posted also were my hand-drawn diagrams showing the true distance and relationships between Willie John Black's doorway and the fountains and the bench where Juliana may have met the suspect.

Then, in the Purple Gallery, we had close-ups of the bruise patterns on Juliana's neck and the fine cutting on her chest, and a series of photographs using reflected UV light that showed the lug-soled design of the boot taken from the skin of her back. For this expertise we had to wait an extra two hours at the Rape Treatment Center while a forensic photographer fought standstill traffic all the way from a private lab called Result Associates, out in Fullerton.

I had assigned young Jason Ripley as administrative case agent, which meant he was in charge of the paper, hauling cartons of printouts from Rapid Start, trying to keep the sub files organized. We were on our knees, hands deep inside the boxes, scraping our knuckles on bristly reams of paper, when I felt a presence behind me and heard Kelsey Owen say, "Congratulations on recovering the victim. That must have been incredibly exciting."

"We got lucky," Jason, the voice of experience, replied.

I sat back on my haunches and rewrapped the scrunchie that held my ponytail, grimacing at the time. "Gotta go."

"Where to?"

"Rick's office," scrambling up and wiping the fine cardboard dust off on my jeans.

"I'll walk with you," offered Kelsey.

I was aching to stop at Barbara Sullivan's, my old pal from the bank robbery squad. They still had real offices on the south side of the floor and Barbara's was still a sanctuary. I just needed to sit in there with the door closed for fifteen minutes, talking carpet installations and flu shots, easy muffin recipes and haircuts of the stars. But now I was late and saddled with Kelsey.

"What's the meeting about?"

"A couple of distinctive things in the Santa Monica kidnapping match the cases that came up on VICAP."

"Why didn't they come up before?"

"Nobody put it together. Nobody alerted Quantico to go back to the local police in Austin, South Beach and DC with what we now know."

"But *you* did. I can see why Rick has a lot of faith in you."

Fawning makes my teeth ache. Too much sugar in the Christmas punch.

"SOP," I said dismissively.

"So how was it for you?" she asked, not going away.

"How was what for me?"

"The investigation. To confront what you were most afraid of?"

"I was afraid she'd be *dead*."

I turned into the office of the kidnap squad.

Kelsey followed.

"Rick inside?" I asked the duo of wavy-haired clerks in miniskirts and high heels.

I took a chocolate kiss from a plate on the counter and smiled vacantly at Kelsey, wondering if she were going to explain to me what I was *really* afraid of. Kelsey Owen never would have guessed it was she. Or, I should say, Special Agent in Charge Galloway's keen interest in her. Why would he allow a rookie to tag along unless he wanted a report? Standing quietly with soft round hands crossed, holding a file, her patience seemed feigned. The move from NSD to crimes against children could not be accomplished in one leap. Besides, she was not that savvy—worn, thin-soled boots and a long flowery skirt with the big soft sweater to pick up the teal? A gold charm bracelet that peeked below the sleeve, shyly asking to be queried over and admired? Galloway, with his herbal supplements and out-of-control daughter, was just paranoid enough these days to recruit a susceptible wannabe to be his eyes and ears on a high-profile case. I really wanted to know to whom Kelsey Owen returned at night.

She trailed me into the supervisor's office.

"Grab the hot seat," offered Rick.

It was so cramped in there you got about two inches of legroom from the desk. Rick was looking expectantly over my head at Kelsey.

"I thought I would sit in. The SAC said it would be a good idea," she announced.

"Really?"

"To learn from you. And Ana."

Rick tipped back in his chair with a questioning look. If this was Galloway's deal, Rick wasn't in on it.

"Karen?"

"Kelsey."

"Aren't you on—?"

"The national security squad." She nodded vigorously as if to affirm the waste of her talents. "But I have a degree in psychology and I want to move over to kidnapping."

My boss rocked his chin at me. "If Ana doesn't have any objection."

How could I have an objection? Balling up the foil from the kiss, I fired it into the wastebasket.

"Nope."

Kelsey settled into the other chair, positioned against the wall where I could not see her, like the goody-goody who always sat behind you, breathing cherry drops and ambition down your neck.

"This is what we've got from Quantico," I told Rick. "At my request they sat with the locals and evaluated the evidence in those rape cases again. First of all, the victimology *is* similar. White teenage girls with long brown hair disappear from a mall. Nice girls, never in trouble, not your liberated types. Two of them are still missing. The victim in South Beach was reinterviewed. The assault took place in a vehicle. A truck. He was into asphyxiation. When he stopped at a gas station she escaped."

"She wasn't drugged?"

"No, but this was several years ago. I'm guessing rape drugs weren't as widely available."

Rick seemed to buy it.

"What if we're looking at a serial rapist," I went on eagerly, "and the reason nobody tagged it is he kept moving out of their territories? He's shrewd. He manipulates these girls at the same time the police walk right by him. He knows how to fit in, not draw attention to himself, because he's *just like everybody else.*"

Kelsey murmured, "This gives me the chills."

"What are the lab results on the Santa Monica kidnapping?"

"They haven't gotten to it yet."

"Hello?"

"I specifically asked them to cross-reference the results. Arnold Reinhold, the head of lab, says, *'We see this stuff by the bushel basket. Maybe a thousand a year,'* imitating Dr. Arnie's hang-loose groove. *'The only way we'd consider it special is if you had a bunch of these cases coming in and the same person in the lab got this stuff.'* I said, 'Come on, you wouldn't notice if some guy was choking girls with a metal chain?'"

We shared a look of cynical frustration.

"Just tell me: why a lab way out in Fullerton? With all the traffic, it's faster to overnight the stuff to Quantico."

"Politics," said Rick, disgusted.

We had recently started using Result Associates instead of the FBI facility back east. Somebody must have had connections, because the Sheriff's Department and the Santa Monica police had switched some of their cases, too.

"The good news is we recovered major physical evidence I think will be significant."

"Such as?"

"The partial impression of the sole of a boot. On her back."

Rick's expression was dispassionate, but there was a silence in the room, as between the ticks of a clock, as we all ran through in our minds the picture of how a man stomps with all his might on the back of an unconscious girl.

"What kind of boot?"

"They're checking the Bureau database of footwear impressions. Maybe a work boot. Or those thick-soled shoes the punkers wear?"

"Dr. Martens."

"Rick, you are too hip for words."

Rick winked at Kelsey, who paused uncertainly, taking notes.

"The victim reported the shoes were shined, so they had to have some kind of leather uppers."

"Keeps his weapons polished."

He winked again, but it was more of a twitch.

"What else do the propellerheads say?"

"They're all excited about examining the reverse side of the victim's T-shirt, but you know, that's what gets them off."

"Gets their rotors turning."

"The inside of the T-shirt might retain skin cells that could be enhanced to show more of the shoe print," I explained to Kelsey.

"I'm sorry," she said. "I'm still lost. When you said—"

Rick ignored her. "All of that's a good evidentiary base." He snuck a look at his watch. There had been an abduction of a minor to Iran that morning. "What was Juliana able to tell you about the offender? Anything about the method of approach? How hostile is this guy?"

I shook my head. "She's still in shock. I know there's more, but her response was guarded."

"I don't like it," Rick said sharply. "If this is a serial rapist, he's going to repeat."

"The nurse was an obstacle," I muttered, hating myself for the lame excuse. Meanwhile, Kelsey was clearing her throat and fidgeting as if anxious to be called upon.

"When's your next interview with the victim?"

"Thought I'd give it a couple of days."

Kelsey was raising her hand.

Rick: "We need her narrative," putting stuff in his briefcase. "Sooner rather than later."

"Can I talk to Juliana?" Kelsey was standing now. "I have experience treating battered women. I know the victim's perspective."

"Up to the case agent."

It was a soft toss, meant to ease my humiliation. Working like this is intimate. You throw out ideas, you have to trust. Alone, his irritation about not yet having Juliana's statement would have been part of the normal give and take; but there was Kelsey, making notes.

"I think it's a bad idea. Juliana has already formed a bond with me."

"A bond," objected Kelsey, "is not the same as an empathetic relationship."

"I am not her shrink and neither are you, and if you think that's what it's about, you've got the wrong idea of what it means to be a federal agent."

"That's a somewhat dated view."

"*Dated?*"

It hung there like spit on a window.

Rick: "Is the victim seeing a counselor at the Rape Treatment Center?"

"Yes."

"Good." He snapped the briefcase. "I hope this was useful, Kelsey. I've got to get to the Iranian consulate."

"I didn't mean to offend you," Kelsey said when he had gone. "I thought we could work together. I'm only trying to share my expertise."

We were standing in the outer office.

"Share *this*."

I didn't say it softly enough or turn away fast enough for Kelsey not to see that I had (unconsciously) made an obscene gesture indicating that if I had been endowed with a penis, it would right now be (symbolically) jerking off in her face.

She saw it, and I saw that she saw it.

"It's okay," Kelsey said, subdued. "It's been a long, hard week and everybody's—" She touched my arm. "I won't bug you anymore."

Juliana could not leave the house. She would follow into the same rooms as her mother, who, for her part, was grateful to be given her baby back, to stay home and bake cookies together and lie in bed watching videos as they had when Juliana came down with pertussis in fourth grade. She sent the nanny to Laurel West for the homework assignments—because Juliana would sob uncontrollably if Lynn were out of her sight—gently reminding her daughter that she still had to keep up in her work because colleges didn't want to see slipping grades.

Juliana was having trouble swallowing. The family would sit down to dinner, expectant, and Lynn would put a plate of homemade lasagna airy with fresh oregano, just for Juliana's pleasure, just to make it special, in front of the girl who would gag, push away from the table in a fit of red-faced choking, rush to stick her head out the back door and suck cool air, panicking her mom and dad as if she did have the whooping cough, ruining their hope.

The bruising had reduced to traces of ocher and the scans of her neck had come back negative for swelling or fracture. Soon she was being served just broth or a protein shake, and then she didn't want to come to the table at all; and nobody mentioned her when she wasn't there, the little sister not unhappy to have the parents all to herself, detailing the ins and outs of nine-year-old friendships with indignant amazement. And maybe it was a relief not to have to extend one's patience throughout dinner, too, have a little break, a glass of wine— but why, reasoned Lynn, continue to cook these elaborate dinners at all if Juliana wasn't able to participate? Spending the whole day in the kitchen wasn't helping one iota, so they began to let the younger sister eat hot dogs and macaroni in front of the TV while Mom and Dad did takeout chicken, whenever, sometimes ten o'clock at night, wondering if there would always be this numbness, it had to be from sleep deprivation, their fifteen-year-old having nightmares, climbing into their bed in the dead zone of the night.

I offered family counseling at the Bureau's expense. They said maybe.

I had to sit with Rick's frustration because there was just no way in.

K elsey Owen is going to have your ass," Mike Donnato warned.

"What is she?" asked Barbara Sullivan, "his new flavor of the week?"

"Oh, he's not sleeping with her," Mike said wisely. "You know, Galloway's in psychoanalysis—"

"No way."

"That's what I heard. Six in the morning. Four days a week."

"How come he's still depressed?"

"Wouldn't you be, if you had his job? He's a new convert to psychotherapy and I think, at the moment, he really believes it's the Holy Grail. Kelsey's an opportunist, and Ana is one big happy dope—"

"The golden retriever of agents."

"Right, so it all works out. At least do something smart, Ana. When you're close to an arrest, call the deputy DA, Mark Rauch, bring him in the loop."

"The guy's a vampire."

"He's ambitious. He can help," said Mike. "You leave him out, he'll suck your blood."

These were my buddies, trying to cheer me up.

We were lounging around Barbara's office. The place had not improved since the baby shower. Everything was curlicue cute—juvenile picture frames with snaps of infant Deirdre, figurines of angels (Barbara collected angels, I collected trolls—what does that tell you?), a haystack of pillows needlepointed by Grandma *(Kiss the Princess, The Princess Is In)*. The personal coffeemaker, where you used to be able to get cinnamon-flavored brew, was silent; now she drank some kind of damn tea that was supposed to give you milk.

Luckily the walls were still covered with surveillance photos of bank robberies in progress, a reminder that this remained the bank robbery coordinator's office, even if she did pump her breasts with a monstrous machine every four hours. Now there was no more sale hopping during lunch, no three-hankie "girl movies" on a weekday night, since Barbara went home to her hungry daughter on the dot of five. Although she had not lost her baby weight, Barbara still wore prim pastel suits with a single pearl on a chain around her neck; oldest of a sprawling Irish family in Chicago, she had been like a big sister until she became a mom. Gradually our lives had grown incomprehensible, and even uninteresting, to each other.

I did not realize how much I would give up by leaving the bank robbery squad and pushing over to C-1. In the old days, before the matrix, we used to have potlucks in the conference room and Mike Donnato and I would flirt outrageously, just because we knew it could never go anywhere. He was still as attractive and elegantly turned out as when he had been my senior partner and mentor. He had a law degree from Yale and wore three-piece suits and a well-barbered graying beard, even though he lived in Simi Valley. He and Rochelle moved the family out there because they were afraid of raising kids in the city. Donnato and I had a special claim to each other. We had put in a lot of miles in a crap brown Chevrolet. Barbara and I had a special claim to each other, too. Those claims do not expire. That's the way it is in the Bureau family.

"You're just fried because the case isn't moving," Mike said.

"I haven't had time to go swimming," I complained. "I don't eat lunch until four in the afternoon. Everybody's always on me, every minute of the day. *Ana!* Where's this? *Ana!* They never called me back! *Ana! Ana! Ana!* I swear, it makes you want to change your name."

"To what?"

"Fritzy."

"*What?*"

"I don't know!" I was suddenly stupid with laughter, sliding off Barbara's couch in a spasm.

They shook their heads.

"How about Ditzy?" Mike suggested, and that really put me away.

"Oh my God." I was slumped on the floor, wiping my eyes. "I don't know why I'm laughing. I don't have enough to profile the offender so my criminal investigative analysis is basically nowhere, and Rick is upset."

"What're you missing?" asked Mike.

Certain people make you feel uplifted just by asking a question in a certain tone. By telling you with their hazel eyes, however lined and worn, there will always be enough to share: their acceptance of you, but rarer still, the willingness to see you clearly, to pause and sit with you through it, even if it's small.

"I can't get the victim statement. She was traumatized to the throat. It's like he choked her into silence."

"Was that his ritual?"

I nodded. "We've got the same MO on a case in Florida. You know he's going to do it again. If he hasn't already a dozen times." And for a moment we fell silent.

Mike gave me a sad smile.

I smiled back. "Don't you bozos have a robbery to solve?"

"This is still my favorite," Mike said, tapping the wall.

Out of two hundred or so photos, he had unswervingly picked the one taken on the robbery where Andrew and I met. It was up there as a joke, and Mike had picked it because it was the most unflattering shot imaginable. As the automatic camera kept clicking away, Andrew and I had been interviewing the managers with our backs to the lens. We looked like a pair of dodoes. He had on the pretentious motor-cycle jacket and his legs were awkwardly splayed like he was getting ready for a broad jump; my trousers were wrinkled and my ass looked enormous.

"Can I take this down now?" I asked.

"You can take it down when the case is solved," admonished Mike as he left. Well, that would never be. Most bank robberies are never cleared.

"Nobody should ever see what their hair looks like from behind," commented Barbara soothingly.

"Do you remember this?" I tapped the photo again.

It was a devilish question, since Barbara Sullivan, whom we used to call the Human Computer, has total recall of every job on the board. That's her gift: matching new information with cold cases.

"It was called Mission Impossible," she rattled off, "because he came through the roof, a two-eleven silent, an early-bird job that came into our office around eight-thirty in the morning, just before the branch was opening. It was in Santa Monica—"

"I remember you saying right away, 'This stinks.'"

"Well, yeah, because it was a new player who was operating. We hadn't seen anything like it before, and when we looked at the loss, it had all indications of an inside job. Remember? He held the managers in the vault?"

"He ambushed them while they were doing opening procedures. They were toast."

Then I recalled Andrew had trained those young managers during that bank security course he gave for the police department. When he showed up, they were so relieved to see a familiar face they fell apart in his arms.

"Definitely an inside job," Barbara was remembering. "They cut the hinges and came down through a hatch in the roof."

The first thing we did, Andrew and I climbed up there, through a utility room jammed with old files and air-conditioning ducts. We scaled a wooden ladder and stepped out into the fresh air, already slightly giddy from the unexpected height and the profound attraction we were simultaneously feeling.

The avenues below were lined with high spindly palms. Cars filled the dealerships and rooftop garages, cars moved at a reasonable pace through the blacktop town. Walls of high-rises blocked our view of the beach but the glittery swell of the sea rose to the farthest sight line. In the low commercial buildings—salmon, tan, lime and brick— there were tiny enclaves of calm: a hammock on a patio, miniature umbrella tables.

"Had a jumper over there the other day." Andrew had indicated a shorefront hotel. "A woman takes a room, jumps out the window. Turns out, five years ago to the day, her daughter jumped from that same room."

Andrew was simply saying it, in a tone that knew burglars who crapped on kitchen tables, grandfathers who molested their grand-daughters, suicides who cut off their own testicles, killers who strangled pregnant women with electric cords or murdered their girlfriends with table legs, kerosene or barbecue forks; a tone that comes of shaking the cockroaches out of your clothes before you enter your house at night, that knows there is no such thing as the bottom, knows there is suffering and concedes to all of it.

But doesn't jump.

That's what drew me to him. He knew things, and saw things, and had fashioned a way for himself to keep on looking at them, because he wanted to help. On one of our first dates, he took me to an Al-Anon meeting (his adoptive father had been an alcoholic)—not the meeting he regularly attended, because that was private to him, but a different one, in the back room of a deli, so I could see what he was about and the road he had traveled, and when we all held hands at the end and said the Serenity Prayer, it was like an aphrodisiac; I was so moved by the ability of this hard man to close his eyes in a group of people, and give in to it. I only wanted more.

The light up there on top of the bank was splendid and all-encompassing, the sun doing double flips between the pastel rooftops and the glossy blue sky, and an ocean breeze flapped Andrew's tie and parted and reparted his black hair so I could see his scalp and the dry-ness of his lips, and then looking became shameful because he was looking at me, too, and I didn't know what he could or could not see but feared he could see everything—my longing, misdirection, lone-someness and rage—and tears gathered in the corners of my eyes, but I smiled and blotted them with fingertips as if it were the wind.

"Something new just came up on that caper," Barbara was saying thoughtfully as she contemplated the Mission Impossible photo.

Some of us can recall that Reggie Jackson hit three home runs on three swings in the final game of the 1977 World Series; Barbara Sullivan can quote the take from every heist on the wall.

"They recovered a ski mask."

"A ski mask?"

"The guy wore a ski mask, right?"

"Right."

"Well, they found it—a janitor found it—kicked behind some boxes. About two months ago."

"That branch was robbed half a dozen times," I said. "Could belong to anyone."

"But Mission Impossible went in through a door in the roof." Barbara had moved to the computer. "Used a Makita drill with a dia-mond blade, like a knife through butter."

"You're amazing."

"Then," said Barbara, laughing at the audacity, "he climbs down a ladder to a utility room, goes out to the second-floor employee lounge and sits up there for a couple of hours watching TV until the bank opens. Life is good."

It summoned up the smell of enclosed waxy floors that had greeted

Andrew and me when we cautiously entered the lounge—empty except for a TV set on a dusty Art Deco coffee table—and a stench I first made as sweat that turned out to be the dead meat aroma left by the McDonald's the bandit ate for breakfast.

"The ski mask was found in the utility room where the ladder was, where you go up to the roof." Barbara nodded toward the information on the screen. "Black nylon, standard-issue army surplus store."

"You know this same guy, Detective Berringer, caught the Santa Monica kidnapping?" I said tapping the photo insistently. "We're working together again, how funny is that?"

"How funny *is* that?" She had instantly picked up on my tone.

That was the devilish part. I had to tell someone. I wanted her to know. This is how we give ourselves away.

"We're going out."

"You're going out with a detective?"

I nodded.

"On a case you're both working?"

I nodded again.

Barbara, the Irish girl, said, *"Oy vey."*

"Thanks for reserving judgment."

"I'm not passing judgment. He looks pretty cute from the rear."

"He's hot."

"Divorced?"

"Twice."

"So when do I meet him?"

"Soon. Maybe. I hope. Things are a little shaky right now. But they can get better."

Barbara was nodding, absently fingering a picture of Deirdre. Up, down, on, off. It wasn't her game anymore.

"Tell him about the ski mask. His case, he should know."

"I will," I said, and forgot about it.

Ten.

Since the night she walked out of the fog, we had been monitoring the use of Juliana's home computer, thinking the suspect might try to contact her again. Or maybe in her personal communications she would reveal some sliver of the attack that had surfaced from memory. Juliana (JMM3) spent hours online, mostly in chat rooms that seemed to attract local kids. The following transcript, posted on Rapid Start, got my attention:

FD-823 (Rev. 8-26-97)

RAPID START

INFORMATION CONTROL

Case ID: 446-702-9977 The Santa Monica Kidnapping

Control Number: 5201   **Priority:** Immediate

Classification: Sensitive   **Source:** Internet Chat
                                   Room

Event time: 11:35 PM
Method of contact: Monitoring of personal computer
belonging to victim, Juliana Meyer-Murphy
Prepared by: Diaz, Ramon   Component/Agency: Tech
                                   support, FBI
Transcript attached.

* * *

JMM3@aol.com 11:35 PM
YOU ARE IN CHAT ROOM **TOWN SQUARE**
MasterMynd: i am so fucked
LiquidFlo: what'd ur mom say?
MasterMynd: grounded don't describe it
TruHacka03: u hear what happened to ethan?
MasterMynd: what?
Truhacka03: took his car
LiquidFlo: away?
Truhacka03: yeah, fool . . .
BlackStar01: be that bitch
MasterMynd: where is she?
LiquidFlo: she a ho on Hollywood Blvd
OoRaver4LiveoO: shut up you don't know shit
OoRaver4LiveoO: is she coming back 2 school?
MasterMynd: if I see her I'll kick her face
LiquidFlo: might help she damn ugly
MasterMynd: why would someone want to fuck that?
OoRaver4LiveoO: I'm out u guys r jerks
LiquidFlo: whining bitch
XxHipHopxx: they're gonna expel 6 kids for weed
BlackStar01: no shit!!!

```
XxHipHopxx: true
MasterMynd: Who?
LiquidFlo: anybody out there know?
XxHipHopxx: Stephanie, Ethan, Kristin--??
BlackStar01: Nahid?
XxHipHopxx: yeah, the towel head
MasterMynd: and she gets off?
XxHipHopxx: she told everything on everybody
MasterMynd: we shoulda done her
BlackStar01: you first
TruHacka03: ugli people should be doomed to hell.
  ugli people should not go out in public
JMM3: why don't I do you all a favor and go out
  and kill myself?
Total online activity: 1.25 hours
```

An hour after reading the report, I was sitting with Juliana on the floor of her room.

"I didn't mean it. It was just to shut them up. Please don't tell my mother, she'll trip."

"I had to inform your parents, Juliana."

"That my friends hate me?"

"These are threats." I was holding up the transcripts. "Threats to hurt you or that you would hurt yourself. We have to take them seriously."

"Like the school doesn't know everybody's smoking weed? They're not *too* hypocritical? Because Nahid's father is a Saudi prince and gave like ten million dollars for the new campus, and he drives to school in a stretch Hummer limousine?"

"I didn't know they had Hummer limousines."

She grimaced at my grown-up ignorance, looked down at her bare feet, toyed with a flower toe ring, trying to hide her face inside the cascade of hair, wavy and dark like mine. She was cleaned up and dressed in a big white shirt and capri-length tights, and the hoarseness had mostly healed, but she was jumpy, hollow-eyed behind the rainbow glasses, like someone weakened after a bout of pneumonia. If Willie John Black's condition were a monotone of gray, Juliana's was a chronic spiking fever. You're okay for a moment, an hour, half a day; then it knocks you flat.

"They don't understand," she said quietly. "You made me."

"What?"

"Tell."

"We already knew about Stephanie and Ethan. Basically they confessed, straight out. We got a warrant and found the stash in Stephanie's locker. They brought it on themselves, you have nothing to feel guilty about." I waited. "Is it hard at school?"

She nodded silently.

"Kids say things about the attack? What do they say?"

"Mostly rude questions." Her eyes rose warily. "Are you going to arrest those kids from the chat room?"

"We are going to investigate."

"Don't. *Please.*"

"They sent you on a fool's errand. They did not have your best interests at heart."

"Your point is?"

"There must be other kids at school you can be friends with. Kids who are worthy of you."

She was picking at the rose-colored carpeting as if to pull it out in tufts.

"I just want you to know," I continued steadily, "you have our protection. Nobody is going to hurt you, okay? Take my card again and *call me* if anything or anyone is bothering you. We have surveillance on your family, and that isn't going to stop until we catch the guy."

Juliana started to gag. It was as if her throat closed up on her, an anaphylactic attack based on no invasion but the air. The impulse was to throw open the windows, flush her passageways with the sweet bright world.

"Can you talk? Talk to me. *Talk!*"

She shook her head. Heaved. Alarmed, I thought she had deliberately swallowed something.

But she was gasping. "I'm—okay." So there was nothing stuck, it was the breath—a living thing, according to my lifeguard friend—being murdered again and again in some cruel posttraumatic replay of the offender's script. He hadn't had to kill her to bring suffering to the max; the repeated assaults had damaged Juliana's brain so that now it triggered its own gag response. This was irony, not plan. A bonus. Anything could replicate the terror. A loud noise. Violent assaultive e-mails. Her sounds were wrenching. I was helpless to stop them, her mother downstairs would be helpless, too (only knowing these attacks would pass had kept me from calling 911), and as I rocked her with my arms around her slumping shoulders, my eyes were closed, and I was listening to a random fragment of the Serenity Prayer which had drifted into my mind—*"To change the things I can . . . And the wisdom to know the difference"*—and the image kept returning of the videotape, the contractions in the lacerated walls of the vagina, how like the fisting in her throat, this tightening animal aversion of the flesh had been Juliana's only poor defense.

She moved away and found some tissues, and we each sat rigid in a denim beanbag chair. She wheezed quietly. I sat. With this child who was not my child. In the big house north of Montana, in the generous room with the sheer white curtains—and computer and clothes, boom box and stuffed animals—and the purple light encompassed us. We were alone together in a cone of purple light.

"What is this?"

I held a get-well card signed with smiley faces, twenty names.

"From the swim team."

"I swim, too."

Neighbors had been leaving things, her mother told me: a flat of strawberries by the front door.

"There *is* good out there," I reminded her.

"Why did this happen? I keep asking the therapist."

"What does she say?"

Juliana's eyes lowered. "That it's not my fault."

I looked up at the dense foliage of a tree outside the window. I could see it was an avocado. The fruit would fall into the narrow space between the houses.

"The man who raped you was acting out his own scenario of power and control. It was all about him. He was brutal, overpowering, clever and deeply driven to do what he did. There's no way you could have stopped him, he had it all planned out. You survived. Because you know something, Juliana? You have a sense of yourself. You've been through an experience your friends cannot ever conceive of."

"That's not right."

"What isn't right?"

"Ray wasn't like that."

She said his name.

Eleven.

I expected everyone to feel the urgency I felt, the surge of momentum that comes with a major break. There would be eager questions, and relief that someone like me, 110 percent committed, was in charge. Andrew and his lieutenant would be there, pumped. Galloway and his ASACs. I was ready for us to bear down and get this guy.

I did not expect to be ambushed.

The briefing was held in our state-of-the-art emergency operations facility. A row of clocks reported the time from the Pacific to the Zulu zone. There were banks of computers, TV screens, a radio console and one-way glass through which the proceedings could be observed. A situation board ran across the front of the low-ceilinged room, a row of chairs before it, facing the troops. It was from those chairs on that platform that Rick and I would address the investigative team.

By 8 a.m., fifty agents and support personnel were grouped around the urns of coffee and cafeteria doughnuts that had been placed on the window ledge, talking shop. To the south, beach cities and teeming flats were bleached by the bandit sun like an overlit transparency.

The hot cityscape seemed to leap up and attack. It hurt your eyes, even through the tinted glass.

Everyone wore sport coats or dresses; I had on the slim black pantsuit. Andrew strolled by, unshaven, the open leather jacket over a midnight blue cowboy shirt, faded jeans and boots, wearing his resentment like the shield on his belt. Nobody but Barbara knew we were going out, but I felt embarrassed where I wanted to be proud. He'd looked pretty sharp for the briefing on *his* turf.

"Where've you been?"

"Caught a homicide."

"Isn't this your most important case?"

"Nothing's more important," Andrew agreed, deadpan.

"I've been trying to call you."

"I called you back," he said.

"Once."

We broke it off as Lieutenant Barry Loomis came over and Andrew formally introduced me for a second time to his boss, whom you also could not miss in a room of clean-shaven straight guys—he'd be the one with the thick brush mustache and Tasmanian devil tie.

"Go get 'em," Barry urged, as if I were some kid in Little League.

Rick and I took our seats, looking out at rows of attentive faces. Andrew, center section, gave me a lazy thumbs-up, chuckled at something Barry said. Galloway, wearing a snowy white turtleneck and holding a dead cigar, was reading from a sheaf of papers on his knee.

Projected on a screen above the platform was a yellow composite drawing, gleaned from Juliana Meyer-Murphy, of "Ray." It didn't tell much: Caucasian, narrow eyes and high cheekbones, thick-necked, short matted hair. Suddenly I felt loose and coasting. After sitting with Juliana on the rose-colored carpet, writing at warp speed, I had been up until two in the morning integrating what she had been able to tell me about the assault and creating a profile of the offender, deep into the marrow of a violent sexual deviant. It seemed insane to be sitting here dressed for lunch, making eyes at my boyfriend in the third row.

"But yesterday, Special Agent Grey was able to obtain the victim's

narrative, included in your packet," Rick was saying, "which you might
want to take a moment to read. Would this be a good time, Ana?"

FD-823 (Rev. 8-26-97)

RAPID START

INFORMATION CONTROL

Case ID: 446-702-9977 The Santa Monica Kidnapping

Control Number: 5231   **Priority:** Immediate

Classification: Sensitive   **Source:** Juliana Meyer-
                                   Murphy (Victim)

Event time: 2:00 PM

Method of contact: Interview in victim's home

Prepared by: Grey, Ana   **Component/Agency:** Kid-
                                    nap and extortion
                                    squad, FBI

Event narrative:

> "The first time I met Ray was on the Promenade.
> I went there to get jeans. I was waiting for my
> mom to pick me up near Wilshire and some
> skaters were grinding on the fountain and this
> guy was taking pictures. He was older. He
> looked regular except he had kind of long
> bleached hair like a rock star and he had a
> professional camera, so I thought he was from a
> skateboard magazine. They're always shooting
> commercials and TV shows on the Promenade. I
> didn't think about it."

> The offender was described as being in his

late twenties, about six feet tall, long legs
but muscular torso, possibly a weight lifter.
The victim is five feet, 110 pounds. She is very
young in appearance, and it is possible the
offender thought she was even younger than fifteen. She described him as wearing a black
sweatshirt, baggy nylon pants and boots that
were shined. (See lab report: shoe print on
victim's back.)

"He asked me if it was all right to take my
picture and I said, 'What's it for?' And he
said, 'I just like taking pictures of pretty
girls,' which I knew was a line so I said something like, 'Yeah, right,' and he apologized if
he offended me and went back to the skaters and
told them they'd better chill before they got a
ticket. 'They bust you for skateboarding but
murderers go free,' he said. 'Cops are idiots.'
He lit up a cigarette and told me I should
never start because smoking could kill you. He
said the cops were a lot cooler in England. He
started telling me about London, he used to
work for an English newspaper and took pictures
of Sting, and I went, 'Is that where you got
that haircut?' and he goes, 'Yes.' But then I
started feeling nervous in case my mom saw me
talking to him, so I said I had to go and
walked up to Fourth Street."

The victim estimated she encountered the
offender on the Promenade three or four times
over the next few weeks. Once he was feeding

the pigeons. Once he was photographing a homeless man. They would have casual conversations.
"I like your sunglasses," he told her one day.
"Where'd you get them?" She named the shop and
he said he knew the owner. He said he could get
her a deal. He never came on to her, he did not
ask her name, but she felt he was her special
friend, an older person who was accepting and
happy to see her while she was experiencing
exclusion at her new school.

On Thursday, the 23rd, the victim had gone to
a commercial venue on the Promenade called
Crystal Dreams, a New Age-type store, desperately looking to buy marijuana to impress the
"in crowd" at school. She was rebuffed by the
owner, who claims to be "antidrugs," and felt
humiliated. As she exited the store she saw the
offender sitting outside on a bench. His appearance had changed. He had cut off the long hair
and was sporting a buzz cut. Despite this rough-
and-tumble appearance, he seemed concerned that
she not put her backpack on the ground.

"He said I shouldn't get it dirty, it was a
nice backpack, and picked it up and put it
between us on the bench. I told him I didn't
care if it got dirty. He asked what was wrong.
'I'm trying to score and that girl inside is
being a bitch.' 'You're trying to score what?'
he asked. 'Weed. Do you have any?' He laughed
and lit a cigarette. 'Let me tell you something
that's going to save your life,' and told a

story about a friend of his, a girl, who shot
up heroin in the neck and died in his arms. I
said that wasn't me, and he said of course it
wasn't and pulled out this album and started
showing me photographs. 'That's you,' he said."

The photos were not of the victim but of
girls like her. Close in age, medium in
stature, long hair, white. She reported that
the shots looked professional, taken in parks
or on the beach or posed with cars. All the
subjects were clothed.

"He told me he'd seen a lot of girls and
picked me out of the crowd right away. He said
I could become a model, like the girls in the
pictures. I shouldn't even think about the kids
in school. 'They're not fit to carry your
purse.' They were jealous of my talent. He used
the word 'talent.' I was feeling better. He
said he had pictures of me in the van. I said,
'No way!' He said yeah, he'd taken some candids
and they really turned out great. The van was
in a parking structure half a block away. I
took my backpack and went with him. It didn't
seem like a big deal."

The van was parked on the roof of parking
structure number five. It was older, dark green,
rear double doors. The victim was not able to
identify the make. Most of the parking spaces
were empty and there were no other pedestrians
visible.

"I felt weird being alone up there with him.

I was hoping someone would come out of the elevator, but I told myself that was stupid, just
a reflex that gets drummed into your head. He
was very polite. He went around to the driver's
side and unlocked the doors, and I climbed in
on the passenger side. There was a camera bag
on the front seat, so I put it on the floor.

"As soon as I was inside his whole thing
changed. He yelled at me to get in the back. He
scared the crap out of me just with his voice. I
tried to open the door, but it was locked. Then
he took out a gun. I never saw a real gun. I
think I went into shock. He said, 'Give me your
money.' I couldn't open the zippers on the backpack fast enough, and he started screaming at me
to hurry up. I started opening my wallet, the
change spilled all over. 'How much do you have?'
I said about ten dollars and my mother's credit
card for emergencies. He stuffed everything into
the place where you put the CDs. He had a bunch
of junk in there. Some wire, a roll of duct
tape, some loose bullets and about three knives.
I was totally freaked when I saw that stuff.

"He told me again to get into the back. I
guess I expected some artsy thing since he was
a photographer, but inside there were filthy
mattresses on the floor and the windows were
covered with black paper and there was like
fishnet hanging. I was really, really scared. He
had the gun to my head. I was crying. He said,
'I'm going to kill you. If you do as I say,

I'll let you choose which way you die.' I said,
'Please don't, please don't,' and said I could
get a lot of money for him, but he said, 'Take
off your clothes.' I took off my sweatshirt. I
had to pull it up over my eyes, and I was sure
he was going to shoot me. But then I could see
him again, and he was right there looking at me,
but it was like his face was a mask. He made me
take off my T-shirt. I don't wear a bra, so he
started feeling my breasts. It was disgusting
and it hurt. Then he told me to put my hands
out, and I did, and he put these handcuffs on
me and that was the worst. I felt like I was a
slave. He said if I made any noise he'd kill
me. He pushed me down on my back and knelt over
me and unzipped his pants. I kept crying and
saying, 'Please don't hurt me,' but he sat on
my chest, put his penis in my mouth, and I
couldn't breathe."

The offender was not able to get an erection.

"His filthy underwear was in my face. He said,
'Are you a virgin?' and I couldn't answer so
he'd grab my hair and make my head nod and he
said, 'You're not a virgin. You've done this
before. You love it. You're good at it. You
love it. Does this do it for you?' and make my
head nod like I was a doll. He was heavy, and I
couldn't breathe, and it went on and on. I could
not believe this was happening on the roof of
the parking structure. I thought I would never
get out of that van alive. It was worse than a

nightmare. He kept telling me what to do, like,
'Suck on it,' over and over and making my head
nod, or banging it against the floor, and this
went on and on until finally he, I guess you'd
say, ejaculated down my throat and all over my
face, and I started heaving like I was going to
throw up and he got off me and said, 'Spit,'
and I spit into a filthy rag, a rag you'd wipe
the engine of a car with, then he rubbed it
into my face and all over my breasts. I thought
at least it was over, I was coughing, but then
all of a sudden he put this thing, they said it
was a chain, around my neck and strangled me
until I almost blacked out. He did that over
and over again. It was like he held me underwater. I tried to fight, but he was too strong.
All I could say was, 'Why are you doing this to
me?' Finally he told me to sit up and quit crying. 'You're my woman now,' he said, which
struck me as so stupid I started to laugh. 'You
think that's funny?' he said, but he was smiling. He tucked in his shirt, and it seemed to
take a long time. He fussed until the buttons
of the shirt were lined up with the buckle on
his pants. Then he pulled a cooler out of the
netting and I thought, Oh my God, what does he
have in there? but it was only sodas and sand-
wiches. 'Want a Coke?' he asked like a normal
person, the person he was like on the bench.
While he was busy getting it, I was looking
around to escape. I remembered hearing you

```
should never, never get into a car with them,
and I knew if we drove away he'd definitely kill
me. I thought if I could get to the back doors
fast I could jump out, even with the handcuffs,
before he turned around, but then he turned
around. I was still naked on top, but also
smeared with oil from the rag and disgusting
stuff all over me. I felt totally filthy and
degraded, but I wanted to live; so I decided to
do whatever he said and try to be nice to him.
I made up my mind about that. He wouldn't let
me hold the Coke. He fed it to me until I drank
it all. Then he said, 'Lie down and die.' I
felt really drunk and passed out."
```

After a few minutes of silence there was body movement and a couple of sighs of disgust. Handcuffs were brought out and fiddled with.

"We believe he drugged her with Rohypnol or GHB," I told the team. "She doesn't remember much of the rest of the assault, but we have forensic evidence—the lab report is also in your packet—that gives an emerging picture of the scenario. The big question now is, where?"

"How about *who?*" cracked Andrew to a couple of guffaws.

I smiled. "Hopefully this guy," pointing to the composite.

"We are fortunate the victim was taken to a rape treatment center where the evidence was collected in a correct and timely manner and the victim was given compassionate care," added Rick. "We all know horror stories of mishandling of evidence. For reference, see the sexual assault victim questionnaire put out by the NCAVC."

Rick, I noted, was a bit of a professor.

"Ana's going to profile the suspect, then we'll talk about assignments based on new evidence. She's been up day and night on this case so I think we owe her our thanks."

Desultory applause.

I stood, notes in hand.

"We're looking at a power-assertive serial rapist. A man whose issues revolve around being seen as masculine. He wants people looking at him. He takes care of his body. He's finicky about it. He doesn't like dirt. These attacks are out of anger.

"I characterize him as a serial rapist because even if we didn't have these hits on VICAP, which may connect him to assaults in Washington, DC, Florida and Texas, statistically there is a good possibility he has raped before. His MO shows there was a definite routine to this attack. He uses a con approach to gain trust. He dresses the part, not like a tourist. He can maybe convince a child he's a big-deal photographer, but this guy's just blowing smoke. Once he has the victim under his control, he has no feeling or concern for her. She becomes something nonliving, a doll, as Juliana described."

The faces were interested. Kelsey Owen was taking notes.

"Our friend Ray has elaborate fantasies of domination, which he acts out like a script. Everything has to go according to this preconceived plan. Clearly, the kidnapping and rape were well thought out. He had the van outfitted for the crime. He had his rape kit, the handcuffs and wire. He buzzed his hair. I believe he was stalking the victim, creating chance encounters, waiting for the right time. The probability is high that when we catch this guy we will find a cache of pornography or detective magazines that reinforce his fantasies. As we know, fantasies are perfect, life is not. It's likely he will do it again and again until, in his mind, he gets it right.

"The man is of average or above-average intelligence, an 'organized' offender, as opposed to the disorganized lust killer, who is generally of below-average intelligence, unskilled, anxious during the crime, socially clumsy and so forth. This suspect has been employed in the field of photography, which was confirmed by the lab report. Analysis of fingernail cuts left in the vagina showed traces of grease under the nails similar to that which is used in cameras. You didn't know cameras take grease, but they do, a very light emulsion. I doubt that he was ever in England, taking pictures of Sting, but he does have professional or semiprofessional experience. I strongly feel the photographs he showed Juliana are those of his other victims, which he took as mementos. Ray has been getting away with it, experimenting and not getting caught. All of that fits into his brazenness. And since he used more force than was necessary to control the victim during the assault—she said she was frightened just by his voice—we can conclude he is deeply compelled to do these crimes. Questions so far?"

Jason Ripley raised his hand. "You used the term 'lust killer.' Does that mean this guy will escalate to homicide, or that he's committed homicides in the past?"

"He's not a lust killer, but it's very possible that a life stress could trigger him to start killing his victims, or that he goes too far and someone dies."

"Life stress meaning . . . ?"

"Loss of job, death in the family, anniversary event . . ."

"Or if he got scared and thought we were onto him?"

"Yes, we are not ready to have this exposed. Eunice?"

"How is the victim?"

"She's experiencing rape trauma symptoms. Afraid to leave the house. Hypervigilant—overreacts to sudden noises; for example, a leaf blower will trigger a panic attack. The forced oral copulation produced an unconscious reflex where now she can't swallow. You know the story. This is going to take a while."

"Ana, do you think she escaped, or that he let her go?"

"He could have turned her loose. He's angry at something that wounded him in the past, right? So I think the message is, *You're going to have to live with this, just like I did. Your life will be like mine.* The point is, people, we have a sadistic serial rapist operating in our area."

Rick wanted to know the results of the liaison with law enforcement in Arizona. Just the word "Arizona" made my stomach clench. "What have you got, Detective Berringer?"

"Me?" Andrew shrugged. "Nothing." He had not taken off the jacket. His heels were stuck out in front of him.

"*We're* doing Arizona," I said quickly. "At the SAC's request."

"Oh."

"They sent us a load of sex offenders. Just starting to sort through the files."

"If you need help, let us know," Andrew offered with audacious sarcasm. "I *think* we're familiar with the alphabet down in Santa Monica. Are we, Barry?"

Lieutenant Loomis laughed. "Maybe you are."

I had to bypass Andrew's resentment and call on Kelsey before Galloway started wondering. She was waving both arms like she had to stop a train.

"Just so you know," she informed us breathlessly, "'lust killer' is a dated term."

There it was again. *Dated.*

"How would you describe it?"

"This man is homicidal," she said, "due to a sadistic personality disorder."

"My way is shorter."

Got a laugh.

"Besides that," Kelsey insisted, "I have to disagree with a lot of what you said."

"What Ana has presented here," said Rick, "is based on the information we now have. That could change. Even though there are over six hundred pages in Rapid Start—"

"I know," Kelsey said, "I've read them all."

Andrew was giving me the "what an asshole" look.

But Galloway was lowering his reading glasses. "I'm curious to hear what Kelsey has to say."

My blood pressure hit the red zone.

"First of all," she began primly, "the offender is not a power-assertive rapist."

"He's not."

"Definitely not."

People were turning in their seats to watch her with a mix of skepticism and bemusement. Most were ready for the meeting to end.

"He has a sadistic personality disorder, which means the purpose of his infliction of cruelty is not to become sexually aroused, but to cause physical and psychological pain—"

"I'm sorry," I interrupted, "but sadistic rapists often *do* need to inflict pain in order to become aroused. Sex and torture of the victim are fused for them."

"This attack," she countered, "*seems* to fit the profile of a sadistic rape. It was calculated. He bound and humiliated her—"

"Yes, out of *rage*."

"No." Kelsey lifted her chin. "It was *punishment*. It was about pain. The more it went on, the more powerful he felt. As a trained psychologist, I need to say that we're talking two fundamentally different personality structures."

"Believe me, I'm aware—"

"Well it makes a significant difference as to what he will do next."

I had to take a breath. I had to take two. I was really, really holding back from taking her apart. But the words that came flying at me— "respect," "experience," "snotty little upstart"—had nothing to do with the argument at hand. We were discussing anger, after all, and I had once pulled a phone out of the wall and thrown it across the bull pen. Things did not end well.

"Maybe Kelsey can explain what she means by 'sadistic personality disorder,'" suggested Rick. "Many of us are unfamiliar with the concept."

Rick long ago had earned his supervisor spurs.

Now she had license to go on for another five minutes. To me it was everything wrong with specialists coming into the Bureau as a second career. They each think their area of expertise is what's going to crack the case, all that matters is whether they, as individuals, get points, because that was the corporate culture they came from, and they'll argue endlessly from their one little narrow point of view. They haven't been around long enough to get the bigger picture of what it means to be an agent.

I have noticed the more specialized you are, the more pompous.

"Okay, we've got two opposing points of view," Rick said at last, "which we have to look at in terms of the best interests of this case. We have to go forward without biases on either side."

I had no idea what he was talking about. All I knew was Kelsey had created a divide in which she, suddenly, had authority. An equal say. And she wasn't even on the squad.

"Pardon me, but this is bullshit." Andrew was on his feet. "Why split hairs, when it's staring you right in the face?"

It threw everybody off. Even Eunice arched her eyebrows and folded her arms skeptically.

"You want academic theory, or how about nailing this cretin?"

I heard some handcuff ratcheting, but I was thrilled. Nobody stood up for you like that at the Bureau.

After a moment Rick composed himself and asked, "Detective Berringer, would you like to share?"

Andrew said, "This guy is former military."

Now there was interest.

"The victim says the shoes are shined, the belt buckle has to be lined up with the buttons—what do you want, dog tags? He's former military out of Arizona. Anybody like to place a bet?"

"Just bring me his dick," said Barry Loomis. "In a paper bag."

Rick didn't like wise guys, but he couldn't argue the logic. Former military made sense. He snapped out assignments: Cross-reference the Arizona sex offenders with military police records. Check for rape charges. Look at the photography angle. Look at the cases on VICAP with this in mind.

The meeting had gone over. We moved out quickly with not a lot of talk. The overhead projector was still running, leaving the amber image of the offender to play against the screen at the front of the emptying room.

All in all, he was having a better day than I was.

Twelve.

You can't go," I told Andrew. "I have something funny to show you."

After the briefing I guess I just needed a little contact, so I guided him to Barbara's office to have a laugh over the bank robbery photograph of our butts, and everything went sideways from there.

Lieutenant Barry Loomis came, too. At first there was professional chatter amongst the four of us, the requisite cooing over Barbara's baby pictures (she gave me the nod—the detective *was* hot), and it was nice after the stress of the briefing just to chill, but while we were looking at the doofy surveillance photo from the Mission Impossible caper, the ski mask came up.

"They recovered another piece of evidence, did Ana tell you?" Barbara said.

Andrew looked at me inquiringly. "No."

"A ski mask," I said.

"Really?"

"It was kicked under some boxes—in that janitor's room, remember?"

"Yeah? When'd they find it?"

I shrugged. "A couple of months ago."

"Where is it now?" Barry immediately wanted to know.

"I guess at Result Associates."

"The lab?"

I nodded.

"Why weren't we informed?" Barry demanded.

I have found that supervisors are supervisors, even if they wear funny ties.

"They're a little chaotic out there," Barbara answered. "About as organized as my garage."

"But they notified the Bureau?"

"Somehow I do remember it coming in."

"Barbara remembers everything."

Troubled, Andrew had turned away and was picking at a spot on the top of his head. Suddenly he refused to meet my eyes.

"We have a problem," Barry said, all bristly. "Obviously we are out of the loop."

"Just call the lab, and I'm sure they'll—"

"Because it was a bank robbery," Andrew interrupted, terse as his boss. "The chief has made bank robberies a priority—"

"And also," Barry cut in, "there is some sensitivity to a federal agency receiving information and not the locals."

We all knew the name of that tune.

"Why the big secret?" Andrew asked, in a voice edged with something I had not heard before. He was still scratching at the same spot on his scalp, snowy flakes appearing on the dark blue collar of the cowboy shirt.

"I just found out."

"You knew it was my case."

"It's my case, too. I've been *kind of* busy."

I did not appreciate his big hulk hanging over me. I felt defensive, like a dog that does not like its head patted.

"If it's such a big deal," I snapped, "let's open Mission Impossible up again."

"Good idea," soothed Barbara. "Make it a positive. I don't believe the case was ever officially closed."

"We'll make it right with your chief," I promised Andrew. To Barbara: "I don't think Mike would mind if I jumped back in on this one," envisioning working both cases, willing to stretch, if that would fix it.

"He'd have you back on the squad in a New York minute," she agreed.

I was waiting for a sign from Andrew that we were still okay.

"As soon as we get a handle on this kidnap deal. All right?"

"We better go," Barry said.

I tried again. "It'll be fine."

"Whatever floats your boat," Andrew said finally.

Well, that was not going to fly. Not with everything else that had been going on. I snagged him on the way out, telling Barry, "I just need Detective Berringer to sign something," and pulled him out a service door into a cement stairwell filled with unearthly moaning, the Corridor of Winds.

"What is your problem, Andrew? You have been acting really strange."

"Man, you fucked me up, bad."

"*I* did?"

"Withholding information."

"How can you say that? I was not withholding information—"

"It is humiliating for me not to know about something *that* important on *my* case with my supervisor standing right there."

"I'm *sorry,* I've had other things on my mind—"

"You're a Fed, you can drop a case with no accountability—"

"What do you mean, no accountability?"

"They can move you all over the map, to fucking Timbuktu, but *I live here,* I don't need this *shit.*"

Suddenly his heavy fist arced the air, so forcefully that I flinched. His shout wafted seventeen floors down.

"Will you cool *out*?" I said. "What's going on? You yell at me over the phone that I shouldn't tell you how to do your job, now I embarrass you in front of your boss. I mean, what am I doing that's so wrong?"

"You're in my way."

I lost my balance then, as if I'd suddenly looked down those seventeen stories and realized I was standing on a ledge.

"If I'm in your way . . . I'm sorry . . . I'll get out of your way."

"No. Look. *I'm* sorry." He took my hands, drew me into a tense embrace. My eyes were open, staring at the cinder block. When he spoke again, his voice was spent. "Got to go," he whispered hoarsely.

I stepped back. "If I'm making you so miserable—"

"*It isn't you.*"

"Then—"

"Later? Okay? Barry's waiting."

"Okay. Listen." Still. The contact. "That was a good idea about the suspect's military background. And thanks for standing up for me with Kelsey."

It took a moment for him to remember. "That? It was just such a waste of everybody's time."

He hadn't been defending me; it was just politics as usual, move the boring shit along. I found myself fighting a dull panic.

"Like your cowboy shirt," running a finger along the decorative white edging that swirled above the pockets. "Want to go for a ride? How about tonight?"

He pulled on the handle of the metal door. A helix of wind sucked it back.

"Sure, when I get off. Around seven."

The hair on our heads flew up in the draft.

*   *   *

We happened to be standing together on line in the cafeteria. It was three that afternoon and I was just getting lunch.

Galloway said, "Are you and Kelsey Owen having a personality conflict?"

"Kelsey? No, of course not."

"I think we should pay attention to what she's saying. She gives things an interesting twist. She's green, but I think she's got some good ideas."

"Me, too."

"So why don't you listen to her ideas?"

"I listen."

"Didn't look that way."

I couldn't focus on how things had looked as far back as that morning. I had tried to be open, or at least appear that way, but now it was past and we had moved on to the next phase, and I was numb and dumb after ten grinding days with no sleep.

"She said you never answer her e-mail."

"You want me to hold her hand, I'll be happy to hold her hand. Whatever you want me to do, Robert, I'll be happy to make you happy."

"It's not about me being happy."

We were at the cashier. He could have paid for me and I could have paid for him, but that's not the way it is.

"I'm going to work in a summer camp," he mused. "I don't want to be the camp director, nothing like that—I'm going to be the guy with the rake, keeping the area clean, where the kids throw stuff out of the tents."

"You don't think the Bureau is summer camp?"

He smiled. We walked outside, and I felt sorry for him, the way the sun burned through to the roots of his curly thinning hair. Wasn't he hot in those turtlenecks? We were each holding our cardboard tray. I had a packaged tuna sandwich and a large black coffee, which would have zero effect. We had been heading toward the main entrance, but now he stopped.

"I'm going to take a break," indicating the outdoor tables.

My cue. "See you later."

But he stayed put. "You think I'm pitiful."

"I don't think you're pitiful, I think you're a great leader."

He smiled painfully. "We're all a team. Part of the Bureau family, and that ain't no jive."

We were squinting at each other against the sun.

"I'll take care of it."

"All right."

About this time I had started to experience blackouts, nanoseconds of sleep that, like it or not, shut down the brain. I was fading in and out, with no defenses. After the grueling and unresolved encounter with Andrew, I could not grasp what else might possibly be expected of me. The rebuke came then, through a flickering daze.

"You were a kid once, too," I heard Galloway say.

I went up to my pod and ate the tuna sandwich. I made some arrangements, and when they were complete, left a message on Kelsey Owen's voice mail, reporting what I had done:

"Hi, Kelsey, it's Ana Grey. I wanted you to know that I had a talk with the SAC about your theories, and based on my conversation with him, I have gone ahead and placed three agents on undercover assignment at different S&M bars in the Valley. Actually, one is a regular black leather bar and two are dungeons run by a dominatrix, where sadomasochists go to be punished with whips and racks, but I'm sure you're familiar with the pathology. I think if we're looking for a sadist, we should look where sadists hang out, don't you?

"By the way, little lady, if you think this is your ticket to profile school, think again. There's a code around here called not ratting each other out that even the brass catches on to. You want to tell me something, have the guts to tell me in person.

"And one more thing. I take pride in my work. It's hard, what we do—to treat people fairly, whether they're the good guys or not. Sitting down and interviewing the victim is one thing. But to sit down and interview a rapist, or someone who has done something that, in your past, you were a victim of yourself, that's something else. That's a result of time on the street.

"Not everyone can do what we do. I'm the kind of person who, when I hear the national anthem, I get all teary-eyed. It's a feeling. Patriotism. I don't know. But whatever that feeling is, you have it or you don't. Like I said, I will keep you informed."

My legs were responding only stubbornly as I passed beneath the portico of the Federal Building, not letting up in their complaints of stiffness and neglect; shoulders and neck were being just as petulant, as I had not been to the pool since the case began, but we all dragged on, discombobulated body parts trying to keep up the march. The evening was muggy and overcast, and glancing at the disinterested sky, I remembered one fragment of a dream in which an owl had put its spiky wing around me.

In the Bureau garage, four male prisoners were chained to a bench. I made them for Chinese mafia. There had been rumors of a deep cover operation about to end in a bust down in Garden Grove that involved the chief of police and a string of sex parlors owned by local Asians. This must be it.

Two of them were businessmen wearing coats and ties, two looked like delivery boys in bad seventies shirts. They were sitting down, handcuffed with arms behind their backs. The handcuffs were locked to a thick chain that ran around the bench. Two agents I recognized from the white-collar-crime squad were walking a fifth prisoner, also wearing a suit, toward the cubicle where he would be fingerprinted and photographed. It was slow going because of the ankle irons.

In the doorway of the cubicle—similar to the office where the manager of a parking lot might tally the ticket stubs—was Hugh Akron, looking like a shoe salesman eager to sell you shoes, but actually he was an English photographer who was working freelance for the Bureau. It would be his job to place the prisoners up against the wall—the most nondescript wall in the world, a little dark from head grease, a nothing piece of drywall—and snap their mug shots. He also did weddings.

A tall, spidery man pushing sixty, Hugh favored oversized blue-tinted aviator glasses and bowling-style shirts made of rayon. He had been doing this a long time and it showed, in the strong knobby fore-arms and curved spine that thrust the narrow head forward, in the practiced joviality of a natural-born hustler. The scams he ran out of the photo lab were legendary.

"Ana of a Thousand Days! Or should I say nights? You're at the office late."

"Hey," was all I could muster.

They brought the prisoner to a box and told him to kneel. The box was covered with carpeting. I wondered if it was government policy not to stress the prisoner's ligaments; the kneeling position kept them helpless as the handcuffs were removed. The man was talking rapidly in Chinese and one of the agents kept repeating, "Do you want a trans-lator?"

Suddenly he fell silent and bowed his head. Spellbound, I watched through the doorway as Hugh Akron inked the man's fingertips, and one by one took possession of their uniqueness on behalf of the United States government.

The man kept his face bent toward the ground. His expression, what I could see of it, was stoic.

I stayed there and watched the whole thing: the ritual humiliation of the prisoner and its mysterious, erotic pleasure.

A ndrew and I never did meet up that night. I wish I had done what I said I would do and just stayed out of his way. Instead, when he didn't call or answer his page, I went looking for him.

The dull panic was rising.

I drove my personal vehicle, a 1970 Plymouth Barracuda convertible, to Wilshire and Third, parked in a red zone and walked by the fountain where Juliana first encountered the offender. It was clever, a dinosaur made of leaves that grew on a wire form. Water cascaded from its snout and collected in a rectangular pool. There was a dark wax stripe left by skateboarders on the edge. A toddler in a pink parka was running along it now. Undercover cops mixed heavily with the crowd.

I paged Andrew a second time, called his cell, got nothing, started to walk down the center of the mix. The sounds were clashing—a keyboard player only yards away from an Ecuadorian band of flutes and tambourines. It was a downhill stroll toward the indoor mall, a palace of dazzling consumption at the very end, during which you passed every manner of marketplace come-on—a mime spray-painted silver, portrait artists, trinket sellers, discount T-shirts off a cart, henna painters and one-man bands, a guy who would carve your fortune on a grain of rice.

We had been over this territory during the kidnapping. It was familiar ground. But the nighttime masquerade suited my mood of self-pity and longing, as I kept hands in pockets, kicking it, scanning for Willie John Black or Andrew, guessing he'd go back to his witness to corroborate what we now knew about the man with the camera from Arizona who called himself Ray.

I swerved down the alleys, asking bag ladies and parking valets if they'd seen the guy who lives on a bicycle or the big cop in the black leather jacket. Nobody knew anything. I passed the bench where we had dreamed of Amsterdam, occupied now by a balding man singing "Happy Birthday" into a cell phone.

We were apart, but we would get it back. We were not rotting meat like the M&Ms, withdrawn to opposite sides of a bleak corridor. Riding the Harley, playing golf, seven-layer bean dip and the Lakers on TV, or just falling asleep, Andrew made everything better. We were alive, we had juice. We genuinely cared for each other. What could be luckier than two buddies who had great sex with no other entanglements? This was a temporary blip. Another case, another bottom-feeding offender not about to knock *us* out. Hadn't we each been stung by garbage like Ray so often that we had become immune?

I felt exhilarated, on a mission, zigzagging up Santa Monica Boulevard and down Broadway, out to the Pier and along the Palisade, maintaining a pace, cleansed in cool damp air, imagining Andrew at every turn. Then I realized it was 11:30 p.m. and I had been doing this two hours, and it had stopped being fun a while ago. The going was much less dense as I trudged up the Promenade one last time, giving up the game and stopping at the police kiosk to do the rational thing, which was to ask if other officers of the Santa Monica Police Department had seen Detective Berringer.

"Who's looking for him?" asked a uniform behind a narrow desk. There were a couple more sitting around.

I badged him. He gave me the lookover and I wondered if rumors of our affair had reached the distant outposts. Or maybe he was just curious to see a female Fed with long frizzy hair wearing a beat-up vintage denim jacket embroidered with peace signs.

"Nope. Haven't. Have you?"

General shaking of heads.

"I think he's mainly doing morning shifts, am I right?"

Shrugs.

"We're working a case together. The Santa Monica kidnapping?"

Empty stares. I decided to go home.

"Tried his mobile?"

I nodded. "He was looking for a transient named Willie John Black."

"We know Willie," said someone else. "The guy with the bike. Usually he's up behind Second Street. In the alley, half a block north of Wilshire."

I felt hopeful again. "Appreciate it very much."

"I'll pass it on to Detective Berringer that you were here. Got a card?"

There was nothing and nobody in the alley where the cop had told

me to look. A Dumpster. Evidence of a nest—trampled cloth and flattened cardboard boxes. A man's shirt on a wire hanger hooked to the
chain-link. If this was Willie's place, he'd taken his contraption and
gone somewhere else.

A shy, stealthy figure appeared, a young Hispanic busboy dumping
a bag of trash. There were no residences here, just the hind sides of
office buildings and a deserted parking lot. A black-running stream
issued from who knew where.

I thought about foul play.

There could be plenty.

I paused, alone, in the middle of the dark alley. Out on the street,
a bus was idling. A string of European tourists ambled past.

The space inside my ears was full of pounding.

Thirteen.

By the following morning we had a prime suspect, Richard (Ray) Brennan. The name had come in the night before, in a fax sent by the Tempe, Arizona, Police Department.

The fax was already posted on Rapid Start when I got to the office, sometime before 7 a.m. As Galloway would say, where else did I have to go? Normally I check personal e-mail first thing—open the curtains, crack the sliding doors, let in the marine layer, look at the boats, grab some OJ and sit down at the glass dining table and plug in—but you can access Rapid Start only from the computers at the Bureau, and stress was waking me up early, anyway. Just before dawn there would be that jolt, as if dropped on the bed from a great distance, the rapid heartbeat and the racing thoughts. The circles under my eyes had gone from puffy to charred black.

We had taken the pile of sex offenders from Arizona, isolated those who were former military, and asked local police to search their files again, using our prompts. It only took one keyword—"sadistic"—to identify Ray Brennan.

FD-823 (Rev. 8-26-97)

RAPID START

INFORMATION CONTROL

Case ID: 446-702-9977 The Santa Monica Kidnapping

Control Number: 5201   Priority: Immediate

Classification: Sensitive   Source: Tempe, Ariz.,
                              Police Dept.

Event time: 2:05 AM

Method of contact: FAX

Prepared by: Conrad, Angela   Component/Agency: Tech
                              clerk, FBI

Transcript attached.

* * *

**Subject: Unknown offender/serial rapist, The
Santa Monica Kidnapping**

From: Sgt. D. Mader

To: Special Agent Rick Harding, Supervisor, FBILA

   **In response to your request to cross-reference
arrests of sex offenders in the Tempe, Arizona,
area going back five years, I found a couple
that fit your profile, which I am faxing to you,
Richard (Ray?) Brennan in particular. I
personally remember this case because it was
out of the ordinary. Officer Kip Ward arrested
Mr. Brennan four years ago on suspicion of
sadistic cruelty to farm animals after finding
evidence of duck feathers and crossbows in his**

residence where he resided with wife and five-
year-old daughter at the time. Basically, the
suspect wounded three ducks in a lake in a con-
dominium complex with a high-powered crossbow.
Brennan is a former marine, which also fits your
profile. He was arrested five times for assault
with intent to commit rape, but the cases never
went anywhere. The DA declined prosecution for
lack of sufficient evidence. I ask you, how does
a guy like that keep getting arrested but never
prosecuted? A search warrant of the Tempe residence at the time turned up 20 semiautomatic
rifles and handguns along with militia literature
and pornography. When he was sixteen, an elderly
neighbor called police to her home on several
occasions to complain Richard Brennan was spying
on her, but no charges were filed and she is
deceased. Brennan skipped bail on the weapons
charge and left this area. Duck feathers nailed
to plywood were also found in the suspect's home.
Let me know if I can be of further assistance.

    Sincerely,

    Sergeant Donna Mader

I sat back and watched the tender morning light stalk Los Angeles, savoring a bite of cinnamon twist and then a sip of French roast coffee. Arizona, the military background, the rape assaults all added up like aces, but it was the wonderful way Ray Brennan had spiked some innocent ducks with a steel shaft going high velocity, then nailed the trophy feathers to some random piece of plywood, that made me know he was my guy. *This* was the twisted, grandiose offender I knew.

I drove against traffic to the Santa Monica Police Department. It was just before 8 a.m. I figured Andrew would be there or on his way. I cannot pretend the move was wholly case-related. I was under siege and running in crisis mode: every encounter held an equal urgency, and I was powerless to stop the stream of guidelines and commands that multiplied and split inside my head. I had a stunning piece of news to present to Andrew which might in some way justify the unsettling search from the night before. That is all I hoped for.

The dewy roofs of cars ticked by as I jogged the aisles of the crowded Civic Center parking lot, skimming for the unmarked burgundy Ford. Instead I came upon Margaret Forrester, sitting in her vehicle, pounding the steering wheel and howling with rage.

Even through the rolled-up windows you could hear it—throat-scraping screams, like an infant in pain. I have never experienced such sounds. They were what you might have heard if you had woken up in primal Africa, the first human on earth, surrounded by a jungle full of hostile, incomprehensible bellowing.

She saw me approaching and popped the door of the gold Lexus sedan.

"Look what he did to me!"

She got out and stood by the car. Her face was clear red, the way an infant's entire body turns red when it's yelling. The door was a barrier that stopped me cold. I was forced to look.

"What?"

She wrenched the back door open, too.

I was unable to detect any damage to the car. Except for the fading scarlet patches in her cheeks, she also appeared intact, a little tousled, the short cream-colored leather skirt and long legs in slingbacks none the worse for wear.

"What?" she mimicked. *"This!"*

And reached into the backseat, dragging out twenty, maybe thirty pieces of fresh dry cleaning in plastic bags, which slid to the pavement in a glimmering pile.

"I have been going there six years. Then suddenly today, out of *nowhere,* he says, 'Take your dry cleaning and don't come back!'"

"Who did?"

"Sam! The dry cleaning man! *I've been going there six years!*"

Instinct told me not to ask normal questions or offer common sense *(Take your laundry somewhere else)* because Margaret's eyes were darting around like little black panicked fish, and I had the sense that whatever she had done to cause trusty old Sam to blow would prove beyond reason, anyway.

"I'm sorry that happened, Margaret."

It was as if she had been pierced with a sharp instrument. She fairly yelped with hurt.

"I don't want your empathy! Don't you dare empathize with me!"

"Hey, look—"

"I'm a widow and my husband died, but that doesn't mean you can empathize with me! Don't you dare. I don't want your empathy. Who the hell do you think you are?"

I put my briefcase down and said, "Let's just pick this stuff up."

There must have been a hundred dollars' worth of dry cleaning billowing around, drifting slowly underneath parked cars.

"It's like this *all the time,*" she complained. "When I was growing up, we had nothing. But people didn't treat you like dirt."

I was trying to lay the clothes on the backseat, but they kept slipping off and there were too many to hang. The Nextel was suddenly as unrelenting as she. Two calls in a row from Rick. Now the pager, too. My arms were full of sticky plastic bags.

"Can you open the trunk?"

"Nobody helps," she said. Then: "Don't help me!"

"Fine. Whatever you want."

I dropped the whole pile on the ground. Now she looked at me, appalled.

"Why did you do that?"

"You said you didn't want my help." I bent to lift my briefcase.

"Don't go!" She grabbed my forearm. "Please don't go," pleading desperately. "He's leaving us, Ana."

These sudden shifts were scaring me—the tossing blur of shining hair and scrabbling fingers seemed out of place and vulgar in the remorseless sun. Was this a hissing fit on a bad hormone day, or could the woman be delusional?

"Who is leaving? Not your husband."

"No, *Andrew*!" she cried shakily, on the verge of tears. "Believe me, he won't stick around while the crap hits the fan."

"What crap?"

"He's going up north, to Fresno."

"Fresno?"

"The Fresno Police Department. I saw a request for a recommendation he passed on to the chief. He wants to get a job up there and—just—never come back."

She covered her mouth with her fingertips and stared at me with a look of alarm.

What sense did this make? My first thought was, no, he would never leave his father's house. Not quit the department this close to retirement.

"You seem awfully upset about Andrew leaving. *If* he's leaving."

And what about us moving in together?

"You don't know," she breathed.

Margaret's eyes were small and wounded with an aggressive kind of deprivation. Her arms were folded and her shoulders pinched as she peered out from a nest of resentment. She was hurting and would find somebody to blame—me, the dry cleaner, Andrew. She would gather her powers and punish us all.

"There's no way you *could* know," Margaret said. "You're not *inside* the department. Andrew is the greatest guy on earth, but he's fickle, very fickle, so be forewarned. He was the exact same way with me, after my husband died. I needed the comfort, understand what I'm saying?"

I did, all right.

"Andrew was the only one who really, really knew me."

Watching her. His best buddy's sexy and ambitious wife. Margaret had retrieved a water bottle from somewhere and was taking a drink, keeping watch on me over the glinting plastic.

"I'm not going to apologize for it. You'll be happy to know, he dumped me, too." She kicked at the dry cleaning. "He thinks he's angry, but my anger is bigger than his. Ha! I am the Thunder Goddess!"

"Is this a joke?"

"What do you mean?"

"I mean, are you a joke, Margaret, or just unbelievably cruel?"

The thing I resented most was how Andrew got us to fight over him in a parking lot.

"No, it's terribly, terribly sad. I'm sad for you because you're going to get hurt."

"Enough." I gripped the briefcase. "I don't want to hear it."

"Woman to woman? You're not the only one on his plate. It's that Oberbeck bitch-and-a-half, too, but that's the way they are. Senior detectives, I love them to death, but they think they're God's gift."

This was something else. Not just lunacy, but lunacy with a barbed point.

"Time-out. Are we talking about Andrew Berringer and Sylvia Oberbeck?"

"Why?" she asked, terrifyingly coy. "Who wants to know?"

I turned around and walked back to my car, making sure to grind my heels as deeply and destructively into as many of Margaret Forrester's slithery garments as possible.

Which way—the freeway, or the streets? *Where was I going?* To the office. *Why?* To talk to Rick. *Rick had called me, right?* He had seen the posting on Richard Brennan and wanted to pursue the lead. It was hard work thinking these thoughts, like lifting fifty-pound boxes, stacking one on top of the other. I was in some kind of a wind tunnel. A hallway. I was doing this work of thinking, stacking up the awkward facts (Margaret was jealous, crazy, unreliable), and at the end of the hallway there was Andrew.

There was Andrew and Officer Sylvia Oberbeck, whose character became instantly revised, from sensitive first responder at the M&Ms' to dumb jock blonde with the fake fingernails and neat French braid that I could never manage, voluptuous underneath the uniform, and canny, too; she never gave it away (neither of them did), but you knew how it worked, she was there every day in the trenches, liked drinking beer and playing pool, a working-class girl with a couple of exes, as lonely and miserable and reckless as the rest of the squad, which she was probably screwing on a regular basis.

He slept with Margaret, too? After her husband died?

Was that possible? Was I *nuts?*

I called him.

"What's the matter? You sound upset. Is it about the case?"

"Are you seeing someone else?"

"What? What are you talking about?"

"I heard you're going out with Sylvia Oberbeck."

"No."

"Tell me the truth and we can move on."

"I'm not seeing Sylvia Oberbeck. Where did you get this information?"

"Margaret Forrester."

"Margaret is pathological."

"I know, but she says you're screwing Oberbeck, and also, get this, that you slept with *her* when the Hat died."

"Listen to me. Ana? Are you listening?"

"Mmm-hmm."

"You're not *crying,* baby."

"Just tell me the truth."

"Do you know what we call Margaret? The Black Widow. Do you know why? Because she killed the Hat. Might as well have. Might as well have pulled the trigger on the gun."

"I thought it was a baseball bat."

"*Whatever!* She pushed that sorry bastard into an untenable situation. And he was a really good man. *Work late. Move up. Volunteer for dangerous assignments. Make money. Money, money, money.* She's a greedy lying bitch, and she doesn't like you."

"That's clear."

"She's jealous as hell because you're the boss—"

"And sleeping with you."

"I'm sorry it came down this way. What can I tell you? This is how she operates."

"I don't care how she operates, all I care about is you and me. Is that pathetic?"

"Ana—"

"I can't talk now, I have to get back. My supervisor's calling. We have a suspect—a guy from Arizona, five arrests for rape, no convictions, name is Ray Brennan. Former marine."

"Bingo."

"Your idea. Good work."

"Feeling better?"

"No."

"What can I do for you, baby?"

"Tell me where you were last night."

"Chasing a Spanish guy down an alley."

"What went down?"

"Pickpocket."

"Where? The Promenade."

"Yep."

"Catch him?"

"What do you think?" Andrew said. "Sixteen years old, runs like a rabbit."

Rick said, "It's about your ninety-day file review."

"I turned in my files."

"And every one of your cases says, *'Unaddressed work due to the Santa Monica kidnapping.'*"

"Be fair, Rick, not every one."

I had not gone into the office. After speaking with Andrew, I had been able to drive no more than a mile from the police station before pulling over in tears. Now I was parked at a meter on the Palisade above the ocean, talking robotically on the Nextel, staring through the windshield into murky space.

"Where are your communications for the past ninety days?"

"They're in hand notes."

"But where are they in the file?"

"Who cares? What about the fax on Brennan?"

"Deal with it, and in your spare time get this assessment up to date. By the way, what is this about you wanting to open up an old case from the bank squad?"

"Nothing. I was trying to help someone."

"The inspectors are coming in ten days."

I forced myself to sit there, gazing at the ocean like the rest of the midmorning unemployed sleazebag degenerates in their trashy cars. I was doing work again, although this time the thoughts came easily off the conveyor belt, greased by their own logic.

Why was Rick suddenly on this? Because he had turned on me, too.

Kelsey got to him.

Through Galloway.

She had not liked my voice mail about patriotism and the American flag. Golly gee.

A Broadway tune came tap-tap-tapping along: *"And good's bad today / And black's white today / And day's night today . . ."* Something-something-*"gigolo."* Was that really the next line? I laughed out loud and put the tan Crown Victoria in gear. Everything was reversed, all right! "Polarized," I think, is the term in photography.

I did go to the Federal Building—not up to the seventeenth floor to take care of the files like a good girl, but down to the subbasement of the garage, down to Hugh Akron's darkroom.

This was now my shadow self, the inverted Ana, passing along the bare cinder-block corridor, following clusters of pipes. Soon the noise of blowers and whining car engines had faded, and acrid film developer had replaced the moldy scent of sweat coming out of the fitness center, and there was Hugh, all bones and lankiness, slicing off the edge of a photograph with the razor-sharp arm of a paper cutter he brought down with a surgical *thwack!*

"Ana-stasia!" He smiled.

That English charm went a long way. Rumor was he had been a pilot in the RAF and a pioneer in aerial photography, whose counter-intelligence was vital to the Normandy landing, but that would put him way past seventy and doesn't make any sense.

I have discovered Hugh Akron knows what to include and what to make sure stays out of the picture.

He always wore a Leica, eager to snap your picture, "Just for kicks," and it was flattering, what the hell. Weeks later you'd get a black-and-white, and there you are, standing by the filing cabinet looking very documentary. The understanding was, you slipped old Hugh ten bucks in American dollars for contributing to your memory book. You didn't really want the print, but you were not about to throw it away. Parking tickets? Play-off games? Wedgwood china? Airline discounts cheaper than cheap? Don't ask, don't tell, see the Brit.

The chlorine smell was overwhelming although the actual dark-room was behind one of the other doors. The counter space where Hugh worked, to a classical music station, was empty and scrupulously white.

"What can I do for you?" he asked, tan cheeks turning an appealing pink.

"I need to run a check through the DMV."

It used to be you could run a background check on anyone who cut you off on the freeway, but there had been so many abuses the Bureau made it a censurable act to make unauthorized use of the DMV. You are not supposed to do this. You are truly not.

Hugh moved to the computer. "Case number?"

"Left it upstairs."

"Let's approximate."

He typed in something. A flute concerto playing on the boom box was blowing notes of unbelievable sweetness like bubbles drifting on the cold, still, pungent air.

"Name?"

"Sylvia Oberbeck."

"California resident?"

"Yes."

His long fingers danced over the keys. He had already accessed the Department of Motor Vehicles database and gone through the security check using, I surmised, not his own ID.

"Driver's license?"

"Don't know."

"Vehicle registration?"

"Don't know. But she's an officer with the Santa Monica police."

"That helps."

I focused on the pleasing music. It was cold and white as a morgue in there.

"You're looking peaked. Have you lost weight?"

"Probably."

"Well, don't lose any more, my love. Not on that tiny frame. What are you working on?"

He knew about the Santa Monica kidnapping because he had processed location shots of the Promenade. I said we had a good suspect who was also a photographer.

"What's his background?"

"He knows how to use a camera. He was in the marines."

"Check *Stars and Stripes*," Hugh suggested. "Might have gone in for journalism."

"Great idea."

Already in progress.

Finally the printer stirred and presented the results.

"Thank you." I folded the page into my pocket. "How's the wedding business?"

"Lovely. Do you know Vicki Shawn and Ed Brewster, the fire-arms instructors? I took their nuptial picture right back there, just the other day."

I stared at the sterile row of doors. "You mean she came down here wearing a wedding dress?"

"Well of course, what did you expect, body armor? This is what I'm really excited about, however, have I shown you?"

He scooped up the picture he had cropped and gathered a dozen like it.

"What is your professional opinion?" he wanted to know, standing back and folding his hands inside the bib of the rubber apron.

A platinum blonde with large breasts was lying tummy down on a bearskin rug, ankles crossed in the air. Another strode a hobbyhorse. Another, the old barbershop pole. It was classic cheesecake, healthy girls wearing nothing but G-strings, in soft-focus studio shots with phony stars of light in their eyes, poses so quaint they would not have offended Abraham Lincoln.

"Are the fifties coming back?"

Alarmed: "What do you mean by the fifties?" He lowered the blue aviators, peering closely at the prints. "This is the hottest thing. The Internet," he whispered. "Hit the jackpot with this lot."

My pits were damp. I wanted to flee.

"Hugh," I said, and his big head jerked. "You've got mail."

I left the money in an interoffice envelope.

It was odd to be on the other side of deception—I had always been the snoop, after all. But it turned out I was good at it, and in this new world of upside-down loyalties and reversed color fields, I moved with remarkable confidence, able to have several conversations with Andrew that smacked of normalcy. It is different when you know what you want. You behave like a phantom, clinging to walls and molding into corners to hear what you need to hear, coax what you have to coax. Unknown to him, our next few phone calls took on a subtle but

interrogatory tone. I fairly purred with newfound interest in his pref-
erences and found out things:

He wasn't at all sure about his birthday; he might go up to see his
sister in the Bay Area. The Harley would need a new muffler. Someone he had gone to high school with just died of a heart attack. He
was swamped with work. Willie John Black could not be located,
which was frustrating because we were soon to get a military ID of
Richard Brennan. Ross Meyer-Murphy was calling Andrew every day,
as he was calling me, demanding that we "get the guy." The department had busted Laurel West Academy wide open with an expanding
drug investigation that would hit the papers any day. Andrew wasn't
even getting to the gym. The most he could manage was a drink after
work at the Boatyard or breakfast at Coffee Craze in the Marina,
where he knew the beach 'n' biker regulars. *That's right near me,
could we meet there?* I asked, guessing the answer. Well, he didn't
really get around that often.

The address on Sylvia Oberbeck's driver's license was a white stucco
sixties apartment building in Mar Vista with a wire sculpture of
three fish and ocean waves over the front entrance. I would take
the G-ride because the Barracuda would have stood out in the residential neighborhood. Still, Andrew had a sixth sense on him, which I had
to take into account, so instead of parking on the street I would pull
into a driveway behind somebody's car already tucked in for the night
and watch the apartment through the rearview mirror.

Sylvia Oberbeck's balcony was the one crowded with Japanese
lanterns and discarded dining room chairs, an old TV. She lived alone
(no other names on the mailbox). I once observed an athletic woman
arriving on a mountain bike, which she hefted onto her shoulder and
carried inside. She then emerged with Officer Oberbeck, and they
drove off in her Mazda. This created a short-lived lesbian fantasy.

I would stay only briefly, not vibrating with tension like the rookie
on stakeout I had once been, but a lazy predator on nature's time. I

was patient, collecting information. I wanted to be immaculately prepared—get it done, if it had to be done, with one swift blow.

Sunday morning I cruised by Coffee Craze and saw them together. They were sitting at a table sharing the newspaper—she in a visor with her hair in a ponytail, he wearing shades, a warm-up jacket and sweats. He sat hunched over his food, the way he does, concentrating on sawing something on his plate, glancing at a section folded back on the table. She lay back, inside the open tent of the paper, hefty legs in black exercise tights, one foot in a dirty old running shoe up on a chair.

Nothing even barely sexy was going on, and after a few nights of unremarkable surveillance, I was beginning to feel relieved. In fact, I was prepared to have a big laugh on myself. So he *had* been chasing a kid on the Promenade. So they *were* two old friends meeting for Sunday brunch. Andrew had been ducking me, but this was not a felony.

I sipped the coffee I had brought in the G-ride, almost ready to walk across the street and clap them both on the back as if it were all a happy coincidence. I watched as they split the bill and got into Andrew's Ford, then followed at a distance as they ambled through traffic and eventually got onto the Marina Freeway, euphoric at the thought that I was just a silly, jealous girl.

The Marina Freeway is basically an access road, a short connection between the 405 and Lincoln Boulevard. It is not well traveled, especially on a Sunday morning. You could, if you timed it right, get three to five minutes of uninterrupted cruise along a straight-ahead stretch that pretty much requires minimal concentration.

And that, apparently, was the plan, for as soon as they turned onto the Marina Freeway, Sylvia Oberbeck's head disappeared out of sight below the front seat, into Andrew's lap, and stayed there.

The speed of the car dropped to thirty miles per hour. It began to wobble along the slow lane.

Instantly, an uncontrollable force like a conflagration consumed both me and the car as one. I revved the engine and leaned on the horn.

Sped up beside them, made Andrew swerve. He saw me. I gave him the finger. Kept honking. Accelerated. He accelerated, but he couldn't get away. We were one on one, expert drivers going ninety miles an hour in high-performance muscle cars. I pulled behind him, kissed his bumper. Drew up side by side, then gunned it and cut him off, forcing him to skid into the breakdown lane. I could see him swearing, spinning the wheel with grim concentration. Officer Oberbeck was sitting up now.

Our cars swiveled to an uneven stop in a hot rain of pebbles. I threw my door open wide.

"Get out," I screamed. "I know you're screwing that bitch."

He lowered the window half an inch.

"Will you calm down? Relax. I'm driving her home—"

"Get out!" I screamed again. "Get out of the goddamned car!"

I yanked the handle, but he had locked it.

Incredibly, I was still holding the coffee cup.

"Fuck you," I cried and threw the hot coffee at his face. He flinched as it slung across the glass, splattering through the open crack and in his hair.

"What the hell are you doing?"

"Let's just go," said Oberbeck. "That bitch is crazy."

"We are talking about *moving in together* at the same time you're screwing her?"

He made a move to open the door, but Oberbeck pulled him back.

"Don't!" she said. "Just get the fuck out of here," and hit the button so the window sealed tight.

Andrew hesitated, put the car in gear.

"Move away. I don't want to hurt you, move away from the car."

His voice was muffled. He let her cut him off from me, and now he was looking up, expressionless, like some red-faced lying civilian, safe behind the glass.

I picked up handfuls of gravel and pelted the departing car. I threw them and threw them and threw them and threw them until they began to slow down and float like shooting stars burning out in the empty air.

Fourteen.

That night the stars were obscured by a scrim of cloud. You could see airplanes, heavy with lights, marching toward LAX, and hear their booming vibration, but the sky was just a formless haze. Lying back on a beach chair on the balcony of my apartment, I wished for the enormity of the heavens to fill my sight, leave no room for anything but misty blue; to feel nothing but the soft worked cotton of my grandmother's quilt wrapped around my body.

It was nearly 5 a.m. No lights were on behind the drawn window drapes of the opposite bank of apartments. Pale beige drapery was standard at Tahiti Gardens, which created a pleasing unity in the ziggurat pattern of jutting rectangular balconies, dark on dark. Some had plants, some had whirligigs and wicker and cats; from my corner unit I could see hundreds of insipid variations on a theme.

I had woken up at four with absolute clarity. The clarity was that I would capture and mutilate Ray Brennan. I would hammer nails into his brain. Shoot him in the kidney so he'd remain alive while strung up by his heels and slowly skinned. *Why should I let you live?* I would ask, and when he tried to answer I would stuff his throat with paper towels. I didn't care for trophies—nipples, fingers, testicles or scalp—I wanted ruined pieces hacked to bits and hacked again, nerve cells active to the twitchy end, and when it ended he would become whole and I would start again with better methods—electric shock and caustic lye—again and again because fantasies are perfect.

I was sipping Baileys Irish Cream and warmed-up milk. Across the path, in the diffuse glow of vintage-looking street lamps, thousands of sailboats huddled close, sighing gently, rocking in their berths. Alternating currents lurched within my body, pitching like the tide; first calm, then whirling violent images of revenge.

A quiet ringing stirred like the wind chimes overhead. It took a moment to understand it was the Nextel, stuck inside the pocket of my robe, muffled by layers of terry cloth and quilt. Voice mail had already been activated by the time I dug it out.

"Um, hi, um, it's me, and I was wondering if—"

"Juliana?" I cut in, puzzled.

"Oh my God! Did I wake you up? Oh my *God*! I thought this was your office—"

"No, no, not at all. I always get up when it's still dark."

"So do I."

"You do?"

"Yeah," she said. "I just wake up."

"How come?"

"Usually a nightmare."

"Did you have a nightmare tonight?"

Juliana hesitated. "This is stupid."

"Nothing is stupid. Things just happen," I told her. "I've been having nightmares, too."

"Really? That is so amazing."

"Daytime nightmares, you know?"

"Yes."

"I'm sure you do."

There was silence. I gripped the phone, as if behind the pale beige

curtains everyone else was dead and Juliana my last connection to the
living world.

"What did you want to talk to me about?"

"I don't know."

"Tell me."

"Really. Nothing. I was just chilling, watching some dumb movie
on TV, I don't even know what it's about."

"How's school?"

"I stopped going. I hate that school."

"What do you do?"

"Stay home and watch TV."

"Juliana, can I ask you something personal? Are you still seeing
the therapist?"

"Yes, I'm seeing the therapist."

"How is she?"

"She's pretty tight."

"Okay. That's good."

Then there was another silence. "So," she ventured, "is it still
dark where you are?"

"Yes. It's dark."

"Do you know when the sun's going to come up?"

"Well, it's coming. You can be sure of that. Do I know when?
You mean, like, what exact time?"

Her voice had become just about inaudible. "How long."

"Hold it. Let me look."

She heard me getting up and panicked. "Where are you going?"

"Just getting the paper."

"What for?"

"They have it in the paper every day. Sunup, sundown, when the
moon comes out, high tide . . ."

With the phone still to my ear I unlocked the door and lifted the
LA Times off the mat. At this hour the corridor seemed cold and unfamiliar as a hotel. I was glad to turn back to the warm stillness of the
apartment.

"Here it is. The sun will rise at five-twenty-three a.m. Not so long to go."

Juliana didn't answer.

"I'll tell you what," I said. "You look out of your window, and I'll look out of my window, and we'll see who sees the sunrise first."

"Okay." She seemed to come to life. "The first time we see even the tiniest drop of sun—"

"The first."

"—it counts."

We agreed. The smallest, faintest ray of light would count.

I stayed with Juliana until dawn, when she finally became sleepy and said she was going to bed. I wished her good night even though I was about to start my day. It would not be the last time Juliana called in the secret hours of the early morning. But instead of inputting a transcript into Rapid Start, I erased the voice mail recording and kept our conversations private; held them and treasured and stroked them like the tolerant stuffed loon.

Now a different portrait dominated the investigation. We had received the marine corps photo ID of Richard Brennan. A color copy looked out at the war room, another was pinned up on my bathroom door with inked-in donkey ears, just so I could look at the bastard every day and tell him, *"We will cut your heart out."*

The photograph was not dissimilar to the composite, which showed short dark hair and a strong neck. Now you could see the power in the face came from the high forehead and big jaw, which conveyed a solid, all-American arrogance, like a college football player from the fifties. You expected him to be wearing a white crew sweater. The nose was pert and the mouth compressed as if he were biding his important time—*I'll stand here and let you take my picture*—while the eyes half closed in drowsy contempt, as if this world were beneath consideration. Or maybe that was just the way the flash went off.

Ray Brennan fit the profile—husky, good-looking, overconfident.

With longer hair and a softer attitude you understood how he could unhinge a girl like Juliana: a diamond blade slicing through a rooftop door, a knife through butter.

Instantly my range of contact expanded like a radar field to include State College, Pennsylvania, where, according to the records, Richard (Ray) Brennan was born. My working day was taken up with faxes and phone calls to Quantico and the Philadelphia field office, trying to figure out which of the cool businesslike voices I could trust with my baby, then working to get everybody on the same page with respect to the most efficient way of obtaining information. Another timeline was begun, a trail through time, that would detail the moves of Brennan's life—lead us west to Tempe, Arizona, through the mirror maze of his psyche, to a bench on a Promenade three blocks from the Pacific Ocean, and finish at that trailer park or ratty little house in whatever mean and shabby sprawl, where we would, inevitably, take him down.

I *just can't sleep.*"

"*I know, Juliana.*"

"*What time does the sun rise?*"

"*Five-forty-four. But it sets at seven-ten. The days are getting longer. What are you doing?*"

"*Painting my nails.*"

"*What color?*"

"*Mango Ice.*"

A s the identity of the prime suspect came into focus, I felt myself emerging from the emotional commotion of the kidnap to the clarity of the hunt. Every day brought exhilarating twists you knew would slam into an unexpected climax—the shocking waterfall at the end of the ride. For example, we had the stats on every 1989 dark green Dodge van registered in Arizona and California. Eliminating the owners by gender and age, there were only a dozen under thirty-five and male. Improbable? You had to believe in your own logic. You had to choose a source of power, or become immobilized. That is why, when I was ready to cash out and close the books on Andrew, I chose the Boatyard Restaurant. The prosecution made it look like I went there only to humiliate him, but logic would say the opposite: after the incident on the Marina Freeway, wasn't it a safer bet for both of us to meet in public?

He was at the bar, drinking with Barry Loomis and a couple of cronies from the department. It was a loud, bright, old-guard kind of joint that smelled of sawdust and beer-soaked timbers, where the steaks were overrated but it didn't matter because the waitresses were slim as trapeze artists, spinning platters of creamed spinach and onion rings at an impossible pace. I think the place must have been there forty years. They say it really was Sal Mineo who carved his name into the table at the far booth.

Andrew was a regular. No wonder he liked the timeless atmosphere, since he was always bitching and moaning about how things changed. How the new recruits, who lived in far-flung developments sometimes an hour and a half away from Santa Monica, did not subscribe to drinking after shift. Hell, they even refused to work overtime, which the veterans considered to be free money. Their work ethic sucked—they wanted to go home and have fun! To them law enforcement was a two-year gig on the way to something else, no longer "a life"—while Andrew and his contemporaries had made one deliberate choice a long time ago, and stuck to it, with what he considered to be a vanishing standard of honor.

When I came up to the bar, he was retelling the legendary story of an arrest of a bunch of drug dealers in a ludicrously bad neighborhood in Compton. The dealers lived in a house with a lot of dogs behind big gates.

"We pull up to the gate and somebody says, *'Where the hell are the bolt cutters?'* Somebody else says, *'The sheriff will have them.'* Well, the sheriff's car is *gone.* No bolt cutters. So now we're into Keystone Kop anarchy. Guys are hopping the fence and getting hung up on the spikes. They could have been shot. Runners are going out the back door—this is what you're talking about when you talk about two agencies cooperating," Andrew was saying as I approached.

His look shifted instantly from unaware to cautious. *Here comes another strange and unpredictable female in my life.* It broke my heart to see that on a face I had held between my hands and kissed.

"Don't worry." I smiled. "I'm not here to make a scene."

"Sit down, have a drink." He offered his bar stool, made introductions to the other detectives. There was Jaeger, who looked like a three-hundred-pound beagle made of melting lard, and a rigid African-American named Winter, both in jackets and ties. They would testify against me at the trial.

"No thanks, I just wanted to talk to you."

"What about?"

"The nine hundred dollars."

This was not the speech about intimacy and commitment I had rehearsed in the shower, but when it sprang out, the number seemed right, a searing response to the way in which *he* had reduced our love-making and closeness and adventure and laughter to another sum in a meaningless progression of conquests.

"Oh, okay." He laughed. I think he was drinking scotch. "I'll give you your nine hundred dollars."

"Good."

"Now will you have a drink?"

"I'll just take a check. You can postdate it, that's all right."

Andrew said dismissively, "Why don't you chill?"

Barry Loomis was leaning in. "How's it going?" he asked. "I got the fax about this scum Brennan."

"See?" I said sweetly. "We're keeping you in the loop." To Andrew: "Come on, you must be making lots of overtime."

"This is not the time and place." Andrew's face was turning dark, uncomfortable with his boss so close to the heat.

"Let's just be done with it and then I'll go."

"Don't go," said Barry, looking to make it worse, whatever it was. "The Dodgers are on."

"You want to mail it to me?" I persisted.

"What?" Barry chortled. "The results of the *test?*" and clapped Andrew on the back.

Clown.

"What did you spend it on?"

"I told you," Andrew said, "the Harley."

Barry and I rolled our eyes at each other, both long-suffering victims of our mutual pal's obsession.

"*Ohhh,*" we said in unison. "The *Harley.*"

Andrew shrugged stiffly. "Had to fix the muffler."

Barry nodded sympathetically. "He had to fix the muffler."

"I know. He treats that pile of crap better than he treats his ladies—*plural.*"

At this, Jaeger and Winter broke up. One of them howled, "You go, girl!"

"Look," said Andrew, hunched even farther over the bar, "I'll call you. We'll work it out."

"Really?" I did not go. "When was the last time you called me?"

Barry, teasing: "What's the matter? Why don't you call the lady?"

"You know what?" Andrew stammered, clamping down on the violence he must have felt pushing out of his throat. He drew out his wallet, pulled some bills, and threw them in my direction while the others started to holler and hoot.

"I'm not the whore, Andrew. I don't go down on senior detectives on Sunday morning in a car."

Barry was bent over double, Jaeger and Winter smirking and snorting and turning away. Andrew was appalled at this betrayal, suckerpunched by his best friend, and for a moment I was ashamed. But as the fury started to work the lines of his forehead, I held his eyes: *See this? This was me when I saw you with her.*

But it did not make anything even or okay, it just made me sick.

"I'll see you," I mumbled, and turned away.

Disoriented, I threaded through the bar crowd and in between the whirling nineteen-year-old waitresses, down the hallway, past the rest rooms, to the rear lot. I hadn't even parked back there. I just wanted to get out fast into the humid cool night air.

"Don't fuck with the Harley."

Hopeful at hearing his voice, I turned with disappointment to see that Andrew had left the leather jacket inside, which meant he wasn't following so quickly because he wanted to talk or reconcile; he really thought I'd trash his bike.

"I wouldn't do that," I said. "See?"

It stood unscathed inside the chain-link.

"Where's your car?" he demanded.

"On the street. What do you care?"

"I want to know what you're doing back here," he said suspiciously.

My arms raised and lowered incredulously. "What do you think? Getting out of your way. Isn't that what you want?"

"What is this bullshit about the nine hundred dollars? You had to bring that up in *there*?"

I put my hand on my hip. "You going to pay me, or what?"

"Is that what it all comes down to for you, too? *Money?* Is that the gig with women?"

I was so angry I could hardly speak. "I don't know, Andrew, you tell me. You're the one who slept with the biggest gold digger of all time. After her husband dies. Very classy. I gave it to you for free. Everything! *Free and clear*," I screamed suddenly, in the middle of the alley.

Andrew ripped the lid off a garbage can and tried to throw it, but it was chained and the whole damn thing fell over, lobster shells and all kinds of crap, and just as ridiculously I pointed my finger at him as if lightning could shoot from it, threatening: "Stay away from me."

*   *   *

t took a long drive around the Marina just to stop trembling. I pulled into the Ralph's and stared into the lighted mirror on the visor, wiping mascara from the blackened crevices underneath my swollen eyes. Drawn to the lights and somnambulant figures beyond the windows of the anonymous market, I took a cart and walked the dead-cold aisles. Regular, bright rows of products put me in a trance.

I had carried the bags up from the garage, unlocked the door and placed them on the counter. It was ten o'clock. I went into the bedroom to change into sweats before putting the groceries away. I had just walked into the room and turned on the light when I noticed some movement in the mirror. I turned around and there was Andrew Berringer, standing in the doorway.

Fear curled inside my gut.

"What are you doing here?"

"We need to talk."

"Did you ever hear of knocking?"

My first thought was that my duty weapon was in my bag where I had thrown it on the bed.

"The door was open."

"It was not."

My heart was racing.

"How do you think I got in here?" But then he waved the whole thing off in disgust. He saw the picture of Ray Brennan on the open bathroom door. "What is that sorry son of a bitch doing there?"

"Just to keep it alive."

"One sick puppy."

"Him," I joked, "or me?"

He went into the living room and sat down on the love seat and turned on the TV. My respiration calmed. I knew this man, his smells, the baseball cap collection, each one hanging on a hook above the dark wood bureau in his father's home, an empty bachelor shrine to his dad, in Sunset Park. He had come here to talk, he said.

"Want something to drink?"

"No thanks." He didn't look at me. "I need safe passage."

"You have safe passage."

"Okay." He swallowed. "We both know, from everything that's happened, that it's time to end it. I'll pay you back the money in install-ments."

"What am I, a credit card?" I tried to keep it light because I was going to cry all over again.

"I told you I was no good in the relationship department."

"Oberbeck I can understand. Sort of. At least she's got tits. But Margaret Forrester?"

"Good old Margaret." His teeth were clenched. "Always stirring the pot."

"Tell me the truth and we'll be clean. Look me in the eyes and tell me. Be warned: I'll know if you're lying. I've been trained."

He looked at me. He had gotten up and was leaning against the wall near the kitchen. I was standing near the fireplace.

"I didn't sleep with Margaret Forrester."

He held my gaze, but that doesn't mean a thing. The only way to quantify deception is with a polygraph machine. He knew that. It was a standoff.

"She's a ganja head," he added after a little while. "Gets stoned two and three times a day. It's a 'spiritual practice.'"

"And nobody knows this at the department?"

"Let's not get off on Margaret."

"She said you were applying for a job in Fresno."

"That's right," he said. "Don't you ever think of getting out?"

"*Are* you?"

"How the hell do I know?" Then, viciously, "The Black Widow. Drove the Hat to death. I'm telling you, she's death."

"Like at this point I care."

He stood up so resolutely that tears sprang to my eyes and I cried out, "Don't go," like a child.

"Pride is important to me," he said sternly. "You keep beating me up."

"I don't mean to."

"In front of my supervisor, my friends—I don't know, is this a thing you have for men?"

"I love men. Is this a thing you have about women?"

He shook his head and laughed bitterly. Another impasse.

"Pride is important to me, too." I took a step forward. "I'm sorry about the thing in the bar, I was just so hurt—"

"You've got to leave me alone," he said almost desperately.

"I want safe passage, too."

I was pleading.

"Go ahead."

Then I didn't know how to say it. "You've changed since we started going out, but especially the past few weeks. Something's different, something's weighing on you and it's not just work. I never know what you're really thinking. You're always holding back."

"That's what my second ex-wife used to say."

"Why?" I replied stupidly. "Is this a pattern?"

I wanted to prolong it, know more, have another chance—I did not want to be discarded like the others—but he was picking up his keys.

"Do me a favor. Whatever you think of her, don't blame Sylvia Oberbeck."

"*Sylvia?*"

"Sylvia's going through a bad time."

He should not have said her name. He should not have defended her, out loud, in my house, at that moment, to me. Like some rajah he seemed to believe all the wives and girlfriends should know the score and be grateful to be poked by him.

"What do you see in that dumb blonde jock?"

"What is it with *blonde*? They all want to be blonde. Can't decide which half?" He gripped the hair at the side of my head and for a moment we were face-to-face. "Dark is good, baby. *Mamacita.*"

Then he let go. I was beyond furious.

"My grandfather was right."

"The racist was right?"

"Yeah, he was right when he said, *'Don't tell anyone you're mixed race. You can pass for white, so pass. Because when you get into a fight, the first thing your husband's going to say is, he'll call you a filthy little spic.'*"

Andrew looked hurt. "I'm not calling you a spic," he protested. "I never use that word. That's not what I said—"

"You're right. You should leave."

"I'm leaving." He was gentle now, and soothing, as he had been with the distraught bank tellers. I had seen more sides of him than a carousel. "Just so we're straight."

"Straight on what?"

"What we have . . . is a working relationship."

"Right," I snorted. "I wish. Unfortunately, the Santa Monica kidnapping is not the only thing we're working on."

He gestured, confused. What was I talking about?

"Mission Impossible," I replied with contempt, as if he were the dumbest fuck on earth.

"That will go away. Barry already forgot about it."

"Not on our end. I officially reopened the case and got creamed for it, by the way."

He had stepped toward me and we were facing each other again, only a few feet away. His hips were square, his hands hung down, deceptively relaxed.

"Why did you reopen the case?"

"To help you out, you stupid *shit*! You say you're in trouble with your boss, the chief of police made it a priority, so here is me, going *out of my way* to go back to a case that I'm not even *on* anymore, in order to *do something nice,* because you were so *upset*—"

"I was *pissed*." His fingers flexed.

"Well, maybe we'll know something. Close it out and be done." I crossed my arms. "The lab is doing the DNA."

"On what?"

"The ski mask they found." God, when would he get it? "Maybe there's dried saliva on the *mask*. Hello?"

He grabbed my collar and held it, tight enough to choke, and fairly lifted me off the ground and put his rock hard knee against my pubic bone and pummeled up and down.

"What are you doing to me?" he said.

I gasped. It was like his knee was penetrating to my bladder.

"Get out of my life. Get out of my business. Stay away from my pussy."

He let me go, and I kicked him.

"You bitch!"

He backed up, clutching his groin.

"Get out of here!" I roared, but instead he sprang forward and grabbed my shoulders and pushed me down on the deep rose coffee table. The edge went into my back and my head snapped. I kept on kicking, and he backed off and was groping himself and spinning around and saying, "You bitch! You bitch!"

I rolled off the coffee table. I could feel warm blood down my leg as if he had ruptured something inside. My intestines hurt and I retched. I was hunched over holding my stomach.

I had instinctively moved in front of the couch, keeping the coffee table between us.

"Stay over there," I warned.

Andrew veered forward.

Inside the drawer of the deep rose coffee table was the Colt .32. I pulled it out and aimed the gun at Andrew.

"If you don't leave right now I'll shoot you."

He looked at me with reddened eyes, leaning over, cupping his groin. The only light in the room was from the TV. He came at me. He kept coming. I fired once, wounding him in the torso.

A small-caliber round, especially with old hard-ball copper-jacketed bullets sitting in there from the time my grandfather had given me the gun, does not produce big holes. Still, I found it hard to believe he was coming at me again, but he was. I fired and he tackled me, and the shot went into the wall. We flew backwards over the coffee table and halfway onto the couch. The gun went off for the third time, hit-

ting him in the thigh. We wrestled for control of the barrel, slippery
with blood and meat. His big heavy body was on top of mine, and I
saw his leg dripping blood. Then he just stood up and got off me. He
walked out the front door and left it wide open.

I staggered into the kitchen. I walked around in a circle, dazed, then
I thought, *Where is he going?* and ran down the hallway after him.

Andrew was already outside at the carport. He had one hand
pressed against his rib cage and with the other he was awkwardly trying to open the door.

"What are you doing, Andy? Please stop, Andy. Andy, *wait*. Please
let me call the paramedics—"

He never spoke. Somehow he had gotten the gun. I didn't realize
it, but I had known, disoriented in the kitchen, something was wrong
because I was no longer holding the gun. Now he tossed it into the passenger seat. I was gripping the top of the driver's door. We had a little
tug-of-war, I tried to pull it open, but he was stronger and jerked it out
of my hands and slammed it and drove away. The glass was streaked
with blood. We must have been out there less than a minute. Nobody
saw us and nobody heard the low-velocity shots over the sounds of
the TV.

I went inside and locked the door to my apartment and stood
there. My insides were burning. I went into the bathroom and uri-
nated blood.

My ankle hurt. My head hurt from where it concussed against
the coffee table. I came back into the living room. There was glass all
over my floor. I picked up three bullet casings. I put a pad in my
underwear to absorb the blood and lay down on the couch. I needed
to call somebody. I lay there in a stream of blood and tears, thinking
someone would come and take care of this, but nobody came.

I swept up the glass. The sun had come up by then. I crouched in
a bathtub full of lukewarm water and then crawled out, clutching my
gut like some primitive thing. Then I got dressed and went to work.

Part Two

SAFE PASSAGE

Fifteen.

I went up in the elevator and got off and used my card to access the revolving entry. I passed through a smudged white door that led to the Corridor of Winds and out to the matrix. Setting the briefcase down, I took off the blazer and hung it on a wooden hanger that went on a peg beneath a brass plaque that said *Special Agent Ana Grey* on a square column of dark wood—a masculine touch, like the posts on a booth in a bar and grill, that marked our territories.

My personal territory that day was a region of numb, disbelieving shock. The ritualized motions of entry and claim did nothing to make it familiar. This was not a place I could have imagined, nothing I had been trained for, a scenario so extraordinary the conscious mind could not hold it all at once, but like a poor clay pot in a fiery kiln, cracked in two. I always thought of working for the FBI as a privilege to serve my community—yet here I was, sitting in my senior-rank ergonomic chair (the chair was a cheap knockoff), scheming like a criminal: *You cannot appear upset. You cannot appear to have prior knowledge of what happened to Andrew.*

Although I may have seemed to be scrolling through e-mail, I was frantic. My head turned. The chair swiveled. It was early, but I could not stop watching for the arrival of Rick and the troops. Would they provide safe passage—or the opposite? If they knew, they would have no choice. It would be *moi* kneeling down on the carpeted box in the office in the garage, hands cuffed behind my back, while Hugh Akron hovered lasciviously with the ink pad. Suddenly it seemed a spectacularly bad idea to be there. *Leave.*

I got as far as the bathroom.

"Put cold water on your face," my grandfather would command, after he had made me cry. I would weep for an hour during his violent verbal tirades. I hardly remember what they were about—boys, virginity—but I would cower on the narrow bed while he stood in the doorway smoking cigarettes and ranting. If my hands weren't clean before dinner, he would spoon dirt from a potted plant onto my plate. He was not crazy, nor a drunk. He was, as far as I can figure it, a rage-aholic, addicted to the power of his own anger. Once, when I was late coming home from a date, he surprised me at the front door with a crack across the head.

"Go. Put water on your face."

Dismissed, I would slink off with mongrel gratitude.

Years later, I had authority and carried a gun; I had long surpassed the status my grandfather held as lieutenant in the Long Beach Police Department, but in the mirror now saw only turbulent red-faced chaos, a guilt-ridden mess for which Poppy would have only had contempt. *"You messed up, stupid."* I willed the tears to stop and when they would not, smacked my own temple with the heel of my hand. I did it again, alone in the tidy rest room.

When I emerged, Barbara Sullivan was coming right at me with bright alert eyes. She had just arrived at work, loaded with shopping bags and cartons to be mailed.

"Do you believe it? Deirdre's already outgrown her six-month stuff. I have to return all these gifts!" she sang, and swept into her office as if I had replied; as if I were not paralyzed with fear of what she might have seen in my face, macabre and chalky-looking from the powder I had hurriedly pressed over swollen eyelids and hot cheeks.

I don't know what impression I gave. But then I had truly become my shadow self, and shadows are tricksters with canny ways of deception. So maybe Ana Grey was standing there beaming, and maybe when Ana settled back at her workstation, others registered a generous sigh of pleasure in sharing her friend's joy.

It seemed a good idea to be looking at something. Files. I counted twelve that needed cleaning up for the ninety-day review, including extortion, an inmate who was stabbed at the Veterans Administration hospital (crime on a government reservation), threatening letters to a software company and three cases of movie stars being harassed by stalkers. The inspectors would pull a document at random and expect it to have met the standards. They would not pay attention to content, only form. The Bureau is all about standards. Standards of behavior. Standards of protocol and language and law.

I was feeling nauseous. Barbara had been, just, *too* carefree. She had not stopped for conversation. Not asked about the Santa Monica kidnapping, nor what was up with Andrew, not invited me for morning tea. This was not her pattern. Andrew must have told them and she knew. Everybody in the Bureau knew. They were getting ready for the takedown and they would do it here, where I was containable. Should I sit it out, or escape through the Corridor of Winds?

Another blackout was coming, and I couldn't fight it. Instead of escape, I dozed in the chair, wondering if offenders shut down in the midst of crimes; if the Mission Impossible Bandit, at the peak of excitement, having made it through the roof and on his way, had not also been overwhelmed by a contradictory torpor; if he had not lain down and slept a while on the warm, waxed linoleum floor of the employee lounge, while the ticking minutes unlocked the vault.

The phone on my desk jerked me awake. It was Dr. Arnie from the forensic lab.

"You told me to put the pedal to the metal on the rape so we cross-referenced the chemicals in the paint flake with particles of soil found on Juliana Meyer-Murphy's clothing. Might have something for you."

I reached for a pad.

"She was probably taken to a post–World War Two house in a loamy area of the coast."

"What do you mean, loamy area?"

"Well, loam is soil that's generally a mix of sand, clay, silt and organic matter."

"I know what *loam* is, it's the *area* I would like more clearly defined."

"You mean, *where* the house was that he took her?"

"Yes. *Where the house was that he took her!*"

"That would be an older residential section, not too far inland, most likely on the Pacific coast, judging from the plant material, which is mainly—"

"Arnie." Struggling. "The Pacific coast of the United States is almost a thousand miles long."

"You might like this better. About the shoe print on her back. Turns out to be an outsole lug pattern on a combat-style boot manufactured in New Hampshire, sometime in the past two years, sold under the name Climbers. Total order seventy-five thousand pairs. I know what you're gonna say: *Hold it, Dr. Arnie! This is what you give me? One boot in seventy-five thousand pairs that walked in an area approximately one thousand miles long, sometime in the last two years?* This is what I say to you: *I can reduce the possible number of boots that could have made that particular impression to six-point-two-five pairs!*"

Hearing nothing in reply, Dr. Arnie continued talking to himself:

"Out of seventy-five thousand pairs, they made ten thousand in size ten, for which four hand-engraved molds were needed. That would be twenty-five hundred left and twenty-five hundred right outsoles from each size-ten mold. The possible left or right outsoles sharing class characteristics of the molded outsole would therefore be twenty-five hundred . . ."

The numbers came at me like enemy fire. They drilled holes in my head.

Where was Andrew? Had he made it to a hospital? Had he told them? Was he dead? Was that possible? Him, inert? I know what dead is. Could I have done that? What a colossal mistake, pulling that gun. What a horrible, tragic, unbearable bungle. Stupid. I messed up, all right. What did I think? He was Ray Brennan coming at me? What was I aiming for? Ray Brennan's face on the bathroom door?

"The same pair of left and right outsoles, bearing the same crime scene impressions, will occur six hundred and twenty-five times out of ten thousand . . ."

I wanted to stand up and scream. An unseen hand reached around from behind and clamped itself over my mouth.

By evening of that day in hell, I had still heard nothing. No grave message from the Santa Monica Police Department. No burly pair of homicide detectives showed up for a private talk.

As an investigator, I'd had to learn patience. It was a skill I worked hard to achieve, since I have the metabolism of a hummingbird—dart here, dart there, get the gist and be *gone*. Now I forced myself to slow down and ask, *What do I really know?*

Andrew had been wounded but had gotten into his car and driven away. Our trainers tell us if you are seriously injured *and you know it* within fifteen seconds, you are likely to survive. It takes a lot to bleed out. Even a critical trauma can be survived if you get to an emergency room within that first golden hour, and the hospital was fifteen minutes from my apartment.

He would seek medical treatment. He would be identified.

The police would know.

It would be easy to find out: call Margaret Forrester on a ruse about the kidnapping and she would spill it, whatever it was.

Like a bad scene from a bad movie, I picked up the phone and let it drop.

Okay, call someone else over there.

Picked it up and let it drop.

I couldn't do it. I was too afraid of knowing, although one fact was unavoidable: Andrew had driven off with my gun.

I left the office at six-thirty-five and drove home, aware of nothing until I was suddenly unlocking the front door. Nobody had been inside, which was good luck, as any rookie would have known she was walking into a crime scene.

There were glinting pieces of glass I had missed with the vacuum cleaner. Furniture was still slightly askew, and come to think of it, there were bloodstained clothes in the laundry hamper. If you missed all that, there would be a bullet hole in the white swinging door between the kitchen and the pantry, which might as well have had a huge black arrow pointing to it.

It was hopeless. All the forensics guys had to do was come in here with Luminol and the details of the struggle would fluoresce in the dark like the answer in the window of a magic eight ball. In a fit of despair I moved to the phone to turn myself in and get it over with. All I wanted was for the headache, like screws in an iron mask tightening over the facial bones, to stop.

I walked around the coffee table (more glass granules on the soles of my shoes) and sat down wearily on the couch where Andrew had thrown his weight on top of me and I had pummeled him with my legs. The absence of that struggle made me feel light-headed. But no, it was the sudden absence of him, as if he had been sucked backward out of my life as quickly as he had been rocketing forward, into the future—a home, shared; a partnership taking root. I missed his loud opinionated criticism of the Dodgers; his puppy love for the Lakers; the puffed-up hyperbole about his job (*"I know all my geese are not all swans")*; the way he would slice a roll the other way and butter each side and put it back together because that's the way his dad did it; the boasting *("I hitched through Argentina and never had to pay for a hotel room")* mixed with self-deprecation *("You can pick my brain. Not much to pick")*; the long, wonderful back rubs; the way he adored my body with his large sensitive hands.

As I hovered, weightless, knowledge came to me that we were too close to go out this way; that stunned awful look he'd thrown as we wrestled for the car door meant to say he was as bewildered as I at how far things had gotten out of hand. I have noticed our destinies are wound around our physical selves: Andrew was built big, big enough to absorb heavy body blows—his, and those of traumatized victims of crime he had comforted during the wearing routine of twenty years of homicide investigation. I sensed that he would take this blow, as well. If he had been sitting across from me in this mess, I know he would have felt just as disoriented, as responsible as I. Neither one of us could have told you what had been true during those scrambled seconds, but we might have said this: We cared for each other. And we shared a code.

Nobody was coming to get me because Detective Andrew Berringer had not turned me in.

I wanted it to be true. It would mean an ending of such happiness.

Lifted by the hope that he was actually protecting me, that we were still in this together, I rose from the couch and settled into the familiar depression in the rattan chair. The laptop sat on the glass table. I believed this was what Andrew was somehow telling me to do, yet logging on to the Bureau website created the most toxic self-loathing of the entire ordeal. I was planning to use classified material on detecting bloodstain evidence to cover up the crime. As it was loading, I came as close as ever to swallowing the gun. It would have made a pretty picture, with the FBI logo shining on the computer screen.

*   *   *

Between the supermarket and a pharmacy in the Marina I was able to get everything I needed. At a hardware emporium it cost almost a hundred bucks for wire brushes, nylon scrubs, wood putty, pine oil cleaner, garbage bags, disposable gloves and a rented rug shampooer.

There was not much blood splatter. I was able to scrub it up with ice water, cleanser and bleach, and then I put on Marvin Gaye and steamed the carpet and washed the floors. It is amazing how much dirt came up. Buckets of black water poured down the sink until the gold flecks in the floor tile winked. I scoured the coffee table and the walls. Threw the cotton bamboo cushion covers into the washing machine. Washed the sliding glass doors. Sprayed the kitchen tile a million times with mold remover, polishing it shiny with rolls of paper towels.

All this time I kept checking the clock, as if knowing the hour were reassurance that I was proceeding on course.

There were so many things to get rid of! The doormat. The vacuum cleaner bag. I unscrewed the swinging door with the bullet hole, *and* the hinges, loaded three bags of trash onto a disposable tarp in the trunk of the Barracuda and distributed the evidence in haphazardly chosen Dumpsters. Then I came back and sanded the marks where the hinges had been, and puttied, and sanded and puttied again. Tomorrow I would repaint the door frame.

At intervals, by the clock, I would call Andrew because there would have been another of those big black arrows pointing to the sudden halt in communication, and left a couple of messages: *"Hi, it's me, just checking in, give me a call."*

Since I could not go to a doctor without documenting my injuries, I took some old antibiotics and leftover Tylenol with codeine. There was fever and my pelvis ached. Peeing was agony. The toilet bowl went red. I waited until after midnight to sneak along the empty hallway, removing traces of the blood trail with my trusty brush and bucket. It took working until 4 a.m. to do all that housework because I was moving slowly and had to rest.

FD-823 (Rev. 8-26-97)

RAPID START

INFORMATION CONTROL

Case ID: 446-702-9977 The Santa Monica Kidnapping

Control Number: 5231   Priority: Immediate

Classification: Sensitive   Source: Culver City
                             Police Department

Event time: 11:27 PM

Method of contact: CDVDB (California Domestic Violence Data Base)

Prepared by: Ripley, Jason   Component/Agency: Kidnap
                              and extortion squad,
                              FBI, Los Angeles

Event narrative:

> **A seventeen-year-old female calls 911 to report
> her mother's boyfriend is beating up the mother.
> Officers find only the girl at home. Suspect she
> has been abused also, but she vigorously denies
> it and denies even making the complaint. Report
> attached.**

CULVER CITY POLICE DEPARTMENT

Culver City, California

Domestic Crime Unit

Complaint Intake

1. NAME   Santos   Roxy   Angela
            Last   *First*   *Middle*

2. ALIASES   none

3. STREET ADDRESSES   3340 Keyes Drive   Palms
CA

4. RACE   (check all that apply)   ☐ Black   ☐ White
☒ Hispanic   ☐ Asian   ☐ American Indian   ☐ Other

5. DATE OF BIRTH   4/23/80

6. HEIGHT   5'6"

7. WEIGHT   123 pounds

8. HAIR COLOR   Blond

9. OCCUPATION   High school student

10. AFFILIATIONS WITH GROUP OR ORGANIZATION THAT MIGHT
BE RELEVANT TO THIS CRIME?   No

11. VICTIM   mother, Mrs. Audrey Santos, age 35
OCCUPATION   Cashier   EMPLOYER   Home Depot

12. OFFENDER   Carl Vincent, age 30
OCCUPATION   Lab Technician   EMPLOYER
unemployed

13. PREVIOUS ARRESTS   unknown

14. TYPE OF ATTACK   unknown

15. WEAPONS USED   unknown

16. FREQUENCY OF ATTACKS   unknown

17. HOSPITALIZATIONS   unknown

Responding Officers: Stewart and Salerno
Officer's Statement: Upon arrival at the home,
the complainant denied making the 911 call that
Carl Vincent, the mother's live-in boyfriend,
had attacked her mother, and instead refused to
make a statement. Several broken bottles were
found in kitchen garbage. Complainant denied
they were result of a domestic dispute. Stated

```
that her mother and the boyfriend were at the
movies. Officers left the premises at 12:40 AM.
```

"Did you see this report?" asked Jason Ripley.

It was the following morning, no news of Andrew. I was sitting rigidly in the ergonomic chair, mind flip-flopping between chaos and a vacuum of black.

"What report?"

"A teenage girl in Culver City says the mother's boyfriend is hitting the mother. Then she retracts the statement."

I did not respond.

"You didn't see this thing on Rapid Start, first thing this morning?" he asked incredulously. "I beat you! First time, *ever*."

"I'm entitled to a late night," said my shadow self with a leering grin.

The idea of the boss on a date seemed to embarrass the young man, and he began talking rapidly about his wife.

"Lunaria is like that, she's a night bird, loves to party. I'm a farm boy, up with the cows."

I nodded. I was supposed to know all the ins and outs.

"She's still back at Princeton. Studying for the bar."

"Right."

"I think we've been together six days since I was transferred out here."

Then I remembered: Jason had married chewing tobacco and whiskey money. His new father-in-law was CEO of some megacorporation that relocated from Illinois to Montvale, New Jersey. The two-hundred-thousand-dollar wedding had been covered by *Vogue*. In exchange, the family kept the girl close. Another of life's mysteries. Jason *was* a shy farm kid, earnest as a mallet, but he was also no dummy, and as he handed over the printout of the report, my eyes fell with charity on the strawberry blond freckled skin below his rolled-up sleeve. If he were still an agent two or three years from now, he would also most likely be divorced.

"We might have something here," he said of the 911.

My brain was frozen. "Why?"

"It's within striking distance of the Promenade."

"Mmm, twenty minutes away. With no traffic."

"Brennan could be using an alias—Carl Vincent."

"That's it? That's 'something?'"

"No, no," said Jason self-consciously. "I have a—theory."

He used the word tentatively, as if he had not yet earned the right.

"Okay."

"What if Brennan split from Arizona when the cops came after him for shooting ducks? He came here for a reason, whatever reason, we don't know."

"We don't know."

"No. But we'll find that out."

"Good."

"Meanwhile," Jason continued, "he's a manipulator. He finds another roost. See," he said excitedly, "here's my theory: I think the *girl* is the one getting beat on."

"Did the officers find evidence of abuse?"

"I don't know, but I have a call in to Child and Family Services. She's close in age to Juliana. I just think she's protecting this fool."

"Afraid of him?"

Jason nodded earnestly and pulled up a chair. We sat knee-to-knee, amidst cartons of files and odd discarded office debris, like a broken Venetian blind lying underneath the next desk.

"Here's another thing. Brennan enacts his ritual to relieve some life stress, right? Well, it says here this guy is an unemployed lab technician. It could be a photo lab. Maybe he's unemployed because he got fired."

The young agent was leaning forward, elbows on thighs, light blue eyes fixed on mine. Suddenly I felt foolishly affected, almost teary, because of the fact that Jason Ripley once had been a ginger-haired little boy and left his mother and learned to tie a tie. That's how whack I was.

"I think it's worth talking to the girl," he continued seriously.

"Convince me. Then we'll both take a ride."

It was a weak lead and I didn't care what he did with it. I was feeling stoned, sleep-deprived, and the low abdominal pain was coming back. He stood uncertainly.

"Is the case still alive over at Santa Monica?"

"What do you mean?"

"Do you think they'll give us someone else? Or are they out of the picture by now?"

"What are you talking about?"

He looked even more uneasy, not sure if I had been mocking him all along—if there were substance to his theory, or if he'd made a mistake in bringing the report to my attention. I let it play. This would be a little test. Either young Jason would work his butt off to prove his point about the connection between this young girl, Roxy Santos, and Ray Brennan, or he would back off and fade away. New Jersey or the stars.

"I mean," he pressed on, "we might need someone else over at the police department because of what happened to Detective Berringer."

Chemical material burst inside my chest.

"What happened to Detective Berringer?"

Quick. An alibi. What did I say about being late last night?

"He was shot."

"Really?"

"Yeah, I think it was yesterday? Or maybe the day before?"

"How is he?"

Before Jason could answer, I began to cough. Dry throat. Closing up. Don't retch. *Breathe.*

"Are you okay?"

I gulped the last of some cold, sugary coffee, wiggling my fingers to show everything was fine.

"Berringer?" I gasped.

"In the hospital," Jason answered.

"Wow. That's terrible. How is he?"

"I don't know—"

"How did it happen?"

"Armed robbery."

"No kidding."

"He was off duty and a couple of guys just came up to him."

"Catch the guys?"

"No."

"How do they know it was armed robbery?"

"That's what he said."

"Andrew said that?"

"That's what he said in the hospital."

"Sorry, I don't know why I'm smiling, there's nothing funny about this." I tried to suppress a giggle and look fierce. "How come nobody told me? I thought I was senior agent on this case."

That made him nervous again.

"Sorry about that, I definitely should have come to you right away. I heard them talking in the radio room—"

"It's okay," stroking his arm. "Now I know."

N ow it was safe to call Lieutenant Barry Loomis.

"I can't believe it," I said over again.

"Things are still touch-and-go."

"Can I see him?"

"He's in intensive care," said Barry. "They're only allowing family."

That would be his sister down from Oakland. Did Andrew say he had a brother, too? Somewhere in Florida? The euphoria that had lifted me plain off the floor at Jason's news that Andrew was *not only alive, but claiming he had been the victim of a robbery,* and we were going to get through this thing, crashed. Now there were frightened family members waiting in a hospital corridor.

"You said he drove himself to the hospital."

"He did, but he collapsed. They rushed him into surgery. One of the bullets pierced his lung."

"Oh my God."

"That was okay," Barry went on, "but then he had a cardiac arrest in the ER."

"*No!*" I shouted.

Barry was saying things like, "Take it easy. He'll make it. He's as tough as they come—"

"I'm sorry, it's just so—"

"It's a shock."

"Why didn't anybody call me?"

"At a time like this," he said stiffly, "you tend to close ranks."

"But he'll pull through?"

"He's in a coma, Ana."

The pain in my kidneys. Everything. I was just undone.

"They don't know," he went on. "They're watching him. Real close. He might have to have heart surgery later on. They found some underlying situation, I'm not exactly clear on that."

I couldn't speak. He let me be with it.

"You okay?"

"I'm okay," I managed. "Thanks, Barry. So, look. Any suspects?"

"Not yet. He hasn't been able to say a hell of a lot."

"Did you recover the gun?"

There was a pause. "No such luck."

"Stay in touch, okay?"

"You got it, hon."

W hat's the matter?" Barbara asked as soon as I walked into her office.

"Andrew was shot. As if you didn't know."

"I *don't* know. How could I know?"

"Jason knows. The girls in the radio room know."

I sank to the couch. Barbara went down on one knee, putting herself below me, as you would not to agitate a child, and asked very gently what happened. I told her about the armed robbery and intensive care but then came a round of tears no amount of head slamming was going to stop.

Soon Mike Donnato was in the room and the door was closed and the two of them were beside me on the couch; their hands were quiet on my hands, their voices low and steady.

These were professionals.

"Are you serious about this guy?" asked Mike.

"I care about him."

"Doesn't sound like a match made in heaven," Barbara said.

"Well, it blows hot and cold."

Mike: "As it were."

Barbara smacked him. "All I can say is, Ana dear, you better know where you were that night."

I winced. "Not funny."

"Irish humor."

"He'll be all right." Mike shifted his head so I could see the constancy in his eyes. "The bullet wounds sound like no big deal."

"What about the heart attack?"

"Same thing happened to my uncle," he said stalwartly. "Eighty-three years old, goes in for a hernia operation and his heart stops. Major alcoholic, so you'd think, *End of story.* Well, he's in Vegas, as we speak."

"In a pickle jar, in Ripley's Believe It or Not," said Barbara.

"He was a good uncle to me."

"Why? Because he took you out and got you laid when you were twelve?"

"Actually," said Mike, "we didn't have sex in our family."

"You still don't," observed Barbara.

"That's not *entirely* true."

"They have a chameleon," was my contribution through a swollen nose. "And the chameleon just had babies."

"See?" said Mike.

"I think there's a cable channel devoted to exactly that sort of thing," Barbara replied. "Why don't you go home, girl?"

"That would be worse."

I never wanted to go back to that apartment again.

"Sit here," said Mike. "I'm going to get you an iced vanilla blended."

"Can I have one, too?" called Barbara as he left. Her phone was ringing. "Nicest man in the world."

I knew that.

"Yes, she's in here." Pause. "Ana, it's for you." Her eyes were sober. Her whole body was sober as she moved to give me the phone. "It's the lieutenant from the Santa Monica police."

"I just spoke to him, two minutes ago." Panicked. "Is it about Andrew?"

She sat down close and put her arm around me.

"Barry?" I whispered.

"Since you asked about the weapon, I thought you'd want to know. Just got word. We think we found it."

"You found it? Where?"

"In Andy's car."

"In Andy's car? How could that be?"

"I don't know, he sure as hell didn't shoot himself, but it's a thirty-two, same size as the slugs."

"Well, that's good news." I turned to Barbara with a madcap grin. "They recovered the gun!"

Sixteen.

The automatic doors swung open, I walked into the deserted lobby, and my knees went out like rubber bands. Eight-fifteen at night is not the time to be visiting a hospital. Not when the rest of the world is washing its dishes and doing homework, families coming together after the day. Night shift in a hospital is the time for separation and good-byes, for facing the hours of darkness, in whatever bed, alone.

Bad things happen in a hospital at night. Knife wounds, sick patients taking turns for the worse, walleyed weirdos on the graveyard shift of the nursing staff. What you did not care to know during the day, you definitely do not want to know now, lost in a maze of empty corridors smelling of institutional mashed potatoes and gravy, buildings and parking structures cloaked in shadow; no escape. To run out of here screaming would put you right into the arms of the dark.

Eight-twenty-three p.m. Visiting time at the ICU would be over in seven minutes. I picked up the pace, although I did not want to see him. I did, and I didn't. I had come late hoping at least the family members would be gone.

Two Santa Monica uniforms, obese Detective Jaeger from the Boatyard bar and a couple of other brown-suited old-timers, were standing
around the nursing station with their hands in their pockets, chewing
the fat in low, irreverent tones:

"—Because he was stupid enough to get into a hot tub and make
sexual remarks to subordinates."

"The picture will come clear."

"No it won't. Not with this guy. He's the fair-haired prince."

"Princes don't pick up their own droppings."

We eyed each other until slowly my identity came into focus somewhere in Jaeger's dog skull. An upward nod of the jowls signaled it
was okay to approach the group.

"Has Andrew said anything more about the assailants?"

Jaeger shrugged. "Couple of guys in a parking lot."

"He's in a coma," one of them said.

"I know."

There was a moment of shared heartache.

"What do the docs say?"

"Not much."

"They haven't ruled out brain damage. He was without oxygen
for some time."

"Hopefully," said another, "he hasn't lost too many IQ points."

I hesitated, looking at the door. You couldn't see much through
the glass.

"Go on in. They know when you're there."

I nodded but did not move.

Jaeger made eye contact and said purposely, "We appreciate you
coming, Agent Grey."

A nurse gave me a gown, and I pushed into a bright room of half
humans, half machines. It was not a bad thing to have been seen here
tonight by four cops, said my shadow self.

There was a curtain surrounding the bed. I parted it and looked.

He was terribly bruised, as if he had fallen down a flight of stairs.
I hadn't been prepared for that, picturing him somehow white and still

as marble. But he was bruised where they had shoved an eighteen-gauge needle into his arm, where they'd pounded his chest, in the areas around the wounds, where he'd hit the floor when he fainted. Plastic tubing formed aerobatic curves above the sheet, rising from arterial lines, draining the bladder and the chest; you could see the expelled blood as it bubbled in an enclosed container.

His eyes were covered with gauze and his skin looked pasty. I touched his fingers, puffy and loosely curled. They were neither hot nor cold. The monitors that stood guard over his vital processes clicked along. Three balloons were tied to the end of the bed.

The sorrow that I felt was ferocious. It fueled the searing pain in my own abdomen. Bending over him, half in spasm, I whispered, *"Oh, baby, what did we do to each other?"*

I wanted to lie down beside him, kiss him, but there was no place to lie down or kiss. A respirator tube was taped over his mouth and the steel rail was up on the side of the bed.

The curtain opened. It was Margaret Forrester, dressed in black.

"He's not going to make it," she said.

A chill passed through me, one of those supernatural moments where you shudder at something you can't explain.

"Why are you here?" she asked.

"I could ask the same question."

"Obviously because he's one of our own."

"In that case, I came on behalf of the Bureau," I replied evenly. "To show our concern."

At least we were not going to reenact the scuffle in the parking lot over the man's hospital bed. Still, I did not like her deep eyes on me. She was clutching a circle of twigs with rawhide strings and feathers hanging down.

"What do you have there?" I had noticed things went better when they had to do with her.

"A Native American dream catcher." Her chest heaved in two big gulps. "So he doesn't have . . . bad dreams."

"He doesn't know a thing," I said darkly.

"NO!" she barked, so loudly that I flinched. Then, "Don't you leave me!" shaking a finger at Andrew. She could cycle up and down faster than a slide whistle. Now she hung the dream catcher on a cardiac monitor, where it would no doubt be removed.

"That looks really nice there, Margaret."

She squinted at her reflection in a metal band around the machine.

"Look at me," grabbing her hair and parting it to the roots. "I'm getting old. Did you know Andrew and my husband were best friends? They were in a Friday night poker game together."

"I heard."

"Wes and I went to Victoria Island up in Vancouver together on our honeymoon and stayed in the most elegant hotel. We had afternoon tea, and went out on those pedal boats? Wes wore somebody's white suit. Not that I thought life would always be like that . . . But I've got two young children." She shrugged as if having two young children were suddenly a big surprise. "Wes should be standing here beside me, right now, today," pounding the bed rail. "*Today*. Instead of me being a *widow*."

"Don't do that."

She was shaking the tubing, the bed.

The curtains swept open all the way and a male nurse came barging through. He was a big soft gay fellow wearing maroon scrubs, a long ponytail and three or four silver bracelets, looking somehow miscast, and peckish about having to play the role.

"Visiting hours in the ICU are now over. You're not supposed to be in here, not with two people and *not* without a gown."

Squirt bottle at the ready, he was about to do something to Andrew's eyes.

"What's that?" murmured Margaret.

"What's *that*?" echoed the nurse, with a disdainful glance at the dream catcher.

He lifted the gauze, revealing dark purple bruises on Andrew's lids.

"Don't touch him!" Margaret shrieked.

"Drops," said the nurse, showing her the bottle. "To keep his eyes from drying out?"

"Don't hurt him!"

"I think we should go," I said.

"Are you a relative?" he asked Margaret, over his shoulder, but she had retreated through the curtains to a chair and was drawing up her knees.

The nurse slapped the bottle down on a tray and went out of the cubicle and grabbed her wrist.

"No, dear, we are not getting comfortable, we are leaving."

"Help him!" moaned Margaret, rocking back and forth.

"I don't have to deal with this," he sighed.

"Hang on," I said and hustled outside, where Jaeger and one of the other detectives were still standing around, having snitched free coffee from the nurses' lounge.

"We've got a situation."

They looked up with alarm.

"Margaret Forrester," I told them. "Flipping out."

They caught the scene through the window: Margaret huddled on the chair. The nurse on the phone to security.

"We'll take care of it," Jaeger said, ditching the cup. "Thanks."

As they headed into the ICU, I fled, through the warren of hallways and down three flights of stairs. I was impressed by their patience—how they had shouldered the thing without question, the way you would an offbeat family member with recurring difficulties, the causes of which you had long stopped trying to guess.

It was the third day, unbearable in its mind-numbing similarity to the last two. I had barely slept, worried about the gun. How would it fit into the robbery scenario? Where did my grandfather get it? Who'd he steal it from? Was it traceable? What about fingerprints?

Nothing happened. No second shoe dropped. Andrew's condition remained unchanged. I was back in my pod looking a shade paler and more withdrawn, less able to imagine a successful resolution: I would get off but he would be a vegetable. He would be a vegetable and I would be convicted. He would recover but remain an invalid. He would recover and point the finger.

Jason, however, was all keyed up.

"Look at this! Look at this!" he kept saying, shaking a piece of paper in my face.

"I can't see if it's up my nose," I snapped.

Jason had done his homework and discovered that Carl Vincent, the unemployed lab technician accused by the teenager, Roxy Santos, of beating her mom, owned a green 1989 Dodge van. The van was registered to the same Mar Vista address. Whether Carl Vincent could be Ray Brennan was an urgent question; even more pressing was the escalating anxiety to get out of the office.

I told Jason, "You passed," and we left without telling Rick or giving a heads-up to Deputy District Attorney Mark Rauch's office, as Mike Donnato had advised. I did not want obstacles.

It was a quick drive to the Palms District, originally a grain-shipping center that had followed the Santa Monica railroad across flat agricultural fields. After World War II, those flatlands were developed into tracts of cheap single-family houses built for returning soldiers. Those were boom years, when the new lawns matched the crew cuts of the new dads who mowed them: young working-class vets could afford to raise a family, and every maple-lined avenue seemed to end at the utopian gates of MGM Studios.

The Santos girl and her mother lived in what used to be one of those tracts. It was still working class, but most of the 1940s standard-issue single-family cottages had been torched to make way for sixties apartment buildings on aqua stilts with carports. A Montessori school caught my eye, an oasis surrounded by tall pines. Bright plastic tugboats and picnic tables were placed around the courtyard of a graceful old Mission-style lodge. Across from the school stood one of those forties-era specimen cottages with a spindly porch and metal awnings, trash on the lawn and pigeons on the roof. It looked abandoned, and I wondered why the corner property had not sold. Something was not right: the windows had been boarded up but there was a new green AstroTurf doormat. That's why. A recluse probably lived there, lost in dreams of dancing in the Technicolor musicals that were made just forty years ago and blocks away.

"What kind of soil do you think these houses were built on?"

"You're asking me?"

"You grew up on a farm."

"We're not in Kansas anymore."

I laughed. Jason reddened at his own joke.

"Dr. Arnie says a paint chip found in Juliana's clothing indicates she was taken to an older house on loamy soil. It had floral wallpaper."

We were sitting in the Crown Vic across from the Santos residence, a vintage stucco apartment building with green fiberglass balconies and giant birds-of-paradise. It was about six inches away from the adjoining structure, a shoe box on legs.

"No old flowered wallpaper in *there*," said Jason restlessly.

"Mylar," I suggested, but I don't think he knew what that was. I observed his squirming. "Let's get something to eat."

A neighbor had told us the Santos family was on a church retreat up in Lake Arrowhead and would be back that night. We had been on surveillance more than four hours by then, endlessly circling the sights: a mustard-colored strip mall, junk shops, plumbing outfits and used car lots, up Overland and down Pico. We must have passed that pile of lime green and zebra-striped beanbag chairs in front of a futon store twenty-five times.

But we *had* located a Jack in the Box, with a Plexiglas security window through which you inserted your money and received your grub like a hamburger bank. It put another attitude on the 'hood.

"Is this where you want to be?" Jason asked.

"Jack in the Box?"

He grinned and crunched some fries. "The C-1 squad."

"I worked my butt off to make C-1."

"Really?"

He sounded surprised, like those broad-shouldered college kids in the fast lane who swim the fifty in less than thirty seconds. What's the big deal?

"When I was coming up, the hottest assignment in the country was the Los Angeles bank robbery squad. I was lucky enough to start from there, but it was still a long haul."

"I really admire the way you do your job."

He said it forthrightly.

"Thank you."

"I mean, you know how to negotiate the bullshit."

"Bullshit makes the world go round."

"When you started out, how did you prove yourself?"

"Well." I had never considered it quite like this. "Made sure I was first through the door."

He nodded.

"You can't show weakness."

"I got that."

"*Never once,* or it will come back to haunt you for your whole career."

"That's not what they say when they talk about the Bureau family."

"We *are* a Bureau family, but let it come out one time that you're weak and see what happens. Male or female, doesn't matter. Once it's out there, they start looking for a pattern. Do you volunteer to go to the back door, or the front? Do you put yourself in a situation where you're less responsible than the others? If your assignment is to be in charge of putting stuff in the evidence log—and if you say, *I don't know if I could do that*—you're finished."

I did not tell Jason, but that is what happened to Barbara Sullivan. Why they took her off the street.

His eyes were narrow behind the mirrored sunglasses.

"You spend your life in an office," he said bitterly. "When do you get the chance?"

"Looking for a chance?"

"Looking for something," he sighed.

I smiled empathetically and glanced at my watch. This was working out well. I had not thought about Andrew in twenty minutes.

"What do you think that thing you are looking for might be, Jason?"

At 10:48 p.m. an older green Dodge van pulled up to the apartment building. It had a dent on the left side.

"Did Juliana say the van was damaged?"

"Don't know," said Jason.

I was sitting up straight now, trying to get comfortable as the last of the codeine pills wore off. My eyes hurt and my back was sore, as if I had the flu.

The van sat there a minute and then a dark-complected woman got out the driver's side. She had a skinny black ponytail and was wearing running pants and a sweatshirt. She looked like a cannonball, big in the bust with a round stomach, and she carried an oversized cup with a straw. She put her head down and worked with determination, sipping the drink as she went around and opened the rear doors.

"Call for backup!" Jason hissed, fingers twitching toward the radio.

"Not yet." I wanted this takedown all for myself.

"Right, right. We don't want to look like idiots."

"Move your butts," the woman was saying.

Two young boys and a teenage girl climbed out. One of the boys started for the apartments.

"Stay here," called the mother.

"I'm tired."

"So am I," she said.

"I want to go to bed."

"Get your sleeping bag. Help out."

"I don't want to."

"*Get your sleeping bag.* I don't want to say it again!"

The boy kept going toward the building.

"If you don't get your sleeping bag *right now*," said the mother, "you can sleep on the floor."

She tossed the cup into the street and started pulling stuff out of the van.

The teenage girl was saying nothing. She had an oval face, ordinary, wore low-riding jeans and was emaciated-thin, tiny breast buds pointing through a tank top too slight for this fifty-degree night. She was holding a plastic laundry basket filled with toys and clothes, a cigarette between two fingers. She had no affect. She just waited.

"Is that someone else in the van?" I said. "On the passenger side?"

We strained to see in the greasy lamplight.

"If Brennan comes out," I said, "I will approach him and you back me up."

Jason waggled in the seat.

We had shifted into high alert. I was aware of the pounding of my heart. I wondered if the camouflage cave was still intact in the back of the van, if the woman was complicit, kept the kids in handcuffs on the long drive to the religious retreat.

"Roxy," she called, sliding the doors shut, "go get your brother."

The girl pivoted obediently on one hip.

"Come back here, cootie head," she said lazily, "or I'll beat your brains in."

The little brother taunted back. "You're ugly. You wear stupid shoes."

"Mom," she repeated with the same lackadaisical scorn, "he called me ugly."

I tried to see in the shadows. Were those bruises around the girl's neck?

The mother did not answer, nor did she attempt to discipline the son, who had ducked inside the apartment building, but heaved a knapsack over one shoulder and picked up two duffel bags. Used to defeat, to carrying the burdens.

The passenger side door of the van opened and a muscular young man climbed out.

"Go for it," I ordered, but as we made for the door handles some-one right outside my window said, "Special Agent Ana Grey?"

I jolted off the seat.

A heavyset man wearing a sport coat and tie was holding up a badge.

"Please identify yourself," he said.

Jason was already out of the car, demanding, "Who are *you?*"

"Chill," I said, looking back and forth to the van.

"Are you Special Agent Grey?" he repeated.

"Excuse me," said Jason. "What's the problem? We are FBI and that is very possibly our suspect getting out of the van." He'd flipped his badge open and held it out impatiently over the roof of the car. "Are you here to help, or to screw everything up?"

"Take it *easy*," I told Jason. "I am Special Agent Grey. What's the problem?"

Across the street the man, about thirty years old, wearing baggy pants and an undershirt, was peering at us nervously from the other side of the Dodge, shifting on the balls of his feet.

"Sergeant Pickett, Los Angeles County Sheriff's Department, spe-cial team. Agent Grey, you are under investigation for attempted mur-der. We have a warrant for your arrest. Please keep your hands in plain sight. Are you armed?"

"What the fuck?" Jason wanted to know.

"Put your hands out the window."

"We're working a kidnap case," I said. "The Santa Monica kidnap-ping, did they inform you of that? We are looking at a rape suspect—"

"Ana?" Jason asked, drumming the roof, twisting toward the sus-pect. "What is going on? I thought this guy was—"

"She's under arrest for trying to kill her boyfriend," said Sergeant Pickett, adding venomously, "He's a cop."

"You guys are nuts," Jason was insisting. "This is Special Agent Ana Grey! She's one of the top . . . the top . . . agents that we have."

"We are cooperating with the FBI, so just put your little prick back in your pants. Believe me, your supervisor knows all about it."

"There goes Brennan!"

And the kid took off, sprinting across the street to where the man had leapt a fence and disappeared.

There were more units now, doors opening, a pair of officers running after Jason.

"Tell them he's FBI!" I shouted.

The sergeant wet his meaty lips. He had shoulders. Flat up the back of the head. You would not mistake him for a ballet dancer.

"I'm still waiting for you to put those hands out that window."

He had a job to do.

I could not, up to that point, unclench my fingers from around the steering wheel. I could not offer up my wrists. But he would not tell those bozos they were chasing a federal agent until I did.

"Let's not make this harder on ourselves."

"Okay, just don't mess up my manicure."

I thrust both fists out the window and immediately the handcuffs ratcheted shut.

"Thomas?" he said into the radio. "This is Pickett. The suspect is secure over here, but her partner is pursuing a rape suspect—"

"—Special Agent Jason Ripley."

"Special Agent Jason Ripley," he repeated. "No, that's the guy from the *FBI*, genius, help him out."

An acid ball was rising up from the depths of my gut and expanding until my throat went numb.

Pickett holstered the radio. "Please get out of the car."

The door opened and I stumbled out. The Santos family was lined up on the curb looking on with glazed expressions as if watching the greatest TV episode of all time. People in the stucco minarets had come out on their balconies. There was intermittent laughter and jeering shouts at the police action in the street.

The sergeant took the weapon from my belt and patted me down.

"We are working a case," I repeated. "That female adolescent over there may have information—"

"I got to cuff you in the back, turn around."

I hesitated.

He didn't.

A sudden jerk on the upper arm twisted my back so it went into a spasm like lightning from hell. The legs went out from under me and I collapsed.

I was proned out, facedown in the gutter. My head turned to rest on a cheek and I caught sight of Jason, now running the other way, gesturing to the sheriff's officers, who seemed to have finally gotten the picture, jacket open and tie flying as he turned in a disbelieving circle of frustration. His bewildered eyes met mine and I moaned and tried to scrabble to my knees to beg his forgiveness, I don't know what, but the sergeant flattened me with one hard cut and my nose rebounded off the asphalt as he recuffed the hands behind my back.

A low-rider had gotten past the perimeter and I could feel the vibration in the ground of its hammering bass. Pickett leaned in close, whispering a stream of filthy brutal threats. A nova was exploding in my kidneys and I didn't care.

Seventeen.

Pickett took a corner fast. Hands cuffed, I slid helplessly along the vinyl bench seat, which stank with an animal stink like fur. We had left the helicopters behind, but the radio still bubbled with confused dispatches from scattered posses chasing the slipstream of Ray Brennan.

"Nice going on the takedown, guys."

Neither he nor his partner would reply. After a little while I said, "My *cop* boyfriend came after *me*. Did you know that before you tried to break my arm?"

"I know that if I were you, I would not make any further statements until I saw my people," Pickett said in a monotone.

After that we hit the freeway and there was no more talk. I watched as factories and dwellings, streetlights, cranes and billboards, roofs, palm trees and riverines of cars slipped by, passing the window of the sheriff's car in a smear of black-and-white, a movie shot you've seen a thousand times, gaining momentum like a train; leaving behind ten

years of work and service to an ideal, until all the constructions that
had lined the road blurred into a single run-on image.

The world was lost to me.

When I saw Galloway's and Rick's cars parked outside the Sheriff's
Department substation, I knew the past few days of anguish in
suspended animation were over—and immediately longed for
them to return. We entered by a side door that opened directly into
the jail.

There were no windows, of course, and when the doors shut they
remained shut, leaving no airflow, so you had the sense of walking
into a large overlit supply closet. It was a cramped area dominated by
a sprawling desk buried beneath logbooks, printouts, overflowing wire
baskets and several TV monitors rotating surveillance shots of empty
corridors. The cinder-block walls were painted lemon, trimmed with
industrial turquoise.

"Ma'am!" called Pickett. "We have a house guest."

It took a moment to locate the custody assistant in the forest of
rules and reminders that were curling off the walls, but there she was,
a small head of dark hair parted neatly down the middle, hidden behind
the desk. She looked up and smiled, a young Persian woman in a dark
olive civilian uniform.

"Yes *sir*!" she answered, echoing the tease in the sergeant's voice,
which had implied just the opposite of what he said: Not a house. Not
a guest.

We stood aside as the custody assistant used an enormous old-
fashioned brass key to unlock the booking cell, an empty ten-foot
square rimmed all the way around by a smooth metal bench. Pickett
walked me in and removed the handcuffs.

"Want a drink of water?"

"Sure."

There was a plastic pitcher on a ledge outside the booking cell.
The custody assistant poured a cup, then I was shown to an interro-

gation room the size of a pea, where Galloway and Rick were waiting. The ASAC sat on the other side of a brown-grained typing table
while Rick stood against the wall. On the table was a yellow pad.

It was 12:35 a.m., still early enough for the faces of my bosses
to hold the contours of the day. Rick wore a windbreaker and jeans.
I imagined him getting the call, strapping on the gun, leaving his wife
and two young girls and driving in from Thousand Oaks at ninety. Galloway looked like he had never taken off his work clothes, dressed in
a white turtleneck and houndstooth sport coat, fingering a dead cigar.
Both were tense and alert.

"Hi, guys," I mumbled, sitting down.

Pickett closed the door and the three of us were locked into the
most uncomfortable space I have ever known.

"I don't know what to say. Sorry to bring you down here." My
voice left me. "This time of night."

"Whatever happened," said Rick, "we know the stress you've been
under. We've all been there."

"I'm *really* sorry about Brennan. He got away? Clean away?"

"We'll find him. How are you?" Galloway asked.

"Not too good. We had a fight and Andrew kneed me in the groin.
I think I have a really bad bladder infection," and winced as I finally
allowed the pain to roll up.

"We'll make sure you see a doctor."

"Okay."

"Have you made any statements to anybody?"

"Not really, no."

"There will be an OPR investigation," said Galloway. "We want
you to talk to the shooting team."

I looked up. "Will that be you, Rick?"

C-1 usually investigated agent-involved shootings.

"I don't know. It's a bizarre situation. Since you—since we work
together."

"We'll get a directive from headquarters," Galloway said smoothly.

"I'm sorry, my mind is still going a mile a minute about Brennan.

We had the takedown, it wasn't Jason's fault, it was the situation of two agencies going in opposite directions. The Sheriff's Department showed up and everything went bad . . ."

Rick's hands were behind his back and pressed against the wall at rest position. His mustache and squared-up bulk made him look like a fireman, ready to rescue you.

"Ana," he said, "stop. You're out of it now. We'll follow up."

"All right," I said reluctantly and took a sip of water. It was cold, with ice. "What do they have?"

"Your fingerprints on the gun. The fact it was fired recently. Matching bullet wounds in Detective Berringer's body."

It was like being buried under truckloads of heavy dirt. First one truckload. Then another and another.

"Despite what Andrew said?"

Galloway stirred. "The armed robbery bit? Well, he was out of it at the time, he was on morphine, then he slips into a goddamn coma."

"You sound like a prosecutor," I said, half joking.

"That's what you're going to face." Galloway inclined his head and caught me in a penetrating stare. "I wish you'd come to me first."

I didn't answer. Then, "How long have you known?"

Galloway looked down at the cigar. You could smell the bitter wetness, like a puddle of dead leaves.

"There have been telephone calls across the top."

Now I stared at him, deadpan.

"Santa Monica Police Department didn't want to embarrass us, because we could turn around someday and embarrass them, so a political decision was made. When the arrows started lining up, a discussion took place above the investigator level. Their commander called me and explained the way it was starting to look to them, how they wanted this to stay confidential, but still keep the Bureau in the loop. At that point we were all stepping pretty lightly."

"Until?"

"Well, until forensic evidence from the gun."

"How did you know it was mine?"

Galloway looked impassive. "As I say, your name had come up."

"From Andrew?"

"We don't need to get into that."

"I'd like to know."

Galloway and Rick exchanged a look.

"Your attorney will be able to tell you," said Rick.

I folded my arms. We had hit a wall. Now I understood why they were ready and alert. A bulletin was out for my arrest and they had been waiting for the call that my car had been located.

Galloway said, "How did you think you would get away with it?"

"I wasn't thinking."

"You were reacting?"

"Look, guys, I would never say this to anyone else . . . This is really hard . . . but, okay, I just thought . . . It sounds pretty dumb now . . . I thought we had a lovers' quarrel, I mean, a *big* lovers' quarrel, but that at the end of the day, Andrew wasn't going to give me up," and sat there, slumped and miserable.

Rick's body flinched against the wall.

"He didn't give you up, Ana."

"He didn't?"

"The tip came from a female employee of the Santa Monica Police Department."

"What's her name?"

Before Galloway could intervene, Rick said, "Margaret Forrester."

I laughed. I just laughed.

"She have a hard-on for you?"

I shrugged. How do you describe someone who gets herself banned from a dry cleaner?

"She's very pretty and very crazy."

"That could work to your advantage."

It was hard to listen. Hard to think.

"How is Andrew doing?"

"He's awake and talking."

"Really? That's fantastic!"

"Well," said Rick, scratching his cheek, "maybe."

"Oh come on, you think he's going to flip? Tell me you don't believe in true love."

Rick just chuckled. "My impression of him was that he had a major chip . . . But I can see what you saw in the guy."

"Thank you."

After a moment Galloway said, "There are always two sides, Ana. We want to hear yours."

"With respect, I think I need an attorney."

"Yes, you do."

"What attorney," I said, "would you recommend?"

"Devon County."

County was a former cop turned lawyer who represented law enforcement personnel, all the big high-profile cases. Police corruption. Murder.

"You must think I'm in big trouble."

They were waiting.

"I'll give Mr. County a call."

"We'll do our best to cooperate with him."

"Thank you."

"And get you out of here ASAP."

"Thank you."

"Get you a doctor."

"Great."

Now Galloway paused. "You know you can't come back to work until this is resolved?"

I nodded.

"We have to take your weapon and credentials."

"I understand."

Galloway drew the pad closer. "Are you ready to make your statement? Want to take a break?"

I hung my head.

"I just want to apologize for whatever disgrace I have caused the Bureau."

Galloway smiled gently. "Don't give away the store."

O ver here," said Pickett, when they had left. We stood before an old wooden cabinet. He pulled a slip from a drawer.

"Special handling," he told the custody assistant. "The lady is an FBI agent."

Her eyebrows went up.

"Special handling," I said. "Is that good, or bad?"

Pickett didn't answer, concentrating on the form. The pen paused.

"Any 'observable physical oddities'?"

"Me," I asked, "or you?"

He snorted.

"Not usually this much fun around here, is it?" I quipped.

They took my fake lizard belt, scuba watch accurate to fifty feet, amethyst ring and gold loop earrings, the leather purse and contents, minus my credentials, which had been plucked out for Galloway and Rick. They might as well have removed my spleen. I signed for my possessions, then we moved to a computer/scanner to enter my fingerprints into the files of the Department of Justice, Sacramento and county.

"You guys are high-tech. All we get are ink pads."

The custody assistant was spraying a screen in the control panel with window cleaner.

"She can roll a perfect set," said Pickett.

The young woman smiled shyly. I was staring at the machine as if it were a huge hypodermic syringe. When I was a kid I once ran out of the doctor's office before he could give me a tetanus shot.

"Ana." Pickett shrugged with that big-eyed cop look I knew so well. "We got to do this."

Afterward, we went back into the booking cell so I could call Devon County.

"Make as many calls as you want," he said. "It only works collect."

There was one battle-scarred phone with an unduly short cord, to prevent death by hanging.

They put me in a four-bunk cell. There were no other arrestees, but even if there had been, they would have kept me isolated. That's what they meant by "special handling." They did not mean the seatless stainless steel toilet or the mattresses made of fire-resistant polymer, or the ham and cheese sandwich and warm apple juice. Those were standard. Knowing the price of wounded pride, they had also put me on suicide watch.

I could not bear to touch the mattresses so I sat on the edge of a lower bunk. The ceiling was very far away. They put it high up to make you feel helpless and small. I thought of Juliana, holding on to the stuffed leopard.

I knew nothing. How long I would be here. If I would go to prison. If the famous attorney would get the message and be paged and take the case and show up. I didn't even know the time.

I sat in the badness. There was no other place to go. I sat and rocked and whinnied and pleaded with God to make the terrible feelings go away, but they gripped me in the windpipe with caustic despair. There was nothing else. No voices to distract, just a deep infant panic for which I do not believe we have yet devised a comfort, one that could possibly equal that annihilation. I had no religious words so I stared at my socks.

I stared at my socks against the ugly turquoise floor and imagined, for diversion, the powers of the colposcope, that with my sight I could penetrate the creamy cotton weave, see through to the spaces. Suddenly I ached for Juliana and the closeness of our morning conversations. Why had I not reached out more? Called her, sometimes. Tried to help.

Juliana, of everyone, would know me, right now.

Eighteen.

By ten in the morning the temperature in the Valley had risen to ninety degrees and swimming in Mike Donnato's unheated pool was like swimming through razor blades—the dead cold chill of the water and the hot sun slashing.

I glided back and forth—four strokes, flip . . . four strokes, flip—across the tiny oval. This was what my world had shrunk to: fifteen feet of icy chlorination. In the current freak show that was my life, I had been turned into a seal, whooshing and snorting empty circles in a tank.

Believe me, I was grateful. Devon County had gotten the bail reduced, from half a mil to one hundred thousand dollars, after arguing successfully that I was not a flight risk, nor, since this had been a crime of passion, a danger to the community. As a condition of the bail agreement, I would be on home detention under the supervision and responsibility of the FBI. Good friend and former supervisor Mike Donnato had volunteered.

As shocking as the daily dive into the frigid water was the realization of how a legal maneuver had taken me through the mirror, made me prisoner, incomprehensibly, of *Mike Donnato's* life, and the choices *he* had made, from marrying Rochelle to having three kids to buying this house way out in the Valley.

"Why don't you take a nap?" Mike had suggested during the long rush-hour slog back from jail.

I lay on the half-lowered passenger seat, staring up at the beige interior, body tissue swaying subtly on the bones. That might have been the low point: humbled and inert, in Mike Donnato's station wagon.

The trees had filled in since I'd been there last, the ocher two-story postmodern had already increased in value by a third. We pulled in at sunset, the twin round windows reflecting like rosy moons, the development bathed in uncertain light. I had been condemned, of all things, to suburbia.

He guided me like a regular guest, between the faux Greek revival columns that framed the doorway, to the floral-scented living room, and soon a glass of red wine, trusting me with a long-stemmed goblet. He dumped a pile of catalogues from the mailbox on the coffee table and went upstairs. Someone was home from school. Soon I heard a halting clarinet.

D
evon County was a former LAPD detective who had become a federal prosecutor and then gone into private practice. Over the years there had been a small growth industry in our town of cops going to law school and then representing their own, mainly because the policeman's union often paid for representation. Devon was smart and capable, and, most of all, he was not a press whore. What everyone at the Bureau respected was how he kept a low profile in a potentially tabloid case where a state senator had been shot and wounded by his male lover, a senior federal agent out of our Sacramento field office who nobody had known was gay. Although he could have made the national news every night, Devon County considered it in the client's best interest to keep that story out of the papers.

I first glimpsed Devon County through the heavy mesh of the booking cell. He was a hefty guy, overweight, with a shaved head and goatee, looking more like a con than a cop. It was barely dawn; he wore a sweatshirt and baggy warm-up pants; you might have thought he was out for a run, except for the crutch. He had become a lawyer because he had been forced to retire from the department on disability after a horrific crash during a high-speed chase. He made legendary use of the crutch in the courtroom.

There was to be no more "special handling." Devon would remain outside the cell, I would be inside, and we would speak through yellowed mesh. When I protested there would be no privacy, Devon said that's the way the lawyers liked it.

"You know why they have this double screen?" he asked. "So you can't spit on your attorney."

"I'd laugh if I knew how."

"We'll try to improve the jokes."

"Devon," I said right off, "you have women on your staff. Shouldn't I have a woman represent me?"

He shook his head confidently. "You would suffer the backlash of the prosecution's theory."

"You already know the prosecution's theory?"

"They will claim the obvious, which is you went after him in a fit of jealous rage. 'Fatal attraction.'"

"Not true—"

He held up a hand. "*Not now.* You need a strong, macho guy as a counterpoint to all the cops they're going to parade out, and I'm as close to macho as we're going to come up with in the middle of the night on a Thursday."

Nor was he unhappy they had made me wait "while suffering unduly" for medical care. Another bullet in the macho ammo belt. I was feeling better after a couple of painkillers and a shot of penicillin from a spiffy young Asian doctor with beautiful shoes. They even gave me a cup of raspberry Jell-O. The bare outdated first-aid room in the jail had seemed like a Club Med vacation.

"You understand that you are being charged with attempted murder. You are looking at potential penalties of twenty-five years to life."

Incomprehensible.

"Apparently the condition of the victim, Detective Andrew Ber-ringer, has been upgraded to stable."

"I wasn't trying to kill him."

"*Stop!*"

I cringed.

"You don't know me, and I don't know you." He was speaking intently, close to the mesh. "We need to have a truthful, but *very del-icate* discussion. The best way I can help you is if we talk about what happened *very carefully*."

"I understand."

"Do you?"

"Yes, you need to preserve your ability to use me as witness on my own behalf. You can't put me on the stand if you know I would per-jure myself."

"Good. So let me ask the questions in my own peculiar way. This is not a tell-me-what-happened. It's not like interrogating a suspect, all right? We have to do this surgically."

"You're talking to a pro," I assured him. "Although it might not appear that way, under the circumstances."

"I never forget who I'm talking to," Devon said.

He produced a leather binder and a Cartier pen with a blue stone in the cap. In the following weeks, I would watch that stone as it whipped legal arabesques around my words.

"If the police were claiming that you were in apartment ten in Tahiti Gardens at nine-thirty p.m. Monday night, would they be wrong?"

"No, they would not be wrong."

"If they claimed you fired a weapon at Detective Andrew Berringer, would they be wrong?"

"They would not be wrong, but—could I ask one thing?"

He waited.

"Is there some legal way I can stay involved with my kidnap inves-tigation?" I told him about the Brennan case and how close we had come to capturing him.

"Not when you're suspended from the Bureau, darlin'."

"The Bureau's going to drop the ball."

"Nothing you can do about it."

"Any way I can stay in touch with the victim?"

"Why would you want to stay in touch with the victim?"

"She's a fifteen-year-old girl. Her world just ended. I don't want to personally let her down."

"Have you been very close to this little girl? Helped her through . . ." He gestured with the pen, indicating spirals of unnamed suffering.

"Yes."

He wanted to know more. After I described our morning talks and how Juliana had opened up to me, his belly jumped and he belched like a bald, satiated Roman emperor, and went back to the shooting.

"If the police were to claim you were a frustrated, jealous woman who was trying to avenge a betrayal by her lover, would you have some other explanation? Yes or no?"

The blue-stoned pen tapped against the pad.

"Yes or no?" he prompted.

"Can we stop playing games and can I just tell you—"

"Yes or no?"

"Yes."

"What would be your explanation?"

"I wanted to stop him."

Devon nodded encouragingly.

"You wanted to stop him from what?"

"From hurting me any more. Physically hurting me."

"Would that involve some kind of self-defense on your part?"

"Yes, it would."

"Would it be true to say you shot him in self-defense?"

I had seemed to lose direction, lost in some elastic loop of time.

"Yes."

"Did you feel in physical danger?"

"I just wanted him to leave."

"Did he leave?"

"No."

"What did he do?"

"He attacked me. He wouldn't stop. I kicked him in the groin and he backed off, and I warned him, but he came back at me. I dropped to the gun. I warned him again. I started shooting. We fought over the gun, and he got it away from me. He never stopped once he started coming at me, and I kept pulling the trigger."

"So he kept coming."

"He did."

"Even when you warned him, showed him the gun?"

"That's right."

"Even when you *shot* him, he didn't run, or take evasive action?"

"No."

"Nothing was going to stop him."

I was unaware of everything except Devon's rapid breath on the other side of the mesh, intimate as a priest's.

"Why," I said, faltering, "didn't he stop?"

"I think it's very possible," Devon answered, "Detective Berringer went to your apartment with the intention of killing you."

"Killing *me*?"

"You thought it was the other way around?"

"I was the one with the gun."

"Yes," said Devon, "that was the surprise."

After a moment I shook my head, as if waking from a dream.

"You're kidding, right? This is one of those outrageous legal arguments—"

"You can't be objective," Devon said. "I can. All I hear is you blaming yourself. It is absolutely not out of the question that this cop, who is used to violence, possibly depressed, despondent, getting older, close to retirement, financial problems, high on drugs, who knows what, finally resents the demands made on him by all the women in his life, and goes over there and takes it out on someone."

"Very creative," I said tiredly. "You should be a writer," totally forgetting that Devon County was also a celebrity author with two thrillers on the best-seller list.

I climbed out of the pool, dizzy with all that flip turning. It was just a few steps from the scorching patio to the cool kitchen, with its light cabinets and vinyl daisy tile and microwave as big as a boxcar. The refrigerator had cold water in the door. Inside the walk-through pantry there were marshmallows and chocolate bits you could chug out of the bag, and a shelf of neon-colored breakfast cereals.

The boys drank Gatorade and powdered fruit punch; there were flats of sodas and wholesale sacks of chips in the garage. All this was new to me, and I was as curious about the stand-alone freezer stocked with chicken nuggets, hot dogs, twelve-pack Klondike bars, whole chickens and racks of ribs as I would have been visiting a family in Japan. I never realized you could buy such huge tubs of peanut butter or cans of soup big enough for the entire fourth grade.

Mike Donnato had taken care of his mother until she died, in this house, of stomach cancer. There were far-flung siblings, but Mike was the only one with the courage to stick it out. She had lived in one of those extra back rooms with a fireplace and TV that nobody really uses, except to dump unfolded laundry and discarded pets. There was a mossy reek from the terrarium that held the baby chameleons; the carpeting, a cheap oatmealy remnant, felt cold underfoot, some dankness having to do with the plumbing.

"Who farted?" was the standard greeting from the Donnato boys.

It was a room without hope to begin with—thinly walled, sliding glass doors opening to a useless jag of the yard, an odd space looking at the back fence. This was where I slept, on a mattress on the floor, surrounded by Mike's parents' effects, which were touchingly arranged as they had been in the hobby room of their big home in Glendale: Dad's preoccupations in one half, Mom's on the other. So you had a Bernina sewing machine, an ironing board and bins of fabric and envelopes of clothing patterns on one side; then a bench with a magnifying glass and all manner of fly-fishing materials and magazines. There were other oddities—a rocking horse, a white cabinet I had not opened, valuable-looking antique wicker chairs, jug lamps, vinyl records *(A Swingin' Christmas)*, framed art posters from the seventies, and the kinds of novels people don't read anymore: *Lord Jim, Catch-22, Shogun, Cancer Ward, The Black Marble, War and Remembrance*. If I didn't feel bad enough, I could wallow in the ash-cold remnants of two extinguished lives.

"Free on bail" was not the way I would have put it. I was free to wander through the living room, lie on the beat-up burgundy-colored sectional (if I wanted to vacuum the cat hair), or sit in Mike's reclining chair and look at cable on a big blurry-screened TV. I could pace the hallway, passing the bedrooms in about four seconds—no daylight, nothing on the walls, except the kids' doors plastered with *Police Line Do Not Cross* tape and puzzles that spelled their names, *Kevin, Justin, Ian*.

I was free to sit on the small deck with the standard grill and white plastic umbrella table, and look up at a patch of milky sky, and know this was a preview, an aperitif, of prison life. I missed my lifeguard friend. I missed the shower talk and the redtail hawks that sailed above the pool in perfect freedom.

Andrew? I didn't know who he was anymore.

The highlight of the day would be the call from the law firm, usually with more bad news.

I learned, one standard-issue hot 'n' hazy valley morning, that the deputy district attorney prosecuting my case would be Mark Rauch, and realized, way too late, the devastating mistake I had made in not involving Mark Rauch in the Santa Monica kidnapping, not paying respects, not providing a political opening for which he might show gratitude, or at least mercy. This might have been the reason Rauch maneuvered to be assigned to this case—or more likely, he saw it as a high-profile opportunity to continue to build a citywide presence for a mayoralty run. So much for keeping us out of the press. The words "slam dunk" were being bandied about the courthouse.

"He's a scary guy," I told Devon.

"Why?"

"Hold up a mirror. He has no reflection."

"He puts his pants on one leg at a time, just like you and me."

"I've seen him work. If you call making little kids cry on the stand 'work.'"

"Come on now, keep that candle burning."

"Say again?"

"That pilot light of competition. I know you've got it in you; maybe it's low right now, but don't let it blow out."

"Is that what the game is for you, Devon?"

"Oh, I've got my competitive streak. I like to know I can beat you at something."

For a moment I felt myself coming alive.

"What if I nailed Ray Brennan?"

"Who is Ray Brennan?"

"The serial rapist I told you about. The case I was working on when—"

"There are seven reasons why you can't go there," he said with such gravitas I believed he had already counted.

"Wouldn't it prove worthiness of character if I went out and found the son of a bitch?"

"It would be a violation of the bail agreement."

"That's minor, compared to—"

"Let it go," he said firmly. "There are other trained and competent people who will continue your work and bring this creep to justice, okay? I know how it is to sit out there alone and have revenge fantasies—"

"It's not a *fantasy*, it's my *job*."

"This is your job: focus and prepare. Things are about to get very real."

I taped the picture of Ray Brennan over the fireplace in the hobby
room.

Now it felt like home.

Sub: Hang in there

From: B.Sullivan@FBILA.com

To: 70Barracuda@hotmail.com

   Just to let you know I am thinking of you and
hoping you're doing okay. My heart goes out to
you, it must be so difficult to face what you
are facing. Your friend is out of the hospital.
I'll come and see you soon.

   Love,

   Barbara

Subj: Santa Monica Kidnapping

From: J.Ripley@FBILA.com

To: 70Barracuda@hotmail.com

   Don't worry, the ball is still in play.
Here's a recap: Brennan remains at large. We
obtained a warrant to search the Santos apartment. In answer to your question, yes, we did
check the shoes, first thing. We did not locate
the actual lug sole boots, but we did recover
size 10 athletic shoes that, according to Dr.
Arnie (what a nut), match the wear pattern from
the shoe print on Juliana's back. So Carl Vincent IS Brennan. He ditched the situation in
Arizona to come here and go hunting. The picture is coming clear of Brennan's deal with
Mrs. Santos. She is an abuser, in and out of

the Program, lost the kids for a while. Social
services has volumes on her. The kids come from
different dads. Brennan worked in Thrifty drug-
store, in the photo department. Met Roxy and
got friendly, cultivated her, like Juliana.
Mother claims he's a great provider. That's a
good one. Fired for stealing. Mother denies he
molested Roxy. Claims they are all religious.
Total denial. Anyway, easy ducks for Brennan.
Sorry for your troubles. Everyone here backs
you up.

Sincerely,

Jason Ripley

Subj: Hang in there
From: B.Sullivan@FBILA.com
To:70Barracuda@hotmail.com
Look at it this way: at least you are missing
the 90-day file review. Galloway is in his office
with a migraine.

Subj: Santa Monica Kidnapping
From: J. Ripley@FBILA.com
To: 70Barracuda@hotmail.com
Just to keep you posted: Brennan's father was
also former military but he and the mom were
divorced. According to Mrs. Santos, Brennan
grew up somewhere around Culver City, maybe the
post-war housing you told me about? Could that
be the answer to the question of why he
returned—*to old stomping ground?*

```
    Yes, as you suggested, we are searching the
homeless shelters for transient named Willie
John Black. Possible Brennan is hiding out with
him or others.
    Sincerely,
    Jason Ripley


Subj: Hang in there
From: B.Sullivan@FBILA.com
To: 70Barracuda@hotmail.com
    Sorry, have to cancel our visit. Two bank
jobs yesterday and the baby has a cold. Miss
you.
    B.
```

Mike Donnato's wife, Rochelle, was a very efficient person who used hot rollers and who, God knows, could track the roasts in the freezer and the kids' activities, both of which she penciled in on a calendar that hung in a nook completely devoted to scheduling. She was a good lady, a scuba instructor, who besides holding down a full-time job in a management firm, which she got after going back to law school, volunteered with a program to teach underprivileged kids to scuba dive. She had been an FBI wife for seventeen years, during the days when postings changed year to year. Their oldest boy had gone to four different schools.

"What happened?" she asked one night in the kitchen.

"I can't talk about it."

"I understand, but this is family."

"My lawyer would kill me. You know lawyers."

"If we're not family," squirting pink dishwashing liquid into a baking pan, "who is?"

Devon had been adamant. *"Don't talk to anybody. If someone contacts you claiming to be a private detective, you say,* Call my attorney. *If it's* 60 Minutes *on the phone, hang up. I've seen it time and time again. Many cases are won by the prosecution, not because of evidence they have at the beginning, but by what the defendant says to so-called friends and family.*"

A natural athlete, Rochelle looked great in nothing but sweat shorts and a little tank top. Her arms were shapely, and she liked her tight gold bracelets. She had an ankle tattoo from surfing days and was fussy about her long red nails—would never pry open a lid without using a gizmo, or wash the pots without big blue rubber gloves.

"You know I'm grateful to be here." I touched her hard freckled shoulder. "If you guys didn't take me in, I don't know where I'd be."

"Mike thinks the world of you."

"The feeling is mutual."

"He has total faith."

Bubbles were rising in the pan. The kitchen smelled like gardenias on a sugar high.

"I'm glad, because it's going to be a battle," I said. "Being a woman FBI agent is bad news."

"You'd think it would be just the opposite."

"*You and I* would," trying to seal a very watery bond. "But females on the jury will resent the fact that I'm—*relatively*—young and free, and sleeping with this hunky cop, and males will think I'm a ball buster."

Rochelle turned with an indignant pout. "*He* came after *you.*"

"That's true. I can say that much. Where does the spaghetti pot go?"

She pointed with a dripping rubber finger. "Underneath." Then, "I don't see why women have to be so jealous of each other."

"Laws of the jungle."

"Look how many hours you and Mike spent together when you were partners—I didn't have a problem with that."

There was an earsplitting crash as all the metal lids in the cabinet where I had been fumbling with the pot fell down, scattering like cymbals.

"Sorry."

"And I *work* with men," Rochelle went on. "My *boss* is a man, we're together all day and after work for drinks with clients—I mean, get a grip."

"Well," I said, on my knees, trying to fit the lids back into a special rack, "usually these jurors are older. Another generation."

"You may not even go to trial."

"I don't know about that."

"Berringer is a big strong guy. You're pleading self-defense?"

"I've got to go into Devon's office and work that out."

"They would drop the charges if your boyfriend said forget it."

"Not with Mark Rauch running for mayor."

"Still." Rochelle pulled off the gloves and slapped them in the dish drainer where the baking pan lay, gleaming and steaming. "What if Berringer stated it was a lovers' quarrel, none of your business, over and out? Do you even *know* what your boyfriend thinks?"

I closed the cabinet and stood. "I don't know anything."

She was already making the boys' lunches for the following day. A whole new meal had appeared on the counter: cheese, bologna, iceberg lettuce, plastic bags.

"Can I help?"

"I've got it. Years of practice," she added, which made me feel annoyed.

"Well, anyway"—I smiled—"it's been great to hang out with you. Except for the circumstances."

"I agree." She smiled back, whirling the cap off the mayonnaise. "When this is over, and you can *talk*—because talking *is* a prerequisite—you'll have to join my book group. It's a great group of girls, you'll love it."

I realized she was afraid of me. Let's face it, she had an unstable individual on her hands, awakening in the early hours, liable to get the dry heaves any hour of the day. When I wasn't heaving I was crying, long emotionless jags in the hobby room. I was down to 104 pounds.

Rochelle had shared some tranquilizers, which laid you down in a cradle of bliss for a while, then tossed you out on your ass.

Hours before dawn, spaced on pills that were rejecting me, I would pace the empty kitchen muttering, *"What do I do now?"* desperate to call someone, but the whole country was asleep, even Donnato, asleep with his wife. Tenderness for him sometimes swelled so hard I had to close my eyes and bear down, but I was practiced at trammeling my feelings for Mike.

Rochelle knew, and it made her afraid, but she sheltered me anyway, because Mike had given her no choice.

Loyalty.

Juliana called the cell phone one of those mornings. I did not tell her where I was nor, at first, what was going on.

"Um, well, this is minor and stupid, but, my swim coach wants me back on the team. And I don't want to do it."

"Why not?"

"It's a joke. My times are *so* bad."

Although speaking to Juliana off the record during the investigation of her case had not exactly been kosher, talking to her now felt very not right.

"The only reason," she was going on, "is they're all in a conspiracy to get me back to school."

"What conspiracy?"

"My parents. The vice principal."

"Maybe it's time."

How long could I stay on the phone without violating someone or something? With Devon's constant haranguing all I could see was Mark Rauch subpoenaing the phone records and jumping on the fact I had been talking to a vulnerable young rape victim at four in the morning, after I was suspended from the Bureau. Who knew what he would make of that, but it would not be an ice cream soda.

"I don't want to go to school."

"What do you want to do?"

"Kill myself," Juliana said.

I closed my eyes and went into hostage negotiator mode.

"Are you thinking about hurting yourself?"

"Don't trip."

"I have to trip."

"I didn't call to get yelled at!"

"I'm not yelling. Am I?"

"Yes, you are."

"I don't mean to yell."

"You're the only one who understands."

Is this what children do? Force you to see the excruciating difference between your real self and who you are pretending to be, you think, for them?

"I—" My voice faltered, which was not hostage negotiator mode. "Juliana, I really, really care about you. Anything you say to me is all right. I'm here for you."

From the quality of the silence I could tell she was fighting tears.

"When people talk about killing themselves, they very often mean it. I need to know what's going on with you."

"It's just an *expression,* for God's sake! I'm not an idiot. I would never do anything like that. Don't you think I know what everyone— my parents—went through just because of the rape? I would never do that. It has nothing to do with what I'm talking about!"

"What?"

"The swim team."

I glanced at my watch.

"Then what's the problem with the swim team? The real problem?"

"The blocks," she admitted at last. "I would almost kind of do it . . . if they didn't make me get up on the blocks. It never used to be a thing."

"But getting up there now, it bothers you?"

"The water's far away."

"I know it is."

"I'm afraid if I . . . I'm afraid I'll be scared and they'll laugh at me."

"Can you talk to your coach? Ask if it's okay to start in the water. Hold on to the wall. You don't have to race right away. You don't have to start from the blocks," I said, "just go for the practices, go down the ladder, one step at a time, how would that be?"

L ater that morning, Devon County called. "Ana?" he said. "It's time to come to Jesus."

Nineteen.

From the bronze-and-steel lobby to the unobstructed view of Beverly Hills, everything about County, Carr, Levinson and Grant said, *We're rich and really happy about it!*

The conditions of release on bail allowed for meetings with my attorney and I entered their swank offices as if having been let out of a cave. Maybe it was a design statement, but diamonds were everywhere—diamond patterns in the sage marble tile, diamonds etched on frosted glass, inlaid in maple cabinets, part of the ironwork coffee tables. The chairs in the waiting room were covered in silk, velvet pillows on the couch. If this was coming to Jesus, sign me up.

The jewels of the kingdom were not shared with the help. A tired-looking young woman assistant in a tattered sweater and jeans led the way to a corner office where Devon sat behind a huge trestle table fit for a warlord. Since I had seen him during that predawn visit in jail, he had gone from ghetto to glitz, a vision of hip efficiency in crisp white shirtsleeves and buffed scalp. The table was loaded with expensive, highly detailed model cars. Cars lined the windowsills and cars rolled by, *outside* the windows, on Santa Monica Boulevard. There

were too many cars in the world, anyway, and considering Devon had
almost lost his life in a car, you had to wonder why he would surround
himself with a fetishistic collection of reminders.

I sat in a cockpit of an armchair made of soft Italian leather.

"It's a long way from the homicide desk, Detective."

Devon smiled. "Ten years ago you could have told me a *mojito*
was a male prostitute."

"You mean a *mojito* is *not* a male prostitute?"

"A *mojito* is a rum drink."

"Oh."

"Apple martinis are out. *Mojitos* are the new LA thing."

"You travel in the right circles, Devon."

His gaze drifted to the immediate view. Ten-million-dollar estates
belonging to new Hollywood and old aerospace were deftly tucked
between neat rows of palm trees adumbrating toward the hills.

"You think as an investigator you've seen it all." He shook his
head. "You would not believe what I see."

"The level of greed?"

"The fucking and sucking."

I guessed we were talking about the same thing.

"The hardest part for you," he continued, in one peculiar segue,
"will be to see Detective Berringer for the first time in court. You need
to prepare for that."

"What should I do? Stare at his picture and give myself electric
shocks?"

"I mean it, Ana."

"I'm not arguing."

"You're feeling defensive."

"No I'm not."

"I can tell from your body language."

I looked down and uncrossed my legs. In fact, the idea of seeing
Andrew in court had made my stomach cramp.

"Better?"

"You've never been on the other side, is what I'm saying. Never

sat at the defendant's table. The DA is definitely going to call Andrew
Berringer. And this man, who you know intimately, is going to basically accuse you in open court of attempted murder."

I reached for a water bottle left by the tired assistant and drank
as if it could give me strength. In the soft field of Mediterranean daylight created by the large windows, Devon, with his white shirt and
shining dome of a head, seemed hyperdefined, like a figure out of con-
text in a dream. Those figures often appear bearing a message.

"Whatever Detective Berringer says, you do not show emotion of
any kind. It is very important," Devon insisted, "if I am to defend your
freedom, to know I'm not going to see you reacting in any way. I don't
want you looking at him with anger, or rolling your eyes when you
don't like something, or—doing like you're doing right now—shaking
your head like I'm a moron."

"I don't think you're a moron."

"I need you to do nothing except take notes on a pad. If there's
something you need to relate to me, write it down. I don't want anyone who might be observing this hearing to assume that you have a
bias either way."

"I'm shaking my head, Devon, because that's impossible."

"What is?"

"For me to sit there and listen to whatever bullshit the DA is going
to come up with."

"Forget the DA. You know how that's played. Let's focus on
Andrew. He's the one who can push your buttons."

I said nothing.

"Am I right?"

"Well, he did. Apparently."

Devon took a breath to observe me in silence. Our eyes held, like
infrared devices connecting and adjusting, sharing information. We
were framing the relationship. Who was in charge? How far would
the other yield?

"If you can't keep it together in the courtroom, the ramifications will be—well, let me remind you. Sometimes clients need to hear it again: Your life is on the line."

Devon let his thick lids fall in a slow, deliberate blink. He wanted me to sit with it, but instead everything I'd been holding back suddenly spurted out.

"I'm pissed at him for getting me *into* this position, I'm upset with myself for *going* there, I feel *guilty, upset, ashamed,*" smacking a fist on the cockpit chair, "and I'm *tripping,* because on some level, I still love the guy! So, I don't know! You tell me! What am I supposed to do?"

"Put on your game face," my attorney advised.

That I understood. From years of interrogation, I understood.

"All right," I said, and took a moment to drop the emotionality, or at least stuff it back into its sack. "Game face on."

He nodded and picked up the pen.

"Detective Berringer is a hundred pounds heavier than you, correct?"

"Yes."

"At least seven inches taller?"

"Nine inches taller."

"Have you seen him before in a state of rage?"

"Yes."

"Did you ever have moments in your relationship when you feared for your safety?"

"I have."

"Talk about those."

Having rendered all this easily, I suddenly discovered I did not wish to reveal more. If there was a pattern of impulsive violence in Andrew's behavior, I had not seen it and certainly did not want to admit that failure now. Here in the corner office, in the uncompromising light of success, I had a deep, vital need to appear as competent and accomplished as Devon.

So I smiled with professional accord and lied.

"Andrew can be opinionated, but whatever minor incidents there might have been, they were nothing you would tag."

Devon was looking at my feet. Always position the suspects so you can see what they are doing with their feet. Often the feet will be dancing to a different tune than the one playing upstairs. Mine were pointing out the door—what does that tell you?

"Give me an example," Devon pressed, "of something minor."

"Driving fast," was the first thing that came to mind. "A lot of people drive fast when they're angry, even though we do our best to—"

"Andrew drove fast when he was upset."

"Angry."

"How fast?"

"I don't know. Ninety? A hundred?"

"This was where?"

"On the Ten, out near Indio. We were coming back from riding dune buggies."

"What set him off?"

"We had a fight."

"Can you recall what the fight was about?"

"Girls. If we were going to still see other people. I wanted to get it clear. You know, where we were. He told me to stop nagging."

Devon's blue-jeweled pen kept looping across the yellow pad.

"What else?"

"What *else*?" I spread my arms. "I was not dating some psychotic maniac."

"I didn't say you were."

"Andrew has a manifesto, in a frame on the wall. 'The Homicide Investigator's Oath,' it says. *'Thou Shalt Not Kill.'* This is a guy who truly believes he is working for God."

"Give me another minor incident."

"Once upon a time, Andrew shot a rattlesnake."

I folded my arms defensively, although I was giving Devon exactly what he wanted. Even through my resistance I could see he was one smart lawyer. The resistance came of my desire, even at this late hour, to protect the truth about who Andrew Berringer was—the *poignant* facts of his humanity that would not be evident in the skewed furniture in the Marina apartment, nor the broken scree of a mountain track.

"We were hiking the San Bernardino Mountains. We see a rattlesnake lying across the trail. He, of course, has to poke it with a stick. I'm telling him not to, but he's like a little boy, he just won't quit, and then all of a sudden he takes out his weapon and shoots the damn thing."

"Was it attacking him?"

"No. It was just lying there."

"What did you do?"

"I told him he was a fucking Neanderthal and turned around and started running down the trail." I had been crying but did not share that with Devon. "He called after me, but I kept going and basically he chased me all the way down. It was not fun."

"Was he trying to catch you? Hurt you?"

"I didn't let him catch me. By the time we got down we were completely wiped and had nothing to say to each other. We broke up for about three weeks after that."

"When Andrew acted like this, what did you make of it?"

I frowned, trying to sort it out, holding on to our most private moments, the way a child hides a clear glass marble in her hand, believing that it is not glass but *crystal*, powerful and made of magic.

"Andrew had a short fuse when it came to anger. Like me, I guess. I thought it was a *good* thing we were so much alike."

"If you were so much alike, what were you doing rolling over a coffee table, trying to kill each other?" Devon wanted to know. "Let's go back. Tell me what happened in your apartment from the moment you opened the door."

"I didn't open the door. He got in. Somehow."

"With a key?" suggested Devon.

"Didn't have a key."

"A duplicate he made without you knowing?"

The idea chilled me. "That would be upsetting."

"Yes, it would."

I told Devon that Andrew had been agitated when he arrived. The lawyer wanted to know what we fought about. It built, I said, small rocks skittering, the way arguments do: The money he owed me. The scene in the bar. Me going after him and Oberbeck. Me intruding into his life.

"What was the straw?"

"The straw was the bank robbery. We recovered a ski mask and were checking out the DNA. This was *his* case, that he could get major credit for, but when I told him I reopened it on my end, he went ballistic. That's when he came over the table at me."

Outside, the traffic glided silently by. The afternoon light had cooled since I'd first entered the office, and the hunched figure of my attorney against the softly glowing cityscape seemed muted as well. The firebrand inquiry had burned out, leaving one core question: why?

"My gut says the intensity of this was not about him being pissed because you didn't like his girlfriend," Devon said slowly. "There was a threat he perceived as so serious he was willing to kill you to wipe it out."

"You keep saying that, but—"

"He kept coming after you, even when you showed him the gun. As a cop, that is nothing I would ever do. You wouldn't normally throw yourself at the shooter, would you?"

I had to admit, "No."

"No!" Devon put down the pen. "Unless you were unhinged." He paused. "Or desperate."

"Desperately what?"

"Scared." Devon shrugged in his white shirtsleeves. "Andrew Berringer was trying to kill you, and you responded in the only way possible, which was self-defense. That is what we need to prove."

I lay back in the chair, spent. "Go ahead," I said, with an ironic wave of the hand.

"I'm planning to subpoena Juliana Meyer-Murphy."

"What does Juliana have to do with this?"

"We might need her as a character witness."

"She's a fifteen-year-old victim of rape who is suffering from post-traumatic stress—she can't even go out of the house!"

"She will help your case."

"Drop it."

"I will not."

"You know what, Devon? I'm starting to lose my game face here."

"I can see that."

"What would it be like for her if someone she trusts, an FBI agent for God's sake, turns out to be an accused criminal, like the guy who raped her, who she *also* trusted—"

"If this goes to trial," he interrupted, "she will see it on TV. The whole fucking world will see it on TV."

"I spoke to her!" I said triumphantly. "This morning! Six and a half minutes on the phone! They could claim witness tampering. You can't go there!"

Devon shook his head dismissively.

"Look, I'm not pretending there are not other implications with having this young lady on the stand. We can't call her as a character witness in a preliminary hearing where the purpose is for a judge to decide whether there is enough evidence to warrant a jury trial, but we *can* have her up there for an innocuous reason that goes to the prosecution's burden of proof. And we can hope, because she's young and emotional, that during cross-examination she will blurt things out about how terrific you are, how you got her through the worst time in her life . . ."

"So now we're exploiting a rape victim."

"If this kid will do something for you, I want to use her, you bet."

"What if, on cross-examination, the DA takes her apart and she's even more traumatized?"

"Ana, when I was a cop, I put rapists in prison. I'm not insensitive and I don't want to hurt anyone, but my sole focus and ethical duty is to my client and my client only, and frankly, I'm not concerned if she has to see a therapist a few times more, we'll pay for it, so what?"

"I don't think I have ever been more offended in my life."

"You don't have to go along with it." He waited, eyes downcast. "You see, we are now at the point where this begs the fundamental question of the relationship between the defense lawyer and client."

By then it must have been five o'clock, the energy of the city draining the other direction, away from the daily battles toward resolution and home. He wasn't exactly putting it on the line, but he was forcing a calibration. Where did we stand? Did I trust his judgment enough to override my feelings for Juliana?

"You're saying if I don't want to do this, you won't force it?"

"My sole concern is in walking you out of that courtroom. If we can't go down the Juliana road, we'll find another way. But as I said, I think she can help you and it's important."

I thought about it for several silent moments until Devon picked up one of the model cars and began spinning its wheels.

"Is that a Porsche you've got there?"

He nodded and spun some more. "A Boxter S."

"Why don't you have a Barracuda?"

"My clients give these to me. I guess I never had a client who owned a Barracuda."

I waited. Finally I told him: "All right. You've got one now."

His eyes rose.

"Call Juliana and ask if she wants to testify. The best thing for her would be to make that decision herself."

"Thank you," Devon said, and a palpable tension left the room.

I sucked the warm, half-empty water bottle.

"How much will the prosecution give us on Andrew?"

"His statement, which is whatever they decide it should be. We can't depose him until the trial. In other words, not much. They sent over a preliminary list of witnesses"—he tossed me a copy—"including someone you know from the Bureau, Special Agent Kelsey Owen?"

"Kelsey is going to testify *against* me?"

"She is being subpoenaed."

"Holy cow."

"What does she have on you?"

"I don't know!" I was really fried. "Nasty voice mails. Obscene gestures. That I'm an asshole because I didn't want her taking over my case?"

"There are two sides to every asshole."

I chortled. "The jokes are getting better."

"That's good."

Devon had taken out a paintbrush and opened the little doors and was dusting the interior of the Porsche.

"How are you going to prove your theory that Andrew was trying to kill me?"

"Investigate him and everyone around him. I've got a string of great PIs who work for me—former cops, an ex-financial reporter who's very good on the computer stuff. We'll look at everything—his marriages, cases. I'm intrigued by that bank robbery."

"You mean what was going on in the police department at the time—"

Devon was nodding. "—that made that particular heist so damn important to everybody."

"And the people he *works* with at the Santa Monica police?"

"Everyone, at least going back five years. Their wives, girlfriends, boyfriends, kids, vendettas, paybacks, who owed what to whom, their mortgages, car payments, bank accounts."

"Follow the money," I suggested.

"That's my credo," Devon affirmed. "The sign on my wall."

Twenty.

Afterward, waiting for the elevator, a soundless voice cajoled me, *Why didn't you tell him about the Sandpiper motel?* It's a private matter that would not be usable in my defense. *How do you know, aren't we talking about Andrew, who he is?* Devon would have discarded it, and I didn't want to see that, his cynical dismissal. *What you don't want to see is your own face in his mirror—* but the voice was silenced as the bronze doors of the elevator parted and my reflection split in two.

I never did tell Devon—and maybe it was a mistake—how our modest plan to drive up the coast to Cambria had to be postponed three times due to one or the other's work emergencies, and how each time I was relieved. How I'd been afraid, after not knowing Andrew very long, that cutting loose on the open road would be a lot different from the occasional night at his dad's house or my apartment, taking us further away from the security of our professional identities, safely cocooned in LA. Twenty miles out of town I was already wondering at the individual who had apparently shed his detective's shield for the persona of some petty delinquent.

"If it's good *to* you, it's gotta be good *for* you," Andrew had said, cracking a beer he'd dug out of the cooler.

"You're crazy."

"Just now figuring that out?"

He smiled, drank, put the icy can between the tight thighs of his jeans.

"I have complete confidence in your ability to drive," I said brusquely, to show no fear. "Under normal conditions."

"If you're nervous we can go back."

"I'm good."

He shrugged. "You won't be the first, baby. Usually they don't make it past that big rock over there."

"Who's the one who is nervous?" I inquired.

"Who?" he asked, completely baffled. Obviously, not him. He was taking the curves out of Leo Carrillo Beach at sixty, palming the wheel with one hand. "Be glad we're not on the Harley, Miss Feebee Chicken."

"Sorry, but I have a strong survival instinct," I said, and pried the beer from between his legs, giving it an extra twist against his bulge.

"Do that again."

"Later. *Maybe*."

I let the brewski trail behind us out the window while he whined, "Oh man, what a waste!" and thought, *My sentiments exactly,* figuring I was on a one-way weekend pass with yet another unrecon-structed sixteen-year-old male.

Oh well, at least the sex would be good. I undid my sandals and put bare feet (pedicured for the occasion) up on the warm dashboard; the road had turned straight and the sun was flat on our windshield as we shot north past Oxnard, Santa Barbara and Goleta, picking up local oldies stations that carried blaring news of used car sales and bluegrass festivals. When we passed a sign for San Francisco, he flashed that irresistible grin and said, "Why not?" and I laughed because I guess I was relieved he liked me enough to imagine head-ing north forever, leaving those cocoons behind all busted open, our friends and supervisors left to guess who in hell was in there, anyway?

"It's because I grew up in Long Beach." I was trying to explain why heading in a northerly direction always made me feel positive, while going south on the freeway was vaguely nauseating. "Not good memories."

Andrew glanced over. "No pressure, you don't have to talk about it."

"It's okay. I was brought up by my mom and my grandfather, who was with the Long Beach Police Department. He was a lieutenant."

"So we're both from cop families," announced Andrew with mock elation. "Equally screwed up."

"Did your dad take you around in the squad car?"

"Sure, but mostly we hit the bars."

"Seriously?"

"I used to do my homework in the Boatyard while Dad had his complimentary afternoon rosé. Ate in the kitchen with the Mexican help. No, listen, I thought it was very cool. What about your grandpa? Nice guy?"

"Not really."

"So your mom was—"

"Lost."

"And there was no dad in the picture?"

"No dad in the picture." That seemed the simplest way. I squinted at the horizon to steady the queasiness in the gut that sprang even at the memory, like a tapeworm. "My dad was from El Salvador. My grandfather didn't like him much."

"Got it."

"It was the fifties. White girls didn't have brown babies. Even light brown. Even *light*-light brown, passing for white."

"One more generation, and everybody in LA is going to look like you. Ana, you're beautiful," Andrew said. "I'm sorry to say it, but Grandpa was a jerk. Didn't know what he had in his own house. I can only imagine—what was your grandfather's name?"

"I called him Poppy."

"—what Poppy must have thought of you becoming a Fed."

I laughed. "I think he was in shock. I was supposed to be a teacher."

"I can see you as a teacher."

I shook my head. "No patience."

"Do you like kids?"

"They're kind of a foreign country. What about you?"

"Had a few close calls." He smiled remorsefully. "But I've avoided giving any child the misfortune of having me as his dad."

"You are so wrong," I said with conviction. "You'd make a terrific dad."

"You're just saying that because you're trying to get me into bed."

"I've been trying for the past hundred miles."

He chuckled. "I like you. You're funny."

"That's good, because you're funny-*looking*," I said, pulling on his ear for no reason. "I don't know why you don't think you'd make a good father. I've seen you work," thinking of the bank managers he had comforted so freely. "You're a natural caregiver."

He made a face. Didn't like the word.

"What about your mom and dad?"

"My mom and dad?" he echoed as if he had not considered them in years.

Then he seemed to forget all about it, involved with the road which was straight as a ruler, fussing with the radio, searching for a water bottle rolling on the floor.

That's when he finally said, "I'm adopted," and I heard the effort in his voice to keep it light, but there was no mistaking the shakiness beneath. He'd thought about it before he told me and now he wasn't sure.

"So growing up, we were both alone, in a way."

"My adoptive parents were very loving," Andrew said quickly. "The most loving people in the world."

My fingers tightened on his knee.

"I couldn't do enough for my dad. Could not do enough," he

added bitterly, and I did not yet know the source, that his dad had been a terminal alcoholic for whom it was not possible to do anything. "You had your mom," he said so wistfully that it moved me deeply.

"She was . . . I guess today you'd say depressed, but really she was young and brokenhearted because she couldn't be with my father."

"Ah, fuck 'em," Andrew interrupted suddenly. "They did their best, right?"

We drove in silence.

"I'm okay with it," I said after a while.

"Your family?"

I nodded, tautness in my throat.

"We think that," Andrew said, "but there's an animal level to things that we can never change."

The sun had fallen to the west, level with the road, so that bright orange rays bored at the sides of our faces and the curve of our eyes. Andrew flipped the visor over to the driver's side window, but it did nothing to block the insistent ginger light that flooded the inside of the car.

"How do you live with it? The animal level?"

"I've had some nightmares," he answered, "that are pretty interesting," and beside us, endlessly to our left, the green ocean burrowed, turned, and groaned with its own weight, restlessly settling and unsettling, seeking the stillness it constantly destroyed.

The Sandpiper Inn was a perky little motel on Moonstone Beach, scrupulously clean, window boxes jammed with pansies and geraniums. There was a decent heated pool surrounded by pine trees and set far enough from the road so all you heard was the cawing of crows and the hum of the pumps. A cheerful old salt wearing a chewed-up watch cap signed us in, urging coupons for Hearst Castle and whale watching.

"Good to see you again," he nodded to Andrew.

We carried our bags into the room and each sat on one of the two queen beds and asked the other what we wanted to do, as it was still the afternoon. I was up for running into the village, getting a nice bottle of white wine and some goat cheese and crackers, coming back here and pulling down the shades and scootching under the covers. His idea was to watch the basketball play-offs on TV.

Alone in this determinedly adorable room, with no distractions, the differences between us seemed unbridgeable: he was too old, too closed off, never went to college, divorced too many times; his loyalty was of a soldier to other soldiers, his self-discipline enormously self-absorbed, I decided, as he lay back with a yawn and clicked on the play-offs, while I sat on the edge of the other bed, really grumpy about not having that glass of wine, and began to count the hours until we could, without too much humiliation, leave. If we got back early tomorrow afternoon, there would still be time to do laundry, get on the treadmill, go to sleep and punch the reset button Monday morning. The odds of working another bank robbery case with Santa Monica police detective Andrew Berringer were nil.

I threw off the cheap thin blanket from where I'd attempted to burrow into the second bed.

"I'm going to take a walk on the beach."

To my surprise Andrew said, "I'll come with you."

"Are you sure?"

"Unless you want to be alone."

"No, of course not. Come along."

And now I was annoyed because I *did* want to be alone, since I rarely have a whole afternoon to walk by the water and think about all the wrong choices I have made.

Although the beach was across the highway we had to drive to get there. It was not a beach but a nature preserve, where wooden stairs descended to an outcrop of black rock. It was low tide and white surf rose and spilled over the tide pools. There were wooden signs describing the migration of shorebirds. We followed a trail through a pine forest padded with silence and emerged at a lookout from which you could see unobstructed views of the teal-dark sea.

It was too cold to stand there, but we stood there, fingers stiffening in our pockets, letting the wind roar over our ears and stream our hair, pour down our nostrils and chill our lungs, scouring the cells of our blood with fresh oxygen as the brutal tide brought in and took away new life from the small carved worlds of sea anemones and starfish.

"Look how nature keeps everything clean."

"Imagine what this coast was like a hundred years ago," Andrew agreed.

"How do the guys in the tide pools hold on? Tons of water falling on their heads, twenty-four/seven."

"They have suckers."

"I know, but still—"

"Hey," said Andrew, shoulders hunched against the spray, "those guys don't have a choice."

"And we do?"

"Sure we do."

"Here's the thing, Andy." I turned so my back was to the ocean and tried to put my elbows on the wooden railing but kept getting nudged off by the wind. "You told me yourself. You come off shift, you take a shower. Two showers, sometimes, you said, to get the cooties off—the TB bacillus from the homeless person, the dog shit from the backyard of a methamphetamine laboratory—"

"So?" He ducked his head to wipe a tearing eye.

"My question is, how do you cleanse the soul?"

"The soul?"

"The stuff we were talking about coming up here. Your dad. My grandfather. How do we ever get past it?"

"You're out of my realm of expertise."

"No, I'm not."

I squinted up at him although hair was whipping across my sight. My heels were planted and I really wanted to know how much he knew. Had twenty-plus years of being a cop washed through him, or had it put meat on his bones? Why was I attracted to this unconventional, craggy face and husky fighter's build that overwhelmed me in

ways I did not always like? What was he made of? I could get past the
petty disconnects if I knew. We were standing on a platform at the end
of the world, and I wanted to know if the trip had been worthwhile.

"You see it every day on the street," I prompted. "Good and bad.
Hell and redemption—"

"It's not that simple," Andrew replied. "Black-and-white."

"What is it, then?"

He shook his head. "It's a job, stop analyzing. I'm freezing. Let's
get something to eat."

He took me to dinner in a nicely restored brick building on the
main drag. Part restaurant and part retail store, it sold hand-knit
sweaters and local jellies and jams, and served up one hell of an
olallieberry cobbler, which we shared from a steaming crock, melting
with vanilla ice cream. Andrew knew the waitress, a middle-aged
teacher who worked two other jobs in order to live in Cambria. She
asked when he was going to retire and move up. "It's just a shot away,"
he joked, quoting the Rolling Stones.

I smiled and sipped my decaf. It was clear to me this was Andrew
Berringer's patented getaway romantic weekend, for those girls nervy
enough to make it past the big rock at Leo Carrillo Beach. All right.
We would be making love (glancing at my watch) within the hour,
and then I would simply walk away and become part of the crowd.

I was still smiling while Andrew retrieved the coconut-scented
candle he seemed to know was kept in the armoire drawer and closed
my eyes and let it happen while his thick fingers cleanly worked the
tiny buttons of my white silk shirt. We knelt on the bed and kissed,
and there arose in me an easy affection for the guy; I understood him,
I thought—a loner who knew what he did and did not want in his life.
Although I had been there only a couple of times, the way he ordered
things inside his father's house—baseball cap collection, weights, garden tools, pots and pans—stayed with me. It seemed a wishful gesture from a man whose daily task was to pull people out of the muck.

He drew me down on top of him and said things that took us away from Cambria, California, to an indeterminate meeting place where isolation and kindness merge. It was a lovely ride and there were no toll payments. We took care of each other.

As we dozed in the wavering white candlelight, Andrew's barrel chest began to heave, at first in small convulsions, then uncontrollable sobs. He lay flat on his back and sobbed.

"What's the matter, Andy?"

He could not answer. Wherever he was, he was in there, deeply. His hands lay palms-up, empty, and his knees and feet were splayed, body open to the grief that seemed to fall on him like rain.

"Talk to me, baby," stroking his wet cheek.

All he could do was put a heavy hand over mine and press my palm to his heart as if to say, *Don't go,* but the lowing animal intensity of his strangled voice, the repeated cries and inability to stop were scaring me by degrees, as the warm serenity of our lovemaking was slowly chilled by layers of rational thought insisting through a drowsy haze that something was seriously wrong.

He began to shiver. It was cold in the room. I covered his body with the brittle blanket and got up and pulled on a T-shirt and fussed with the thermostat. Instantly a gas fireplace in the corner roared into flame. When I turned, Andrew had gotten out of the bed and was standing at the open door, buck naked, staring out at the parking lot.

I laid a gentle hand on his arm. "Where are you going, buddy?"

"You can hear the ocean."

He seemed so completely dream-bound that my anxiety rose to a panic. My fingers tightened around his hard wrist, breast up against his arm, legs braced, as if he might slip loose and run.

"Listen," he insisted.

A rhythmic whisper carried from across the road, tiny, like a fountain in the neighbor's yard.

"I'll bet that water's chilly." I was thinking of jellyfish, billowing and diaphanous in the bitter gloom. "I'll bet it's fifty degrees."

It was getting damn chilly standing in the open door, half starkers. The other rooms were dark. The motel office was closed, but rose-colored lights strung along the roof were shining in the mist, and the sky was powdered with stars.

"What is it, hon? Do you want to get some air?" I asked. "Let's get dressed and take a walk."

It did not matter that it was one in the morning. We could pick up the highway at an unspecified point, like the beginning of that movie where a woman is running along the white line of a darkened road, wearing nothing but a raincoat.

Andrew's hands moved over his sticky groin.

"I have to take a shower first."

"How about a bath?"

We turned from the doorway.

"Did I tell you that my dad committed suicide?" he said.

He was fifty years old, a strapping, handsome guy—had the boat, the house on the lake, everything going for a beautiful retirement except one thing: when he drank, he did it to excess."

We were wedged into the motel bathtub, facing each other, his legs on the outside, mine on the inside. My feet were on his belly. He rubbed the puckered soles absentmindedly as he spoke. My thumb massaged his ankle. The shower curtains were pushed back carelessly and the door was closed, mirrors dripping with steam. The only source of light was the coconut candle on the vanity, now half melted into the shape of a woeful ghost.

"On a Saturday night he went out with some pals to this place that used to be down in Venice, isn't anymore—a whole group of guys met, a number filtered out, Dad stayed, another group filtered in. They drank until the place closed and went in two cars to another party supposedly somewhere up in the Palisades Highlands.

"On the way over there, the other car, the one his friends were in, starts driving erratically, and a *third* car, driven by civilians, starts honking and getting into the mix, so at a stoplight, they all stop—everybody stops—and my old man gets out. He's this big guy, right?"

Andrew paused to cup hot water, let it draw down his reddened face.

"So my dad instructs the civilian driver to pull over. He was always a team player, standing up for his buddies, you see. He goes up to the driver and he's got his gun out. Big, big mistake. He's going to pull this guy out of the car. He's not in uniform, he's drunk, the civilian doesn't know what's going on, his friend cell phones the cops. They have a vehicle in the area, and they swing over in seconds, and they seize my dad. Take him into custody."

"Where was this?"

"Pacific Palisades. LAPD."

I nodded.

"In trying to get the story from a bunch of inebriated witnesses, all they focused on was that my dad had a gun and tried to pull this guy out of the car. So they book him for attempted car jacking and put him in jail.

"I'm a rookie, I'm living with two roommates in a dive off Pico, and I get the call from my lieutenant on a Sunday morning. '*Your father's in jail.*' Not only in jail but on a felony charge. You have to remember, nothing like this ever happened to my dad. This is like Sandy Koufax robbing a bank. It just doesn't happen. Turns out, they called the office, verified his status as a captain in the Santa Monica Police Department, and now I go over there to bail him out.

"He's okay, he's sobered up, a little chagrined but not majorly, or so I think," Andrew said, wagging a reproachful finger. "So we go and have breakfast at Rae's, and I drop him off at his house and go play basketball. That's what I do. I play basketball."

He took a jagged breath.

"When I go back to the house later on, I find he's penned a note, indicating that he wants me to have all his possessions"—Andrew's voice cracked—"because I've been such a good son . . . And he says he's going down to the beach."

He waited. I held on to his shins.

"So I call the department and I say, 'You've got to find him, he's going to blow his brains out,' and they did find him at the end of a strand, he's sitting on a rock, two uniforms approach and talk to him, and he's not responding, and he pulls out his service weapon, and he did kill himself."

Again he lifted cupped hands like a chalice and water ran down his face.

"I'm so sorry."

"All his life my dad wanted to be a police officer. He thought that at the end of his career he would go out under a veil of shame, and he couldn't live with that. It got to the point very quickly where he decided to take his own life."

"It wasn't only that."

"What?"

"How did he feel about retirement?"

"He *wanted* to retire. Planned for it for years."

"You can still be afraid of what you want."

Andrew just sighed, exhausted.

"You have to forgive yourself, Andy."

"Doesn't matter to me."

"You're a loving son. Remember that."

"Oh, he wasn't even my real dad, why should I care?" Andrew smiled ironically and quickly tweaked my toes, to show it was a joke, a painful joke. "Who are you?" he mused. "How did you come into my life?" and whispered my name just to hear how it sounded now that everything was different, and slipped farther, chest-deep, into the warm suds, sloshing water on the floor. We stayed so long in that common pool that when we slept entwined in each other's arms that night, it was as if we had become transparent to each other.

Twenty-one.

Devon County simply lied to Juliana, assuring her she would not have to talk about the rape on the stand, and so, after several more conversations involving her parents, she agreed to appear for my defense at the preliminary hearing. Juliana said she would do anything to "help me out" (that's the way Devon put it to her), but the deal was sealed when he promised to send a limo to pick them up. The girl wanted to know if the limo had a TV. Luckily, I was not aware of any of this, as I had been banned from talking with Juliana until it was over.

The Honorable Wolfson H. McIntyre presided over the courtroom that was to become our theater, our coliseum, on the fifth floor of the Criminal Courts Building in downtown Los Angeles.

Judge McIntyre, who was about seventy years old, with a ruddy beak enlarged by rosacea, wore a bow tie that was pressed tightly against his Adam's apple by the yoke of his black robes. He had sparse white hair parted on the side and combed in ridges. He would not be the trial judge, if we went to trial. All he did, all day long, for the past quarter of a century, was preside over preliminary hearings. He was the traffic cop, sending folks this way and that. Final destination? No interest.

But that did not mean you were going to get away with anything. Judge McIntyre was tenaciously anal, which made him a great traffic cop. He reminded me of an art history professor I had at UC–Santa Barbara. A pompous egomaniac who wore a three-piece suit at the podium, I had once surprised him in his office, slumped at his desk in a worn cardigan sweater, lining Ritz crackers up in a row and ritualistically squirting each one with a rosette of American cheese product from an aerosol can. He had looked up with rheumy, accusatory eyes . . . and you did not want to think about it any further than that.

Judge McIntyre's windowless courtroom was paneled in dark oak beneath square modular ceiling lights, which illuminated everything with democratic pallor. We had an American flag and a California flag. We had the Great Seal of the state. An exit sign and a thermostat switch on the wall. I spent a lot of time staring at that naked, proletarian switch. It spoke to me, in eloquent detail, of exactly what it would be like to be in prison.

I was not in my right mind during the hearing. Could a doctor remain sane, forced to operate on himself? Facing charges in a courtroom before a judge was the cruelest reversal so far in this unlikely pageant, which would turn into a full-blown Roman circus, should I be held to answer those charges at a jury trial. Meanwhile, we were doomed to be part of the sideshow.

The judge had a twin brother who sat in the back of the courtroom. It was explained to me the brother came every day to bring the judge his lunch, and sure enough, there were two identically folded brown paper bags on the floor near the gentleman's polished Oxford shoes. He wore a tweed jacket with leather buttons and sat straight and calm, head up like an eagle, while his brother fussed over pages on the bench, getting dandruff all over his black robes, the brother's hooked nose pointing north, the judge's pointing south, like two faces of destiny.

The judge had a clerk who was so obscenely overweight his belt floated around his belly like a hula hoop. His shirt was too short, so when he turned around you could see his butt crease. We had an audience of twitchy high school students on a field trip, prodding and smirking, while the middle-aged male teacher read *Chicken Soup for the Teenage Soul*. Then there were the watchers, a boozed-out clan of bowlegged cowboys and cowgirls wearing dress boots with taps who *also* brought their lunches, and the other defendants and their families awaiting hearings, including a young male with four sticking-out braids who hunkered down in the seat and kept his hands in his pockets while his lawyer discussed with the mother the possibility of drug rehab instead of jail.

"This place is a zoo today," said the mother, wiping her forehead.

"Gotta do something about this justice system," muttered the son. "Something wrong with it."

"That's what Judge Judy says."

The son snorted and shook his braids.

"Just *think*," said the mother, cuffing him, "what kind of justice you'd get with Saddam Hussein!"

Deputy District Attorney Mark Rauch made his entrance through a side door, pushing a trolley laden with stacks of books and files like a man with an awesome and holy burden. Those tablets could have been made of stone the way he huffed and puffed, in a detached Scandinavian way. A bully in an austere town out of a Swedish art film is how I saw him, the angry kid without a mother who keeps punching the other kid until there is blood in the snow. He was over six feet tall, forty, flattop hair, wearing a blue suit with an iridescent blue tie. There were dark manic rings beneath the eyes, and he moved with the lanky urgent stoop of a preacher crackling to put things right.

Detective Andrew Berringer followed in his wake, looking grim and uncomfortable in an olive double-breasted suit as if, I feared, his stitched-up wounds were aching under whatever bandages they still keep on several weeks after surgery. I wasn't supposed to look, but I could not help watching how he walked so heavily, listing to one side, thinner, slower, paler, sapped. Despite our preparations, his presence was jolting and I think I gave a little cry, as I felt Devon's hand compress my forearm, tighter, telling me those tears had better not run down my cheeks, so I kept my eyes wide and stared at the thermostat switch until they absorbed.

In contrast to Rauch's dark melodrama, Devon was playing the wounded policeman hero, a role he had fine-tuned over the years. The handicap sticker on his mondo black BMW assured great parking spaces, and he had no objection to being pushed in a wheelchair when the family went to Disneyland. People in wheelchairs went to the head of the line, he told me, so his kids could always get on the rides first.

It was therefore no ethical leap for him to assign two young attorneys to solicitously carry the briefcases while Devon hobbled ahead, and for them to make a big show of settling the maestro, opening books and fetching water as if he were some ailing Marlon Brando, laying his crutch as reverently as a vintage carbine M1 on top of the defense table.

I wondered how the judge facing south and his mirror image facing north would view these charades and turned to see the one sitting with the spectators was smiling with delight.

Rauch was in fact carrying the burden of the day. The prelim is a mini trial heavily weighted by the prosecutor's presentation. It is his job to convince the judge the charges are compelling enough to warrant a jury to hear them. Usually the defense does not put on witnesses, which meant Juliana Meyer-Murphy would not be called unless we were pushed to the wall. Since the judge would not allow a pure character witness to testify, Devon's ploy was to use Juliana to corroborate times—and then edge into how I had saved her life. Just knowing she was downstairs waiting in the cafeteria with her mom caused shivers of apprehension on her behalf and a gushy, emotional gratitude.

The bailiff called the court to order. As the attorneys sniffed and pissed (Devon yawning ostentatiously during Rauch's opening statement), a cold disappointment seized my heart. Smart and skilled as they were, they were about as inspiring as two mongrel dogs squaring off. You knew exactly what was going to happen. The ruffs went up, the growls and snaps. Justice had nothing to do with it. This was blood sport, and the goal was to win at all costs.

I had my game face on, and my heart was hammering. Andrew, on the other hand, was looking more and more relaxed, joking with the prosecutor, with whom, as a detective testifying in a criminal court, he would have often waltzed to the same tune. Although forbidden to look at him, I was still foolishly hoping he would sneak a helpless glance at me, and when there was not the slightest subtle nonverbal acknowledgment, I felt a flare of anger and betrayal, as Devon's theory that *he* had attempted to murder *me* began to work on this paler, more languorous Andrew, who was seeming somehow not quite so delicate as cunning.

"Is that him?" whispered one of the courthouse secretaries who had gathered in a giggly group in the front row. "He is pretty cute."

You still look good, Andrew, I agreed, darting my eyes away. *You could still do it to me, old pal.*

The girls in their nylon dresses and cheap platform heels were all aflutter with their game. When hunks were sighted anywhere in the building they would call one another and duck away from their desks and rush courtroom to courtroom to check out the goods, their flushed childlike excitement revealing how much they did not yet know about men and women.

CRIMINAL COURT OF LOS ANGELES

PRELIMINARY HEARING

DEPARTMENT C

444-8743—Bailiff—H. Solanas

The Honorable Wolfson H. McIntyre

Attempt 187

Transcript of Proceedings page 4

BERRINGER: I told her I wanted to do the right thing.

RAUCH: What was the right thing, Detective Berringer?

BERRINGER: To end the relationship. I knew it would be hard for her because she had become dependent on me.

RAUCH: Can you give us an example?

BERRINGER: She'd call all the time when I was on duty. Show up at my house. Have a breakdown and come to me for solace—which I was happy to give—but then it started to get crazy, and I realized, this woman is obsessed, she's making it impossible.

RAUCH: What kind of breakdowns, Detective?

BERRINGER: Angry, saying she was depressed and life wasn't worth living, she didn't want to be a federal agent anymore.

RAUCH: How did you react to that? When she said she wanted to kill herself because things were bad at work?

DEVON: Objection.

JUDGE: I can hear what the witness is saying without embellishment from you, Mr. Rauch.

RAUCH: Sorry, Your Honor.

BERRINGER: I worried about her. I talked to her about not quitting her job. I said we'd break the case. But it got to the point where I couldn't deal with it inside myself any-

more. Toward the time of the shooting incident, I was
becoming extremely uncomfortable with the relationship.

RAUCH: Have you witnessed this sort of behavior before, in
your professional life?

BERRINGER: Sure, I've seen depressed people, suicidal people,
schizophrenics, alcoholics, the whole gamut.

RAUCH: Did Agent Grey fit any of these categories?

DEVON: Your Honor, Detective Berringer does not hold a
degree in psychiatry.

JUDGE: Get to the point, Mr. Rauch.

BERRINGER: I think I can short-circuit this, Your Honor.

JUDGE: Do us all a favor.

BERRINGER: Ana was having a lot of trouble at work. We
were both involved in a very stressful case. It was a case
of rape and kidnapping of a juvenile, and it would be
upsetting to anyone. It was upsetting to me. The victim
was brutalized, we believe by a sadistic serial rapist, and
quite frankly, the Bureau wasn't getting anywhere close to
solving this thing, and Ana was the lead agent, so she was
under a lot of pressure. I understand that, I really do.

RAUCH: As a law enforcement professional, you've been there?

BERRINGER: I've been there, but she couldn't handle it. She
was falling apart.

RAUCH: What did you observe?

BERRINGER: As I stated, she became obsessed with me.

RAUCH: Why you?

BERRINGER: Well, I'm such a handsome guy. Sorry, Your
Honor, I don't mean to joke, it's not a joke by any
means, but—I don't really know. I was there, I guess. We
were working together. You know how it is.

RAUCH: You mean the long hours, the forced intimacy . . .

BERRINGER: She's an intelligent, attractive woman, and I guess—we got along. We understood each other. We were both uninvolved, free adults, and we knew what we were doing—or at least, I thought she knew. It was just a casual thing.

RAUCH: Did Agent Grey agree it was casual?

BERRINGER: I don't know.

RAUCH: Can you go back to this obsession? Give us more examples, if you would, please.

BERRINGER: She'd show up at bars, where I went to unwind after work with my fellow officers, and she was . . . demanding . . .

RAUCH: Are you all right, Detective?

BERRINGER: Yes. I'm sorry, I—

RAUCH: Take a moment. Is this testimony difficult for you?

BERRINGER: Give me a minute.

RAUCH: I'm surprised, Detective. You often testify in court. In fact, that's part of your job. Is this case different?

BERRINGER: I'm fine, let's go on.

RAUCH: Why is it different, Detective Berringer? Is it because you cared about Ana Grey?

JUDGE: We'll take a fifteen-minute recess.

RAUCH: Are you ready to resume, Detective Berringer?

BERRINGER: Yes, I apologize, Your Honor.

JUDGE: No need. Go on.

RAUCH: You were giving an example of Ana Grey's obsession with you.

BERRINGER: Ana said she wanted the nine hundred dollars back that she loaned me to fix my Harley. She picked the time to tell me this while I was at the Boatyard Restaurant in Santa Monica with my fellow officers, relaxing after work. She confronted me in front of them and the other patrons. It was embarrassing for the Santa Monica Police Department, which I take a lot of pride in, and to me personally. She verbally abused a woman friend of mine, also a police officer, who was known to everyone at the table, and made remarks about this woman's character that were potentially damaging to her professional reputation.

RAUCH: This is Officer Sylvia Oberbeck?

BERRINGER: Officer Oberbeck.

RAUCH: What is your relationship to Officer Oberbeck?

BERRINGER: We are friends, colleagues, we came up together, she's an excellent policewoman, and I have the highest respect for the way she does her job.

RAUCH: Are you romantically involved?

BERRINGER: We have been. In the past.

RAUCH: Did Ana Grey know you were romantically involved with Officer Oberbeck in the past?

BERRINGER: Yes.

RAUCH: What was her reaction?

BERRINGER: She went out of control.

RAUCH: What do you mean by "out of control"?

BERRINGER: She followed Officer Oberbeck and me in her car—her official Bureau car—and tailgated us up to speeds of one hundred miles per hour on the Marina Freeway. She pulled up behind us to the bumper of my car. She was very aggressive, revving her motor and honking the horn, forcing us onto the shoulder. When she got out of her car she was agitated. She said, "I know you were fucking this bitch and this is a perfect example." Officer Oberbeck

was terrified. I was pretty scared myself. She was pounding on the window and throwing rocks and ultimately
tried to scald Officer Oberbeck with hot coffee.

RAUCH: I'm sorry, I'm lost, you were on the freeway and she
had hot coffee . . .

BERRINGER: She had a cup of coffee in her hand when she
got out of the car and she threw it.

RAUCH: What happened to Officer Oberbeck?

BERRINGER: The window was closed, it didn't touch her, but
that's an example of how out of control Ana was. Completely out of control.

RAUCH: Was she out of control the night you came to her
apartment to break it off?

BERRINGER: At first she was sad, upset, whatever, said she
couldn't take it, we had to make this work out, it was the
only good thing she had left in her life.

RAUCH: What did you say?

BERRINGER: I said, baby, I love you, I care about you, but
that's just not going to happen. That's not where I am
right now. I've been married twice, I want my freedom, I
told you from the beginning.

RAUCH: How did she respond?

BERRINGER: Again, she became more and more agitated. She'd
been crying for a while—excuse the expression—she was
really pissed off.

RAUCH: Officer Berringer, why did you go to Agent Grey's
apartment that night?

BERRINGER: She paged me.

RAUCH: Where were you?

BERRINGER: I needed to do some cardio training, so I was
running the steps in Santa Monica Canyon when the

pager came through. The signal wasn't strong enough—
reception isn't good in the canyon—but I was eighty-five
percent sure it was her, because she'd been trying to call
me all day, so I ignored the page and finished the workout, and as I'm driving in my car, on Ocean Avenue, I
became aware of someone pulling up in back of me,
fairly close, putting on their brights. At this point I
assumed it was Ana because I'd had that experience
before, of her following Officer Oberbeck and me. She
pulled up beside me, made eye contact, and gave me a
hand motion that meant, Follow me. She then pulled in
front of me and I proceeded to follow her to her apartment in the Marina. She pulled into the garage, and I
pulled into the visitor's spot outside her place, and we
walked in together. She went into the kitchen to get
something to eat. She wore running tights and running
shoes and a spandex top and a jacket on top of that and
she had her hair pulled up. She said, "Hi." I said, "Hi.
What's going on?" And we had a general conversation.
She offered me a drink, I said no. She said, "What's
going on, where have you been? I've been paging you."
She wasn't being aggressive at that point. I said I've got
things on my mind. She said, "Like what?" I said I
wasn't comfortable with the relationship anymore. She
put her arms around me and told me she wanted to move
in together. I told her that wasn't in the cards.

RAUCH: Then what?

BERRINGER: She started blaming me for everything that was
　　wrong in her life. She got on this theme of everyone screw-
　　ing her over, including everyone at work. She said I was
　　screwing her over and she was tired of it. I saw things

going south real quick and I didn't want a confrontation. Her arms were still around me. I said, "What do you want me to do?" She said we could start over. I told her no.

She became infuriated. She was breathing hard. She was tense all over and you could see her going off the scale, the most upset I've ever seen her. Then she came back to me for the last time. "What are you trying to tell me?" she said.

I didn't have anything else to say, so I started walking toward the exit, and she turned away in the other direction, to the coffee table. I never made it to the door. I was looking back to see what she was doing. I wanted to make sure nothing was going to be thrown at me. She bent down and stood up and suddenly there were two bright flashes, and it was as if someone shot me with a drug. I don't remember hearing the gun.

RAUCH: But you knew you were shot. What were you thinking?

BERRINGER: I was thinking, I know I can win this.

RAUCH: Can you explain why you thought that?

BERRINGER: It might sound corny, but Teddy Roosevelt said, "Those who are willing to enter the arena are always preparing themselves for the battle." I'm a police detective and I take my job seriously and I like to think I'm always prepared. First of all, you know your body's going to help you out. Fear is your body responding in a high state of arousal. Fear is okay. What you want to avoid is panic and indecision.

RAUCH: You did not panic?

BERRINGER: I thought, Okay, this is just like in training. Everything was moving slowly. It was like when I was knocked unconscious once when I got hit riding the Harley. Everything was woozy except I had this incredible tunnel vision. All I saw was Ana taking aim with the gun for round two.

RAUCH: And you were how far away from Agent Grey?

BERRINGER: I was almost to the door. I was in the dining room area. She was back near the coffee table, near the fireplace on the other side of the room.

RAUCH: So you were at least fifteen feet apart.

BERRINGER: Correct.

RAUCH: Go on.

BERRINGER: I felt a burning along the lower right side and noticed my shirt was just beet red, full of blood, and I ran toward her.

RAUCH: Why did you run toward her and not out the door?

BERRINGER: That's my training. In my training guns are made for distance. You run from a knife but not a gun. I could have gotten hit in the back. I tried to get the gun from her. I kept saying, "Don't shoot me. Why are you trying to kill me?" I got my hand on a piece of the gun, but she was pulling away. She fell over the table between the table and the couch. I'm still maintaining a piece of the gun, the barrel. I stumbled over the table myself and ended up wedged between the table and the couch. She was lying down and I was kneeling with one leg on the couch. The gun went off again, to my right thigh, above the kneecap. I said, "You're going to kill me, I'm going to die." I was feeling pretty bad. I've seen people die for a lot less than what I had. I was feeling like I'm getting ready to check out. I ended up with the gun and went toward the exit of the residence. She remained crouched in a fetal position, to see if I'd turn the gun on her—which I didn't—and I went out to my car.

I opened the car door and got in. I reached over to close the door and she followed me out there and wouldn't allow me to close it. I said I had to get help. She said, "Where are you going? Stay here, I'll take care of you." I just started to drive, I figured she'd get out of the way, and I guess she did because I closed the door and drove away from her location.

Everything was like a dream, from the time I was shot. I felt as if I were getting ready to die. I saw I had the gun and it was pointed toward me on the seat. It scared me but I couldn't do anything about it, I just kept driving, started to recognize where I was. I was wheezing, sucking air, couldn't breathe very well. I saw the hospital and pulled in. From that point on, I have no idea what went on. I think I passed out in the ER.

I've had a lot of injuries from sports and street duty, but this was the most painful of my life. I had a tube draining blood from my lung into a bucket. Tube in my throat. Tube in my nose. I didn't get any sleep. It was the most miserable time I had, ever. It was just terrible.

RAUCH: Do you remember what you told investigators at the hospital when they asked what happened, how you were shot?

BERRINGER: For the first three days I was on constant medication because of my injuries, and for a while I went into a coma. I wasn't fully aware of what I said until I got out of the hospital a week later. I couldn't remember anything.

RAUCH: You said you were shot in a holdup that went bad.
   Why did you say that?

BERRINGER: I have no idea. It must have been the drugs.

RAUCH: At what point did you tell the investigators you were
   shot by Ana Grey?

BERRINGER: I never told them it was Ana.

RAUCH: You never told them it was Ana Grey who fired at
   you *three times in a row*?

BERRINGER: I never gave her up.

RAUCH: Is that because, until the end, you were doing your
   best to protect Ana Grey? Because you cared about her,
   Detective Berringer?

BERRINGER: The police department investigators and the FBI
   already had information that implicated her when they
   questioned me.

RAUCH: You mean, you were shot and Ana Grey was immediately a prime, number one suspect?

BERRINGER: I didn't say that. I don't know how their investigation was going.

RAUCH: Thank you, that's all.

The court stenographer's fingers worked at a rhythm of their own.
From the same fashion era as Judge McIntyre, she wore a white blouse,
a blue blazer, a pleated skirt with polka dots and white high heels.
After his performance, Rauch's shoulders hung at an exhausted angle,
drooping like a Dickensian scrivener's. Andrew's face was pasty and
filmed with sweat. The judge turned his head like a turtle inside its tender jowls.

In the rear of the courtroom, his brother watched with patient,
kindly interest.

*   *   *

On cross-examination, Devon tried to impeach the witness, using incidents I had told him to paint Andrew as an angry, burned-out peace officer prone to violence—one hundred pounds heavier, nine inches taller—who had attacked a petite female with intent to inflict great bodily harm because he was angry at women, having never been able to sustain an intimate relationship or marriage. He meant to silence me—why else would he have charged a loaded gun? I had defended myself, according to my training.

Devon emphasized that in the struggle I, too, had been critically injured, with a severe pelvic infection that could still possibly lead to sterility. Andrew was surprised by hearing that, said he had not known, and deftly used that surprise to express regret at his actions.

Even as Devon maneuvered himself elaborately back into his seat, grimacing with effort, we knew the argument had not worked. Andrew had come across as affable and sincere. The women-hating thing just did not play. We had hinted at darker motives but had no proof.

What we did not know was that I was not the only one in that courtroom who was trapped between the good face of the law and the bad. Andrew had become ensnared by the shooting in a way that went beyond the events in my living room. Although for one teetering moment he had shown conflicting emotions up on the stand, he had regained his resolve, for he must have known the only way for him to survive, as I had scrawled in frustrated silence to Devon across the yellow legal pad, was to bury me in a pack of *"LIES!!"*

The ER doctor, a knockout Brazilian woman, slender and beautiful as a model although she said she was running on four hours of sleep, described Andrew's injuries and how they were treated. She confirmed he had been receiving heavy doses of morphine when he stated that he had been shot by bandits, but later, even when he was lucid, she said she never heard him mention my name in connection with the shooting.

"True or false?" I wrote facetiously on the pad.

*   *   *

As Devon predicted the very first night, the prosecution rolled out a chorus line of cops unanimously insisting I was jealous, violent and obsessed with Andrew Berringer. The guys who had been in the kiosk testified I had been "emotionally distraught," searching for Andrew at midnight on the Promenade. We heard outrage from Detectives Jaeger and Winter about how I'd humiliated Andrew in a public restaurant, and then, remorseful, "bullied" my way after hours into the ICU. Lieutenant Barry Loomis, sporting the walrus mustache and a Betty Boop tie, described me as "behaving in a manner that was suspect" when we spoke on the phone while Andrew was in the hospital. He said "bells went off in his head" when "out of the blue" I guiltily asked whether the weapon had been recovered, although on cross-examination admitted anyone in law enforcement would want to know the same thing. In his version of the confrontation in the Boatyard, I came at the senior detective like a bloodsucking harridan. He omitted the fact that he had been teasing Andrew and egging us on.

"Loomis just killed us," Devon whispered, and as soon as we broke for lunch, he hobbled out ahead of the crowd, to personally escort Juliana Meyer-Murphy and her mother. She would be our first witness after the prosecution wound up its case.

Andrew and I avoided eye contact or any other kind of contact during the awkward scramble from the courtroom. I was very engaged with the zippers on my briefcase, anyway.

A small crowd had gathered in the corridor, looking out a window. In the street, five stories below, a car in the middle lane had unaccountably flipped over on its roof. There were no other wrecks, no barricades or obstacles or pedestrians that might explain how a two-thousand-pound vehicle could turn completely upside down.

"*Do you think that's a Honda?*" someone said.

"Could be. My wife just bought a Honda. She loves it."

"Have you seen the new ones?"

"No, are they pretty much like the old ones?"

I had no appetite. I went back and sat in the empty courtroom. Twenty long minutes later, Devon's associate entered alone.

"Where's Juliana?"

"Oh," said the jumpy young attorney, who had not yet learned from the master how to lie, "no problem."

"Where's Devon?"

"I think he's grabbing a cup of coffee."

"Is there a hang-up?"

"No, not at all. Just a last-minute pep talk. They'll be up in a minute."

The associate smiled the vacant, noncommittal smile of a subordinate covering badly for his boss.

"Do me a favor? If Devon shows up, tell him I went to the ladies' room."

I walked demurely through the doors, then hit the stairway.

There was only one place to get coffee inside the building, and that was the dilapidated cafeteria, but when I arrived out of breath the grill was closed and the place half deserted.

Afraid I had missed them, I was about to run back upstairs but noticed through the rear doors of the cafeteria there was a patio. Sure enough, a cappuccino cart. A few courthouse workers sitting on wire chairs were taking their breaks, bent over sliding leaves of newsprint or sitting back with heads tilted toward the sun, hands wrapped around the universal paper coffee cup.

Juliana, wearing dark glasses and a heartbreaking little pink suit, legs crossed, long dark hair blown out straight and looking about twenty-five years old, was sitting in the shade with her mother. Devon had pulled a chair close and was speaking intimately. Juliana's arms were folded and she appeared to be staring straight ahead, turning guardedly as I neared.

"Hi, Juliana. Great to see you."

"Good to see you, too."

"Ana," said Devon, "you're not supposed to be here."

"I just want to say thank you. Can't I say thank you?"

"No, you cannot be seen talking with a witness!"

But I was already shaking Lynn Meyer-Murphy's hand. I think it was the first time I had smiled in about a month and the fresh breeze blowing through the courtyard smelled like spring.

"Thank you for coming and for bringing Juliana. I know this is hard for her and I really, really appreciate it."

"Ana," said Devon, standing up so his chair moved back with a scrape, "go back upstairs."

A long time ago I had stood on the threshold of the Meyer-Murphy home, shaking the hand of a woman wearing mismatched clothing who was deeply in shock. Her eyes squinted and her affect was blank, but after a brief moment's nod toward her discomfort, I was impatient to get inside and go to work. Now it was Lynn's face that was composed, and *her* fingers that withdrew first and went to the calfskin shoulder bag and took out the car keys.

"Are you leaving?"

"We'll be up in a minute," Devon assured me.

"What's the matter, Juliana?"

"I'm having a panic attack," replied the girl.

I saw her rigid carriage was effort, not composure. Her face was flushed and beneath the defiantly crossed arms her chest was heaving.

"It's okay. It will pass," she said bravely.

"Ask for a recess," I told Devon. "The witness is ill."

"Juliana wants to go for it now," my lawyer replied urgently.

"I'd rather get it over with," Juliana said, breathing through her nose.

"What do you think?" I asked her mother.

"I've been told to let her make her own decisions," she said in a voice that was raw with self-pity.

Lynn was also wearing a suit, royal blue, and the two looked as if they should be lunching at Café Pinot, except for the obvious anger crackling between them that made it hard to imagine them even sitting at the same table. Despite her equanimity, Lynn was clutching the car keys so tightly her knuckles had turned pink.

"But she's sick," I protested.

"I'm not *sick*. It's just a panic reaction to being in a big room in front of people. It's a feeling, not a fact. The fact is, I'm safe. I'm safe here," Juliana repeated, apparently as she had been taught.

"Let's roll," said Devon, looking at his watch. "This judge likes to go home at four."

Juliana and her mother stood up.

"No," I said, "no. Thank you, but no."

"No, what?"

"I don't want Juliana to testify."

Devon, used to all manner of sudden turns, adroitly steered into the skid.

"I know how protective you feel of Juliana, and you've spoken very touchingly of your concern that she'll be further traumatized by going up there and talking to the judge—"

"She's in no shape to do this."

"She wants to. Don't you, Juliana?"

Juliana nodded, clutching a tiny black handbag in front of her, as if about to fall off her feet.

"Listen to what this young woman is telling you."

Devon stood with one hand on the round wire table to take the weight off his bad leg. The awkward posture thrust his upper body forward, made him look gracelessly eager.

"Do they know the prosecutor has a right to cross-examine?" I said. "Do they know he can question her about the rape? He'll make her relive it and he'll put the blame for being raped, for being kidnapped by Ray Brennan, on her."

"No," said Lynn, looking back and forth to Juliana. "Nobody told us that. What would that have to do with—"

"I am acting in your best interest." Devon's voice was raised, he was plenty steamed. "I am defending your freedom. That's what I do.

It's in your best interest to have Juliana on the stand, testifying on your behalf."

"And how you get her there doesn't matter?"

Devon spoke deliberately, sarcastically, annunciating every word: "She-says-she-can-do-it."

"She has no idea. You're putting her up against Mark Rauch? No," I said. "No way! He'll malign her character," turning back to Lynn, "so the judge won't take what she says seriously. I can't believe you weren't briefed on this! He'll make her look like a pot-smoking disenfranchised spoiled Westside kid looking for kicks who got in over her head. Who's been bullied into testifying by the big bad scary FBI agent and her lawyer. Maybe it will set her back, maybe it won't, but look, I shot the guy, there's no question that I shot him—"

"Shut up, Ana," said Devon County, former LAPD. "You're fucking yourself, excuse my language."

Juliana shrugged. Her mother looked confused.

"You'd rather go to trial?" asked Lynn, dubious. "Because, well, that's what Mr. County said. He said, if the judge thinks you shot this policeman for a not very good reason—you'll go to trial, right? And maybe go to jail."

A thousand replies sprung up at once. "I'll take that risk."

"We have to get back," interrupted Devon, grabbing his crutch and making for the glass doors. Awkwardly, he held them open, challenging us to follow. Only Lynn walked on ahead.

"Mom?" called Juliana, waiting uncertainly, holding on to the mini purse.

She turned. "It's up to you."

"Since when has anything ever been up to me?" Juliana catcalled back.

Lynn's lips compressed and her eyes were blinking rapidly.

"You told me to stay out of your life."

"Ladies?" Devon implored.

"He's talking to you," Lynn repeated, in a voice as jagged as a shard of glass, suddenly a weapon capable of cutting.

It seemed impossible this same woman had sat on the kitchen floor and wept for her lost daughter.

"Lynn," I asked, "what's going on?"

She straightened her back and fixed her sunglasses. But before she could reply, if she were going to reply, Juliana said, "My parents are getting a divorce."

The lazy sunshine, relaxed figures, polished fruit and chrome fittings on the espresso machine parked between two shaggy trees made a hopeful frame for an urban oasis, but it wasn't, really, not for these two. Where there had been connection, now there was emptiness. Where there had been a family with all its gnarly, snotty, tear-filled, heated, cleaving, lustful, playful, painfully shared aliveness, now we had disembodied individuals hurtling into space.

You see, the actions of Ray Brennan had caused this to happen to the Meyer-Murphy family.

We are drawn to the nexus of violence. Everybody's hot to reconstruct the crime scene—crawl inside the bore and ride the spiraling projectile; pilot the factors that brought so-and-so together with so-and-so at such-and-such a time and place. I have noticed small attention paid to the aftermath, the shock waves released into the human atmosphere, more deadly than the original event because they have a wider range; an infinite range, if you think about the physics.

"I am so sorry about your marriage, I cannot say."

"A long time coming," Lynn Meyer-Murphy sniffed.

"Mom?" said Juliana. "What should I do?"

"It's up to you," she repeated, tiredly this time. She was worn out by it and had nothing left. "I know you care for Ana and you want to help. That's very admirable. I'll support you. Whatever you want to do. I have a Xanax in my purse if you need it."

In response, Juliana raised her chin and marched toward the door that Devon County patiently still held open.

"No, I'm sorry," I said, "it's not for a fifteen-year-old to decide to put herself in harm's way," and stepped in front of Juliana and put my hands on hers. They were quivering with the tension of holding on to the purse.

"Please go home," I told her gently. "If you want to do something, do that for me."

Then I took her in my arms and told her that I loved her.

Upstairs, I put my forehead against the marble wall of the corridor, imploring Devon, "Why did you do that?"

"I came very close to firing you," he said.

"The feeling was mutual."

"Take it easy," he said, echoing my own words to Lynn the first day of the kidnapping: "We're only at the beginning."

It was like a doctor telling you there are only five rounds of chemotherapy ahead.

"This morning was pure hell, Devon."

"I know."

"And now I get to be beat up by that poser Kelsey Owen. She's nothing." I felt weak and close to tears as I thought of Juliana and her mother, already on the freeway, driving away in the silent depths of the limo, "Nothing."

"Owen? Your friend from the Bureau? She wasn't called."

I rolled my head off the wall. "She wasn't?"

"No."

"Then who is their final witness?"

It was Margaret Forrester, and she had dressed for the occasion, in a tight-waisted black suit, black sheer hose and heels. The suit was not new, it had wide shoulder pads, but she looked intriguingly attractive, thick brown hair framing her cheekbones and one of her more dramatic creations—a choker of pink shells and purple stones—breaking up the black. Her nails were red. She sat up straight. She was the Thunder Queen.

Andrew did not return to the courtroom after the break so he did not hear her testimony, although he certainly would know what she was going to say.

FORRESTER: My job entails a lot of responsibility. I'm the
widow of a police officer, and I have two small children at
home, so I have to be thinking about a lot of things all day
long. You have to be a "people person" and know a lot of
rules and procedures and the way a police station operates.

RAUCH: In your job as police liaison with the FBI you worked
with Special Agent Grey on the Santa Monica kidnapping. What was your experience?

FORRESTER: Difficult.

RAUCH: Difficult, how?

FORRESTER: She was demanding. Always wanting to do
things her way. She had no understanding of how hard it
is to do *my* job.

RAUCH: You've worked with FBI agents before.

FORRESTER: Yes.

RAUCH: Was Ana Grey any different?

FORRESTER: No offense to the *nice* people I've met at the
Bureau, but Miss Grey had a chip on her shoulder. She
thought she was better than you.

page 215

RAUCH: Was it common knowledge at the police station that
Ana Grey and Andrew Berringer were dating?

FORRESTER: I was shocked, but I wasn't surprised.

JUDGE: He's asking you if other people knew, not your personal reaction.

FORRESTER: Yes, Your Honor, it's a fishbowl, everybody
knows everything in a police department. I said I was

shocked because Detective Berringer is such a quiet guy, a guy's guy, and usually goes out with quiet women, but I wasn't *surprised* because I'd seen Miss Grey get her fingers into anything she wanted.

Cross-Examination   page 249

COUNTY: Mrs. Forrester, your late husband and Detective Berringer were good friends, correct?

FORRESTER: Best of buddies. They did everything together.

COUNTY: How was your husband killed, Mrs. Forrester?

FORRESTER: He was attacked by a gang.

COUNTY: And did you receive any payments on his death?

FORRESTER: He had life insurance.

COUNTY: What about his pension?

FORRESTER: We were denied any pension my husband accrued after eighteen years of service.

COUNTY: Why is that?

FORRESTER: They ruled that he did not die in the line of duty.

RAUCH: What is the purpose of this line of questioning?

COUNTY: The relationship between Detective Forrester and Detective Berringer goes to the attitude of this witness. Mrs. Forrester, did you have a sexual relationship with Detective Berringer?

FORRESTER: No! Of course not!

COUNTY: After your husband died?

FORRESTER: No.

JUDGE: Take it easy, Mrs. Forrester.

COUNTY: It would be understandable that you would seek comfort with someone who knew you well, almost as well as your husband.

RAUCH: He is berating this witness.

JUDGE: Go on.

COUNTY: Do you recall an incident in the parking lot of the police station during which you were very upset because of an altercation with a dry cleaner?

FORRESTER: He was extremely rude to me.

COUNTY: The dry cleaner was rude and you were angry and you encountered Ana Grey.

FORRESTER: I don't remember any of that.

COUNTY: You dropped your dry cleaning, and she picked it up. Do you remember the incident?

FORRESTER: I'm not sure.

COUNTY: Is it true in the parking lot, when you were very upset about the dry cleaner who told you never to come back to his shop, you told Ana Grey that Detective Berringer was sleeping with Officer Sylvia Oberbeck?

FORRESTER: I thought she should know. Anyway, like the other gentleman said, it was "common knowledge," I was not letting the cat out of the bag.

COUNTY: I see. You were only repeating what everybody knew.

FORRESTER: That's right.

COUNTY: And did you also tell Special Agent Grey what everybody knew, which was that after your husband died, you had an affair with Detective Berringer, and that he would ultimately leave her as he had left you?

FORRESTER: No! Absolutely not! That is an insult, you are attacking me, you are attacking me and nobody is doing anything about it.

JUDGE: We'll take a fifteen-minute recess.

COUNTY: Your Honor, I'm almost done, and then we can wrap it up for the day.

JUDGE: Do you think you can answer the questions, Mrs. Forrester?

COUNTY: Didn't you say to Ana Grey, of Andrew Berringer and Officer Oberbeck, "I slept with him before that bitch," or words to that effect?

JUDGE: Mrs. Forrester? Answer the question.

FORRESTER: She's lying, she's a liar, she is out to get me and I have no idea why.

COUNTY: Really? I think that statement should be reversed because, Mrs. Forrester, *aren't you the one who told the investigating officers Ana Grey shot Andrew Berringer? Aren't you the one who first pointed the finger at Ana Grey?*

FORRESTER: They asked if I had any thoughts on the subject.

COUNTY: You had "thoughts."

FORRESTER: Yes, I did.

COUNTY: But no facts.

FORRESTER: I knew.

COUNTY: Were you there at the time of the shooting?

FORRESTER: No.

COUNTY: Did you have any direct knowledge of the shooting?

FORRESTER: No, I didn't.

COUNTY: Then you couldn't *know*. You guessed, is that right? You conjectured. You wished. You were jealous. You wanted revenge because this big strapping handsome detective was finished with you, and his current squeeze was Ana Grey. You told the police not out of knowledge but spite, is that correct?

RAUCH: I'm sorry, we have to stop—

COUNTY: That doesn't make you a very objective source about Special Agent Grey's behavior, does it?

JUDGE: I think this witness has had enough, Mr. County.

We stood in the corridor. The upturned car was gone, and traffic was jammed up as usual in the late afternoon. Devon's cell kept ringing and he kept ignoring it. The two other attorneys were talking on their phones down the hall.

"The prosecution's case was overwhelming," I said. "The judge did not buy ours."

"Don't worry, the jury will. This was just practice."

"*Practice!*"

"We know a lot more about their witnesses. We know how Andrew comes across in the courtroom—"

One of the young attorneys interrupted in a hurry. "Devon? Breaking news."

"What's up?"

"They found a body."

I almost laughed. This, after all, was the criminal defense attorney's gruesome stock and trade. Bodies here, bodies there. Must mean another client!

"Teenage girl," he was saying, "in a park in Mar Vista. The crime scene guy is saying sexual assault."

The door to the courtroom opened slowly, and Judge McIntyre and his twin came out and our little group stepped back.

"Good evening, Judge," said Devon, and his associates echoed the courtesy.

"Good evening," said the judge. Dressed in street clothes now, he looked like any number of anonymous older men who wear hats and go about their business with a certain air, a burden of knowledge, that says they may have had experiences that belong to a different time and place, but they have understood those experiences in a way that we, still in the midst of life, have not.

Slowly, Judge McIntyre led his twin by the hand. His brother, it was now apparent from the lopsided shuffle and darting eyes, was mentally retarded and needed guidance through the world.

Twenty - two.

The river oaks had been planted in two rows, shading a dirt
road that still ran along the far reaches of the park. Their
slender trunks all tilted in the same direction, and the shape
of their foliage was vertical and tall; as if once upon a time a family of
gnomes fleeing an evil wind had become frozen in flight, and their
stubby legs had been turned into tree trunks and their tangled masses
of hair into leaves whooshing fearfully up.

It was spooky, this dark grove at the edge of the playing fields, out
near an old white stucco wall long covered with tents of ivy. Blown
leaves and granular red dirt had accumulated near the foot of the wall,
forming a dry mulch thick enough to dig through, unlike the hard-
packed earth of the baseball diamond whose backstop sat at the edge
of the oak shadow.

A six-year-old boy chasing a foul ball had discovered the victim
between the trees and the wall. In this narrow space, the killer could
have worked unobserved all night. When the crime scene folks carted
the leaves away, shovel marks were visible like uniform bites around the

edge of the grave. The killer was meticulous. He had come prepared—
yet the grave was shallow, as if meant to be discovered. This showed
ambivalence about the death. The clothed body was curled on its side
in a green trash bag that did not quite reach over the head, so long
thick brown hair extruded in a bunch. The hair was the oddity that
caught the boy's attention, visible through the leaves. He had thought
it was the tail of a dead animal, encrusted with flies and blood.

Her name was Arlene Harounian, sixteen years old. From the condition of the body the coroner estimated she had been dead four days.
She lived in a worn-down working-class city called Inglewood, about
six miles from the park, an hour bus ride and a world away from
Laurel West Academy and the Third Street Promenade. The father
reported her missing, and a detective, already working three homicides, had been assigned to the case. Arlene had been especially beautiful, with dark tanned skin that added to her exotic look, a wide
smile and confident, infectious energy. She was a popular honor student with a 4.0 grade-point average, who also played basketball and
ran track, described by friends as "independent" and "a person who
knew what she wanted, which was to go to college and make a difference." Newspaper photos showed grief-stricken classmates hugging
one another on the steps of the high school. Arlene had been the kind
of kid who could recharge a cynical, burned-out teacher just by walking into the room.

Everyone on my legal team had the same thought: What if Arlene
Harounian were another victim of Ray Brennan? Although there was
no obvious link between them, she and Juliana Meyer-Murphy were
similar in age and appearance, and the coroner was talking sexual
assault. If the two were connected, her death could yield important
facts that might have bearing on the charges against me. I was hoping
it *was* Brennan just so we could nail him. That is the warped agony of
the serial crimes investigator: sometimes the only way to move forward is for the offender to do it again.

While Devon's office pursued their sources, I pounded Jason Ripley with e-mails and phone messages until finally he agreed to meet in the park where the body had been found.

It was a Saturday, ten days after the crime scene had been released, which meant the tennis courts were busy and slow-pitch softball games back in play. Jason could have been another gangly new dad coming through the crowded picnic area in which every table held a different multiethnic birthday party, scrawny ficus trees enveloped by a haze of smoking hamburgers and roasting skewers of yakitori and chorizo.

When we made eye contact, instead of breaking into the usual shy-but-eager grin, Jason ducked his head deeper under the bill of his cap.

"How's it going?" he asked somberly.

"It's going."

"Sorry for your troubles."

I nodded. He put a running shoe up on the seat of the picnic table, and we stood there awkwardly. What I really wanted was a big soft hug.

"So," rubbing his farmer's freckled hands together, "how can I help?"

I squinted over the acres of playing fields to the small, twisted procession of river oaks and what had been hidden there, diagonally across from tables full of toddlers reaching eagerly for birthday cake.

"Let's take a walk."

Jason glanced at the site uneasily. "I've got to get back to the office, got a ton of three-oh-twos."

"Sure," I said, surprised to feel how much his terseness stung. "What are we getting from the lab?"

"In terms of what?"

"Cause of death?"

"Haven't gotten the autopsy results."

"Why not?"

"Backed up, as usual."

"Give me a break, it's a high-profile case."

"All I can tell you is what they tell me."

"I like it," nodding with mock approval. "Where did you learn to put on the spin?"

Jason reddened.

"Okay, then, what's the buzz? No reason we can't gossip, talk about what you're hearing in the halls."

"The buzz is sexual assault."

"Any links to Brennan?"

"Nothing confirmed."

"If there were," I asked with a tight smile, "would you tell me?"

"Ana, you know, I'm kind of in a tough position here."

"Where? Who's listening?"

An ice cream truck had backed into the picnic area piping idiotic circus music over and over.

"I just can't . . ." His lips curled in against his teeth, a sign of refusal if there ever was one. "I just . . ."

"You feel disloyal because you're talking to me? About our own case?"

"It's not exactly your case," he muttered, "or mine, really, anymore—"

"I'm only on suspension."

"But if you go to trial . . ."

"If I go to trial that's another deal, but meanwhile, girls are getting murdered and what the hell is the Bureau doing about it? That's what I want to know. What is the status? Because I learned from experience that when the lead agent doesn't keep the pressure on, the whole thing evaporates. So is anyone still tracking Brennan? Is anyone going to put this case next to the Santa Monica kidnapping and the hits we got in VICAP—Washington, Florida and Texas—or, when there's *another* sexually assaulted body of a teenage girl, am I going to spend the rest of my life pacing around Mike Donnato's kitchen like some demented bride of Frankenstein, saying, *I told you so?*"

Jason laughed. "You're a real character, you know that?"

"It's not about me, it's about the Bureau. You want to be loyal to the Bureau, help me keep working this case, because all indications are this guy is into a cycle of repeating."

"We don't even know if it's Brennan," Jason began.

I found myself rubbing my face all over with my fingertips, like putting on cold cream or taking off a mask.

"So why did you come here? To tell me you can't tell me anything?"

"I came because I like you," he blurted. Then, "I don't know what went on with you and your boyfriend—I'm just hoping it all works out for you in the end."

"And . . . ?"

"And . . . nothing."

He was leaning one forearm on the bent knee that was up on the table, looking at me sideways, trying to hide behind the green sunglasses.

I waited.

"They want you to back off," he said finally. "They want you to go away. You shot a cop, no matter what the circumstances." He added quickly, "You're a problem, and they want it gone."

"Is this a message from Rick?"

"I'm just trying to explain why I can't share information. I know you care a thousand percent, but until your court case is resolved— and believe me, everyone is pulling for you—it's just too political."

The guise was gone, as Jason seemed to vent on behalf of the whole field office. "We've got so much shit coming down. Bank robberies are up, the spy scandal, the 'alleged terrorist' who died in custody, the 'misplaced' assault rifles—how could that happen? Hackers busting into our secure files. Everywhere you look, the Bureau is taking another hit."

"Can we get away from this clown music?" I said of the ice cream truck. "It's driving me nuts."

The young agent straightened up. "I've got to get back to the office."

I put my bag on my shoulder.

"What about Brennan?"

"Brennan is over," Jason said firmly. "We recovered the victim of the Santa Monica kidnapping," holding up a hand to stop my protest. "That was our job. We did our job. If the locals want our cooperation, cool, but it's their homicide. That's how the brass sees it."

"How do you see it?"

Jason shrugged. "I feel for you. I feel for the girl. It's hard."

"You know, we're about ten blocks from Brennan's apartment," I said after a little while. "I drove through the neighborhood on the way over. Strange mix. You've got the old abandoned houses, the apartment buildings . . . I'd love to talk to Mrs. Santos after this," nodding toward the oak trees. "See how safe she feels right now for Roxy."

Jason's foot thumped, but he did not take the bait. He was changing. I had actually watched him change, that was the amazing thing, like all the new agents who come in looking like Clark Kent until they realize all those other Clark Kents are getting in the way. The ginger-haired little boy had grown up.

"Remember what we talked about? Proving yourself?" I asked. "It's hard these days, even knowing how. What's important? What's political? Are you the good son who's loyal to the organization, or do you go out on a limb for what you believe? Don't worry about it, Jason. Either way, you've got a great career ahead of you. Two different paths, is all."

"That's not *at all* a fair evaluation," he called after me.

I walked toward the parking lot, past an empty swimming pool and a brand-new roller-hockey rink. It must have been a youth league tournament because the bleachers were filled with cheering parents on their feet with fervor and excitement; the high protective mesh strung with red, white and blue balloons.

I s this Dr. Arnie, the mad magician of Fullerton? Hi! It's Ana Grey!"

I was lounging at the white umbrella table in Mike Donnato's backyard, sipping a mint-flavored *mojito,* which I had fashioned from a recipe in the *LA Times,* the morning sun just creeping across the deck.

Hip, all right.

"Ana," said the lab director, "I've been meaning to get back to you."

"No problemo. I know you're under it."

"*Hello?* Am I talking to the real Ana Grey, or is this a clone? The *nice* clone, who doesn't put your testicles in the wringer the minute you don't have an answer in twenty-four seconds?"

"Am I really that bad?"

"On a good day. On a *bad* day, you don't want to know from it."

"Speak to me of shoe prints."

"Don't you love shoe prints?"

"I do," wondering if they were drinking *mojitos* over at the crime lab, too. Maybe everybody was. The entire Southland. Starting around breakfast. They contain lime juice, a good source of vitamin C. "Did you recover any shoe prints from the homicide in Mar Vista?"

"Of course we got shoe prints. What do you think, we're *incompetent?*"

"What size?"

He clicked computer keys. "Ten."

"Like Ray Brennan."

"*Your* guy, Brennan?"

I could hear the surprise. "Is it a match?"

More anxious clicks. "The problem is, the outsoles are different and we couldn't get the wear characteristics off the impression on the skin of that first rape victim. It was a herringbone pattern from a tennis shoe we recovered in the park."

"But the same size?"

"Correct. And, obviously, he asphyxiated her, wasn't that the ritual?"

"He did? The new victim?"

"Where have you been?"

"Out of town."

I had called Dr. Arnie on the odds that news of my preliminary hearing situation had not yet reached Fullerton. Propellerheads live in a parallel universe from ours; parallel to most.

"We sent a full report to the Bureau last week."

"Last *week*?"

"Sometimes we do our job."

Jason's look came back to me, the averted eyes behind the green lenses.

"But you're not prepared to say it's Brennan?"

"Not conclusively. Look, I'm sure it's all up on Rapid Start."

"I'm not in the office."

"Want me to fax our report to you?"

"You're an angel."

I placed the glass with the spent mint leaves in the water and watched it float.

Three hundred tiny lights from three hundred candles grew brighter as the sun sank behind the gymnasium building. The memorial service of Arlene Harounian was held late on a cloudy afternoon in the football field of the high school, where a stage had been outfitted with microphones and floral arrangements. The stage was big enough to hold the school orchestra, which played with heartbreaking finesse. The kids were good. They had accomplished something.

Silently they stood and carried their instruments off and the madrigal singers filed to the microphones, like everyone else wearing ordinary teenage grunge, boot-cut jeans and wind pants and baggies and T-shirts, underdressed for the gathering chill. It had been sunny in the morning. The few dozen grown-ups there, old enough to have read the weather report, came wrapped in scarves and winter coats.

The singers lofted into "Ave Maria," and I began rooting around in the pockets of my leather jacket for tissues. Man, why was I there? To tap into that spring of grief that ran underground, seemingly always just beneath my feet? There must be a river of sadness below the pavement of our cities. One after the other, for at least the past hour, friends and teachers had stood at the podium and universally described Arlene Harounian as a girl with unusual promise, whose smile "lit up the world," who "wanted you to feel better." White doves were released and her basketball jersey retired. The team showed it to us from the stage, horribly laid out flat inside a frame.

Her parents sat on folding chairs with the other siblings and did not speak. The father had a wild head of madly blowing black hair and big teeth that snapped shut like a nutcracker into a stupefied smile. The littlest sister read a poem Arlene had written in seventh grade called "I Am," which they printed in the program: *I am purple sunsets / I am the sick child who wonders why / I am a bell / I am a big sister who sometimes wants to be a little baby / I am a leaf . . .*"

A history teacher called for the study of nonviolence, a boy played a keyboard solo. Two girls holding each other for support took turns recounting how fine-looking Arlene was, but how practical about her gifts. She had determined to become a model in order to pay for college. They wanted to be models, too, but she was the one who actually went out and had a portfolio made. It was dark by then. The little paper cups on the end of the candles, which sheltered the flames from the wind, glowed in the evening like homespun orange lamps. My fingers were caked with melted wax from turning the candle to keep it alive. Here and there the cups would catch on fire and be stomped out. Nobody giggled. A screen had been raised, and someone clicked a laptop, and we were watching a montage of slides and rap songs that told us all about Arlene Harounian's life, from a dark-haired tyke on a bicycle to a confident young woman in a lacy cutoff top holding on to a tree and arching her back, but whose look into the camera said, *I'm in charge, not you.*

Then it was as if that kid with the keyboard had come back for an encore, ringing out chords of dissonance and rage. I sat up straighter and straighter, as if the conviction growing inside would fill the stadium, as if everybody must know, as I knew then, that the amateur modeling photos we were looking at on the screen were the work of Ray Brennan. All the loveliness of Arlene swirled like a crescendo of discordant notes into an artifact not of her, but of what had taken her, and that was the greatest injustice of all.

E ven before I reached my car, the cell phone was ringing.

"The judge handed down his decision," Devon said.

I did not even hold my breath.

"The judge is holding you to answer. He has found reasonable suspicion that you committed this crime, and you are held to answer for attempted murder." He paused. "Ana?"

"We're going to trial," I repeated.

"No surprise," Devon rolled on smoothly. "We expected this. We've heard their witnesses, and now we punch holes in every single one. It's clear Andrew Berringer was lying. And I have investigators going after Margaret Forrester, there's obviously a screw loose there. You'll be happy to know Mark Rauch has already come back and asked the judge to raise bail."

"On what basis?"

"Now that you know you're facing trial, you're supposedly a greater flight risk. It's a bogus argument, of course—"

"Devon?" I said calmly. "I'm fairly certain of the fact that Ray Brennan killed Arlene Harounian. The girl who was found in the park. She was his most recent victim, and I'm sure there are more. Let me call you back."

I stood unconcerned in the middle of the parking lot as cars zigzagged and honked. In the stadium they were taking down the screen and carrying off the floral arrangements. The father had stepped down, clutching his wife's hand. Awkwardly tucked beneath his other arm was a basketball signed by the team.

Brennan had photographed both Juliana and Arlene. He had posed them the same way, according to his own ritualized and private reasons, holding on to a tree with their butts sticking out. The photo of Juliana we had up in the command center was identical to this one, of Brennan's latest victim.

Juliana looked scared.

Arlene looked assured.

I had found stillness.

Twenty-three.

If I were working the case, I would jump all over the photography angle. I would show Ray Brennan's picture to everyone in Arlene Harounian's life until we could pinpoint how and where they met. I would redraw Brennan's "hunting field" to a twenty-five-square-mile grid on the map in the command center—west to Culver City, south to Manhattan Beach—and all the eager new agents would say, *Ahhhhh.*

But I was not working the case. I had been held to answer, and the trial was coming now like a pair of headlights when your power steering has died. A sense of fatalism replaced whatever moxie I had felt in court. Devon might wave his crutch, but nothing would stop Mark Rauch's head-on prosecution now.

Also, the story broke in the papers: *FBI AGENT TO STAND TRIAL IN LOVE SHOOTING—Veteran Agent Ana Grey Allegedly Wounded Police Detective Boyfriend in Marina Del Rey Apartment.* As my lawyer kept reminding me, the slightest violation of bail would be a public relations jackpot for the other side.

I returned to the prison of the hobby room, with the brown carpeting that had the flat cracked nap of an old sheep and smelled like an old sheep, and sat on the checked sofa and stared at the empty fireplace. We had lost our motion to prevent cameras in the courtroom. The trial would be televised, and after that, even if the verdict were not guilty, my career would be over. The Bureau did not deal in damaged goods.

There was no longer a reason to leave the house or even get dressed. Aside from a call or two from the law firm every day, I would sit on the couch in my pajamas and make obsessive checklists concerning the Santa Monica kidnapping. I would meditate on Brennan's watery picture over the mantle, then reconstruct the assaults on Arlene and Juliana, noting time and date, location of the victims, method, physical evidence, laboratory findings, and make spiderlike diagrams showing possible connections between Brennan, Arlene and Juliana.

There was one promising link. The lab report faxed by Dr. Arnie said tiny chips had been found in Arlene's hair—the same sandwich of floral wallpaper between two layers of old paint that had collected in Juliana's clothes. Both girls had been taken to the same 1940s-era house "in a loamy area near the coast."

The link that did *not* make sense was that one of the girls was dead.

Killing the victim did not fit Brennan's known pattern. He had wounded the ducks; strangled Juliana to the point of unconsciousness and let her go. Why? Guilt? Torture? Ambivalence? Another clue was the grave. If he had meant to hide the body, he would have done that. If he had meant to show it off, he would have done that, too. This was hasty and halfhearted—maybe, I scribbled, because it was not part of the plan. Perhaps she had asphyxiated accidentally during the sex act. His ritual is interrupted. Suddenly, he finds himself not in control of the game. He swallows the rage and reverts to his military training—a quick burial, leave 'em by the trail, go on to accomplish the mission.

That compulsive drive—to finish the act at all costs—might prove stronger than the intelligence that had protected him so far, the canniness that had allowed him to set up his victims (it could be dozens, including those from back east, never put together by local law enforcement because he would move out of their territories—attack and withdraw to safety).

He would be overwhelmed by the uncontrollable need to find another girl.

Now.

Who could I tell? Who would listen? All connections with the Bureau had been stripped. There were no more encouraging e-mails; hell, nobody even returned my calls. When it was announced that we were going to trial, Galloway must have come down hard. I couldn't talk to Mike. For weeks we had stalked around each other in the confines of the house, avoiding mention of the case. He was my final sanctuary. I would not put him in a position of disloyalty now.

It was about two in the morning and I was awake, as usual, barreling through an old Donald L. Westlake mystery, dug up from the dad's side of the hobby room, although not even a hilarious band of thieves could distract for long. I put the book down and finally, with restless despair, threw open the white cabinet that had been standing as an enigma all this time amongst the old possessions of Mike's parents. Inside was a jewel box of sewing notions: a hundred rolls of thread lined up in rainbow order on hooks set in Peg-Board. There were drawers of bobbins, scissors, glue and markers. Scraps of crocheting and spools of ribbon, each in their places; a clear box just for Christmas glitter and felt.

Here was a marriage. Mike's dad had built this cabinet for his mom, I was sure. He had made a place for her pleasure and her work, and she had done her work, and there were the garments, hanging on a rack—half-made blouses with the patterns still pinned. I sat down on the rancid carpet and allowed myself to become lost, handling old cellophane packets of bindings (twenty-five cents each), unrolling silver lace, finding peace, like an orphan, in the fairy-tale world of the phantom parents. It scarcely mattered whose parents they were, so deep was the yearning to be comforted. I dug into the cool layers of the button bin, letting them sift through my fingers like stories.

Then, emboldened, I pulled out a drawer in the sagging file cabi-

net that held the trout-fishing magazines. Burrowing into the one spot
in the left side of the couch that still had spring, in the light of the fat
brown-shaded lamp, I studied yet another watercolor rendering of a
steelhead trout. Over and over these magazines showed the trophy,
and it was always the same trophy. And what about those hours tying
flies beneath the magnifying glass, only to have most of them, *and* the
trophy, lost? What could I, as an investigator, learn from this?

I went back to the fishing magazines. Then I discovered that hidden
behind them, way back in the file drawer, was a pile of *Playboy*s dating from the sixties. The top cover (Miss February) was coated with a
perfect layer of dust, as if the secret stash had lain untouched for thirty
years.

Miss February's interests were "tennis and kittens." For the center-
fold, she wore a G-string sewn with tiny hearts and stroked a white
fluffy cat. She had enormous pinkish breasts that barely fit on the page.
She'd be a grandmother now. What I loved most were the one-inch
ads in the back of the magazine that whispered to the anxieties of the
male psyche: *"Helps you overcome false teeth looseness and worry"*;
"Bill Problems?"; *"A Timely Message to the Man with Hernia"*; *"How
to Speak and Write Like a College Graduate"*—and a classic pictorial
essay on "Favorite Valentine's Day Gifts," featuring Playboy bunnies
and red satin sheets. Then I saw the photo credit.

There was a soft knock on the door.

"Come in."

It was Mike.

"Saw the light on, so I thought . . ."

He handed me a cup of milk and a bag of chocolate chip cookies
with macadamia nuts.

I said, "Wow."

"What are you doing?"

"Snooping into your parents' lives. Did you know your dad read
Playboy?"

Mike took the magazine looking somewhat confused.

"Am I shattering your illusions?"

He broke into a grin. "God bless the old man."

"Look who took the pictures," I said excitedly, pointing to the photo credit. "Hugh Akron."

"*Our* Hugh Akron?"

"Got to be. Do you think he'd want to have this?"

"What? This magazine?"

"For his personal collection."

"Sure, if he wants to buy it, the slimy tea bag. He ripped me off for Lakers tickets. The *scalpers* were selling them for less."

"How does a creep like Hugh Akron get girls to take off their clothes?"

Mike was lost in the magazine.

"Where does he find them?" I went on. "These cute twenty-year-old girls? You know, he still does this stuff? Cheesecake, on the Internet. Did he ever show you?"

Mike abstractedly shook his head. "Uh-uh."

I dipped a chocolate chip cookie in the cup and sucked out the milk. "My grandfather read *Playboy*. Those were the days when they put centerfolds up at the police station."

Mike lowered the magazine and kind of nodded, as if he had been only half listening. He was wearing plaid cotton flannel pants; mine were the same navy blue skivvies from Quantico I'd had on for days. I pulled the sweater close around my chest. As he stood there unmoving, I became uncomfortably aware of both our sex parts loose inside our pajama bottoms.

"Would you mind listening to something?"

"Sure."

He fished a microcassette from his pocket and flickered it in the air.

"From the answering machine. The one in the hallway," he insisted. "Right when you come in the door."

I nodded, wondering why the location of the answering machine was important at two in the morning.

He sat down on the opposite side of the couch and fitted the cassette into a small tape recorder.

"*Wacko bitch. Why didn't you take a two-by-four and do a Sam Shepard, do something to yourself big-time? If you had the guts, you'd shoot yourself with a service revolver and claim you wrestled the gun away. You could strangle yourself and leave marks. If you had the guts. Do you have the guts?*"

"Who is that?"

"I don't know."

The tape chattered along on fast-forward.

"*I saw you in the courtroom. I thought you looked at me kind of hot. I'm up for anything, sweetheart, and I know you can show me the way. Do you think I have ulterior motives? I don't have ulterior motives. Ask me if I do. I'd love to hear your sexy voice . . .*"

Eventually it clicked off.

"How many are there?"

"Seven."

"*Seven?*"

"Now they're coming two times a day."

"Did you put a trap on the phone?"

"I will, but they won't call again."

"Why not?"

"They know that's exactly what I'm going to do. These are cops, Ana. This is intimidation."

It was late, my brain running slow. "Andrew's homies, you think?"

He shrugged. "Got to be someone who knows where you are and how to get an unlisted number."

"Screw them."

"Right, except that Ian"—referring to his middle boy, aged ten—"took that message off the machine."

Chocolate burst inside my mouth, the last taste of bittersweet.

"I am so sorry, Mike."

"I have to ask you to leave."

The world stopped then. I tried to nestle deeper into the arm of the couch.

Mike said, "I'm sorry. This is just too close to home."

I nodded, stunned. My only thought was, *I will go to jail.*

"Is it Rochelle?"

He admitted, "She's upset."

"I hope I haven't—"

"No, no," he said quickly. "Nothing to do with that."

He stayed on his side of the sofa. We looked away with embarrassment at what had been left behind a long time ago, when we were partners chasing bandits.

"You've gone way beyond the call of duty as it is."

His eyes filmed and so did mine. He was a decent man, trying to do the decent thing. "We'll figure out another place for you to go," he promised.

"Depends if Devon can renegotiate release terms and conditions."

We were silent. There had been a moment, when his marriage went bad, I had thought it would be Mexico. Lobsters and tequila and an endless beach.

"I can't tell you how sorry I am. I've been up thinking about it," he said.

"Family is family," I replied on cue. "I love your kids, I don't want them exposed to this crap."

Suddenly Mike stood and ripped down Ray Brennan's picture.

"Hey!" I said.

"*This* is crap! I don't want it in my house!"

"You're right," I said, taking the crumpled photo from his hand. "This is bad, bad, toxic stuff. We can't let it contaminate your family."

He gestured helplessly.

"The problem is, this guy kills girls. I know he did the one who was found in the park."

Mike rubbed his hair. "Which one who was found in the park?"

His ignorance of the latest murder confirmed what Jason said: the Bureau had dropped the case.

"Another victim, named Arlene Harounian. She was asphyxiated, possibly during the sex act. Ray Brennan took her picture, just like Hugh Akron takes pictures of girls, promises them modeling careers—"

"You have to give this up."

"I know Brennan photographed both victims. The question is, where? How does he find them? How does he get them to pose? Because, I'm telling you, he's going to take another girl."

"Jesus Christ," said Mike suddenly. "I have to be up in three hours."

I told him I would be out by the weekend.

The next day Mike called from the office.

"Hugh Akron says there's a thing called photo swap meets. They have them every two weeks, at different locations around southern California. They're like swap meets, where photographers and models get together. It's supposed to be legit. He says that's where he goes to meet models, and he'd be pleased to take me along."

"You declined."

"There's an organization."

Mike gave me the website.

I understood that it was a parting gift.

```
Subj: RE: PHOTO DAY
From:moose@sunshinephotoclub
To: 70Barracuda@hotmail.com


Dear Ana,
    Don't call it a "swap meet," we are not a
"swap meet," since "swap meets" are places
where photographers trade and sell camera
equipment. No shooting is done at a "swap
meet." Our club sponsors Photo Days, which are
actual photo shoots, for photographers and mod-
els. Are you interested in modeling? The female
```

```
models are admitted free. All of our models are
female, as men don't like to take pictures of
other men. Our next Photo Day is this Sunday.
Click on the link. It's a lot of fun. I would
like to welcome you personally. Please provide
a physical description of yourself.
```

This would be one of those subcultures where you'd want to put on rubber gloves before typing a reply.

I downloaded the Sunshine Photo Club's calendar of events. Counting back every Sunday for two months, I got to the week of Juliana's abduction. There was a Photo Day scheduled that Sunday in Veterans Park. Juliana had been taken the following Tuesday. She had never mentioned a photo shoot. She did not say she wanted to be a model. If the theory was that Brennan stalked these shoots, why had he been trolling the Promenade?

I flipped back through my personal calendar and noted that was the weekend when Andrew and I were supposed to ride his Harley in a police fund-raiser. But we did not ride the Harley because it had rained. It was raining all weekend. It had rained the weekend before.

I had gone swimming in the pool in the rain.

The police fund-raiser had been canceled.

The photo shoot was undoubtedly canceled, too.

Ray Brennan was hungry. His pattern had been disrupted and he had to look outside his comfort zone.

The Promenade was not his hunting field. We had been misled by our own assumptions. Juliana had not been the pattern. She had been the *exception to the pattern.*

I dug out the crumpled program for Arlene Harounian's memorial service, which was still inside my jacket pocket. The two girls who had spoken about Arlene wanting to be a model were listed in the order of events as *Remembering Arlene by Jane Latsky and Muriel Fletcher.*

Directory assistance gave me four Latskys in the area. I told young Jane I was a reporter for a local paper and wanted to know if her friend Arlene had ever attended a photo day.

Yes, said the girl, all the time. Once in a park in Manhattan Beach.

The next upcoming photo day, according to the website, would take place in a Japanese tea garden in Glendale.

They couldn't bust me for going to a park on a sunny day.

Twenty-four.

The Japanese tea garden was located in a recreation center in Glendale, at the end of a palm-lined street in a neighborhood of nicely landscaped older cottages. The park was tucked up against the Verdugo Mountains, in a shady oasis that included a public library. A table had been set up, blocking the Shinto gate. You had to sign in.

"I'm looking for Moose," I told the wiry fellow on guard.

"Who's *Moose*?"

"One of the organizers."

"*I'm* the organizer," he claimed. He was about fifty, rugged, too-tanned features and shoulder-length hair, wearing a water bottle belt and short shorts to show off his developed legs—one of those deeply California characters whose past would probably read like a parody of West Coast fads: hot tub installer, dope dealer, surfer, yoga teacher.

"Moose said he'd be here."

There was a beat of numbskull silence, and then a mountainous person who had been standing nearby said in a deep announcer's voice, "I'm Moose."

"Great!" shaking his hand enthusiastically. "Just as great as you said it would be."

So was he. About six foot four, three hundred pounds.

"See, we're fenced in here," said Moose, indicating the manicured garden. "No looky-loos."

"Are all these photographers full-time professionals?"

"Amateurs. The word for this is amateurs," he admitted reluctantly and sighed.

"They all have other jobs?"

"Like me. I have another job."

"What's your line of work?"

"Cleaning supplies."

"Ahh. So, Moose, how do you become a member?"

"The models get in free. The photographers pay twenty dollars at the door."

I had seen them in the parking lot unpacking their equipment, overweight middle-aged men wearing fishing hats and elaborate vests with dozens of pockets. Some were sporting lenses the size of the Mount Palomar telescope, others had tiny digitals. Half were white, half Asian, and they all seemed to know one another in the forgiving, easygoing way of hobbyists.

"Anybody can walk in here with twenty dollars and a camera?"

"We are totally legal," interjected Mr. California. "We have never had an incident. Who are you?"

"She just wants to look around," mumbled Moose.

Mr. California became distracted by trouble with a barbeque and I took the opportunity to lose myself in the strangely peaceful garden. I had already picked up flyers for other photo days from other clubs and saw there was a circuit. You could find one of these shoots every weekend at some public location somewhere in the Southland. Although that expanded Brennan's hunting field considerably, it brought the comfort of a plan: I would go to every single shoot. I would show Brennan's picture to everybody there. If someone turned up a credible lead, I would pursue whomever I had to pursue, at the Bureau or the local level, I didn't care, in order to set up surveillance for the next time Brennan showed. I would do this meticulously, until my trial was over, until the last appeals were spent, until they put me in jail.

The photographers lumbered slowly and with prerogative along the winding paths, while the female models—young made-up faces bright as flowers—waited under the ginkgo trees, with their mothers, to be picked. They were all picked. This was a dance where everybody danced. Someone would position a girl and half a dozen men would shoot over his shoulder, paparazzo-style.

"Give me that laugh again!"

"Would you guys mind if I moved her into the shade?"

For twenty bucks you could get a sixteen-year-old to bend over a pagoda and stick out her butt.

It was supposed to be clean family fun. A young lady with seductive eyebrows, wearing a cheap strapless evening dress, was wrapping and unwrapping a shawl around her body, liking the attention, while a bunch of sad sacks stood around snapping. One of them, who wore a dirty baseball cap and a big bushy beard, slipped her a pair of mirrored sunglasses and shyly asked that she put them on.

I could picture Hugh Akron, all right. He would ace these geezers, a pro amongst the clueless. Ray Brennan? He'd do just fine, sidewinding through the innocent façade. And Arlene Harounian thought she could handle anything.

If I had my credentials, I could have worked the situation in fifteen minutes. As it was, all I could do was saunter around smiling and engaging folks in casual conversation, asking if they'd seen the man in the photo, using the ruse that Ray Brennan owed me some prints, occasionally taking a picture with my Ricoh to look authentic, but I was the only woman with a camera and kept getting apprehensive looks from the moms. I was not liking civilian status one bit.

"Photo day is a handy place to test out your technique," a retired engineer named George told me.

"Great to test your equipment," added his friend, who had an automatic camera with no settings.

"Do the models and photographers get to know each other?" I asked dully.

"Oh no, not at all," insisted George. "This is a very safe place. There's no direct contact. We only go by first names. We e-mail their pictures to them, but usually to a friend's computer. You have to be careful."

"In this day and age," intoned his pal.

They were gray in the face with thin sloping shoulders, wearing closely related plaid shirts.

"I'm looking for Ray," showing the picture once again. "Met him out in Riverside," another location on the circuit. "Ray Brennan? Or he could be using another name."

Like everybody else, they shook their heads. By now there were maybe fifty hobbyists and half as many models clustered in little groups near flowering trees and stone shrines. It was becoming sultry and humid in the tea garden. Maybe that is why the photographers were moving so languorously. Or perhaps they were all about to drop dead.

No, wait, there was some excitement by the pond, where a narrow girl in a red cowboy hat, short denim jacket and low-riding jeans was placing one red high heel on the lower rung of a bridge, causing a reaction amongst the photographers like goldfish to crumbs.

"Smile, honey! *Pose!*" shouted a strained woman's voice.

"Are you the mom?"

Of course she was the mom, who else would have laid out a blanket piled with head shots?

She looked not much older than her daughter, ruddy face, wide at the hips, an infant over one shoulder, a toddler wearing a butterfly costume prancing along the path.

Like they said: family.

"I'm Sonoma's mother," she said self-importantly. "Sonoma has her own website."

She gave me a card. Her nails were long and white and sparkled. The only sparkly thing about her.

"I tell my girls, use your looks while you have them. You won't have them forever."

The butterfly had scrambled onto a rock, hands clasped to her chin, flashing a demented smile at a guy with a mustache and a tripod.

"You don't mean the little one," I couldn't help saying. "Losing your looks at three?"

"Oh no," said the mother, "Sonoma and Bridget. That's what I say to *them.*"

She pointed with the toe of her running shoe at the glossies on the blanket. Sonoma was blonde. Bridget had long dark hair, like Juliana's. There were dozens of shots of them in halters and short skirts. It made you appreciate actual models.

"Bridget is Sonoma's sister?"

"Eighteen months apart. I have to be careful they don't get competitive. They like to dress the same, but I tell them, you should each develop your own look."

"The cowgirl look."

"They do it different every time. They love it," she assured me. "We all the time go on a shopping spree before we come to one of these."

It turned out they lived in the desert, three hours away. The drive was no problem. This was, according to her, how the actress Heather Locklear got started.

"Last week Bridget earned a hundred fifty dollars."

"Really?"

"Through an agency on the Internet. They get paid twenty-five dollars an hour, two hours minimum. I make sure I'm always at the photo shoot," she said firmly. "And it has to be nonglamour, not lingerie."

"Is Bridget here?"

"No, she's working with one of the gentlemen."

I looked around for another doll in a cowboy hat.

"Where?"

"She went with him for a little while," the mom explained, shifting the infant to the other shoulder.

"Where did they go?"

"To his studio."

"You said you're always present at a photo shoot."

My heartbeat had kicked up to a hundred thirty.

"I am," she said haughtily, "but I have the babies."

I was angry enough to nail her to a tree. She never went on shoots. And you know Bridget never got the hundred fifty bucks; it's how mom kept the girls tied up inside her own spandex dreams.

"Is this the photographer?"

The lady peered at Ray Brennan's picture.

"That kind of looks like him, but this man's name is Jack."

"Kind of, or *is* it? He might have changed his hair color, or his facial hair. He's six feet tall, weighs about two hundred, in good shape."

I might not have the creds, but I had the attitude, and it was rattling her.

"Let me ask Sonoma."

I stood there, knowing. It was like suddenly being encased in ice.

Sonoma minced over, walking on toes to keep the high heels from sinking into the sweating grass. She was the older one, not so pretty close up.

"What is the problem, Mom?" she snapped, looking at the picture. "That's Jack. Who else would it be?"

"Don't use that mouth," the mother whined. "I just wasn't sure."

"It's chill," the girl told me. "My sister knows him really well."

"How well?"

"He's come here before." Then, less certain, "I know she's talked to him . . ."

I realized why the other photographers claimed not to have seen the hard face of Ray Brennan in their garden. They had not wanted to see him. He was forty years younger, stronger, pumped with male vitality, capable of getting real girls to do the real thing.

"Bridget left with this man? How long ago?"

"Half an hour. Forty minutes."

"They'll be right back," the mother assured me.

"Where is the studio?"

They looked at each other.

"—Somewhere close."

"—Five minutes away."

"—He said it was at his mother's house."

I t was not supposed to be this way. Not without an arrest plan, or a warrant, for God's sake. Not without backup. I sped down the 134 Freeway while punching the address book on my personal cell phone.

Donnato.

Jason.

Barbara.

Galloway.

Vernon.

Eunice.

Voice mail. Voice mail. Voice mail. Voice mail.

Donnato was at a wedding with his Nextel turned off, but where the hell was everybody else? What did they do on Sunday afternoons? Damn, they were probably *all* at the ceremony—it was Vicki Shawn and Ed Brewster, the firearms instructors who had posed for Hugh Akron in their wedding clothes. I roared out loud with frustration. It would take too long to go through the rigmarole with some rookie on the switchboard. I needed to connect in the next two minutes with somebody who knew the Brennan case.

Fingertips on the wheel, I reached back with my other hand and felt around the rear seat for the envelope of files concerning the preliminary hearing. The files were in folders, which took the finesse of a bomb squad expert to extract from the envelope at eighty-five miles per hour in a convertible. Glancing from the gyrating road to the pages flapping in the open air, I located the list of witnesses, and there was Kelsey Owen's home phone number.

I guess she was not invited to the wedding, either, because she picked up on the first ring.

I explained as concisely as I could: Ray Brennan had taken a teenage Juliana look-alike from a photo shoot less than an hour before.

"Where are you?" she shouted.

"Almost to the Ventura Freeway. They said he took her to a studio in his mother's house. I'm guessing his mother's house is somewhere around Culver City or the park—"

"What do you want me to do?"

"I didn't mean for it to go down like this—" I was yelling.

"It's okay, Ana. Calm down. You're doing good. I'm here and I'm going to help you. Tell me, clearly and slowly, what you want me to do."

"Go to Rapid Start. Either on his military record, or on one of the three-oh-twos, it's going to say his *mother's maiden name.* You'll need it when you run the title search because the parents were divorced—"

"I can't go to Rapid Start from here!" she interrupted, trying to stay calm. "I'm home, remember? You called me at *home!*"

"—He's got this girl, and he's at the killing house. He has to finish the ritual—" The cell was cutting out. "How fast can you get to the office?"

Her reply was garbled.

"*What?*" I said. "What did you say?"

"—West. Keep going west."

Twenty agonizing minutes later Kelsey called from the office, just as I was curving onto the 405.

"Look," she said, "I need to say that I take responsibility for what's been going on—"

"*What are you talking about?*"

"Well, the tension between us—I'm wondering if you've been feeling it too—I've been sad about it, and I just wanted to say—"

"Screw that! We are so past that!"

"Are we, really? Because I need you to know I was never going to testify, no way. You see, I do understand about loyalty, and if they called me, I was going to be a hostile witness and they—"

"Yes, yes, we are totally cool. I'm sorry, too!" I bellowed over the screaming wind. "I really, really am. Just give me what you've got!"

His mother's maiden name was Connors. Lilly Connors. The title to the house was in her name. It had taken Rapid Start about a half a second to retrieve it.

Step by step, I walked Kelsey through the procedure, while simultaneously accelerating the Barracuda over an overpass like a toy race car that defies gravity on the loop-the-loop. By the time I was peeling off at National, she had run an emergency property search and come up with the address in Mar Vista. His mother's house. Where Ray Brennan had grown up.

T he moment I pulled up, I wanted to bang my head against the dashboard.

It was a house I had seen before, when Jason and I were on surveillance. I just didn't know what I was looking at.

It is like that, often.

It was the house on the corner, across from the Montessori school, a small stucco bungalow sun-scorched to indiscriminate gray, with a porch supported by thin white posts—a suggestion of a porch really— and rotted concrete steps. A rusted TV aerial was perched on top of a sloping roof. The lawn was dead, the place had looked abandoned, but there was a bright green AstroTurf doormat. I remember thinking when Jason and I were there the first time that something was not right.

I have noticed when the hairs go up on the back of your neck, and you think something is not right, something is not right.

There were two windows on the porch side, two on the left where a front bedroom might be. The windows were not boarded up, as I had hastily assumed, but blackened in, with paint.

I had been looking at Ray Brennan's darkroom.

His roving abduction-mobile was parked out front.

"I see the van. I'm at the address," lifting the latch on a chain-link gate. "I'm going in."

"Wait!" cried Kelsey over the phone in my ear. "Culver City police are responding!"

"He's got a girl in there, *now*."

"Are you armed?"

"They took my gun, remember?"

I was heading up the weedy path.

"If he's into it and you interrupt him, he'll go into a rage and he'll—"

"Where are the cops? The cops aren't here! He's doing her, you think I'm going to stand outside and wait? I'm going to distract him," and cut it off.

I pulled back the creaking screen door and knocked on the peeling wood until my knuckles hurt, then picked up a piece of cinder block and banged. Finally there were footsteps.

"Who's there?"

I said: "Do you believe the Bible is only a book?"

"What the *hell*?"

The door opened.

It was Brennan. He was wearing clear oval glasses, a studious look that went with the dimples you could not see in the photographs. His light brown hair was military-short, and he wore a tank top and baggy camouflage shorts and the polished boots. Hunting. Behind the glasses, his lucent eyes went to the curb, where a unit from Culver City police had just pulled up, siren *whupping* quietly.

"What's going on?"

I did not turn. I tried to maintain eye contact and just stay still until he could be subdued.

"Nothing to worry about, I'm sure."

I heard the latch on the gate unlock behind me.

"Ray?" someone called.

"Who the hell are you?"

"Culver City police. We just want to talk to you."

"Bullshit!" he shouted. "This is CIA harassment!"

"Now come on Ray, we're just local police—"

Then he had me in a headlock, up against his chest, a knife to my throat. I could smell his personal sweat. His forearm was rock hard and gritty, his skin on my skin.

The uniforms on the pathway froze.

"I'll kill the bitch."

"Take it easy, Ray."

"Try me, assholes."

"No problem," said one of the cops, lifting his hands to show they were empty. "Hear that, buddy? You're the man."

Ray Brennan pulled me inside and kicked the door shut.

Twenty-five.

He started yelling his head off and threw me across the floor. *"Goddamn son of a bitch! Oh, you goddamn bastard!"* My hip hit first, I tried to roll with it, slammed a shin into the bulging leg of a sofa. The floor was rough old redwood with protruding nail heads here and there. Where my jeans had snagged, blood was darkening the denim; my palms had turned abraded and raw.

In the small daylight coming through random scratches in the black-painted windows, I could see we were in a tiny living room, empty except for a green fleabag couch. The walls had mostly been stripped, but flayed sheets of wallpaper still curled away from the studs—delicate garlands of flowers on stiff old-fashioned backing. Paint chips had collected near the baseboard. The house smelled cold, as if it had been empty a long time. Our footsteps echoed. There were white beams in the ceiling with rows of hooks—for plants.

Ray Brennan had dead-bolted the front door and was pacing and cursing, suddenly wheeling and stabbing the knife halfway into an exposed beam.

"Take it easy."

"Shut up, bitch."

Slowly, watchfully, I got to my feet. Immediately my hip flexor gave out, causing an excruciating buckle of the leg.

"If I were you, I'd stay away from the window."

"Oh, shut up. I was raised by nuns, I don't need you to tell me what to do."

"That's not why—"

"Shut *up*."

He was coming fast with fist cocked and I was cornered, just managing to twist away as the blow grazed my shoulder, bouncing my temple against the denuded plaster as I scuttled behind the couch. Now they would find paint chips in my hair, too. Infuriated, Brennan picked up one end of the couch and tossed it.

If he rapes me, I'll survive. I'll let him do it and survive.

"They have night vision!" I shouted hoarsely. "The police snipers! They can see through the windows!"

It was a lie (night vision works only at night) and he knew it— "Bullshit!"—but it distracted him enough so I could move farther behind the angled end of the couch and maybe start a dialogue that showed I cared about his welfare.

"*Seriously,*" I managed between chattering teeth. "Stay down."

He nodded several times as if listening to someone else not in the room—*Okay, okay*—then squatted low and crab-walked like a Russian dancer to the wall space between the windows. I saw how young and lithe he was, younger than Juliana had described, young as a recruit who signs up to save the world.

"I know who you are—"

"Me? I'm Superfuck."

A wave of nausea spiraled up my gut. The hip gave out again. I was not certain I could remain standing.

". . . the schedule," he was saying.

"Is someone back there? I thought I heard something."

A phone began to ring.

The mistake the Culver City police had made was calling him Ray. You never wanted to call him Ray. You wanted to ooze respect. You called him "sir."

"Are you going to answer the phone, sir?"

"Sit the fuck down."

I sank to my haunches and drew up my knees. The phone, an ancient black rotary, sat on the floor between us. Its rings were coarse and jangling, as if dragged through the wires from another epoch. I held my breath, as the echo of each became another lost opportunity for connection to the outside.

Brennan was sitting on the floor with his legs splayed out so I could stare at the lug soles of his boots. He was playing a high-speed game of mumblety-peg, flipping the knife so it landed perfectly, pulling it out and flipping again, making small quick cuts in a circle on the soft redwood planks.

He had spent a lot of time at this, activating and reactivating his obsessions.

The ringing stopped.

My breath was coming fast and shallow. I told myself I was not alone. Culver City had witnessed the abduction and called for SWAT, which would first set a perimeter. They would soon have the house surrounded, although their positions would not be visible all the way around, giving the illusion of escape through the back. The snipers would maintain a low profile on the roofs.

Meanwhile, Culver City and LAPD would be huddling, trying to figure out what they were looking at. *How many hostages? What do we know about this guy?* It appeared they had the phone number and were trying to open a negotiation. Let's hope the Bureau had gotten there by now with a six-hundred-page history of Ray Brennan and his alleged acts. That should tell them his ritual had been interrupted, he was in a panic, and the ringing would only agitate him more.

As desperately as I concentrated on what *they* would do, I hoped they were focusing on me. I hoped Galloway, or Rick, or someone was out there saying that despite recent events in her personal life, we have a trained negotiator inside with that piece of shit: we should trust that if she is alive, she will follow procedure, so let's all play this by the books.

"How are we doing, sir? Is everything okay?"

"What do you think?" he asked sardonically.

"I don't know, sir. You tell me."

"I'm being torn to pieces."

"You're feeling torn apart?"

"—Yeah, now that you brought the whole miserable world with your *stupid* religious bullshit—"

"I'm sorry that happened. Is there anything I can do for you now?"

"Go away."

"Let's go together."

"Are you shitting me?"

"Let's walk out of here, right now. Nothing bad has happened yet."

He sneered and picked at wood grains with the flashing point of the knife.

"Is that a KA-BAR knife?"

"Uh-huh."

"You must be former marine."

"I served my country. I love my country."

"You love your country," I mirrored approvingly. "You know what? I love my country, too. My name is Ana. What can I call you?"

"*Me?*" He looked incredulous, as if I had asked a different question. "This is *my private property*. I'm not the one violating someone's private rights and busting into their own home with a bunch of cops."

There was a thump and a crash and breaking glass. Brennan and I both scrambled to our feet. The sound had come from the back of the house.

He got up on his toes and roared, "Stay away from me!" throat cords straining.

"It's not them," I said calmly. SWAT would not breech, not yet. "It's not them! Listen."

There was no more banging, just guttural inhuman sounds trying to get out of someone's throat, then silence.

"Maybe we should check that out."

"It's the other one," he said.

"You mean there *is* somebody else in the house?"

"There's a girl. She's back in the studio. I was going to kill her," he stated flatly, "but she begged me to let her pray first."

"I see. So there's a girl back there, and she sounds pretty much okay, like nothing bad has happened yet. It doesn't have to happen, sir—"

The phone again.

"—You can make it stop right now."

But the phone wouldn't stop. Brennan had shied away from it sideways, as if he were wired on something. Angel dust? Chain-smoking marijuana for eight days straight?

"It's just the phone."

Bridget was in one of those rooms, possibly dying on me. The only way I could help her was to keep in control of myself although I could feel the situation breaking loose and fragmenting with the metal-on-metal shriek of a nightmare out-of-control merry-go-round going tilt, beginning to lift up off its rotors.

"It's just the phone," I repeated. "You can answer it or not. You have the choice."

Give it up! I thought-beamed to the negotiators outside. Brennan was in a state of acute stress, frozen still like a terrified animal.

My eye was on my leather purse, which had been thrown into a corner. Inside the purse was the cell phone. I took an unauthorized step toward the bag.

He lunged, I twisted, but he grabbed me around the waist. We wrestled into the hallway until he threw me down in a narrow kitchen—open cupboard doors and shelves littered with dry blown leaves and pebbles and white enameled cabinets streaked with rust. Again my head slammed. He got his hands around my throat. I surprised him with a quick release, knocking his arms apart, but did not kick or grab because I did not want him to feel attacked; he would overpower me in an instant with a mindless homicidal fury.

"No sir, don't do it, I'm with the FBI."

I scrambled toward the front room, he dug his fingers into my back, my waistband, I rolled and broke the hold, but then my strength was ebbing, something I had not imagined in fantasies of kung fuing through the air.

"I'm a federal agent, I can help you—"

I kept up evasive action as best I could, trying to get to the purse, writhing away by inches, dragged back, trying to get him to hear me.

"Sir! Don't mess! I'm a *federal agent,* you'll get the death penalty, I'm a *federal agent—*"

I must have said it, choked it, twenty times even as he climbed on top of me and put his thumbs on my eyes in some bullshit marine move, and I slammed his inner elbows so his torso fell on mine, his spit all over my face, and he reared up again and I saw myself dead on the floor in that putrefying kitchen with cockroaches swarming the drain, and my mind kept repeating, *It's only pain,* and, *The wisdom to know, the wisdom to know*—until suddenly he stopped and said, "It's no good."

Oh God, what was this? Was I saved because Ray Brennan could not get an erection? Could that be true? The same thing that happened with Juliana in the van? *Saved?* By some crazy, unbelievable irony? Saved, by *impotence?*

It wasn't that. It was crazier: "I just can't hurt you if you're going to fight."

I waited, thoughts pinwheeling, breathing the breath of this stranger.

"Then can we . . . get up, please?"

He shifted off me and I hand-over-handed my way up the cabinets and would have vomited in the sink if it weren't for the cockroaches.

I had reason to believe he had hit his upper limit and would now press the reset button and regain control. I knew a lot about Ray Brennan. Had this been an UNSUB I would have lost my urine when he pulled me through the door, but this was old home week, reuniting with the crazy brother whose psychotic breaks and hospitalizations you know so well. *I just can't hurt you.* Unless you are drugged unconscious, or playing dead, like a doll . . . or really dead.

Juliana said: *"He banged my head as if I were a doll."*

Sometime in there the phone had stopped ringing.

"This is what is going to happen," I said in the stillness. "Sir? Do you hear my voice?"

He had retrieved the knife from where it was sticking upright in the floor.

And I had my leather bag.

"The negotiator wants to talk to you. That's why they're calling. His job is to get you out of here in one piece."

I did not mention Bridget. This was Ray Brennan's moment in the sun.

"They want to talk to you, sir. They know I'm in here. I'm one of them, and *you* know, because you're former military, that we take care of our own. It comes down to this: if I'm not alive, you're not alive."

Brennan had stopped his slow advance, knife in hand, and shook his head, as if shaking off a dream.

"Run that by me again? You're telling me you're *not* one of those nuts who tries to get you to believe in Jesus?"

He had taken a while to dial it in, but that was fine; I had managed to reach unobtrusively into the bag and hit 911.

"I talk to God," he was saying, "so I don't need your crap."

"I don't sell Bibles. I'm a federal agent."

The phone inside the bag was lit. The screen was active. I was betting the farm that a well-trained emergency operator had picked it up and stayed on the line and that we now had an open channel to 911. Someone would be listening and relaying information to the team of negotiators, ten or twelve of them sitting in a squad car or having commandeered a neighbor's kitchen table, roughing out their situation board, putting together a picture they could convey to SWAT.

"If you're from the FBI, where's your gun?"

"I'm not armed. Obviously."

"Your badge."

"Don't have it."

"And I'm Warren Beatty."

"They took away my credentials."

"I'm supposed to believe you?"

"Look—okay—" I used the old negotiator's line: "Do you want me to lie to you, or do you want me to tell you the truth?"

"Hell, I can't tell one from the other at this point," and broke into a grin that was free of anger or guile.

"The truth is, I shot my boyfriend."

He laughed, and I saw the appealing, easygoing world traveler Juliana had met on the bench.

"No shit?"

I smiled and spread my hands. "I'm not jiving you, man."

"Was he screwing another woman?"

"Basically."

Brennan shook his head. "What'd you shoot him with?"

"A thirty-two."

"That don't do nothing. You should've called me."

"I'll remember that."

"You didn't kill him?"

"He's alive and well and testifying against me."

"So"—the suspect wasn't stupid, he could put two and two together—"what the hell are you doing here?"

"I've been after you, sir, for a long time."

He liked that.

"I didn't know I was so important to the FBI."

"You have created a lot of interest in our office, sir."

I did not want to feed his grandiosity even more by letting him know that the whole world was there—the suits from Culver City, LAPD and Santa Monica, as well as our SWAT team chief and the

highest-ranking supervisors in the Los Angeles field, all gathered in a
makeshift command center, all focused entirely on him.

And soon we would hear the helicopters from the local news.

I smiled at Ray Brennan, genuinely, and don't know why. Perhaps
because I saw his desperation, in the skittering tiptoe strut between
the front windows and back, checking here, checking there, like a rat
constantly smelling the air. Perhaps because, beyond whatever happened to me, I knew the way it would end for him: what SWAT guys
call a "head shot," quick and sweet.

I also knew the psychology of the bond between assailant and
victim and so discarded what I was feeling for him, which was compassion. How could that really be? The naked house was unnerv-
ing—opposite to what a house should hold—and it was clear he had
grown up exactly in this cold-wall emptiness, mother with a wooden
tit. It was more than passing strange—Ray Brennan in his phantas-
mic tank top and camis, and I in black T-shirt and nail-torn jeans,
standing almost casually together like strangers at a cocktail party
who have just hit on a connection: I shot my boyfriend. He kills girls.
What now?

We were not completely strangers. Over the long pursuit and
struggle, had we not come to know each other well—both outsiders,
way beyond the norm? Would those civilians in the crowded apartment buildings all around us, spooning mush into the mouths of
babies, counting dollars from their minimum wages, ever breathe the
pure oxygen of risk, of *going over the edge,* knowing superhuman
power over other human beings, dancing easily across enemy lines
because they were *smart, smart, smart*?

Ray Brennan smiled genuinely back, as if this were true and complete, and we were man and woman of a different race.

Like strangers at a cocktail party, we were lying to each other and
ourselves. The difference was that I knew this, and he did not.

"Inadequate personalities," a New York City police negotiator
once told me, "need to be told what to do."

"Show me the other girl."

He indicated with the knife that I should go ahead down the hall.

"On the left," I said for the folks I hoped were listening. "That would be the north side of the house. Is that your studio? I bet I know why. Because of the light. Artists' studios will generally face north," I reiterated as clearly as possible, but the babble halted as we entered the studio and my breath caught in my throat: "You're quite an artist, sir."

For the next five and a half hours I sat on a metal chair, hands bound behind my back with flex cuffs, in a room white and clean as an operating theater. It was an ordered sanctuary where time made sense because time had been turned into action that was repetitive and understandable; you could contemplate the passing of the weeks in the razor-straight rows and rows of photographs of sexual assaults. The dates were right there, printed with bold precision, in the right lower corner of each shot.

Bridget, the girl from photo day, had apparently fallen off a chair and hit a rack of lights, which crashed while we were in the living room. She had been lying unconscious on her side in a mess of broken glass when we entered. She was still fully dressed, in cowgirl garb identical to her sister's—denim jacket, tight jeans and red high heels—dark hair half covering her face. She had been bound wrists to ankles and gagged with her own red kerchief. Small rivulets of blood from superficial cuts made by the broken glass crisscrossed her forehead and ran down the side of her nose. A black Stetson hat and a small leopard purse stood on a counter beside a six-pack of Coke. One can had been removed. I saw the cooler Juliana had described on the sanded and finished floor.

Brennan crossed his arms and fingered his elbow skin and gave an appraisal of the quarry: "This one is an eight. Maybe an eight and a half. My preferred type has fuller lips. But she was trusting, the most innocent creature," he said thoughtfully, gazing down at the sleeping girl.

"I'm concerned about her. Are you?"

"What for?"

"Well, is she all right? She's bleeding, and she looks like she was drugged."

"She's happy."

"You think she's happy?"

"Yeah."

"It makes you happy to look at her like that?"

"Not really."

"Should we do something to make her look better, sir?"

"I'll take care of that," he said.

"You know, if you're hungry, the folks outside will get you something. Pizza. Anything you want. All you have to do is pick up the phone."

"That's okay, I brought my lunch."

"Is it in the cooler?"

"Yeah."

And so it went, a hiccupping conversation, alternately dreary, charged, flat and hostile. They talk about "seeing the face of training" during situations of high alert, and I did. I saw the smooth kind face of the singer Harry Belafonte, who resembled our hostage negotiation training officer, whose name I had forgotten, and heard the trainer's gently ironic voice—*Don't forget to ask the guy to come out*"—and it was a secret refuge to remember the time he admonished our class to set fitness goals: *"Here is my challenge to you: If I don't lose twenty pounds in six months, I'll shave my head."*

So the face of "Harry" was with me in the photo studio, where the studs had been drywalled and painted over, and on the drywall was pinned Ray Brennan's collection of photographs, some from magazines, some glossy and fresh, some downloaded from the Internet, of female suffering inflicted by the mutilation of female anatomy or, in close-up, of Brennan himself in the act of anal or vaginal penetration, or demonstrating his famous strangulation techniques. There were rows of chains and belts neatly hung on the same portable rack I had seen in the Bureau darkroom that Hugh Akron used for strips of negatives.

If your hands were tied and you had run out of tactic options, "*Be a good witness,*" Harry had said.

Two cameras were set on tripods trained on the chair from which Bridget had fallen.

I could not look closely at the pictures because if I had seen what he had done to Juliana (it was documented, on the south wall), I would have gone into my own mindless homicidal rage. I had noticed—and narrated into my purse—that the back entrance to the cottage was barricaded on the inside by a security gate. He had foreseen the possibility of escape. The mission, I repeated to myself, was to keep him calm until SWAT could make the shot.

So I asked endless questions about photography, digging around in the brainpan for scraps of photographic factoids. The name Walker Evans bubbled up. Which did Brennan prefer, digital or film? Film, we agreed, was for the serious professional. Did he know crime scene examiners still went for the old four-by-five-inch cameras? You got the best detail. Brennan's work, I observed without looking at it, was "Impressive."

"You mean I'm a sick fuck."

"Is that how you see yourself?"

He scoffed and shook his head. "What would any normal person think?"

"They'd think you care about your collection."

"You know how much *money* these shots are worth?"

"You tell me."

He whistled, as if the sum were too shocking to say. "A lot of sick fucks out there."

"But this is *your stuff.* It's special to you."

"Uh-huh."

"The next time they call, maybe you should answer the phone."

"What for?"

"So they don't bust in here and torch it."

He considered this, as I considered whipping the remaining rack of hot explosive lights into his smug, clean-shaven face.

"When you shot your boyfriend, Ana, was it a turn-on? Did you get aroused?"

"No."

"Sure you did. Let's face it, you're a little girl. You brought down a buck. Don't tell me it wasn't a thrill."

"It wasn't a thrill."

"Can I share something?" Brennan was sitting against the wall again, with the lug soles in my face. "Big hair is out."

"You think this is big hair? I don't have big hair, it's just wavy."

"I prefer a ponytail, with the ears showing, and tiny studs. What did your boyfriend like?"

"I don't know."

"You don't know! That's the problem, right there! And you say you two were in *looove*?" he crooned mockingly, flipping the knife between his legs.

"I cared about him."

"Of course you did, you're a good person, you have exuberance for life, I can tell that."

"Can you?"

Talking about Andrew made me sweat; a couple of dozen cops and FBI people listening.

"Did you like it when he made love to you?"

I didn't answer.

"Did you tell him that you liked it?"

A voice jumped out of my throat. "Shut up!" I screamed. "It's none of your business!"

He startled, on his feet and going to the pistol in his belt.

"Shut up? You're telling me to shut up, lowly bitch?"

"You know what I would like?" I said fiercely. "I would like my boyfriend to come in here and beat the crap out of you."

Wrong, all wrong, you are totally off the track—

"That's not about to happen, is it?" Brennan replied, and now he was pissed.

Wrong, to get him all worked up with a male challenge. What are you doing? That is exactly wrong—

The phone rang.

As if they knew! As if they *were* listening on 911 and heard it escalate and tried to cut it off.

"Answer it," I whispered. "Your collection."

He ticked the barrel of the gun back and forth at my face and went into the living room and picked up the phone.

"How are you?" the negotiator said on the tape.

"Leave me alone."

"I'm just curious to know, how is everybody in the house?"

"Everybody's fine."

"How is Ana Grey?"

"Ana?" he smirked. *"Ana is not in a position to talk right now."*

"Besides you and Ana, how is everybody else in the house?"

"I've got two!"

"You've got two ladies?"

"Yeah, that's right!"

"Why don't you let one of them go?"

"No way!" said Brennan. *"No way ever. You're going to have to come in and get me."*

It was night by then, and the grinding roar of helicopters vibrated the bones in my head. Outside, beyond the perimeter, the media waited with turned-off lights; they'd flood the place when there was action. SWAT could see Brennan now with night vision, and I was tormented at why they did not take the shot while he was in the living room, edging the metal chair closer to where my bag lay on the floor, trying to poke it open with my feet. Brennan was back before I could see if there was glow on the blue faceplate, if it still held charge, or if I were talking to the dark.

"Did you tell them what you want?" I asked tiredly. From the booming headache that had begun even before the helicopters, I was certain that I had a concussion.

He did not answer. He was crouched between the painted-over windows, sunk into some inner negative space, features gone flaccid and eyes dull.

"I want everyone to go away."

When a suspect wants something he will say it over and over. Brennan had wanted nothing, over and over. They would have noted on the situation board, *NO DEMANDS,* and worried because that was not good. Keeping us here—Bridget still knocked out on the floor— was not good, either. It meant he was going to finish.

"Sir, I'm curious to know what's going on with you, and if there's some way I can help."

He held up a hand. "Ana," as if we were old pals, "stop. I know exactly what you're doing."

"What am I doing?"

"Trying to create a psychological profile of me."

"Give me a break," I said, "I can't even spell it."

He smiled. "I know I'm a freak."

Then, for some reason, he took off his shirt.

I did not like that, at all.

I did not like seeing the thin, hard physique and the pinched nipples. I didn't know what that message was supposed to be.

"So you and your friends in the FBI have been looking for me?"

Did he need more strokes?

"You're a priority, sir."

"I'll bet you didn't think it would go down like this."

I acknowledged my situation: "Fantasies are perfect. Life is not."

He smiled at that, too.

"There's my baby. Now she's getting up."

Bridget's eyes had opened to a dull stare. The blood on her face had flaked dry.

When the phone rang again, he went to answer quickly.

"Bridget!" I hissed. "Are you okay? The police are here. We're going to get you out."

Then Brennan came back, pouting.

"They said no."

"No to what?"

"All I wanted was to see my sister."

"They wouldn't let you see your sister?"

He shook his head. Hard-asses. They had probably admonished him for breaking contact. Tried to reestablish the rules. I was hungry and my head was throbbing. In despair, I could only support the choices they had made.

"That's it, then. They're not going anywhere. As long as we're here, they're here."

"You told me to tell them what I want."

"Yes, but you have to give them something in exchange."

"You see, it's all a stupid game, like Russia and the United States."

"What's going on with Bridget?"

She was awake but not moving. Pink froth gathered at her mouth.

"She'll be paralyzed for a little bit longer," he said, kicking her leg. "Then she'll be fine."

"The difference between you playing their game or not," I said quickly, to distract him, "is you on death row, or not."

Bridget had begun to moan.

"I love my sister."

"Let me talk to them. I want to tell them what an exceptional job you've done in keeping everyone safe."

He looked up with sad eyes, meant to uncork my sympathy. If you had met Ray Brennan on the street, your heart would have been touched by his core loneliness.

"My sister understands. She forgives my sins."

"Right," I stuttered, imagining what role his sister had played—or been forced to play—in this tragic madness. "She knows who you are." I tried to wet my lips. "You're a good person who . . . who . . . I don't know, sir, but something happened . . . Something really bad . . . But it happens to all of us, in some way. Did you know that?"

Big fat tears of humiliation and exhaustion had escaped and were rolling down my face. If I could crawl over to where he was sitting in the other metal chair and embrace him, he would stab me in the heart.

"—It happens to us all."

"Like you and your boyfriend?"

"Me and Andrew," I confessed.

"Andrew." His lips began to quiver as if I had held out a sweet. "You miss him?"

"Yes."

"It wasn't you who did it."

"No," I said, and he agreed: it wasn't him who did things, either. He watched me, with bright and curious eyes.

"Do you think," he asked, after a moment, "God forgives every-body?"

I sniffed and wiped my nose on my shoulder.

"Yes," I said, "yes I do, and I think, sir, that now we're really friends, okay? Because you and I have been to places none of these other people are going to see . . . So let's help each other out, as friends."

His eyes, behind the oval lenses, still held the question.

"Yes," I declared with all my soul, "*God forgives you,* but you have to ask. You have to show God you're sorry. *I* know you're sorry, so—let's show him. Let's walk out of here . . . like you know your sister would want you to do."

"I have work," he said uncertainly.

"Let's help each other out. Let's go now. God is listening."

"How long will I be in prison?"

"Um, well, you'll have to accept some responsibility for your actions, sir, but I know the judge is going to be lenient when he sees how serious you are about making this right."

Docile and repentant now, he freed my hands and helped me rise stiffly from the chair.

"I'm sorry," he whispered. "I shouldn't have done that to you. I'm sorry for my crimes."

"You're doing the right thing, sir. I'm proud of you, I am. We're all going to walk out of here. I'm going to call them on the phone and tell them. Then we're going to walk out the door. There'll be a couple of guys right outside who will tell us what to do and where to go. Okay? We just do what they tell us. Are you with me?"

"Let's do it," he said with a lift of the chin.

"Put your weapons down, sir. Place them down on the floor, over there, away from the girl."

Brennan squatted and laid the KA-BAR knife and pistol on the ground.

"Thank you, sir. Now back away, please."

He did, and I snatched up the weapons, light-headed and delirious with a sudden total body rush.

"They'll shoot me."

"They won't shoot you because we're going to do everything slow and easy. How're you feeling?"

"Weird."

"That's okay. It's all pretty weird when you think about it."

I tried not to hurry as he shuffled ahead to the front room. When I picked up the heavy receiver of the old black phone the primary negotiator was right on the line.

"Is the suspect armed?"

"Negative. He's here with me, by the front door. I'm telling him that we appreciate the fact he's going to surrender," I said over the phone, "and I told him there will be some people out there by the front door—" Then he turned and sprinted back down the hall.

I screamed, *"RAY!"* and fired clumsily, and missed.

The front door flew out, ripped off its hinges by a cable that had been strung between the doorknob and the winch of a truck lurching backward on command. I kept out of the way as our tactical SWAT team, like Ninjas from hell in their Danner boots and black Nomex flight suits, and black balaclavas that secret the face, armed with H&K

MP5s and Springfield 1911 .45s, batons and wicked knives, blew past the uncleared doorways in a hostage rescue speed assault to the hot spot which they knew, from my description, was the studio, in back on the north side. At the same time a second team charged through the brittle blacked-in windows with an implosion of splintered sashes and flying glass, dominating the house from both directions, and the air was filled with concussive flash-bangs set off to disorient the subject, and then screaming—*"Drop the knife!"*—and he did, a hair's-breadth nanosecond before he would have been *such* a pouffy head shot, before the honed edge of the kitchen knife he had pulled from the cooler could kiss Bridget's throat.

He never did finish his business.

Although the cops wore shirtsleeves and the neighborhood crowd was in T-shirts that mild night, I was so cold my teeth were chattering. They put me in a patrol car with a blanket around my shoulders, where I kept fumbling and dropping the cell phone until a kindly paramedic dialed the number.

"We got him," I said.

On the other end there was a yelp, and then Lynn Meyer-Murphy burst into sobs.

"Juliana! Juliana!"

The phone clunked down and she seemed to have forgotten about the call altogether as her cries receded to a distant point in the house, and there was ambient noise—a dishwasher, maybe—and I hugged my knees under the blanket and smiled.

"Ana!" It was Juliana's bright lilt. "You got him? Oh my *God*!" she squealed as if she had just won a car. "Is he dead?"

"He's not dead, but he is in custody, and he is not going anywhere for a long, long time. You're safe now, baby. You're safe."

Twenty-six.

The following day I picked up a message from the dad, Ross Murphy, apologizing for not calling immediately, but he was late getting the news as he was no longer living with the family in the Spanish house on Twenty-second Street. He thanked us and thanked us again for capturing Ray Brennan, said he was proud, just unbelievably fucking proud, to be living in America, and that the Federal Bureau of Investigation deserved all the credit in the world, and then some, and vowed to make that fact publicly known because "Nobody gets it," although, apparently, now he did. The bewildered hurt in his voice told you that he did.

The sweetness of victory barely lasted twenty-four hours, when Devon County summoned me to his Beverly Hills office to say that I was going to jail because my participation in the takedown of Ray Brennan had been in violation of the bail agreement.

I was skeptical. "Do you know the meaning of the words 'Oh, please'!?"

"You were not supposed to leave the Donnato residence," Devon replied severely. "You were not supposed to be working that case. You were suspended from the Bureau, remember?"

"Yes, and I'm going to get a letter of censure and be dinged big-time for violating Bureau policy, but, oh, *please!* If I didn't knock on that door he would have done her."

"Others could have done the knocking."

"Not *really.* Nobody else was *there!*"

"You were warned."

"I was *warned?*" I hauled out of the leather cockpit armchair. "What is this, prep school?"

In fact Devon was tapping a pencil against the hood of a miniature BMW and frowning.

"Why did you have to be the first one in?"

"It was personal."

"With you, everything is personal."

"Damn right. He had her picture on his damn wall."

"Whose damn picture?"

"Juliana Meyer-Murphy!"

"Good." Devon bounced the pencil so hard it flew out of his hand. "And she really came through for *you* at the preliminary hearing."

"*Ohhh,* no," I warned. "Don't go there unless you *really* want to piss me off, and I'll walk out so fast—"

"—You're not walking anywhere."

"—I told you not to call her as a witness—"

"—And I told *you* that you were looking at fifteen years."

I picked up the pencil from the floor and slammed it down on his desk.

"I wanted that creep dead, or in jail, all right?"

"Well," he said primly, "you achieved your goal."

We glared at each other.

"Why am *I* on the defensive? You know, when we were in court at the prelim, I saw this kid, African-American, who was there with his mom on a drug charge. 'Something wrong with this justice system,' he said, and she hit him upside the head. Let me tell you, that boy is my bro now."

Devon pushed the BMW away in disgust. It hit the Porsche.

"It's a no-brainer, Ana! Rauch doesn't have a choice; this would be a slam dunk for any prosecutor. You violated bail on an attempted murder charge. Try to see that clearly. You handed it to him! The attempted murder charge is entirely different from the Santa Monica kidnapping. You don't get extra credit for solving that case just because—"

"The credits are nontransferable," I interrupted sarcastically.

"That's right. They're nontransferable."

We were at a dead end. I was going to jail because I had saved two lives. Devon sighed with deep irritation. I stared defiantly out the window.

"Rauch wants you in custody now. It's newsworthy, coming on the heels of the arrest of a serial rapist."

"Great."

"He's going for a warrant, the SOB."

Devon raised himself up from the chair and loped slowly across the room.

"Hip bothering you?"

"Stress."

"Tell me about it."

We stood close together, mesmerized by the sparkling traffic; so close, the surface of my skin could sense the tight muscle mass of his worked-out upper body, and at the same time, the effort it took to balance his lower withered side without the crutch.

"Why don't we sit?" I took his arm in a gesture of reconciliation. Lowering to the couch side by side, we were once more allies in the long winter of a treacherous campaign.

"The best use of our energy," he said, "is to prepare for trial. Our task right now is to discredit their witnesses. The background reviews are on my desk. Take a look, see if anything pops."

I sprung up and got it.

There were reports from Devon's private investigators on the ER doctor who had testified, the thoracic surgeon, Lieutenant Loomis and two other Santa Monica detectives, Margaret Forrester, the Sheriff's Department stiff who would no doubt say I resisted arrest . . .

"Margaret Forrester does okay for a police widow," I said, staring at the bottom line on her IRS form.

"She's got that business on the side." Devon rubbed his bald pate. "What is it, jewelry?"

"Seashells. 'Body ornaments.' She nets thirty-eight thousand dollars a year?"

"Her stuff is carried by some big stores. Fred Segal. Barneys." He caught my look. "Surprised?"

"I didn't think Margaret could get it together to do something like that."

"She had help getting started. Look at the financial statements."

I sat beside Devon and his manicured fingertip showed me where. Fourteen months ago Margaret had made a deposit of $52,674 into a money market account.

"Where did she get the dough?"

"Her husband's pension."

"Are you sure?"

"The dates connect—the deposit was made a few months after he died."

"But she stated in court that she was *not* eligible to receive his pension."

Devon had both hands on a quad to support the leg while it stretched.

"The husband was killed by a gang."

"He was killed off-duty, and they never proved it was a gang. It was never crystal clear to me how exactly the Hat died."

"We'll get it clear." Devon made a note, glanced at his watch.

"How long do I have before the marshals show up at the door?"

"We'll file for a hearing. It will be postponed."

"*How long,*" I insisted, "can you keep the balls in the air?"

"I can't say for sure—"

"Because Mike Donnato kicked me out of his house."

Devon stopped writing. "When did this happen?"

"A couple of days before the Brennan thing went down."

I told him about the threatening phone calls and Mike's kids.

"You'd have to ask for new terms and conditions anyway."

Devon looked seriously unhappy now. "I hate giving Rauch another fat one over the plate. Can you find someone else of equal stature to stay with?"

"You mean someone else from the Bureau who will vouch for me?"

Devon looked up. The blue stone in the pen matched the intensified blue of his eyes. He meant it. He was not being ironic.

"Is there anyone?" he asked.

Instead of ducking suavely into the Bureau garage, I had to wait in the visitors' section of the outdoor parking lot, signal flashing, while a family of Russian immigrants squeezed into a slouching old yellow Mercedes sedan in the midst of a whopping intergenerational argument. I gave a toot and eight stormy faces glared at me with unified indignation. I guess that ended the argument.

Sprinting up the steps to the US Federal Office Building, I was ambushed once again by the same stomach-tightening anticipation I had felt every day on the job. Of course, they would not have let me past reception. Nor could I have tolerated the looks of rank curiosity, had I run into people I knew, hustling in a group to a meeting, peering out from behind an attachment they took for granted, or even begrudged, while I wanted nothing but to belong. Better to stay outside, lost in the impersonal scale of the flat-faced building, another ordinary citizen wearing ripped-in-the-pocket Levi's and running shoes, entitled to the safeguards of democracy.

The Human Computer would take lunch between twelve and one, hurry across the sunshiny plaza into the fumes of the garage and down the cinder-block passage to the ancient and pungent gym. Now that I thought about it, why should hardworking agents be condemned to that claustrophobic space? Even the franchise health club across the street had a view of Wilshire Boulevard. They should do better. They deserved it.

They.

"Barbara!"

She was carrying the black Lancôme tote bag we both had gotten "free" the day we ditched work and went to Robinsons and spent hundreds of dollars on makeup.

"Mother of God!" she gasped. "You scared me."

"Can I walk with you? Pretend I'm a homeless person."

"Don't make me feel guilty."

"For what?"

"Not calling you." She squinted against the sun. "I'm sorry. With a new baby your life isn't your own."

"Hey."

We avoided each other's eyes.

"Outstanding job on the serial rapist," she said finally.

"Thank you. Deirdre good?"

Barbara's face lit up. "Almost walking. Cruising on the furniture, you know . . ." Then her voice dropped, as if I wouldn't know. "So where are you off to?"

"Jail."

She laughed. "Oh, come on!"

"No joke. Mark Rauch is arguing to revoke bail as we speak."

"Why on earth—?"

"Violation of the agreement. Because I went after Brennan."

"What a crock."

People kept padding by. Overweight men wearing windbreakers and carrying briefcases. Tiny Asian grandmothers in black. Suddenly I knew I could never ask her to take me into her home.

"Well . . . I just wanted to say hi. See your smiling face."

She saw the hurt and put her arms around me. "I feel so bad for not calling."

"Don't," I sniffled. "You're not the only one."

"Tell me. Quickly. How are they going to argue? I have to interview another new baby-sitter, or else I'd—"

"It's okay. Another time."

"No! I don't care, she'll quit in a month when her boyfriend gets back from Tibet."

"Tibet?"

She blocked my way. "I want to hear."

"It's over for me, Barbara. I'm looking at hard time, for real."

She insisted on that zany Catholic optimism. "What is Devon County doing for you, *right now*?"

"Background checks on witnesses."

"So he's just getting started!"

I snorted. "It's great bedtime reading. The dirt on the dirtbags. Remember that Margaret Forrester, the dame Andrew slept with— one of many—at the Santa Monica police? I told you about her."

"Kind of."

"She's the one who ratted me out."

"Jealous?"

"A nutcase. Turns out she's making a ton of money selling sea- shell jewelry to yuppie stores . . ."

"Aside from the police job?"

"She was awarded $52,674 when her husband died in the line of duty, although apparently—"

Barbara pushed the blowing hair out of her eyes. "When was this?"

"A year and a half ago. Why?"

She had that Barbara look.

"It's a funny number, that's all."

"How funny?"

The Human Computer is never wrong about numbers. Never wrong about anything that has happened during a bank robbery, if it is in our files, in the last five years.

"That's the same take as the Mission Impossible caper."

"The *exact* amount the suspect took from the bank?"

Barbara nodded, brows furrowed with concentration.

"There was more in the safe deposit boxes, but he didn't find it or he didn't have time . . ."

The details of the robbery would have continued to spit out like runaway ticker tape if I had not stopped them by suddenly gripping her arms.

"Oh, Barbara," I whispered.

B arbara ditched the baby-sitter and came with me to the apartment in the Marina because, she said, it would not be a good idea to go back there for the first time alone.

The key turned happily, as always, in the brass faceplate that was worn yellow in the spot where the rest of the keys had hit every day for the past ten years. These are the marks we leave on the world.

"They wouldn't trash it," Barbara kept promising during the drive, but still I pictured desolation and ruin left by the crime scene techs. When we got there I hesitated with the key, giggling foolishly, because I was afraid that once we opened the door the loss would be overwhelming.

All that was missing was a piece of carpet, a neat surgical square out of the center of the living room where there must have been blood-stains, but there were black fingerprint powder smudges left on the walls, and the furniture had been moved and put back in a haphazard way. It looked as if they had been messing around in the garbage disposal. Like Juliana overcome by brutal flashbacks, I was hit with spiking memories of the destruction that had happened here, as if nameless obliteration were still shaking the floor, as if Andrew and I had been citizens caught in some mistaken blitz: *What in the name of God did we do to each other?*

"Don't cry," said Barbara briskly. She dropped her purse on the glass dining table and strode to the windows and yanked the curtains back. "Let's get some air in here."

When the light swept in, and the white-hot view of the brilliant boats and the sharp smell of kelp and gasoline, I saw the place was still mine—the bamboo furniture I had chosen, the TV with its trusty remote—but were I ever to live there again, room would have to be made now for a smoky melancholy. I could not even look in the direction of the coffee table and the couch.

"Where do you keep your plastic bags?"

I pulled out the drawer for Barbara, who was brave enough to open the refrigerator. "Don't worry, I'll take care of this. You do what you have to do," she instructed, holding out the Baggies.

I stared at the box with the certainty that we had reached the end, the place in the river so treacherous it could not be crossed.

"I can't do this to him."

"Do you want your home back? How about your freedom? He's more than ready to take your freedom away from *you*."

In the bathroom, the bars of soap were shriveled and dry and the towels were gone, taken for evidence. I had to hold on to the wall as the image came of Andrew and me playing in the shower before work, teasing who would get to rinse their hair first, bending to lather his strong long toes and legs, working my way up, warm water pulsing on my back.

As I stared into the mirror it seemed to fog up with that very steam, and then, as if I had wiped that steam away, I saw in an arc of clarity, Andrew and me. Our hair was wet, cheeks ruddy, his big naked shoulders inches higher than mine; we were ritually washed for the workday, but no longer playful—rather, patient and solemn, as we had never really been. I steadied myself and the impression faded. Two toothbrushes still hung in the holder. One green and one blue. His and hers.

Andrew had bought the green one, fastidious Andrew, who kept a change of clothes in the car, whose tools were always clean and hung in rows. Solitary Andrew, whose mind worked like a clock, with ruthless omission of whatever it is that must be left out.

Ruthless?

I removed the green toothbrush and slipped it into the plastic bag, allowing myself to hear only the part of my mind that was quickly calibrating which route would be fastest to the forensic lab in Fullerton this time of day.

Twenty - seven.

The azaleas in front of Andrew's house were trimmed as usual into perfect ovals of red, white and pink, like mounds of psychedelic candy brightly pulsating along the path to the door. The path was newly wet and fragrant with cedar chips still moist in the shade of a mimosa tree, whose featherlike leaflets trailed languorously in light ocean airs. Everything would be in working order—the tight screen door, the chiming bell—and it would take several more seconds for him to unsnap all the locks and chains. In those seconds we could still turn back.

But then he was standing there, with nothing between us, vivid and three-dimensional in the immediate plane: greasy day-off hair, old sweats with cutoff sleeves, as if popped there whole. Behind him I could sense dark wood and cool rooms, and the poignant scent of gardenias was blowing across the interior through open patio doors.

"What's up?"

I could have handled the cop face much better, the shut-down superior detachment, but instead he was giving off uneasy suspicion, as any home owner would, to find an unpleasant character from the past unexpectedly on his doorstep.

"Can I talk to you?"

There it was, the scan, the intuitive check for psychotic unpredictable vibes. No, he decided, it was just Ana, as surprisingly flesh-and-blood ordinary as he.

"Want to come in?"

"Are you in the middle of something?"

"Just working out."

Stiff-legged, I crossed the threshold and hovered by the back of a couch, fingers scratching at the cracked leather.

"Want something to drink?"

"I'm fine."

Twenty-pound barbells had been taken from the rack near the sliding glass doors and were resting on the dhurrie rug.

"Sorry to interrupt."

"I wasn't exactly on a roll. Hard getting back."

"I know what you mean," and let it fade.

He was still shockingly underweight. His cheeks were stubbled and gaunt, the biceps that showed out of the cutoffs were not Andrew's iron signature, but belonged to a different man, a sick man, the flesh of the muscles deflated and pale.

"I'm sorry," I said again, and willed myself not to flee.

"Sure I can't get you something? Coffee? Juice?"

"Maybe just some water. My throat is kind of dry."

"It's dry," he agreed. "Come on in."

The kitchen was just the same—spotless Mexican tile and family-size jug of dishwashing liquid on the wiped-down aluminum sink. Plants in the window, a white embroidered valance above the plants. The reason the curtains went so well with the house was they had been his mother's, still starched by the same cleaning lady.

He pulled a bottle from the pantry and tore off the cellophane.

"Oh. Did you want ice?"

I shook my head and drank the water.

"Look, I don't know how to say this."

"I can't drop the charges," he interrupted. "Even though you got Brennan. It's in the prosecution's hands."

The sincerity and swiftness of it caught me off guard, as if he had been waiting for me to show up just to say this.

"I wouldn't even suggest that."

"Once it got rolling, there was nothing I could do."

"Of course. I know."

"I never gave you up."

He had begun to breathe hard and through the nose with little snorting sounds and his finger pointed at my heart.

"I did not give you up. I wouldn't do that."

"It didn't matter anyway, because—"

"Yes, it does. It does matter. Even at the hospital. When they came to me, ready to go out and kick ass, I *still* gave them cock-and-bull about who did it."

"I know, and I'll never forget." My voice broke, and I had to clamp my fingers over my lips. "Anyway, there was Margaret."

"There was Margaret," he affirmed with no attempt to hide the bitterness.

"She told them it was me."

His voice was thick. "She thought she had something to protect."

"You?"

"Whatever. Who knows what's in her mind?"

"Also," I went on perversely, "they recovered the gun, so you had to know, sooner or later, they'd come to me."

"Just like old times," said Andrew. "You're listening but you're not hearing."

"What's the matter?"

Abruptly the color had drained from his face. He reached for a bottle of pills. There were many bottles, collected on a tray.

"Are you all right?"

He took the water bottle and gulped some tablets, then squatted and put his head between his legs. I went down beside him and stroked his hair, his bristly cheek.

"Hey? Hey, partner. You okay?"

He allowed himself to slide all the way down until he was sitting on the linoleum. I hunkered beside him.

"Good thing you keep your floors clean."

We rested there until his breathing calmed.

"What's going on?"

"I've got a heart condition. Nobody knew about it until I almost bought the farm."

"In the ER?"

"Yeah."

"See? That's why it was a *good* thing I shot you. Otherwise, you'd never know you have a heart condition."

"You really fucked me, baby. It hurts to get shot," he said, and slapped my thigh with an empty laugh.

Fear had begun its paralyzing creep. I had not been afraid like this even in the house with Brennan.

"What does the doctor say?"

"It's called IHSS—idiopathic hypertrophic subaortic stenosis. See, the old fart can still learn new words."

"Congratulations. What do they mean?"

"There's a thickening in the walls of the heart that blocks the flow of blood. No symptoms, won't show up on a physical exam, it's only when you're under stress and shock and your blood pressure falls to a dangerous point that it becomes significant."

"Well . . . we just won't let that happen again."

"I'm supposed to have no salt, no booze, no sex."

"Are you kidding me?"

"The medication wipes out your sex drive. Can you imagine me, without a hard-on twenty-four hours a day?"

I smiled.

"Here's the other thing." He paused for the worst of it: "No bike."

"No way!"

"If I got into an accident on the bike, it could happen again, I could have another 'cardiac event,' so I'm not supposed to ride the Harley."

"But you will."

"I don't know if I will. This kind of shit makes you old."

He was lolling the back of his head against the cabinets, looking up, one transparent tear crawling down his cheekbone.

"I feel," he said, "like I'm at the bottom of a well."

I put my arm around him.

"We fucked up, Andy. We fucked up really bad."

"I'm the one," he said, "I'm the one who fucked it up—"

"No—"

"Can you forgive me? Please forgive me. I want to make an amend to you," he cried desperately. "If I hurt you in any way—"

"Yes—"

"If I caused you to suffer because of my actions—"

"*Yes,* I forgive you."

"I made a mistake, Ana—"

"Forgive me, too. I did something terrible, I don't know how I could have, actually, aimed a gun at you, I'm not *capable of it,* it must have been—"

"It's okay, it's okay—"

Then we were holding on to each other as tightly as humans can grip.

"We were meant for each other," he whispered and we cradled and rocked.

"Oh God, Andy, this is really, really bad."

He stroked my hair. "What is it?"

"I need safe passage."

"You have safe passage, baby doll."

I had to get my breath. I had to find my voice. It was 1:47 p.m. He waited, slow and easy. "Go ahead."

"I know you robbed that bank. Mission Impossible. It was you."

He lifted his head and smiled sadly.

"You know, huh?" and touched my chin. "How do you know?"

"I ran the DNA on the ski mask. You dropped the ski mask, you stupid dope." I hit his arm, but I was weak as a kitten. "Your DNA is a match to the DNA in the dried saliva on the mask."

"Pardon my ignorance, but how did you get my DNA? Did you sneak in here in the middle of the night and cut my hair?"

"Your toothbrush," I said softly. "The one you always kept in my apartment. It was still there."

"My toothbrush." He shook his head in ironic acknowledgment of all the petty bullshit that makes the world go round. He sighed and we released each other.

"Andrew—"

"It's okay. I would have done the same thing."

"No, you wouldn't. You just said you would never give me up."

"If I were facing attempted murder? And I wanted to prove self-defense? The guy came at me because I had the goods on him? You bet I would," but it was bravado because now he was afraid, too, I could feel it.

"Nothing would have happened if we didn't have that fight—"

"I came at the wrong person," he shrugged.

"I never would have put you together with the ski mask. I never would have had a reason—"

"Shhh. It's done. It's survival."

"Survival is ugly."

He laughed. "So is a newborn baby. You think you arrived on this earth any different?"

The house was immensely quiet. All the clocks had finally stopped.

"We've run out of time, Andrew."

He nodded. "You're wearing a wire?"

"No, I'm not wearing a wire. But I'm armed."

"Right."

"I told them to give me half an hour."

"I'll make you a deal." He smiled faintly. "You and me. Take the money and run."

"I wish. I really, really wish."

"Let's go. Come on. It's not too late. You know you want it."

"I want it, all right."

"I can get the money. We can go right out that back door now. They never cover the back door—"

I laughed.

"—One of the most common tactical mistakes."

The look in his eyes was meant to be hopeful, but his rakish despair was breaking my heart.

"Oh, Andrew, this is so making it worse. Don't try to do this now. Don't try to—oh, God, I just want it all to go away."

"We can, baby."

"What are you talking about, anyway? You gave the money to Margaret. Why *her*?"

"I was practically a godfather to her kids. Cute little kids. The boy's a natural athlete."

"Is that why you robbed the bank?"

"She got screwed by the department," Andrew said. "She should have been compensated when the Hat died." He sounded tired. "The guy had almost twenty years in."

"So you robbed a bank?"

"Somebody had to take care of the kids."

"Really? I think not. I think she was blackmailing you. Emotional blackmail."

"For what?"

There was knocking at the door. I startled. No, wait, stop—it was too soon and too late at the same time.

"Listen," I said with crazed desperation, "you can make a good deal."

He replied with a doleful look. "I used a weapon in the commission of a bank robbery. That's twenty-five years, no questions. And I'm a cop." He shook his head.

More knocking, harder now.

"Ana? You okay? Andrew! It's Barry. It's me, buddy. We've got to talk."

We smiled at each other. He had automatically locked the door.

"I hope he brought a tape recorder because I'm only going to say it once." Andrew put a hand on my shoulder. "I'm glad it's me, not you. Going to prison."

"I'll stand by you," I promised. And then I felt a great liberation, as if an old, worrisome question had been resolved.

"Andrew, let's get married. I love you."

He kissed me, hard.

He would not surrender in his father's house. He would not surrender to his buddies, knowing it would be something they could not live with afterward. Out of deference, because he was a cop's cop, they gave him a break and took his weapons, and we all followed in a caravan—my car, him in his car with Lieutenant Barry Loomis, and two vans of Santa Monica officers, over to the closest strip mall we could think of that would be in Los Angeles County, out of the jurisdiction of the Santa Monica police.

It was one of those neighborhoods where the haze is always hanging low, scouring the eyes and the hoods of dented cars with patched-up ten-year-old paint jobs, where wide commercial avenues, built for a dense mix of fast food and retail, instead are empty and scrawny as cheap Christmas trees. Everything seems to be on a slant. Signs are broken or defaced. Figures do not walk upright, unless they are mothers dragging double loads of grocery bags; buses don't stop very long and drivers keep their eyes straight.

There was a Laundromat and a Lucky supermarket, a used record store, a bright blue Caribbean restaurant with beaded curtains and exuberantly painted suns and moons and fiery cockatoos.

Andrew's car pulled into the center of the lot. It was mostly empty, the middle of the afternoon, except for indigents who were lounging at the outdoor tables at McDonald's. Too early for the hookers. Barry got out quickly, turning his anguish into clipped, efficient movements, getting on the radio and telling everybody where to go.

The vans had rolled in and the guys were keeping their distance, waiting for the LAPD captain to arrive.

"Ana!" Barry snapped his fingers. "Andrew wants to say goodbye."

Why don't you go back to the seventies? I wanted to say to him and his ridiculous mustache. *I don't need orders from you about when and where I should talk to Andrew Berringer,* sashaying past the uniforms, who were still trying to make sense of what was going on.

Andrew was sitting alone in the car, fingers drumming the steering wheel.

"How're you doing, babe?"

"I've had better days," he said.

"I am serious. I want to marry you."

He snorted. "Is that your ambition now? To be a prison wife?"

"I don't care. I love you."

"I love you, too." He gave me an unreadable look. "Do I have safe passage?"

"Always," I assured him, and waited for the question.

It was not an answer that he wanted but a promise.

"One last time?"

"Don't say that."

We kissed through the open window, then he turned the ignition.

"You better not do that."

He had me by the neck—

"Andrew!"

—and pulled me halfway inside the car and with the other hand, he steered.

"Andrew! Please! Stop!"

It was a muscle car, in seconds we were going in treacherous, widening circles.

"Stop the car!"

My feet were lifted off the ground, yet I was pinned through the window by his desperate strength.

"Kill me," he said.

We were going faster, wider, a death spiral.

"No, I won't, I love you—"

But it didn't stop anything or change anything. Figures were scattering and weapons were drawn and there were shouts, *"Get down, get down! Police action, get down!"* Andrew's teeth were clenched, but with effort, not rage. Our foreheads banged, I bit my tongue.

"Kill me. Please, just do it."

There was shouting. Gunfire. They blew out a tire and the car veered crazily.

He pulled tighter so I could not breathe. My body flew like a rag doll as he relentlessly and with purpose kept doughnuting the car in wilder circles. The glass façade of the supermarket came rushing at us, gleaming shopping carts and spinning women grabbing babies. *"It's all right,"* he said, and I pulled the nine-millimeter Sig Sauer and his eyes were closed so I closed mine, and point-blank put it in the only place where I could reach, against the side of his rib cage, underneath the armpit, and fired.

His hands dropped. His head slumped forward. He lost all animation, his foot put no pressure on the gas. The car slowed and coasted into a parked truck and I rolled free, to stare up at the empty sky. Andrew's buddies tried to cover the hole, but the contact shot had penetrated the aorta and spinal column. He did not have fifteen seconds to imagine that his life might continue; that the wound might not be grievous, his case might be dismissed or won, or that he could save his partner or his father, or be given any other kind of freedom, any kind of chance. In an instant, oblivion, not love, had flooded his chest.

Twenty-eight.

The sky was growing lower, as if it would touch the ground and reclaim the planet, sucking up the horizon and everything that lay before it in streaming tunnels of ashen cloud. Whippy branches of ocotillo cactus jerked in spasms in a sweeping wind-colored brown. Raindrops sleeted the windshield, and then it went dry. I detested California.

We were moving at a good clip down the slick highway—a sheriff's van, the prisoner in an unmarked sedan and then the coroner. We were hunting bodies. Andrew's funeral had been the day before, but the harvest was not done. There were still more corpses in the ground for the digging, or at least that is what Ray Brennan had boasted to his cell mate.

I was free. The DA dropped the charges based on Andrew's confession, taped in the living room just before his surrender, in which he stated that he had attacked me with intent to commit bodily harm because I had knowledge of the Mission Impossible bank robbery. Our relationship was falling apart at the time, he said, and he was fearful that I would expose him.

Andrew took sole responsibility for the heist, providing details of how he had planned it, all the way back to the class he gave on bank security. He trained those two managers so when he appeared as a robber wearing a ski mask, they would unwittingly follow his commands. He used a weapon to threaten them, so he would not have to speak; so they could not recognize his voice. He had severed the hinges in the rooftop hatch weeks before, waiting until he knew there would be a large delivery of cash. Since Andrew had taught the opening procedures, he knew exactly how many minutes he had inside the vault and how long it would take for the police to respond. He expected a take of over a million dollars, but all he finally put in the trunk of his official car before driving to the police station to report for work that morning was $52,674 because the rest had been locked in empty safety deposit boxes overnight. He had given the money as a gift to Margaret Forrester to care for her children in the aftermath of the death of his best friend.

Deputy District Attorney Mark Rauch was forced to concede that I had responded to the attack in self-defense, and except for the obligatory blast from Galloway for violating policy, and serving time off without pay, reinstatement at the Bureau had all the drama of renewing your driver's license. There were mumbled condolences, mostly avoidance, taking refuge in the work. Now I was rolling in the sedan with Ray Brennan and Special Agents Todd Hanley and Jason Ripley on a tip from the snitch who had been placed in Brennan's cell, a giant three-hundred-pound murderer named King Tut.

King Tut had been a popular and lovable custodian, a really sweet guy, who bludgeoned two kids to death with a shovel when he found them having sexual intercourse in the high school parking lot after a basketball game. King Tut had sad, puzzled eyes like an elephant who does not understand what he did to deserve being an elephant. You might mistake the look in those eyes as kindly, when actually they just rolled around in their sockets like wet black marbles, expressing nothing. When you had two head cases locked up together, neither could read the other anyway, like blind men batting sticks.

Brennan had to brag, had to tell his secrets. Not a surprise. Nor would I have been surprised if the things he told King Tut contributed to the coronary that ultimately felled the big guy. King Tut read the Bible daily and so did his wife, who told the prison minister her husband had been put in a cell with the devil, and could he please do something about it?

Brennan told King Tut he had raped twenty-seven girls and women and been forced by circumstances beyond his control to murder three. We already had leads on eight more victims and corroborating evidence on the young woman who had been abducted from the Georgetown mall, so twenty-seven was not an impossible number. Brennan described sadistic dreams and visions that made King Tut sweat as he repeated them to us in an air-conditioned interrogation room. He went through an entire carton of Kit Kat bars. Brennan claimed to have taken jewelry from the victims and buried it with the three bodies out in the desert near the military base at Twentynine Palms. That would have been sacred ground to him.

The Sheriff's Department had driven the prisoner to the alleged burial site twice before. Each run had to be orchestrated in advance so the fact this one fell the day after Andrew's funeral was one of those random kicks in the head the universe occasionally deals.

The night before he was to show us the bodies, Brennan refused to eat and became so agitated in his cell they called off the search, but then he calmed down and slipped into some kind of zombie zone. In the car, he slumped over, sleepy and mute in handcuffs and leg irons, as if neutralized by whatever antipsychotic cocktail the docs cooked up. His hair was matted. He had not shaved.

I fingered the tiny metal box in my pocket that held dirt from Andrew's grave. I had stolen it, after the thousand-man entourage of police officers and media people and girlfriends and family were gone, after watching the spit-and-polish parade to the cemetery from a doughnut stand across the street, a landmark from the fifties with a sagging sculpture of a doughnut on the roof. When you looked closely, the painted fabric that covered the wire had weathered off the frame, as if these biting desert winds had zipped a hundred miles west to pick off any remaining life, until it had become the gesture of a doughnut more than anything else.

The big clock had begun to tick again as I sat in that plastic chair, half smothered by the heavy bouquet of sugar and coffee and yeast, in the heat of the sun intensified by the plate glass window. If I can make it through this second, I can make it through the next; the duty weapon sat on my hip like a living thing.

All I wanted was to be beside him, inside that coffin.

My foot was tapping to an inaudible tune like the bagpipes beyond the glass I could not hear. Margaret Forrester and Officer Sylvia Oberbeck were at the grave site, dressed in black, and I did not begrudge them. It was not that Andrew Berringer had been heartless or insatiable—he had needed us, all three. Margaret was the hellcat, Oberbeck his friend—and I? I was Andrew's mirror, we were mirrors for each other, like twins, who simply know. I just had to look inside myself to see what Andrew wanted and why he'd set it up the way in which he had, but as I explained to him from the doughnut shop, he had to understand the ball was in my court now. It was his game and he had left me with the goddamn ball.

The pillbox had belonged to my mother. There was a rose enameled on the lid. She used it to carry saccharine tablets to sweeten her coffee, and I associate the box with the waxy scent of red lipstick that would spiral out of its mysterious cylinder, that could transform her worn face into that of a movie star. Funny, isn't it? Now we know saccharine causes cancer, and my mother died of cancer, but she would drop those minuscule pills into the wide black pool of her coffee with such élan—and sometimes I would do it for her, fascinated by the miniature tongs that came with the box for that purpose. The tongs were lost now and the box filled with dirt, and I held it in my pocket on the drive through the desert.

Jason Ripley was in the back with me and the prisoner, Todd Han-

ley was up front with the driver. Nobody talked much during the
two-hour ride. I did not think it would ever get easier with Jason, but
it didn't matter. Neither of us needed the other anymore.

We made a pit stop at a gas station that was the only service for
fifty miles. It was part general store—racks of white bread, huge bags
of ice—and part tourist trap, with bins of quartz crystal and fossils
and skeletons of small desert animals in plastic bags. There were real
scorpions inside crystal paperweights.

I headed for the ladies' room, thinking about the kind of person
who would catch those nasty scorpions, took down my khakis and
heard the unmistakable sound of stainless steel on porcelain. My handcuffs had fallen into the rest stop toilet bowl. Well, that clinched it.
Fishing them out, I knew I would soon be over and done with it all.

We went half a mile down an unmarked road to a place where
two boulders met, for no reason, at a right angle. They did nothing to
block the wind and scree, which blasted from every direction so our
hair whipped madly and we had to shout, and the cold cut through
our parkas, as if Brennan had brought us to the cauldron source of all
winds.

The dogs squinted against the blow and their ears were up and
they trotted the area, pawing the sand where it had been dug before.
Brennan pointed here and there and stood with shoulders hunched, a
stream of snot running from his nose. Motorists doing ninety with
their windshield wipers on might have gambled one or two seconds
on a glance at the small circle of vehicles; we were out there while the
rain came and went, while lightning raked the charcoal clouds moving in from Arizona, while six more holes two feet deep were dug by
the sheriff's men, and Brennan went down on his knees weeping and
saying he was sorry that we could not find his stash.

Finally the rain was pelting hard enough that we retreated to the
car, wet as the dogs. Brennan sat between me and Jason, quiet, his
head sagging, shoulders stooped.

"What's up, Ray?"

He did not respond.

"Disappointed? We're disappointed, too," I said. "We thought we could trust you, Ray. After driving out this far. You know, you don't show us some results, we're not taking you out for an airing anymore. Is that the game?"

"It's not a game," he said. "I just don't know exactly where it is. Could I lie down? I'm feeling very stressed right now," and laid his head in my lap.

Brennan's hands were still cuffed and he was in ankle irons. His face was turned away so all I could see was oily hair, dark at the roots, spiked in all directions, and a small perfectly formed reddened ear.

"Sit up, pal," said Jason, reaching for his collar.

Brennan dug his teeth into my thigh and hung on like a pit bull.

I screamed and pulled him off and slammed his forehead against the back of the front seat. In a moment Brennan was out of the car, facedown in the sand with two deputies kneeling on his back.

"The son of a bitch tried to bite her," Jason gasped breathlessly.

"I'm okay."

His teeth had not penetrated the heavy khakis.

Jason was peering at me from underneath his whipping hair. He wanted me to find his eyes and mark the message there.

"Get him up," Jason said.

They hoisted Brennan to his feet. He was spitting mealy-colored gunk and shouting hoarsely that we were all spying for the CIA.

Jason spun from the hips and while they held him, smashed a fist full-force into the side of Brennan's nose, and blood and teeth spurted out as if from a squirt bottle.

Then the young agent turned to see what I thought of this action. His breath was coming hard, and his face was red and shiny with rain. He wanted to know if it were done now, if his initiation were complete.

I would have answered that there was no beginning or end to this. The intimate desperation I had shared with Brennan in the house had meant nothing but a tactic in an arrest. He and I and Jason and Todd

Hanley were just interchangeable parts and would encounter one
another in different guises again and again. I would have told him
that, sooner or later, everything you care about ends up in the crapper.

"Over here!" someone yelled, and we slogged to where one of the
shovels had overturned a black nylon strap. Lifting carefully, we found
it was attached to an old discolored day pack, barely recognizable as
yellow.

"That belongs to Willie!" I shouted.

"Willie who?"

"The transient we interviewed on the Promenade! He knew Brennan!" I was pointing, using sign language over the scream of the wind.

I thought of Willie's stained white beard, how he had painfully
lowered himself in the doorway of the old bookstore. The sad, lost
look in his flat eyes. With icy fumbling fingers I unbuckled one of the
pockets. Inside was a handful of sparkly girlie hair clips and ponytail
scrunchies, cheap beaded bracelets and dime-store rings.

"This stuff isn't Willie's!" I shouted. "It's Brennan's trophies. From
his victims, like he said!"

"Where is Willie?" Jason shouted back. "Is he out here? Did Brennan kill him, too? Is he dead?"

I did not answer but watched as Jason, carrying the pack, lumbered through the blustery sandstorm to the van where Brennan was
receiving first aid for the injury he had suffered by falling down on a
rock.

I turned to the open desert, its monotone mauves blurred by rain.

"Willie!" I bellowed. "Wil-*lie*!"

And lifted my arms and stood up on my toes and felt the wind
under me.

The house was near the Venice canals, in a funky working-class
pocket. It was, amongst Spanish shacks and Victorian clapboards,
a two-story remodel painted blue, with all sorts of adornments
hanging off the eaves—whales and wind chimes and snowflakes and

a whole school of angelfish. Carved into a wooden oar were the words
Welcome to the Forresters. A boat was still hitched to a trailer in the
drive. On the porch a table was laden with young plants in flats from
a nursery; above them, an American flag. On top of a pole, like a
totem, sat a pelican with head tucked. I wondered how they'd gotten
a sculpture up there, but then the wind ruffled its feathers and I saw
that it was a real bird.

"Who's there?" Margaret Forrester demanded, impulsively opening the door before hearing a reply.

The air had a swampy, cabbage smell, which must have carried
from the languid, slow-moving channels that ran beneath arched
bridges to the sea. People who lived in the expensive houses on the
canals kept rowboats and canoes. But that upscale neighborhood
was several blocks away.

"Ana Grey, with the FBI."

"I know who you are." She stepped out. "What are you doing
here?" Then she saw the police.

"We have a warrant for your arrest."

She folded her arms and laid her weight back on one hip.

"Is this about the guava trees?"

"It's not about the guava trees."

"—Because I've had it *up to here.* Have you met my neighbors?
Obviously you have. I've told them if the fruit falls on their side, keep
it, *what* is the problem? These are the oldest continually producing
guava trees in Venice!"

"You are under arrest as an accessory in the murder of your husband."

The eyelids began to flutter, the eyeballs circling uselessly as if cut
loose from their stalks. She whimpered like a child.

The police captain said, "Ma'am?"

Now there were sharp intakes of breath as if she had found herself in a gas chamber.

"I'm sorry. I was up until five a.m., working in my garden."

The captain said, "What is it, a moon garden?"

"She has guava trees," I explained.

"I'm going to read you your rights," he began.

Margaret cried, "Andrew is the one who killed my husband. But he's dead, too, so what is the purpose? Why are you doing this to me?"

"What did Detective Andrew Berringer have to do with the death of your husband?" I asked, although I knew.

I knew because during preparation for the trial, my attorney had obtained the coroner's report on the death of Wes (the Hat) Forrester. He'd had it reviewed by an expert in tool and weapon marks, who found significant discrepancies in the stated cause of death. Lividity showed the body had been killed in one place and moved to another. Also, there were two kinds of wounds. One was consistent with a whack from a baseball bat to the back of the head; the second looked more like a hit from the riser of a stairs. The riser had caused a sub-dural hematoma, which had killed him. The baseball bat came later. The expert stated there was no bleeding in the margins of that wound, which meant Margaret or Andrew had hit him over the head to make it look like gang revenge after the heart had stopped pumping.

"Your husband came home and found you two together."

"We were together." She nodded, unaware of what she was confessing. "The detective and I—"

"In bed."

"—And they got into an argument, two big angry men. Their faces were this far apart, I couldn't stop them, it was terrible." Her voice twisted up and she grabbed her own hair. "Stop that, Margaret!" she scolded herself. "I don't want to be like this anymore!"

During the fight the Hat had fallen down the stairs, hit his head and died. Andrew and Margaret panicked, covered it up, but made a mistake. They did not pay close enough attention to the time. They waited too long to move the body. What went on between them— arguments, declarations, deals—during those minutes or hours cannot be known. But afterward, even after he gave her all the money from the bank job, the Thunder Queen was not assuaged. She wanted Andrew, and he wanted out. He thought a million bucks in cash would buy his freedom, but things did not work out that way, and when Margaret was threatening to come apart all over the map, he tried to appease her with more money. My money.

"Mom!" called a voice, and a little boy was at the door staring at us with resentful impatience. He had a faint milk mustache and buzzed hair and was eating a croissant. A TV was going in the background and the sounds of a video game. He wore a soccer uniform and had strong legs. "Mom!" he demanded. "When are we going?"

The captain had finished his recitation. "Please turn around, ma'am," he said.

"Please, please, don't do this to me."

The boy ducked back inside the house.

The captain and I exchanged a look. "Do you own any firearms?" he asked.

"I'm a widow," Margaret wailed. "My husband was a policeman, just like you. It was an accident. It was an accident."

"What was an accident, ma'am? Your husband falling down the stairs, or his skull being smashed with a baseball bat?"

The sharp inhales had become vocal sounds, like braying. She stepped back from our approach, and her body went stiff and her eyes went wide with the most God-awful desperation.

"You're going to jail, lady."

"No!"

"I'm going to ask you to cooperate, ma'am," said the captain. "Out of deference to your deceased husband, we'd rather not drag you from the house in front of the neighbors, do you hear me? But we will if we have to. Think about your children, okay, Mrs. Forrester? Who is going to stay with them? You got a family member we can call?"

"Ana," she said. "Help me."

Two officers were coming up the steps.

"Excuse me, gentlemen." I put myself in her face. "Andrew never gave you up."

"What is the purpose?" she said, and her legs buckled.

"He never gave you up."

They held her upright.

"No please," I said to the officers, "let me."

I unhooked my handcuffs off the back of my pants and felt their weight and the smooth familiar heft of a useful and reliable tool and put them on the woman's wrists and listened as they ratcheted shut with a delicate sound, like the winding of a clock.

"Remember," I told the captain, "I want those back."

Bright plastic flags strung over the entrance to the pool snapped and pulled in the canyon breeze. I was used to getting there by 7 a.m. for the workout anyway, but by seven-fifteen on the morning of the swim meet there was no place to park within half a mile, and you had to walk all the way up from the beach. I was shocked to find the pool deck jammed with four or five hundred children and adults on blankets and beach chairs cheek-to-jowl, extended families from as far away as La Canada who had moved in for the day and brought all the comforts, from thermos jars of steaming rice to beading projects for the younger siblings doomed to remain bored and dry the rest of the day.

It was disorienting to find my comfort zone overrun, like walking into the wrong apartment identical to yours. Added to the reassuring scent of wet concrete, for example, was the splatter of sausage from an open grill, where the dads were turning out big fat pancakes.

It was becoming futile to keep searching for Juliana in the milling crowd of shivering children and grim adults who crowded the event schedules as they were posted. The swimmers were indistinguishable in their caps and goggles and there were so many of them warming up, the pool looked like a frothing overpacked aquarium. The PA system cut in and out and the chaos of high-pitched voices was torturous. The odds, I had known starting out that morning, were that Juliana was not ready and would not show.

Since I had been back on the job there had been only one or two calls. It seemed she no longer needed to talk. She was in school and her parents were still split; yes, she had new friends—but her tone was guarded, as if she finally had stuff going important enough to keep safe in a private treasure box. The fear, however, could not always be contained. Sometimes, she admitted, the nightmares could still be so bad she would find herself out of bed and writhing on the floor.

I did not share my own nightmares with Juliana. I did not tell her how every day I looked into the mirror that was Andrew and me, and every day I was surprised. I had not guessed that either one of us was capable of what we had done, but every day I saw that same reflection. "Good morning, killer," I would say, and in that way, we would always be joined.

The national anthem blared, and the meet began. The sun had risen, and people were taking off the heavy jackets. The deck had begun to steam. Somehow every part of my body had already gotten wet—pants legs, soft lambskin boots—and there were meltdowns amongst the contestants. A petite blonde girl about eight, wearing a navy team suit with a bolt of lightning on the chest, was curled up in a towel on a beach chair, sobbing.

"She just doesn't want to," shrugged the embarrassed mom.

It was itchy to be wearing street clothes with the water so close and beckoning. Only a few weeks ago I had started to swim with the team again.

"Welcome back, Ana Banana," said my lifeguard friend, standing up in the next lane. In goggles and white cap, he had looked like a grandma who had somehow been endowed with broad glistening male shoulders.

"Been a while," I said, breathing hard.

He nodded. "The water senses it."

I laughed harshly.

But he was serious. "When you're flailing, the water senses it," he said, and dove neatly under.

Girls twelve years old and older were being called for the one-hundred-yard freestyle, and out of the mob of competitors that had gathered at the west side of the pool for their starts, I noticed something interesting. Two swimmers were helping a third to the blocks.

They were all wearing glossy violet suits, and other members of the same violet team were pushing past the judges seated at lane one to shout encouragement. The girl who was going to swim the race held on to the arms of her mates and very carefully, one foot at a time, climbed up onto the tilting platform, from which she stared down at the water with knees locked. You could almost see them quaking. I knew that body.

Shoving through the crowd to the edge of the pool I shouted, *"Go, Juliana!"* She couldn't hear me, but I kept on shouting, *"Go, baby, go!"*

Her skin was mottled white and blue. She bent over and pulled the cap down, and pressed the goggles firmly to her face, and the whole team of teenage girls—lumpy, long-legged, talented or not— was screaming, *"Go, Juliana! Juliana, you can do it!"*

A lot of folks had come out here to cheer for Juliana.

"Swimmers, take your mark," came the announcement.

In the tense space between the silence and the buzzer a few excited shrieks erupted from the team, and then there were shushes, and Juliana's whole body was trembling, her fingers stretched behind her like fluttering wingtips, in a crouch so tenuous it looked as if she might simply fall over. The distance before her was unbroken; the water still, and knowing.

Above us, the redtail hawks traced their arcs of freedom.

ACKNOWLEDGMENTS

Thank you to the law enforcement professionals who generously gave their time and expertise:

First of all, to FBI Special Agent Pam Graham, Negotiator—the inspiration and guiding angel of this book. Her insights were invaluable, her accomplishments impeccable. I was proud to be in her company.

To other outstanding members of the FBI Los Angeles Field Office: Special Agent George Carr, SWAT; Special Agent Hugh Coleman, Principal Firearms Instructor; Special Agent David A. Kice, ERT Coordinator; Supervisory Special Agent Chuck Joyner; Special Agent Mark Voges, Fireams Instructor.

To those based in Quantico: thanks to Arthur E. Westveer, Violent Crime Specialist, and John Jarvis, Behavioral Scientist, Behavior Science Unit, for essential technical advice.

To Special Agent Mark Llewellen, Retired, of Executive Shield, Inc. Also Special Agent William J. Rehder, Retired, the world's foremost expert on bank robberies, and Special Agent Nick Boone, Retired.

Gratitude, once again, to Don Mauro, as well as to Captain Richard Odenthal, Retired, and Detective Sgt. Ken Gallatin, both of the Los Angeles County Sheriff's Department. It was a pleasure to know Barry A. J. Fisher, Crime Lab Director, whose range of knowledge is as awesome as his generosity.

Santa Monica Police Department Captain Gary Gallinot and Detective John Henry provided skilled understanding of criminal motivation and police procedure.

The work of Anna C. Salter, Ph.D., was helpful, as was William J. Bodziak's *Footwear Impression Evidence,* and *Practical Aspects of Rape Investigation,* edited by Robert R. Hazelwood and Ann Wolbert Burgess.

Without the compassionate assistance of Gail Abarbanel, Director of the Rape Treatment Center, Santa Monica–UCLA Medical Center, and clinic coordinator Amy Tishler, RN, NP, this book could not be in any way true. The RTC is a model facility that provides free, state-of-the-art emergency medical care, forensic examinations, counseling and legal support for victims of sexual assault and their families, twenty-four hours a day—but that scarcely describes its humanitarian reach or the urgency of its mission. For victims who suffer in silence, confidential care is available at www.911.rape.org. My greatest hope is that these words reach out to them.

I am deeply obliged to the brilliant defense attorney Blair Berk for legal strategies and to Walter Teller for continuing counsel. William F. Skinner, M.D., was an unfailing source of medical authority and comradeship. My son, Ben, was the creative voice behind the portrayal of teenage life—making me sound more chill than I could ever aspire to be. Thanks to my daughter, Emma, for sharing many spirited adventures; and to Douglas, ever yours. To my East Coast friends and family, always in my heart.

As for agents of another kind—Molly Friedrich is, quite simply, the best; Robert Graham and Matthew Synder at CAA, equally anchors in the storm. Paul Bogaards and Pamela Henstell have done a wonderful job at Knopf—thank you for your support all these years; and to Vrinda Condillac for keeping us all on track. But there is no greater privilege for any writer than working with Sonny Mehta. I remain indebted to his wisdom and enthusiasm.

ALSO BY APRIL SMITH

NORTH OF MONTANA
An Ana Grey Mystery

After Ana Grey pulls off "the most amazing arrest of the year," her squad supervisor—who is clearly sexist—snags her on a technical detail and gives her an official reprimand, instead of the promotion she deserves. Then, as a test, she is assigned an incredibly complex case involving an aging Hollywood starlet. It doesn't take her long to understand that in the eyes of her higher-ups this "is not a case" but "a political situation waiting to explode." As the boundaries between the private and professional begin to blur and Ana's own world collides with her investigation, she is forced to confront uncomfortable truths about the nature of stardom and her own past.

Crime Fiction

JUDAS HORSE
An Ana Grey Mystery

FBI Special Agent Ana Grey returns to infiltrate the volatile core of an ecoterrorist cell in the Northwest. Only months after a traumatic shooting incident, Ana is still emotionally unstable when she returns to work and learns that a fellow agent—and former lover—has been killed by a group of domestic terrorists operating under the name of FAN (Free Animals Now), whose alleged purpose is to free the wild mustangs of the west. Ana goes undercover as an animal activist and encounters Julius Emerson Phelps, the charismatic leader of a "family" of anarchists in rural Oregon, whose secret past could blow the Bureau sky-high. Ana meets her match in Phelps, who draws her into a deadly game of cat and mouse as he prepares a cataclysmic act of terrorism using Ana, in her undercover identity, as bait.

Crime Fiction